A VIKING AGE TRILOGY

PART ONE
AKSEL'S ODYSSEY

A HISTORIC PLAY ON THE VIKING
ERA OF TURMOIL,
ACCEPTANCE OF CHRISTIANITY VS
THE GODS OF OLD

A SAUCY LASS STRIKES
A WILLFUL PRINCE,
A SAIL AFAR TO LEARN
A JUDICIOUS KING TO BE.

A Viking Era Trilogy © 2013
All rights reserved by Ann McDeed

A-Argus Better Book Publishers, LLC

For information:
A-Argus Better Book Publishers, LLC
9001 Ridge Hill Street
Kernersville, North Carolina 27285
www.a-argusbooks.com

ISBN: 978-0-6158770-9-9
ISBN: 0-6158770-9-5

Book Cover designed by Dubya

Printed in the United States of America

Cast of Characters
A VIKING ERA TRILOGY
PARTS ONE, TWO & THREE
By Ann McDeed

Aksil's Odyssey
Kaja's Angst
Harmony and Tribulation

A historic play on the Viking era of Turmoil
Acceptance of Christianity VS the Gods of old

Cast of Characters

BOOK ONE, AKSILS' ODYSSEY

Aksils' Odyssey Chapter One, Alfhild
King Ivar of Alfhild, father of the three below
Mother, Queen Alva
Margrethe (ill daughter, 16)
Kaja (recovered daughter, 12,
Jorgan (recovering son, 10)
Frode, wizard
Prince Aksel, (18), from Heborg, son of King Gregors:
Karl, Aksel's cousin, (16) Companion
Ingvar   an older knight - companion/protector

Aksils' Odyssey Chapter Two, Iceland, Noble Virtues
King Gregors, Aksel's father - king.
Unne Arason, old friend of King Gregors
Finn, a young local lad
Ulstead, Chieftain at Althing
Lam, young lad on trip to Althing, his mother (unnamed)
Young lass and her sire on trip to Althing (unnamed)

Aksils' Odyssey Chapter Three, Iceland, the Althing and Sagas
Unne Arason and spouse Ingeborg
Young boy frightened by saga's.
Law Speaker and Chieftains, Godar's and citizens (no names given)
Herrick charged at Althing

Aksil's Odyssey, Chapter Four, Iceland to Ireland
Captain Sune of merchant ship
Bjarke, fisherman in Iceland
Yrsa his wife
Ejsten, 11 year old son
Liz, 4 year old daughter
Verner Eskild, of Kaupang, Norseman trader
Various seamen about 16 unnamed
Evoch, Norweigan found in Greenland
Kyush, Inuit lad cared for by Evoch
Inuit natives of Greenland, unnamed

Aksil's Odyssey, Chapter Five, Ireland
Tyge Holsten of Dublin, born of Norsemen, fighting with the Vikings
Friar Magnussen, teaches Christianity in Nordic tongue.
Knight Armage to King Baru
King Brian Baru Monarch of Dal Cais to south
Kiev, young lad in fort, beat by his uncle.
Uncle Skorre, who beat him
Angelica, Kiev's mother
Farmer's lady who gave them food for journey, unnamed
Neighbor who helped them find transportation, unnamed
Traveling Merchant
Captain who takes them across channel

Aksel's Odyssey, Chapter Six, England

<u>Wulf</u>, Irish freeman who serves them.

<u>Harald Ringnes</u>, local Norseman farmer

His daughter, <u>Gerda</u>, who Karl weds

His spouse <u>Lady Ringnes</u>, and a younger sister and brother (unnamed)

<u>Aksel's Odyssey, Chapter Seven, Return to Norway</u>

<u>Asmund</u>, Ingvar's neighbor

Older couple, neighbor of Gerda's parents when they lived in Norway (unnamed)

<u>Erik,</u> Ingvar's son

<u>Dagmar</u>, Ingvar's wife

<u>Queen Hulda</u>, Aksel's mother

BOOK TWO, KAJA'S ANGST

<u>Kaja's Angst, Chapter One, Alfhild</u>

<u>Aunt Gudrum Eskild</u>, from Kaupang Queen Alva's, sister

<u>Sigred</u>, Kaja's friend from village

<u>Thora</u>, Kaja's friend from village

<u>Fridley</u>, Pig Herder

<u>Munk and Punk</u> 2 hunting dogs

<u>Sir Esben </u>(young knight escort)

<u>Sir Vig </u>(young knight escort)

<u>Two urchins, their mother and sisters </u>(unnamed)(Agge in Pt.3,Chpt. 6)

<u>Hega</u>, guardian to Kaja, at puberty

<u>Kaja's Angst, Chapter Two, Alfhild (Winter)</u>

<u>Godvin</u>, son of blacksmith from Alfhild, teaches Kaja to play the harp.

<u>Jakob</u>, young knight in Alfhild

<u>Poul</u>, young knight n Alfhild

<u>Sir Knud </u>(mentioned only)

Two wild sables. And two guinea pigs

Kaja's Angst, Chapter Three
King Havard, whose son is too young for Kaja (mentioned only)

Kaja's Angst, Chapter Four
Jannike, Kaja's maid servant when she becomes queen.
Ostman, Head Gardner,
Gaius & Jorunn & their mother 2 boys who pulled plants.5 years and 2
Friar Kristoffer, who marries them
Alf, companion dog to King Gregors'

Kaja's Angst, Chapter Five
No new characters

BOOK THREE, HARMONY AND TRIBULATION

Harmony and Tribulation, Chapter One
Joseph, the weaver and newborn son, Gustav
Magda, lass who wants to learn to play the harp.
Thomas, Squires son, mentioned only Jannekas betrothed.

Harmony and Tribulation, Chapter Two
Broder, leader of barbaric Norsemen
Ramgerd, barbaric Norsemen who kidnap Kaja
Torben, Alf and Edmond - Knights in Heborg guard
Lad, unnamed, who helps Kaja
Bue and Ernst, Ramgerd's men
Skjold, man from cave in the altitudes
Asbjorn, man from cave in the altitudes

Harmony and Tribulation, Chapter Three
Lady Eirene, a siren visiting the realm
Lodin, Karl & Gerda's infant son

Bjorn, Kaja and Aksel's first born
The Alliance -Peaceful organization of Realms.

Harmony and Tribulation, Chapter Four
Sten the builder in charge of church
Hjordis' old friend of Aksel's
Slovene, his wedded pregnant wife
Birgitta, illegitimate daughter of Aksel
Lady, Berit, who took care of Birgitta

Harmony and Tribulation, Chapter Five
Rolf, (skilled w/bow & arrow) indentured slave
Helge, babe Janne –his wife and child (Kaja nurses babe Janne)
Toras a farmer whose brother set fire to the grain in barn
Stak & Pank, 2 hunting dogs.

Harmony and Tribulation, Chapter Six
Lady Clausette – King Gregors second cousin arrive.
Dorte daughter of Clausette. (Marries Frode)
Gregors, Kaja's second son
Svend, Frode & Dorte's son
Agge, urchin from Kaupaung (also Part 2, Chapt 1,unnamed)

Harmony and Tribulation, Chapter Seven, Heborg and Alphild
Farmer Vitolf, brewed strong drink, dies from drink
Khora, his visiting niece, dies from spotted fever.
Alexandria, Jorgan's newly wedded spouse
Unne, third baby prince
Queen Mother Alva dies

Harmony and Tribulation, Chapter Eight
No new characters mentioned. Citizens of Heborg (listen Aksel's confession) not mentioned by name.

Church complete.

Harmony and Tribulation. Chapter Nine
Stig, pet guinea pig
Sara, lass assigned by marm to be pleasant to Aksel
Vagn, her sire, mentioned only here.
Aslaug, claims to be a saint, barbarian evangelist w/army of men.
Emanual, leader of contingent of men from Degfinn.

Harmony and Tribulation, Chapter Ten
Edvard (17) Havards son
Georg (15) Havards son
Arne, Kaja/Aksels 4th son
Giedde, soldier who rescues vinum slaves
Sunesen, his missing brother
Many soldiers and vinum slaves

Harmony and Tribulation, Chapter 11
Sir Borghild, who tried to kill Aksel in battle.
Ulrika, Hjordis' lady
Margarethe, Kaja & Aksel's daughter

Harmony and Tribulation, Chapter 12
Kaja is killed in childbirth
Daughter Kaja born just as mother killed.
King Tornekrans from the Alliance
Queen Alvilde, his spouse
Thorkild their son 15
Ditlev their son almost 14

CHAPTER ONE

ALFHILD, NORWAY

"Do I behold a young lass jousting with a young lad?" Prince Aksel asked in a disparaged tone of voice as he paused on top the hill. His companions nodded in agreement as they gazed down into the pleasant valley below, the sun reflecting off a rather large lake with ditches draining into the nearby fields of grain and planted vegetation. It had the look and comfort of a thriving realm with a neat, small castle to one side and the thatched roof cottages of thegns and ceorls nearby. A small herd of cattle grazed in a distant field along with evidence of barns and fenced areas for flocks of chickens and barnyard animals.

"It so quiet – no one work about. It so still," Prince Aksel observed aloud to his two companions, Cousin Karl and Sir Ingvar, a strong older knight, as they carefully followed him down the uneven path while watching the jousting activity below.

Aksel was excited with anticipation as they rode their stallions in closer to the courtyard. After two years of waiting he would meet his promised maiden, the beautiful princess his sire described to him. The stirrings of his youthful manhood rose in eagerness of seeing her for the first time. Will she be as lovely as he said or did he exaggerate to make her sound more enticing than she actually was?

"I hope this not be my lady," the prince said over the noisy clopping of the horses on the rocky downhill path as they approached the young pair. "She look a skinny young lass with her smock tied up so she can joust with ease."

Cousin Karl turned to give him a smile, "This skinny lass be but a child, surely your lady will be a maiden of poise and beauty, she be almost sixteen."

Aksel approached and called to the two jousting companions, "A word with you there young lad and lass!" When they didn't respond, just continued with their jousting, not even hearing him by the looks of it, he dismounted, unsheathed his sword and placed it between them to break their concentration.

"What you do?" The startled young lass shouted up at him and slammed her small wooden sword against his metal one with all her might. Aksel's sword flipped into the air - he almost lost it. He was surprised at the force she used, for such a young lass. "You interfere with our training session, Sir Knight. Leave us be!"

"Training session you say? You, a maiden, seriously training with a young lad in the art of jousting!" he mocked. "This hardly be a fair fight."

"And you, a knight, interfering with sword of steel on two novices with wooden sticks be fair?" she loudly complained. "Do you intend to use your sword of steel to make me stop? If not, you best sheath it or I will take it as ill meaning."

"I will, young lass, but give the lad a rest afore he collapse from fatigue."

"Yes," she said in agreement, sighing, "he be tired, we make him move to gain strength. This be my brother, Jorgan."

"And do you have a name?" Aksel inquired as she raised Jorgan's arm, placed it around her shoulder to help him toward the castle entrance.

"I be Kaja, second daughter of King Ivar of Alphid," she replied, not looking up at them, intent on her brother as they slowly walked through the empty courtyard toward the castle. The men dismounted and followed them into the long hall. Jorgan collapsed on the couch as Kaja left the room and returned shortly with a mug of goat's milk for her brother and helped him drink it slowly. "You will drink it all or I ask Frode to feed you. You must get better and stronger. You must take sustenance, now drink all the milk," she insisted softly in a begging, stern voice.

She completely ignored the three men who patiently waited for acknowledgement. They looked about the large comfortable accommodations, admired the many carvings of mounted knights and wild beasts, displays of ancient weapons and tapestries of scenes from battles that hung on the walls. They heard footsteps approach – a woman and man carefully supported a young maiden between them, flushed of face, barely able to stand. They coaxed her to walk down the stairs to the couch where the young lad sat. Jorgan moved aside to make room, hugged her waist gently as she weakly acknowledged him with a light touch. Kaja returned again with milk for her sister and helped her slowly drink in little sips.

The man noticed the three knights and approached them, "I be King Ivar of this realm, forgive me, I not see you arrive. The fever has struck our entire village. All keep to their cottages and many fled to the countryside to escape the illness. It best you not stay here exposed to the fever."

"I be Prince Aksel, son of King Gregors of Heborg. I come to claim the hand of your daughter as my sire arranged the promise two years ago."

"Margrethe, your promised maiden lies here very ill, in the last phase of fever." He indicated the maiden lying on the couch. "If she live the night, she may recover; but be so frail, I fear for her. My son has not recovered completely. My youngest daughter has recovered well. Come with me, I will direct you to Frode. He will accommodate you outside the village where it be safe from harm of fever. We will bring food and drink to refresh you."

Prince Aksel dwelled on the Lady Margrethe where she lay on the couch with unseeing eyes, feverish of color, chest rising and falling erratically with shortened breath, her golden hair spilling from a white wrap around her head. As he gazed at her, desire aroused within him, a yearning for the lovely maiden who would be his wife. He followed his companions with sadness. What a rare beauty he mused, his sire chose well; she would be a pleasure to wed. Surely the gods will help her recover he prayed within himself.

- - - -

"The Princess Margrethe did not survive the night. She will be buried this morn along with two others of the village," King Ivar announced to the prince and his companion the next morning. Jorgan and Kaja wept while their mother, Queen Alva, held them close and King Ivar comforted them and another family at the gravesite where mounds of dirt from fresh graves of victims of the plague lay one after another. They sobbed quietly, found it hard to control their tears. The burial was quick, short and without ceremony, they do not dally among other mourners, for fear of spreading the fever. A few words were said for each deceased, for Margarethe and the two young sons of a farmer. Tears flowed as they slowly walked away, it was a sad time for the realm, the death toll rising.

Prince Aksel watched in disappointment, so lovely a maiden, he mused. As the morning passed, the disappointment turned to resentment at the turn of events, he became angry inside; he had intended to wed the lovely princess *now*! There was no other suitable maidens of station about. They were either too old or too young like Kaja. Where could he look for a maiden to wed now?

He felt the need to escape, to ride fast and far. His irritation mounted and he vented at the young attendant in the barn, "What takes you so long to saddle my steed, you lazy lout?" Weak from the aftermath of fever, the attendant apologized to the young prince and forced himself to move faster as Cousin Karl stepped in to assist him lift the heavy leather saddle. Prince Aksel mounted the animal, cracked his crop and his steed bounded forward in a cloud of flying dust and stone. He looked neither left nor right and followed the path at top speed into the rolling hills of the countryside. He reigned in his distraught steed along side a small fresh-water pond, dismounted and threw himself down on the ground among the weeds and wild flowers disturbing the insects and butterflies around him. He was not accustomed to waiting for what he wanted, he desired a wife *now*. He was eighteen and needed a maiden of his own for wife to love.

When the prince returned from his wild ride, Kaja and Jorgan stood beside the barn seeking comfort from Frode, their teacher, who lovingly held them close, speaking softly. They had to jump aside to escape the frantic steed as it came to a halt rearing up on its hind legs, neighing loudly. The steed foamed at the mouth,

beyond control from the hard run and would not be stilled. Frode stepped in, grasped and held the reins so the prince could dismount safely. The steed still reared in a dangerous manner while Frode softly talked to the animal in an attempt to calm him; he had the touch of compassion recognized by all living things. Prince Aksel raised his crop to flog the horse in an attempt to control the animal. Frode held up his hand to allay him, which angered the already raging prince who cursed and struck Frode with the whip rather than his steed.

Kaja, witness to this, was aghast and shouted, "Stop!" and threw herself on the Prince. She struck his chest with both her fists and verbally attacked him for abusing Frode. "You not use your whip on our wise man. You be mean, nasty, no less an animal than your steed."

The Prince horrified at her attack, forcefully held her arms. "A lady does not strike a prince who will someday be king," he said indignantly. "You will learn to behave as a lady before you come to my castle."

"I will not go your castle! A true knight would never strike an older man, a wizard smarter than himself will ever be," she raged.

Thunderstruck by her attitude, Prince Aksel released her as she shook loose from him and turned to help Frode and tenderly checked his wounds. She found no blood; his clothing had kept his skin safe from the lash of the crop. She dipped the edge of her smock in cold water from the drinking trough and soothed the red welts on his shoulder.

"My dear lady, Kaja," Frode spoke softly, "be calm and polite to the young prince. He may return someday to claim you for his wedded wife."

"I will not wed a man who hurt a defenseless person. He best listen to your wisdom and not dispute it – not abuse you."

"You must understand that the young Prince not know me as such."

"He be nasty and mean," she insisted. "He whip his horse, he whip you. I not be careful of every word I speak just to keep a mean, stupid prince from whipping me on every whim!"

Later that day, Frode related to his King the confrontation and that Kaja disliked the prince because of it. He felt her sire should know what occurred.

By evening, the prince had regained his composure and was relaxed after a pleasant meal of venison, fresh garden vegetables and a mug of ale. King Ivar talked with him as they strolled through the courtyard and the still empty village streets. He spoke to him about the whipping incident and why his daughter felt it necessary to take the wizard's position. He explained Frode's place in the realm. "He be a very learned man. All the

people learn from him, skills that aid them become better farmers and workers in all phases of life here in the village."

"Even in jousting," Prince Aksel retorted cynically with a laugh and toss of his head, "for the ladies?"

"Jousting taught to young men, yes, not usually ladies. Kaja enjoy competing with them in many things. Now she jousts with Jorgan, her brother, to keep his body active and strong, to fight this malady and make him well. This be the best defense against the fever after it waned." The king continued, "Frode be a wizard, a wise man, highly learned. He scribes a journal of observations, records plantings, results of experiments, problems and solutions which others reference in future as the need arises. We highly respect him here and other nearby realms. All benefit from his knowledge. The young learn to read and write, which even I never learn when I be young. We treat our wise man with respect. If you disagree what he says, tell him so, he will convince you with words. However, do not abuse or punish him in any way unless the king approves. This, be for his protection. He be too valuable for us, all of us. You understand this?" He strongly stressed in a quiet voice to soften his tone of displeasure at the prince's actions. They walked in silence for a while through the narrow streets lined with the thatched-roof homes of the people. None of them were out and about as the fever was still a very strong threat. The shuffling and sounds of their flocks and animals could be heard in the yards behind their cottages on the still, calm night.

As they turned back toward the castle, the prince did not answer King Ivar's question, did not reply even to defend his actions. King Ivar softly said, with a choke in his voice, "Since your betrothed has been taken from us, you may have Kaja as wife when she be of age, as be the custom," he paused, "If you so desire."

Prince Aksel turned and looked at him with a startled expression of dismay on his face. *Take that wild lass to wife?* he shuddered to himself.

King Ivar felt relief, did he read that expression, under the dim light of the torch above the gate, as a negative response? For Kaja's happiness, he prayed so as he found the prince's willful demeanor not to his liking for a husband to his beloved daughter. He well understood Kaja's dislike of this young willful prince.

Prince Aksel, lay awake for many hours before he fell asleep, thinking of the cruel turn of events which left him without a bride. He could find a lesser lady perhaps, a cousin to royalty as was his cousin. He still felt offense when the sun rose the next morning and decided to leave, not knowing if he would ever return. He told his companion as they headed up the hill away from Alfhild and those seeing them off in farewell. "Let us be gone from this place. I continue search the country for a more agreeable lady. One who strikes me and fights with me be not to my liking; women are for a man's pleasure, to make babies, sons and daughters and prepare a comfortable home." He did not look back as they climbed the rocky path they had descended just two days before.

Karl with a mischievous gleam in his eyes, asked his prince, "If you find a docile lady to your liking, Cousin, may I claim this young maiden? Did you not see the beauty of her sister; the fullness of body, the hair of spun gold, fairness of skin and beautiful green eyes? Kaja yet a child, will grow lovely in time and be a pleasure to behold. Yes, I venture to say, a delightful pleasure indeed, a saucy green-eyed lady." He smiled broadly as he looked back, waved and bowed to her from his saddle, with a flirtatious flourish of his arm.

Kaja felt relief to see them leave, hoped they never returned, and waved back as they headed up the path. "Papa," she asked with deep concern in her voice, "do you really think he will claim me when I be old enough to wed?"

"He did not say, dear Kaja, but yes, he may return to claim you," her father acknowledged.

She looked up at him, a pained expression on her face, "If he does come to claim, may I refuse him?"

CHAPTER TWO

ICELAND AND THE NOBLE VIRTUES

Aksel raged for the manner his sire, King Gregors, escorted him, his son, to the longboat and ordered him to "Get in the boat or I will lift you and throw you in." Aksel looked at his father, standing firm of demeanor, whose jaw was set as hard as his own. He looked at the contingent of men his sire had behind him. He knew what his father would do, had seen what he could do when someone needed strong discipline. *Did he want those men putting him aboard the longboat by force?* he asked himself. *The indignity, I a prince! My father be doing this to me?* He looked again at the anger in his sire's face. *Yes, he do this, even to his son.* Aksel slowly climbed aboard, with Cousin Karl, Knight Ingvar and a purse with coins enough to keep them traveling and fed for several years.

His king gave Sir Ingvar orders to "Travel the seas to many lands, observe how kings rule and men live together in peace or harm throughout their lands. Return only when the willful prince has learned to be judicious and can stand proud among the greatest of men."

Aksel turned his back to his father, the hurt and hate he felt for him rising within. He did not look back to his land of birth as the ship slipped out to sea, roughly bouncing over the waves. *Perhaps,* he thought, *I will never return.*

Aksel huddled, weeks later, in the bow of the longboat among bundles of cargo, headed to the Viking Colony of

Thingvellir, Iceland, where an old friend of King Gregors was last known to reside. He was miserable with the unrelenting lurching of the boat, the constant wind howling and blowing in the sail, the horrible stale bread, salty smoked meat, occasional raw fish and mug of ale presented to him daily. He watched as the ship's crew rowed ceaselessly to move faster toward their destination, fighting against the current. He watched as Ingvar and Karl took a turn at the oars, rowed for a short while, then tired and begged to rest. He noticed they rowed longer at the oars with each turn, as their bodies and muscles become stronger and accustomed to the strain. Aksel stiff with inactivity, thought to row to ease the stiffness of his bones, but decided not, thinking – I *a prince, not a slave - men of station do not do slave labor.*

The winds turned favorable, with warm currents of air flowing from the south, heralding the advent of spring as it blew them along. For many days they saw no land, at night they saw only the stars and moon and Captain Suni explained how to read from the pole star to find which direction they take. Sometimes, with a fair wind in the sail and no need to row, the men played games of chance or strength to amuse themselves and occupy the time.

Ingvar boastfully displayed the muscles in his arms, "I have not muscles like these since a young lad. Come Aksel, get up and row. It build your body, make you strong - give you the look of a man. Your sire will look on you with favor when next he sees you."

Karl chided his cousin to join them. Aksel stubbornly resisted, but shortly finds himself bailing sea water from the bottom of the boat when needed. Moving about did loosen up his joints which were stiffened from inactivity in the cold, relentless wind.

It was a long, uncomfortable sail across the ocean. Weeks of living in a cramped longboat with nothing to occupy the time, Aksel eventually ventured to try the oars. He was positioned back from the others to give him room to get in synch with the rhythm as had the others. He became discouraged at the first try and gave up, but Ingvar coached him the second time, sat along side to instruct and work together pulling on his oar. Ingvar slacked off as Aksel became more proficient and strong, taking complete control of his ore. Ingvar gave his prince a firm pat of approval. Aksel swelled with the feeling of accomplishment and pride, he had earned approval from his strong, admirable protector. Yes, in time his body felt stronger, much stronger as well as vibrant and alive.

The boat was laden with merchandise to sell among the people of this distant, isolated Iceland. It is icy cold as they approached the shores of Iceland, their cloaks not warm enough to ward off the last cold blast of winter. They landed on the southwest coast and once on shore away from the wind, the warmth of the sun enfolded them.

They were surprised to find the settlers were Norsemen who spoke their language. They found a few they did not understand, were these Celts? They inquired along the shore for King Gregor's old friend, Unne

Arason, with no success. With the purchase of the small, strong Icelandic breed of horse, they ventured out into the countryside to explore the region. They met many citizens who welcomed them and told them of hot springs nearby, which were a pleasure to soak and bathe in - an opportunity to cleanse themselves of the stench of weeks at sea. Finn, a young local lad, led them to the springs where they enjoyed the luxury and soaked for hours. They splashed like children in the water, and strayed into the depths, which was dangerous as they did not know how to swim like a fish. Finn brought them a log to hold on to in the depths, clean clothes to wear and took the dirty ones to his marm to launder. His marm made room for them to sleep the night in her barn among the sheep. It was not restful or quiet, the animals were not still the whole night. They worried they were not safe from their hoofs. The strong, obnoxious smell kept them from a sound sleep. They wakened the next morning smelling just as bad as before they had bathed. Grateful and appreciative as they were for the hospitality, they felt justified to leave and traveled north to inquire for Unne, still without success.

They beheld many sights, many wonders of nature as they continued to travel along the coastline, the beautiful blue water rolling up along the shore in wave after wave of crashing seawater on the sand and rocks. They turned inland toward rugged mountains laden with glaciers that fed the rivers; the melting ice raced down the beautiful waterfalls to fill the clear blue lakes below.

Often they traveled days without seeing any man and needed to hunt for wild game or fish to feed their empty bellies. Spring berries of elder, thorn and rowan abound among the underbrush, but they needed to be careful of wild animals who desired not to share the fruits of their land. Joyous they were when they came upon a settlement and were welcomed among the citizens. They shared stories of adventure and accomplishment. They saw fields of grain, many goats and cattle wandered nearby, some with the swollen-belly promise of young to come. It was a sight to give comfort and happiness to the heart – the nature of a peaceful, prosperous land.

Ingvar expounded, "This be the glorious God-given beauty of nature, fruits of the fertile land and water to nourish the body and plants of earth. Even with the frozen glaciers of winter, it be more glorious than our own land. Look about you, see how wondrous it be, it be good!"

Aksel just looked at him without expression. He was still the willful prince, who did not want to be there. Karl would nod in agreement on occasion, thinking on Ingvar's mental condition. "You be not a skald, you a knight, a warrior!" he would let him know.

As they approached the next settlement, all was astir. It was time for the annual meeting of chieftains to settle grievances. Ingvar listened closely, "Meeting to settle grievances. What this be? Something we should see and listen? How think you?" he asked his charges. "We go this meeting, see what it do, what purpose it serve?"

Aksel said naught.

Karl charged, "We go, even if not want to. You take us! This be what our sire, King Gregors say we do, learn how other men settle dispute and live together in peace. This be right?"

Ingvar smiled "It of importance, yes. We go, join them and learn how they govern this land." He spoke with the local Chieftain Ulstead, who agreed they should join his entourage of men, women and children which would leave in a couple days. A wagon full of favors, gifts, foods and supplies, to last many weeks for the journey and social functions, had left the previous week to arrive before the travelers. It was a long journey to cross the island, west toward Thingvellir, and the oxen-drawn wagons loaded with supplies moved much slower than the convoy of people.

Ingvar rode alongside the men, spoke with them and asked after Unne Arason. They laughed, "Sure Unne Arason be there, he be punished for wrong doing many years gone and come again every year to charge again of the injustice done him."

"What he do, kill a man?" Aksel asked.

Ulstead laughed, "Nah, who remember? It be many years, he be an old man now. Try always to live in the law, but angered he be wrongly charged. He talk at Althing every year, hope someday he be judged right. He come to Althing, he not stay away."

They travel through the valleys, alongside the rivers and lakes of clear blue water shining and sparkling in the sun. Cold as the water is, they wash often, fully dressed so to clean their clothes also. They were

given cloaks to cover themselves while their clothes dried, less the young lads and lassies giggle at their nakedness - living in the open left little privacy for all.

The families enjoy jesting with the young knights and Karl and Aksel become more pleasant in manner and jest back with them. They challenge and play with the young. Ingvar instructed the young lads how to perform many small duties and tasks to aid their elders, trap small game and skin them, make a fire by striking flint to cook the game over the open flames.

Aksel challenged lads to "Find sticks to burn, find more than I do!" and one day young Lam carried more than Aksel did back to the camp. They gave a strong handshake together, like men do, with a friendly slap on shoulder.

"Prince Aksel shook my hand!" Lam proudly boasted to his friends, and Aksel glowed inside remembering how proud it made him when Ingvar praised his rowing efforts aboard the longboat.

Of night, Ulstead spoke with the three, "Your Sire charge you learn how men live in peace? I tell you of rules we bring from Norway help live a better life, honest life, hard working life, be proud to show before the gods. Nine rules, name of Noble Virtues." He called them off from memory. "Honor, Truth, Courage, Perseverance, Fidelity, Discipline, Hospitality, Industriousness and Self Reliance. Each night after sustenance we discuss one virtue, define it and give meaning." Others about them sat and listened, as well as asked questions and added to the discussion so all learned about the Noble Virtues.

"First Noble Virtue be **Honor** – this be how we feel of ourselves, value of self, be we noble, show respect, give respect? We have worth among men? Do people come to you with trust in your word? All things die, animals, kin, each one of us will die, but our deeds live on - they show our honor – for good or bad. Our good works say that we be worthy of respect of others. These live long after we die, whether in worth or shame."

Ingvar listened, thought on it, then asked, "You say honor have worth among men. How we know we have respect from others about us. We work hard, do what need, what be assigned by sire. Be this enough?"

Ulstead said with a smile nodding his head, "We know when we have honor among men. Do any ask your thoughts, desire your knowledge to make decision, listen your words or follow advice you give? This show they know you be true, worthy, honest. They have regard for you. You be an honorable man. Your sire, King Gregors, trust you with his son, you think he not honor you? If he not honor you, he not trust you with son on dangerous voyage across sea. You think?" he asked, smiled at Ingvar who slowly nodded his head. Yes, he understood.

Aksel hung his head, he was ashamed to look at Ingvar, did not feel himself to be honorable when he thought of his actions. He be a willful lad, not a fine prince.

"Next Noble Virtue be **Truth**. Speak honest in all things, say only what we know true, what we see be true. But beware, do not be fooled into speaking true when others lie to you, not accept the lies of others, not respond true when others lie to you. Man be good as his word. The ancients valued truthful speech. We must not say more than what be true as when tell tales of feats of gods or men. When boast of strength of body, when boast of deeds done for good or evil, be wary to make story full true."

Young Lam, say to Chief, "What of saga of Grettir who lift great stone to show his strength to friends at Bjarg. Stone be bigger than he, heavier than he ever. Not that be a lie? He not boast?"

"Ah, saga of Grettir be like all sagas, like stories all speak through ages. It be hard to believe any man strong enough to lift that rock, many sagas hard to believe. Many sagas start true, each time it told, it be embellished and as time pass be not always fully true."

Lam nodded his head to agree with Ulstead, as Aksel considered what was said. He remembered many times he had not spoken true to his marm, his sire, even as a young lad he often not speak true. He felt shame in his heart.

On the third day, it rained and fell harder as the day progressed. Ulstead decided, "We not ride our wagons in the muddy path ahead, it be treacherous." They made camp on a somewhat higher knoll early in the afternoon, prepared shelters of limbs and leaves covered with leather skins to keep them dry. All wear cloaks and skins for warmth, drink hot beverage and mead, then gather under their shelters and cloaks and listen to another virtue.

We speak of **Courage** this rainy day. Courage be bravery to do what be right at all times. It brave to live by the Noble Virtues. Have courage to tell when man do wrong. Have courage to do what we know be right, to stand by our beliefs, our kin and not have faint heart. You know any who be brave, show courage?" he asked the young who cuddled close to him to keep dry under the shelter.

A little lass looked at him, said, "Sire be brave, he chase away a mean beast who want eat me."

"What sire be that?" Ulstead asked.

"My sire. He chased a bad lion who would eat me." she repeated.

"That not lion, my lass, that be a wild goat who thought you be her calf. I told goat you my babe and send her away to find her own babe."

"You told me it a lion." She looked at her sire accusingly.

"Yes, I did, to be sure you not go with goat. You stay aside me and your marm," he reassured her. "Goat not know how to care for little lass."

"I be cold, sire. You care for me now, make me warm?"

"Yes, I care for you." He lifted her to his arms and cuddled her close, wrapped in his cloak to keep her warm and content. It wasn't long before she fell asleep.

Carl and Aksel smiled at the love of the little lass. Ingvar thought of his son and yearned to hold his own young lad back in Norway.

They traveled early the next morn, as the rain had stopped and the water sufficiently drained from the dirt pathways over night. They traveled a great distance that day and it was late when they stopped for the night. All were tired and retired to bed soon after sustenance. They rose early the next day, the sun was shining high in the sky, hard bread and warm goat's milk broke their fast as they moved on.

Ulstead spoke the next night of **Perseverance**. "It be how we do well, keep trying even when we fail. Try again, 'till we succeed. In war, if enemy defeat us, we retreat, build up strong and try again to defeat them.

In life when fail, if our grain not grow, if no rain or too much rain, we try again next season till crops grow well. Not give up if fail once, even twice, keep trying till we succeed. Who do we know who never gives up?

Lam looked up at him "I know Chieftain. It be Unne Arason."

"Yes," Ulstead agreed. "What did he do that he not succeed, not quit?"

"Speak grievance at Althing!" Several children shouted loudly in unison.

"Yes," Ulstead laughed with them. "Unne persevere; will try again this year, maybe he will succeed. You think, maybe?" They giggled, laughed and clapped their hands for Unne.

Aksel thought, Ya *Unne be as my sire. He persevere, send me away to make me a better man. I not always listen to him, but do I learn from what he say? Do I remember his words of wisdom? Am I still a willful prince? Yes, I still be a willful prince who need change his way, grow strong in mind and spirit like other men, like great men.*

The next night they speak of **Fidelity**. "This be loyalty to each other, our spouse, sires, marms. True to one's self, our friends as to our gods - be they the gods of old or the one God of Christianity. Troth be an oath of fealty to family, friends, our gods - a sacred contract for wedded vows not to be broken. Generosity be part of fidelity - give gifts to one's family and friends and receive gift in return - both ways, even in marriage.

Vengeance be not a virtue, but an obligation for murder of kinsmen, a duty. Take revenge or make a heavy fine to prevent a blood feud. To make fine be better. Best not do murder on one another. Murder be not good. One man killed, than another in vengeance and again a third to avenge the second – it go on and on. When will it stop? Yes, heavy fine be more acceptable. Then put feud aside so all can live together like good neighbor."

This silenced everyone, no one needed to say more. The sun set in the west as they retired to their shelters for the night.

The days and nights marched on as Ulstead spoke of the other virtues.

"**Self Discipline**," he said "give us strength to do what need be done for ourselves and to help others, so good be accomplish for all. We must be strong on ourselves to set good example and lead others, so all will follow. Discipline keeps us true to virtues, keeps us on the path of virtue to be true to principles and be free of dependency on others. Self discipline provide will power to remain faithful to the path of Asatru."

Aksel within his thoughts again, wanted to ask a question, but did not know what question to ask. *How do I discipline myself? Sire discipline me, take ungracious, willful prince and send him into the world to live and learn among men. Be this the way of self discipline? I need do this, make myself to think and live by noble virtues? Can I do this? I make myself do this? Do I have courage to do this? Yes, I must discipline myself if I will be a king someday. I must learn how to be a judicious king.*

"**Hospitality** be a virtue to take seriously," Ulstead began. "When guest come to your house from near or far, offer drink and sustenance to make comfort. We share with friends and strangers who visit. In old times, the Gods of Asatru be known to wander in human guise - you never know who a guest really be. It be necessary when traveling long distance to open our door to friends and strangers. When we travel a long distance, they open their door to us. Host provides a warm place to stay, a guest provides news, tales or a song to amuse or perhaps a small trinket or gift. This be friendly, pleasant. This be hospitality."

"Yes," Ingvar said, "as the hospitality you give me and my young charges, accept us in your travel, show us the way to Althing. We be one with you. This be hospitality. We do the same in Norway when you come visit with us." Aksel and Karl nodded and smiled in agreement.

"**Industriousness** means working hard, always strive to be efficient. Activity be vital, to work hard to achieve goals - to work hard to accomplish assigned tasks, at fun and at play also. Enjoy free time – it help to keep us happy. Keep mind free, body strong. All reap rewards of work - eat well, play hard to keep us healthy

of body, strong of mind and have wealth to share among us, so all citizens be happy. Children see parents and grown people work hard, they do same to be industrious. If want to drink mead, must first collect honey from bee. If want to drink ale, must first sow grain to brew. If want to eat, need to till the land, plant seed to grow crops to feed our bodies and raise animals for meat. If we want a clean house, must sweep the dirt and wash the cloths. A strong active body, be a happy, healthy body."

"Yes," Lam's mother said, "Listen to what he say children, not dispute when marm or sire ask you to feed sheep, fetch eggs from nest and be careful not to break them, carry wood to the fire, help sweep dirt from the floor and do the chores needed for house and barn. It be the work of gods. They like to see young lads and lassies help their elders work. You hear?" She spoke true.

Aksel did not remember that he ever did work when in the castle and quietly spoke to Karl who did not remember doing work either. "We work on longboat from Norway, we rowed the longboat hard. See, I have big muscle now." Aksel proudly displays them, pulling up the sleeve of his smock to show his muscles.

They laughed at his muscles, "They not that big!"

"No, maybe not big as Ingvar's, but they're bigger than afore!" he laughed with them.

"**Self Reliance,** the last virtue, to be dependent for oneself, for family, for clan, for all tribe and nation. To ensure we care for self first, then all family, those we love, for whole nation, to share hospitality, be industrious. Do tasks yourself, not wait for others do them for you. If not know how, learn how, have someone teach you how. Self reliance make us strong and independent. Use intellect and wisdom of Odin, the God of Wisdom. Use wisdom, not power or force," he emphasized.

"How a King show self-reliance?" Aksel asked. "I never see my sire work himself. He give orders, others do work, he watches and collects taxes."

"King be leader of the realm, yes," Ulstead replied. "Not labor much, he enforce laws as he see right. If he be judicious, he give his freemen and slaves the tools to work and prosper, and take only sufficient in tax for himself to live in comfort and protect them from harm. If all do the work assigned them, the realm be strong for all, can help others and each other in time of need. A happy realm will be wealthy and healthy, be not that the importance?"

The three found themselves engrossed, listened intently and wondered about the virtues. Karl spoke to his companions, "We never speak of these things, never speak of honor, courage, discipline, reliance. It give much to think and ponder. How be these Icelanders so smart?"

"There be a new creed, Christianity, a faith with the one God of heaven who sent his son, Jesus, to earth to teach us how to live in peace among men," Ulstead continued. "This a loving faith, one to help men achieve happiness among one another and aid each other. It be said it will become the one religion of Iceland, afore long. It be a better religion than the gods of old." Ulstead told them. "Soon we have a friar to teach us how to live, be Christians. Some have a Friar in their midst now, soon he will come to teach all of us."

Aksel mused to himself, *Christianity – Ya, we hear of this. Ulstead say he brought virtues from Norway. I never hear of Nine Noble Virtues afore. Who teach these in Norway? Not my sire!*

CHAPTER THREE

ICELAND, THE ALTHING AND SAGAS

They arrived in the valley north of Lake Thingvallavatn, the chosen place of assembly for the yearly Althing. They prepared their stone walled booths with branches across the top to support the grassed-over roofs to protect articles to be sold or gifted to others and to prepare feasts to share. Friendships, made over the years, enjoyed this time to visit and catch up on news of births, sorrows and happy occasions from the past year.

Ingvar, Aksel and Karl were taught by the lads to pre-pare a shelter for themselves using limbs to build a support wall and cover it with the skins they were offered to use to keep rainwater out; boughs of leaves to hold it in place and to protect them from the elements. "This how we always make shelters for many years past," Lam said.

Ulstead told Ingvar, "Unne Arason shelter be in the field on far side of large rock with those who have a charge to present before the Althing. He be man with big belly, little hair on his head, but full grey beard on chin and a red horse on tunic, you see."

Ingvar walked over to the other side of the grassy field, beyond the large rock. He saw many men with big bellies and full gray beards, but no man with a red horse on his tunic could be found. "Unne be here, he does not wear a red horse tunic. He wear dark tunic," a lad told him, "with silver sword on it."

"Ya, I be Unne Arason," he roared when Ingvar approached a large, strong man. "Who you be?"

Ingvar introduced himself proudly, "I Ingvar, Knight to King Gregors of Heborg, Norway, who charge me take his son on voyage over the sea to show him how men live for good or harm, to help him grow to a man. He say we start in Iceland to meet friend of his youth, to show what a good man be."

"Gregors send you? Send his son to meet me? Where this son not yet man?" Unne sounded incredulous at the request, but pleased, proud his friend would show him to his son as a "good man."

"He be on other side of the meadow with Ulstead - angry still at sire who send him far away to sea."

"Ha," Unne roared, "he be like his sire, of strong will, he grow a good man soon. Come take me to this son not yet man. I see for myself. Come wife," he called to his woman, "I show you lad from Norway, son of my old friend, Gregors."

Ulstead saw Unne coming and hailed him, "Unne, you ole buzzard of a man, still fight your neighbor over that old mare you say he steal?"

"Till I die! Horse come home to my barn always. Be not that sign he be mine, you old cow thief?" Aside, he explained to Ingvar, "Small horse of Iceland be strong, smart, know way home to barn of master. All here know this. Some say horse like gods. Some stories say they be gods."

Ingvar introduced Aksel and Karl. Unne looked at them, "Which be prince? None look like Gregors, you both skinny, where the muscle? Huh?"

Aksel felt insulted, "I the prince. When you know my sire? When he fat old man like you?"

Unne roared again, "Yes, you be prince, sharp tongue like your sire. It good you not him, I take sword to you, trounce you good. This lad be cousin, you say. You both not look like your sires, you have the look of your marms? That not bad," he mused with a shrug of his shoulders. "Me had the look of my Marm, but the muscle of my sire. Ya, you need grow muscle to be a man!" he explained with vigor in his voice. "How be that old goat of a King, your sire?"

"He angry with me, but is well."

"You not anger of him?"

"No anger. Hate him, he call me 'blemish of a man', send me afar - not want to see me more," he explained with resentment.

"Nah!" Unne laughed brashly. "He want see you **grow a man**, you be fine, look about you and learn what be good and what be bad. This a good place to learn - at Althing. Watch how men speak problems in court and chiefs rule who wrong and who right.

"They not fight among each other. Well," Unne paused a moment and shook his head, "sometimes fight anyway, but still speak problems before all to hear! You listen - this help make you wise when you become king and judge for good or harm." He turned to his woman, "This be my spouse, Ingeborg. She be fine woman, she keep me happy." He smiled broadly at her as he patted his belly in contentment.

"All I need do, be to keep food to feed him on table and he happy," she said with a smile. "You all be welcome to join our meal this eve."

Ingvar gratefully accepted without hesitation or consent of the others. "Ya, we be ready for food to make a man happy. Enough of eating food not cooked proper while we travel on the paths."

Unne, well versed in Viking lore of Iceland kept them entertained with his tales of the outlaw, Gisli, and his faithful spouse, Aud.

"Gisli be trapped, he must avenge the death of his faithful friend, who be his wife's brother. To do this, he must kill his sister's husband, who did the murder. Come the dark, he steals into his sister's room with his great spear named Grayflank. He took Thorgrim gently, who thought it be his wife, Gisli's sister. Gisli pulled back the cover and thrust his spear, Grayflank, through Thorgrim so the spear stuck into the bed. Gisli ran! He now be outlaw.

"For many years, some say fourteen years, he hide in cliffs and valleys near his wife, Aud's, farm at Geirthjófsfjörður. Gisli hide from his enemies, but not hide from dreams of a good woman and bad woman who haunt him. He see a bad woman who wash her head in blood, 'til it make him fearful of the dark. "Enemies find his secret hiding place and follow his footsteps in the snow. Fifteen came - he be pierced with spears from both sides. Before he be done, eight enemies lie dead in snow, he speak a verse before all, killed one more with a sword to the skull and leap off cliff to die. He die a heroic Icelandic death.

They whiled away the night listening to his stories and drinking the ale Ulstead provided when he joined them, as did many others who heard the merriment. Many slept the night where they sat - fell asleep from the ale. Ingvar's young charges hung on him and stumbled as they walked back to their shelter to sleep.

There were three men with heavy heads in the morning. They did not eat or drink and were afraid to move lest they stumbled. They groaned with the aching head and grumbling stomach. They were not accustomed to drinking ale all night.

All laughed at their discomfort, as did Unne, "That help you grow a man!" he shouted to them.

As several chieftains had not arrived, the Althing proceedings could not commence, so they traded goods with one another from the different booths. Karl and Aksel marveled at the assortment of articles for sale or trade. They each bought a linen tunic and pants so they could have clean clothes to wear when they washed the dirty ones. They saw a wide variety of designs embroidered on the tunics and had a difficult time deciding which to choose. Ingvar admired a small, sharp knife with a beautiful gilt bronze handle which matched the design on the tunic he chose. Aksel approved his choice and purchased one for himself - Karl looked at them as though he should have one also.

That night many joined them and brought ale to get Unne to tell a tale of yet one saga after another.

"Hallgerd be beautiful wife. She refuse to save her husband Gunnar's life by twining her long golden hair into a bowstring for him to fight his enemy. His mother called her 'an evil woman whose shame will long be remembered.' Hallgerd still became famous among strong Icelandic women.

"There be Gudrun, loveliest woman in her time, also of great intelligence. She be courtly, shrewd, best spoken of all and of generous disposition. She be manipulator, divorced and married many times. She in a love triangle with foster brothers. She tricked one brother to kill the other, who then be hunted and killed. This a great love story of the sagas. She marry again and then be widowed. In old age she be Christian, a nun in Iceland and buried in the holy mountain, name of Helgafel.

"A great warrior, Hrŭt was smitten by aging queen mother, Gunnhild, who ordered him to her bed. He obeyed but was homesick for Iceland and the desire to return to his lovely betrothed Unn. Gunnhild let him go

"With gift of gold bracelet, a kiss, and a curse. She make spell on him, he can never enjoy his lovely betrothed in Iceland who he set his heart to. They had much passion and desire but he could not consummate their love, so went their different ways." Unne spoke lightly with a flourish of his hands and a sad smile.

The next night, Lam said to Unne, "Tell us story of Grettir. He strong man from north who lift huge boulder, show strength to friends at Bjarg. That my favorite story."

"Yes, he be a strong man. He tough, willful, cold, cruel, scornful and ill-behaved when a young lad like you. Strong as he be, even as a young lad, he not work. He kill young goslings, scratch his sires back with a steel comb 'til the blood flowed and flayed his sire's horse." Unne accentuated with gestures and expressions meant to put fear into their hearts.

"When grown he did battle with a ghost, bear, troll, and giant." He paused after each name spoken in a scary voice. "These had placed a spell on all the countryside and Grettir was the only one who dared to kill the monsters - then he stole the ghost's treasure." Unne guffawed and looked about him at the scared young faces.

"Next he rid a haunted farmhouse of a ghost named Glam, who walked about the house on the roof and made noise with heels banging so hard he nearly broke the roof.

Men feared to go near. Grettir stayed the night in the house, pretended to sleep and seized Glam when he entered. He fell through the door fighting and Glam lay flat looked up at moon which scare him so bad his eyes roll round and round." Unne embellished his words with his hands, going around in circles as he spoke. "Grettir weak, not fight. Glam made curse on Grettir. 'You no longer be hero, your deeds no make you known by all. They bring you ill and misfortune, you be outlaw and you live alone. You will see these eyes of mine before you always, they horrendous, drag you unto death.' Grettir struggled one last time and cut off Glam's head. As Glam said, Grettir did make mistake, Althing vote him outlaw, he lost all he owned, lived alone, no one help him. He hungry, stole farmer's livestock to eat, stole things not his to use. A reward be put on his head, he fought all and killed many. He tried to sleep, but see Glam's eyes before him. They haunt him everywhere he go – he saw many phantoms in the night.

"He escaped with his young brother, Illugi, to an island, name of Drangey. It be an eerie island of rock which came straight up out of sea, 150 feet. Lived many years on island, ate birds, eggs and mutton from sheep that grazed there, and water to drink from one spring. Many try to climb the island to kill him - none succeed. Thorbjorn had old mother who knew witchcraft and use her to help put curse on him. Grettir threw rock and broke her leg. She came back when leg healed, put curse on wood that Grettir use in fire. He swung axe to cut wood, but axe cut him to the bone. It fester and he become weak. Thorbjorn and many others come the night, cut off Grettirs' head and kill his brother. That be end of Grettir."

"You scare me," a young boy cried out. "That not what my marm say of sagas, they be nice fairy people who sing and dance in the moonlight."

Unne nods his head, "There be some, yes, but more of other. There be elves and fairies about Iceland, many people see them. If you be good boy, if you grow to be a good man then someday you will see fairies, maybe." He nodded his head. "Trolls live in canyon of rocks near Bolugil where water falls down from hill."

Aksel wondered, *I be willful prince like Grettir, I grow like him?*

In time, all the chieftains arrived, the parliament convened the next day and the elected Law Speaker climbed upon the Law Rock to recite from memory the Law Codes of the Althing.

"He not forget no single code - they not let him," Unne was loud to proclaim. "If he not speak one Law Code, it no longer be law. So we tell him when he forget to speak one, less it be our favor not to speak," he chuckled with a mischievous grin.

All sat attentive while the man-of-important-position of Althing spoke the codes and then went on to review settlements of past years to be sure the law was being obeyed in proper order. As none complained, the court separated in their four geographical divisions so Godar's, the chieftains of each division, could adjudicate old and new grievances as they were brought to the attention of the court.

Unne waited his turn to speak. It wasn't till the third day before he could stand to make his complaint. When he stood, the Chieftain asked, "You still fight over that horse you sold your neighbor?"

"No, maybe yes," Unne politely replied. "He still not pay for mare, not even one ell. Horse still return my barn after I take her back to Herrick's barn. Now she be with foal, sired by my strong stallion of good blood. Neighbor not ask to use stallion. Mare keep coming back to my barn, stallion took her when she ready. Do I not earn some reward for service to his mare he not pay for, always come back to my barn and eat my oats. He take mare he not paid for to his barn, keep mare with foal sired by my stallion not paid for. This be fair?" he demanded of the chieftains.

"Be Herrick here to speak on his behalf?" the Chieftain asked the assembly.

Herrick's name was called among the citizens many times. He did not answer. The chieftains discuss the case and came back to Unne. "You have honest complaint. You take foal from mare in her time, keep foal. If neighbor still wants mare, he keep mare, but if mare returns your barn again, you keep mare. Make him pay agreed price to get her back. That content you?"

Unne looked hard at chieftain, slowly shook head, "That sound like good rule, but neighbor not listen. He take mare in night and hide her in the woodland."

Chieftain thought, then spoke, "I speak with Herrick, tell what we decide in Althing. He will abide our decision - I make him pay what he owe. Or, next time mare come your barn, you keep her. Lock her in barn – she be yours with foal. All hear what we say? You all be witness to Althing decision!" he shouted so all could hear.

"If he not settle price, I settle with him my way," Unne threatened. "It be two years. He think me fool? I show him not deceive old man who fought alongside Gregors of Heborg in raid on Britons."

This quieted the assembly, they never heard Unne speak harsh of his neighbor. He always spoke well of his neighbor until he had a grievance, as he did now.

The three men listened to the charges and counter charges of the Althing assemblies and Aksel dwelt on this method of governing. He addressed Ulstead, Unne and the other chieftains, "Would Althing Assemblies work in Norway, would all the realms abide by one agreement of laws for all? Would one king accept the decision of another king where there was conflict amongst them?"

The chieftains looked at one another, thought about it and discussed it among themselves, but could not give Aksel an authoritative answer. "Perhaps, it depend," Ulstead finally concluded. "Kings be of one mind, listen only to their own thoughts and not make compromise lest others think them weak. It be wise to try, see if you get some to agree to one set of laws. If it works, others will know it be good and join also. You think to try this when you become king?" he questioned.

"I dwell on it. It be a fine way to rule. I not know how do this, must think, speak with wise men and other's who rule. Do you scribe laws?"

"Have one scribe, yes, but not have instrument to scribe with – so we remember laws and speak them in front of all at Althing."

Thus, Aksel had much to dwell on. He spoke with his cousin and knight protector who gave him even more to think about. They listened to the last of the disputes and rulings and enjoyed the social life for the rest of the fortnight with the Chieftains, Godars and citizens of Iceland. But minded not to drink too much ale while socializing the night long.

They were invited to travel with Unne to see inland and investigate the rock formations, basalt columns among the remains of icebergs along the way. They took advantage of available hot springs, soaked their bodies and washed their cloaks and pants with the soft cleaning liquid Ingeborg gave them to remove the dirt. They enjoyed the soft, creamy liquid. It cleansed well and removed soil from their clothes. They inquired of what it was made and marveled as Ingeborg showed them how to crush the root of a soap plant from the nearby woodlands and smash it well, until it softened and could be rubbed on their skin and clothes for cleaning.

"You will stay with us in our cottage in the country. We have a nice farm, work hard. It be beautiful during summer and our friendly neighbors come to talk and feast," Ingborg said. They were made to feel at home with Unne and Ingeborg, and enjoyed the pleasant, quiet life. The three men worked the fields with their host and thralls to produce food for the coming year. Aksel and Karl flexed their muscles and enjoyed the strength in their bodies as they grew stronger and competed with Ingvar in many ways.

Eventually, Unne met with his neighbor, Herrick, who came for the horse not paid for. "Godar speak with you? You will pay for horse now? You also pay for my stallion's service?" Unne quizzed.

"I speak with Godar, yes. I not have money to pay for mare. You keep her, she now with foal, be useless for hard work. You won't have anger now?"

"Not have anger, Herrick, we be neighbors." They shook hands and Unne brought him up to date on the Althing activities and asked him, "How you feel to accept Christianity as religion for all Iceland? Do away with many Gods, have just one God of peace?"

Herrick agreed, "It be discussed by many and we will soon become land of one God. Not know how to feel about it, need to dwell on it. Have neighbor who proclaim it be better, he accept it. We should talk with him to learn more."

Unne introduced his neighbor, Herrick, to his guests after they listened to their discussion. It was becoming a more interesting subject for them, this Christianity. Aksel still wondered and questioned it.

Soon thereafter the cold winds threaten from the north and the three take leave of their gracious host and hostess to travel astride their stallions southwest back to Thingvellir on the coast. "It with heavy hearts we leave your land. It be marvelous country where all are ruled fairly among men. If you ever come again to Norway, you and your spouse be welcome in my father's realm, Sir Unne," Aksel held his handshake for a long time, "Yes, you be welcome." Turning to Ingeborg, Aksel hugged her close and gave her a kiss on her cheek. He had a tear in his eye, "You were a marm to us. We appreciate all you do for us, for welcoming us. May the gods look with favor on you and protect you."

Ingvar looked at his willful prince with a nod of approval; he was learning to be gracious, thoughtful and judicious. "Ya, the young prince learne much from the hospitality and laws of Iceland," he told Unne.

"He be better prince now, soon will grow into good king." Unne was quick to agree. "Happy I am to meet and know the young prince of my friend, happy to help him grow to be a judicious man. Give his sire my regard and pray he be well and his spouse, Hulda."

They rode hard to the coast and inquired along the shore for passage to the east coast of Ireland. A vessel was available on shore. The captain had to wait several days for the arrival of a merchant with merchandise to transport back to Norway before he could set sail to the southeast.

CHAPTER FOUR

AT SEA, ICELAND TO IRELAND

"It will be a week before the merchant arrive, stores his wares secure and proper aboard the longboat," Captain Sine told Aksel, Karl and Ingvar when they arrived at the seacoast.

Aksel was in a foul mood for the delay. The air had turned cold, the wind blew from the north in gusts, threatening to bring an early winter to the land. Captain Sune tried to be patient with the aggravated, still willful prince. "The merchant be a frequent trader. I be obliged to wait for him, lest I return to Norway with an empty longboat and no profit."

So Ingvar attempted to keep them occupied locally. They rode their horses about the outskirts of the city, chanced upon a local fisherman on the river inlet who was in need of help, as his thrall was ill with chills and fever from the cold.

"That lazy lout get chills and fever every year when the first cold blast of winter come upon us. My name be Bjarke, supplier of fish to all in Thingvellir. You know how to catch fish? Be you gentlemen of leisure? Do you look for work and lodging to keep body and soul together?"

"We fish some, yah," Ingvar told him, remembering their experience when they first came to Iceland. "We not do well. Perhaps if you show how do, we can help. We need to leave soon when longboat be ready to travel to Ireland. We wait for merchant to bring his trade goods to ship to Norway."

Bjarke taught them how to place the brushwood weirs to trap fish in their funnel shapes in the nearby inlet as the tide carried the salmon up river. They spent four days with the fisherman and his wife, Yrsa, working the weirs on the in-coming tides and were fortunate to catch a considerable number of large salmon. They feasted on the salmon Yrsa roasted over the hot coals and also enjoyed meeting their two young children, four year old Liz and ten year old Ejsten. Liz took a liking to Karl and followed him around whenever she could. Karl was flattered the little lass wanted him to play with her, but how was he to play with a little lass? He just contented her by taking her hand and going for a short walk to see what her sire was doing with the boats for the night.

Ejsten was learning how to work the nets and they were amazed at how capable he was and enjoyed watching the lad haul them in. "You surely be strong to help your sire fish. Someday you will catch more fish than he?" Aksel encouraged.

Ejsten laughed, "It be long time afore I catch more than my sire, Prince Aksel, but work hard, try best I can. Fish be good to eat, I like to eat much. Do you fish in Norway among your people?"

"No, there be no sea where I live – there be lakes and river. Sometimes my people fish there, but we not catch big salmon as do you here. We have traders who bring us salted fish to eat, but it not good as fresh salmon caught from cold Icelandic sea."

There time of waiting over, they bid Liz and Ejsten farewell, invited them all to visit in Norway and mounted their steeds to return to the coast. They sold their steeds to a farmer as they left the countryside and walked to the shoreline with a supply of salted salmon wrapped in a woven sack that Yrsa provided. Captain Sune was pacified with their delicious contribution to the ship's food supply. He tried to conceal it from the crew, but it did not last long once they caught sight and smell of it.

The trader's stores were laden aboard the merchant vessel and tied down inside the belly of the ship. "Will the ship sink?" Karl asked the captain. "I not see one so full afore."

Captain Sune laughed, "Have no fear, the ship be stable and secure," the merchant assured them and was amused by their unwarranted concern. They set sail as the light from the sun rose above the trees early the next morning and rowed out, away from the haven of land, where the wind caught in the sail. Karl and Aksel worked among the oarsmen until they tired and then took a turn bailing water from the bottom. The wind picked up the third day as the first blast of winter found them and the ship skimmed over the water to the southeast with full sail.

Captain Sune walked the length of his ship, checked the wind direction, the ropes that held merchandise fast, found all well and prepared to retire to his cot. He spoke to his mate, "Not sure I can sleep sharing that small space with the young prince. He demands his convenience. The two traveling with him are accommodating and the merchant a pleasant man of means, but the prince be a thorn in my side."

The prince's cot lay vacant, Captain Sune thought perhaps the young prince fell overboard. None would expect him to try a rescue in these heavy seas. He smiled with the thought.

Prince Aksel lay down earlier in the evening. His stomach sending mixed messages. On the one hand he ached for food and on the other - just the thought of it left him nauseous. He dared not test it - he swallowed a few mouthfuls of water and collapsed onto a bear rug nearby. Ingvar covered him with a fur skin for warmth. They all slept the night in discomfort of the cold wind and lurching ship.

The clouded sky obliterated the north star so the ships mate could not find direction. They could not determine what direction they were being drawn. The current and the wind pulled them in unison. Even with the sail furled, the ship skimmed over the sea with the strong surge of water underneath and continued through the night. The men on watch felt fortunate the clouds partly cleared so the bright half-moon lightened their path part of the time.

Come morning, Aksel opened his eyes, rose forward on one elbow to peer over the side of the ship to look at the sea. He peered hard trying to see through the mist sprayed up from the bow. He looked about at the others still sleeping, even the watchmen sat in the stern their heads bobbing with the lurching ship. He reached over, shook Karl who lay beside him, "Look, Karl, look. Do you see what I see, be that land on the horizon? Have we reached Ireland? So soon?"

Karl groaned as he turned over, his eyes stung from the bright sun in his eyes. "Where?" he mumbled. "I not see land the sun too strong."

"No, the other way," Aksel paused, a look of alarm suddenly appeared on his face as the realization of what that signified sunk in. "That be to the west, the sun rise in the east. What land be to the west?"

Karl turned to see and he, too, became alarmed, and quickly went to the Captain who was just stirring. "Captain, there be land - to the west, there be land. Sun rise the east." He pointed, "The sea move us to west, all night long the sea move us to west! We be going the wrong direction!"

Captain Sune rose slowly, controlling himself to show the least amount of concern. "Not to fret, we be safe. If the current take us to land, we take to shore 'til the wind become still or shift to the east." He did not know what land they had come upon.

In short order, they beached on the rather desolate icy shore and carefully secured the boat. The merchant was concerned to lose his merchandise and fretted about while Captain Sune and crew did the best they could. "The tide be coming in so we pull boat up on shore as water rise," he explained. The rough water was still a threat as they saw nothing close by to secure the anchor.

They walk on the snow, uncomfortably, their footwear did not protect them from the snow and ice. The temperature was extremely cold, their heavy tunics were not adequate to keep them warm. They saw no sign of life and ventured into the sparse wooded area nearby to escape the wind.

Several crewmen took their axes and ventured further into the woodland to look for animals they could kill to eat, while others searched for dry wood and cleared a place to build a fire. Stones were abundant nearby, but the cold made it hard for the flint to spark. Perseverance succeeded eventually.

"Captain Sune," a crewman called, "I find a trap made of wood sticks. It caught small animal in it. There be people living here about, but where?" It was a puzzle no one could figure out. They also discovered traps strung further up along the shore to catch fish in the ocean. The land was occupied – by whom?

Aksel had been venturing along the woodland looking for something, he knew not what. He noticed several round mounds covered with snow and was startled when he saw a section of the snow-covered dirt fall outward and a man climb out. Fully clothed in fur skins, the figure stood up, replaced the sod section into the mound and moved away into the woodland. Aksel froze in his tracks undetected behind a tree, didn't know what to do. He walked back to the others and spoke to Ingvar and the Captain of what he had seen.

"Did he see you?" Ingvar asked.

"I think not, he never turned around, climbed out, went into the woodland and disappeared among the trees," he replied.

Captain Sune, Ingvar and Aksel walked cautiously back to the snow-covered mounds and observed them for a short time, no one appeared. "He walked this way into the woodland," Aksel said and led them in that direction. It wasn't long before they heard the ring of an axe hitting on a tree and the sound of a felled tree landing on the ground. They came upon the man Aksel had seen. The man was startled at the sight of them and stared with the look of one not believing his eyes.

"I be Captain Sune, a seaman from Norway," the Captain introduced himself. "We came ashore the morn, blown by the strong wind from the east and not know where we land. Be you a Norseman? You have the look of a Norseman." He smiled and spoke to him slowly and politely so as not to appear threatening."

"I be Norseman," the man confirmed. "I not see Norseman in many moons. Your ship be well secured?"

"Yes," Captain Sune answered. "We leave soon the winds turn favorable, we travel from Iceland to Ireland. How you arrive here? Where be this land? It a strange land of ice and snow. You make a home here?"

"Traveled with Vikings, we land here in storm many moons ago. Longboat destroyed by strong wave which throw it on rocks ashore. I be the only one who alive - others drowned or froze in sea. I live here now with peaceful tribe who make me welcome. I work with them, help them, cut much timber to warm shelters underground. They be short people, strong, but small. Live here many, many moons. I learn to understand what they say, they travel from far west and settle here. They have name for country, but I not understand how to say it. It be a strange manner they speak." He rambled on delighting in speaking his own language to someone who understood.

Ingvar was fascinated with the man and what he told them. "How you live in the ice? Do you raise pigs? Grow corn? How you eat? What be your name?"

"My name be Enoch. We do farm work, but eat walrus, seals and many fish from sea, trap small hares to eat and kill musk oxen, wolves. I not like this place, there be no warmth, no comfort. I leave when find a way. You take me when you leave? I be good oarsman, I strong to fight the sea, the wind?"

"Will the people here miss you, let you leave?" Captain Sune was hesitant. "I not want make bad feelings or make problems."

"They will let me go," he assured them. "They know I not one of them. They welcome me, yah. I work with them, yah. But want return to Norway where my family be. They wish me well."

The native leader greeted them and they were welcomed by the people of the land of ice and snow when Enoch returned to the mounds and introduced them. They could not speak with them, except through the marooned Norseman, who was able to make the natives understand the Norsemen would be leaving when the weather turned favorable. The natives rarely saw foreign men, were curious about them, as the Norsemen were curious about the natives. They enjoyed socializing with the friendly people, playing with the children and their smart breed of pet dogs with beautiful, full, thick coats of fur. They feasted with them on the fresh fish from the sea and clean melted ice water, but no mead or ale was available to warm their blood. Captain Sune didn't offer to use the supply from his stores for fear it would be needed at sea.

The air warmed up slightly in the afternoon, the tide was coming in fast. Captain Sune questioned Enoch, "The tide rises fast? We leave on the out-going tide this night, if the wind be stilled. Get a good start with the tide, row the night and pray the winds be favorable the morrow. Will this work?"

"If we get far away from the land and take advantage of the current at sea, yes, that be good. The sky shouldbe clear to read the north star. You try this night?" When Captain Sune nodded, "Ig go with you?" Enoch asked.

"Have you talked with the people who accepted you, how do they feel?"

"Yah, I talk with Chieftain, he say I go. He smiled and said, 'Yes, go with your people.' He understand, I return my home land," Enoch smiled happily.

Captain Sune shook his hand in agreement. "We will have another man to pull the oars. This be good."

The winds from the northeast calmed enough by evening, the daylight lasted far into the night as it had in Iceland, also. Enoch spoke his farewell to the peaceful tribe who had accepted and aided him in his trial and shook the hand of the men. A young lad, hugged him gently, spoke words of farewell and gave him a small object which Enoch gazed at for a long moment. He was pleased and gave the lad a smile of happiness, a fatherly hug in return and a manly handshake of appreciation. Tears filled the lad's eyes. Enoch knelt, held him close, hugged him tight and the lad babbled at him in his foreign tongue clinging to his neck. The native leader spoke to them and the lad nodded his head and clung even harder to Enoch's neck. He stood up, lifting the lad with him. "He want to come with me. He be like a son to me these many moons, his sire and marm be dead. We become like father and son. He has one relative who say I can take him to my land if he want to go. Be there room for one little lad, one good little lad?"

Aksel looked at his companions, who nodded in agreement, the crew was non-committal. The merchant spoke up, "He not take much room on ship, won't eat much, but need to tie him to the post so he not fall overboard when ship lurches about," he jested.

They were given a supply of dried, smoked fish to add to their stores and fresh water to fill their kegs. The men were grateful and bid farewell to their pleasant hosts and shoved off into the outgoing tide in the half light of the artic night.

They wakened the next morning, a strong wind filled the sail and pulled the longboat smoothly eastward

The men kept occupied as best they could, then played a game with dice. Karl and Aksel joined them, gambling for half-pennies. The game was lucky for only one seaman and strong words passed among them which then erupted into a fight. Captain Sune put a stop to it when one man pulled a knife, "We'll have no bloodshed on this ship, I'll cast you into the sea," he threatened.

At the end of the third week the wintry winds again escalated to a steady gale, unrelenting with occasional pelting rain. Prince Aksel huddled between cabinets aft, held tight to his knees and groaned in agony as his stomach lurched again in miserable fashion. "May the Gods look down and calm these seas, I cannot lose more. My stomach be empty to make me miserable." He watched Cousin Karl who enjoyed the wild movement of the ship as the waves tossed the longboat on high, then low into the depths. *Look at that madness* Aksel thought, he *swing back and forth from one rail to another, daring the rough seas to cast him into the deep. It maks my stomach lurch just to watch him.* He found the young lad, Kyush, had come in close to him holding fast to his tunic for security.

The seas and the waves remained rougher the night long and through the morning. Captain Sune assured the merchant, "Your stores have not been disturbed. We will check them shortly to be certain." He told his crew, "I not certain where we be, no land sighted since we left the land to the west. Clouded skies hid the stars all the night, so cannot see to find direction." The Captain's mate told him, "No large ice floes crossed our bow the day or night. We must be south of glacial temperatures. Some huge whales challenge our right to the ocean, but they too pass. The wind still blows the same course from the northwest, but the seas have settled."

Prince Aksel wakened to the milder movement of the longboat thinking, *I not experience such a debilitating two days my whole life. My strength, my self-sufficiency be challenged. To be sick and dependant on others belittles my self esteem. Karl and Ingvar tend my needs, I be gratified yet humbled. I not enjoy being beholden to them in this fashion. I not sick sailing to Iceland. None about me suffer the debilitation. Even little Kyush not feel the movement. I not belong at sea? Be this a sign?* he asked himself. *Dare I admit failure to my sire? The son of a Norseman King unable to sail the seas on a Viking longboat? The shame! I not speak of it, even to Ingvar or Karl.*

Ingvar, like an older brother to him, tended his needs when he rose. They consumed the last of whatever food was left and forced the miserable cold gruel down – it was that or nothing. They were overdue to reach port on the shore of Ireland.

Prince Aksel politely took up conversation with the trader traveling with them, who had kept to himself most of the trip, speaking only to the captain. "I be Prince Aksel of Heborg, this my cousin Karl and Knight Ingvar. Your name, sir?"

"Verner Eskild, of Kaupang, trader of carved wooden articles, precious stones and metal appliances from foreign countries in return for farming tools, fine cloths of linen and many other articles to sell. Also, a small supply of dried meat."

"You say dried meat?" Prince Aksel interrupted. "Be it edible, will it make us ill?"

"Not so. It be a very substantial food consumed by people for many years, perhaps centuries. I learn the process to preserve the meat," he emphasized. "I offer the process to my spouse's family to experiment in the preparation and use. They be intelligent, with a learned scholar among them. They will test the accuracy of the assessment of drying the meat with smoke and heat, not with excessive salt, so it keep for indefinite length of time. If it do well, they will produce it so I offer it in trade to others. It be a wondrous boon for travelers."

"Well can we buy some to eat now?" Karl demanded, looked at Aksel for agreement. "We be famished for good sustenance!"

"I pleasure to offer you some, but must wait to get it from my supplies so others not know. I can offer only you a small amount of my limited supply," he insisted. We will be in port within another day, if all go well, where food be plentiful for all."

"How soon can that be?" Ingvar inquired, "I could eat a whole pig to salve my hunger."

"The Captain intends to check my stores for damage from the weather. I get some then, if possible. Be silent of it. It have very strong aroma, it be advisable to eat it aft wind." He cautioned them in a hushed voice, "Meet me aft when I return."

The four men sat in the shelter of the stores, their stomachs fed of dried meat and toasted the gentleman of means with mugs of ale. Even Kyush joined them, since Enoch was rowing. Captain Sune allowed his men to open a small keg of the precious drink to keep their stomachs content in place of solid sustenance. The sailors had greeted the keg as a favored prize and were completely oblivious of what Verner retrieved from his stores.

Now they sat with loose tongues chiding their young prince of his follies. Verner gleans from the conversation, "You give the young prince an education in living by traveling the world," he asked, "to become knowledgeable by watching other nations rule for good or harm? You do this to prepare to succeed your father?"

"Yah. We see Iceland, they have no king, but rule with chieftains who assemble every year to make and review laws, hear disputes and settle them among the citizens. It do well. We travel to the isle of the Celts next." Aksel told him.

Karl interrupted, "We also find Aksel an acceptable maiden for wife, hopefully in the Land of Celts or perhaps Britain."

"No," Aksel said firmly, "I will find a maiden in Viking land. One I can talk to and understand, not of foreign tongue."

"Yes, a pleasant, docile lady who will 'Yes, Sire' to you, give no grief or harsh words. Do you think to find one among the strong women of our land? Like the little lass who struck you? Called you 'no less an animal than your steed?' "

Ingvar interceded, "For uncommon reason, cousin. Aksel grieved loss of his promised bride, might not you counter in like manner?"

Karl looked at him, "A beautiful disappointing loss, but then the younger sister will be as acceptable in time. She survived the fever, be a strong lass, even jousts with her brother. If he keep his wits about him, she might accept him, but now?"

"She may still," Ingvar replied. "King Ivar offered her." Aksel ignored them. "Perhaps in time our prince will forgive the transgression and look at a mature maiden from a peaceful realm, fair of hair, taught by a wizard. Aksel lay whip to her honorable wise man, she responded in kind," he explained to Verner.

."Yah," Karl gleefully retorted. "Kaja struck him for using the whip on her wise man and named him animal," he repeated.

Verner's ears perked up, he realized they spoke of his nieces. He could no longer just listen to them talk disparagingly of her. Verner knows Kaja as a delightful, intelligent young maiden, a lovely prize and felt the need to defend her. "Perhaps this young maiden too young to be a lady, to act a lady?" he asked politely.

"Yes," Ingvar responded for Aksel. "A very young maiden and they allow her to act much as a male child. I do believe the king, her father, and her queen mother will see that she be properly refined now that her older sister not available."

Verner studied his words, "Do not be hasty to look elsewhere until you see the young maiden as a mature princess. You say she survive the fever, strong of body and spirit," adding incredulously, "can even joust?" Verner smiled, recalling Kaja trying to be ladylike, enjoying still the interaction with the sword, much to her mother's chagrin. He did not tell them he was Kaja's uncle by marriage.

They spent many hours that last day together. They discussed different subjects and found many things in common to speak of, shared experiences from their travels and actually enjoyed each others company. Young Kyush sat with them and listened though not understanding.

The prince being receptive of his words, Verner resumed the earlier conversation, "I see many countries on my travels. If learning to be a leader you seek, to spend time in the Britons, to observe their approach to governing and commerce, be a beneficial learning experience. They advance well, seek to rule fairly, use the skills of the people to better their lot, benefit in trade among each other to improve the realm."

"We will travel there after we see the Celts," Aksel told him. "The Celts practice this new religion, Christianity, a more peaceable way of life I be told. Some Icelanders be Christian, but the old gods still prevail. We observe how Christianity fares among nations. We see the Britons and return after to Norway so I can find a proper wife," he emphasized. "Enough of this miserable sailing the seas, fighting the elements."

"Are you aware the profits of peaceable trade between countries and realms within a country, to share knowledge with benefits beyond belief?" Verner asked. "This I do. Bring new knowledge and many things back home, like the smoked meat that keeps well for long periods of time, better than the method now used by Norsemen. It amaze me the methods seen in even the most remote areas, even this land of snow and ice. The way people devise ways to overcome obstacles in their path, a remarkable tribute to man's intelligence, his vision. Observe and learn. Ask questions, others are willing to speak of their customs and methods and hear yours in return." Verner paused a moment and ventured, "What do you look for in a maiden for wife? Beauty you seek? Perhaps, a learned, good hearted lady to aid you, sit by your side with love? There be advantage in the later if you seek a peaceful realm. If you find both beauty and learning, all in one, you have all you need, you be a blessed prince, a fortunate man and king indeed."

They heard, "Land Ho!" from the captain. He called, "We be ashore afore dark."

They part as friends and Verner is proud the young prince actually listened and accepted advice on many subjects. He goes from one to the other grasping each hand in farewell. He held the prince's hand and looked him firm, "I found you to be harsh and negative, by first impression, Sir Prince." He paused, "After the stormy seas, perhaps, nature's rampage humbles us, as it did me many moons past, made you feel vulnerable, at the mercy of the elements, the gods. A prince, yes, but still just a man, and as all men, subject to the ravages of nature and circumstance. You do well. Continue your quest, you will find your lady and your destiny."

Verner clapped the young prince on the shoulder and prayed he had given him thoughts that would help him become a judicious man and king, especially if his niece, delightful Kaja, was to be his wedded wife.

CHAPTER FIVE

IRELAND

In the kingdom of the Celts they chance upon a brigade of Vikings traveling the road ahead of them. "What be your destination?" Ingvar asked a young warrior straggling at the rear, dragging his encased sword beside him as he struggled to catch up to his companions.

"We return to Dublin. The Christians fight us to take back control of their church at Clontarf," the warrior answered.

"Be that reason for war? The Christians a threat? I thought they a peaceable lot."

"Except when they refuse to worship our gods: Thor, Odin and Freyr. They fight to the death! Which they did," came his odious reply as he continued walking on laboriously.

Prince Aksel came along side, "You are tired from your journey young knight? Come ride behind me. My steed be strong to carry two men."

The warrior welcomed the invitation and used the stirrup and hand, which Aksel made available to him, to lift himself up onto the horse.

"I be Aksel of Heborg, what be your name?" he asked.

"I Tyge Holsten of Dublin, born of Norsemen here in Ireland, fighting with the Vikings to hold this fort against the Celts. They be a fearsome lot and hold strong to their faith."

"Yes, Christianity be known in Norway, soon the old gods will be no more," Ingvar responded. "It has merit; a peaceable, righteous creed, to bring people together in peace and love. What be gained from warring on each other; pillage, murder, enslavement. In our travels we see both peaceful and conflict, the peaceful approach make a better living among all people. To live in fear of our neighbor be not good."

"What your name?" Tyge asked.

"I be Ingvar of Heborg and the other Karl, also of Heborg."

"A word of advice – do not expound on that view in Dublin, you not survive the night," Tyge told him. "Our Vikings take no patience with Christianity, to hear it from a Norseman will start a war among us."

"Yah, I know, but it will be, we Norsemen like it or not," Ingvar insisted and nodded his head in emphasis.

As they neared the gate to the city, they caught up to the brigade of tired marching men who looked forward to their quarters, sustenance, a pint of ale and rest for the night. They wait their turn to enter the fort.

The warriors at the fort welcomed the brigade. Tyge left them explaining, "I be grateful for the ride, Aksel. I leave you now. I not want to be amongst Christian loving people, lest others discover it and I be charged."

The three spent several weeks in the area, visited different parts of the very extensive, prosperous city and walled fort that the Vikings had built and settled.

They ventured out into the countryside and observed the Celtic farms, spoke with the farmers when they found one who understood them. They observed their methods, talked to local leaders inquired of rules and laws, listened to and attended the religious services, prayers and attempted to understand their Christian customs. They joined a group of people who were being instructed in the Norse tongue, in the Christian faith by a local friar, Friar Magnussen, and found it even more acceptable than before. They listened to the stories and gospels of Jesus with interest and tried hard to understand them. The Friar gave detailed explanations so they would be more likely to comprehend and accept.

"It take faith to understand the teachings of Jesus, you must come to know him and love him. "They speak of how we look one upon another, in malice, anger, slander, sorrow, love, humility, fear. How we be obedient to God's laws of repentance, gluttony, lust, pride, prayer and simplicity. It remind me of the Nine Noble Virtues learned in Iceland. It bring us peace to the mind and spirit," Ingvar said to his charges.

"The Irish be a happy, carefree people; sociable and willing to accept us, even invite Norsemen into their homes. We find many Norsemen married to the Celts, many living in harmony and others in disunity. If we call ourselves Vikings will we be made welcome? Why be it ever thus?" Karl went on with his observations as they returned on their steeds to Dublin and the Viking Fort, after having enjoyed the calm, peace and quiet of the countryside among the Irish for many weeks.

"What would you think if I find a bride among these Celts and take her back to Heborg?" Aksel asked his companions.

Karl looked at him disbelieving, "You jest?"

"No, just a thought, they be mighty sweet little maidens," he countered, smiling.

"To play with perhaps, but to wed and become a queen in Norway? You best think about it longer, my Sire." Karl gave him a hard look of concern for his cousins' sanity. "Remember I jest aboard the longboat to pick a maiden from our travels, and you spoke strong against it. What changed your thoughts?"

Aksel spoke naught, just smiled impishly at his cousin. Ingvar raised his eyebrows to Karl, decided it best not say a word, his cousin spoke it well.

Aksel and Karl enjoyed drinking ale among the merry lassies as they learned the dances of the Irish. Ingvar drank ale and thought of his family back in Heborg and muttered to himself, *When will my young Prince hurry and finish with his travels and mature in his mind so we can return home? My wedded wife be lonely and my young son, now a young lad will not know his own sire This be enough for me.*

As Ingvar watched his charges play and dance, a large, strong Irishman came, sat nearby and asked him with guarded words, "You be a strong man, have the look of a knight. You travel through Dublin?"

Ingvar looked him straight in the eye, thought perhaps he was trouble. He did not say a word, just a nod and grunt. The Irishman spoke in Norse, not Irish, so he understood what he said.

"I be Armage, Knight to Brian Boru, Monarch of Dal Cais to the south. One day he will be high king to all of Ireland," he paused, "I have watched you close. You have the look of a man on a mission. Will you tell me what that mission is?"

Ingvar looked at him again straight in the eye, perhaps this Armage make story? He make me talk, then kill me? "Why need you know who I be, what my mission be? I not do harm, have no malice for Irish. I watch young men at play, drink ale, enjoy dance with lassies. Be this of harm to you?"

"No, not harm. Stranger come, I watch for my liege, talk. They be friend, perhaps foe."

"You say name Brian Boru? I not know this name, not know the names of monarchs in Ireland. I be a Norseman, on mission of love for my liege, King Gregors of Heborg. He have willful son who has need to learn how men live for good or harm so will grow to be a judicious king. He trust me take his son afar, then return home safe. We see Iceland - land of no kings, chieftains rule by parliament, make laws to live by among each other. It be good. We now see Ireland, land of kings, much as Norway. Always, one king fight another king, no peace among men. This not good. Next we go to England. What we see there, do you know?" he paused while Armage sat with lost tongue. "I not foe to any man, we look for peace, knowledge, justice and regard among men," Ingvar added,

Armage still sat with lost tongue, "How I know you speak true?"

"I speak true," Ingvar asserted. "This be one of Noble Virtues we learn in land of ice. I gain nothing with story. I speak true."

"Noble Virtues? What be this Noble Virtues, I never hear this before?" Armage asked.

"There be nine – Courage, Truth, Honour, Fidelity, Discipline, Hospitality, Industriousness, Self Reliance, Perseverance." Ingvar said these slow and sure so Armage could hear them clearly. Ingvar repeated the virtues again, while Armage listened again. Ingvar then said, "There be many rules that speak of how we look at one another, in malice, anger, slander, sorrow, love, humility, fear. How we be obedient to God's laws of repentance, gluttony, lust, pride, prayer and simplicity. This be the new Christianity the Celt's expound. You know these? You be Celt?"

Aksel and Karl returned to the table with three little lasses in tow, laughing,

"See Ingvar, ladies show us how do Celtic dance. We have fun, drink ale. Come join us, there another lass here for you to dance with," Aksel persuaded.

"Who be this gentleman, he join us the night?" Karl asked.

Ingvar introduced, "This be Knight Armage to King Brian Boru, who ask what our mission be."

Aksel said, "It a pleasure to shake hand of knight to king. Ingvar be knight to king, my sire, Gregors of Heborg. You join us, dance with pretty lasses, drink a pint? Get this old man up from his chair to have fun, dance." He called the lasses to him to introduce them. They giggled and flirted with the men, but stood aside.

"Your knight has mission, cannot look away, must keep watch on young prince so he not go astray," Armage spoke in understanding. "He has duty and perform it well. You sleep now. Tomorrow I take you to meet my king who be camped nearby. He be pleased to meet the young prince who learning to be a judicious king."

"What say, Ingvar, we do this?" Aksel was quick to agree, received Ingvar's nod and accepted the invitation. "It will be our pleasure to meet your sire in the morn."

"We lodge in chamber behind alehouse, where you be lodged?" Ingvar asked and arranged where to meet in the morning. They bid good day to the young lasses as they scurried to their quarters for the night.

Ingvar was cautious when they rose to meet Knight Armage. He found no need to fear as Armage led them many miles down the road where the fields of green stretched out before them. There they found the camp of Irish soldiers, met their King Brian, sat among them, discussed their travels in Iceland and then Ireland. King Brian listened to their tales, listened to their nine Noble Virtues and explanations. He agreed, they were good virtues to live by. Brian told tales of his own conquests, his plan to be king of all Ireland. He planned to speak with a rival Monarch to join with him and make one king in Ireland. The three travelers joined Armage with his small army of men and traveled north toward Dublin.

It was a pleasure to march alongside, until they met a contingent of men of the King of Ui Neill, a rival monarch. The two groups stopped steadfast, face to face, until one shouted to the other, another shouted back.

The two groups attacked, had a round of dodge and charge, charge and strike and go round many times. The combatants moved to an open field nearby and fought among themselves, almost as though at play.

"What this be?' Ingvar asked Armage. "You dance not fight!"

"Yes," Armage laughed, "we be rivals. When meet, we test one another - see if they know how fight against strong army. It be a game. Play awhile, then rest the night, fight again in the morn, and then go on to next rival, keep in practice. You want to get in the fight?"

"No, I not a rival. They try kill me for sport."

"You sword fight for sport? Armage countered. "We fight a round or two with sword with a dull point. Just touch to chest be strike. Three strong touches make the winner of the round. Watch, my men give demonstration." He spoke with a group of young knights and asked them to joust a game to demonstrate. All others sat back to enjoy the games. Eight men paired off, spared one pair at a time, then the winner's paired off to fight, until the last two spared for the championship of the game.

Karl was excited, wanted to get in the sparing game. They were allowed to join, to make another group of eight which included Armage and Ingvar. Armage and Ingvar were deprived of another turn because they had two strikes each and came together in unison for the third strike, which was a dead match.

Karl being a stronger knight than Aksel won their first bout. Karl also won his second bout, but was beat in his third match. He was defeated by their very best swordsman who hailed Karl as a strong adversary, as they shook hands.

The three Vikings spent many days among the two armies, learning that they would converge into one realm when Boru made his bid for High King of Ireland. The armies headed north while Ingvar and his charges returned to Dublin to continue their adventure in learning. Aksel was in high spirits from their adventure with the Irish army of Brian Baru. Karl, too, was exhilarated with the sparring demonstrations.

As they entered the fort, they chanced upon a burly Viking beating a young lad mercilessly. "Hold there, Sir," Karl called to him. "What this lad do to warrant such a whipping? You intend to render him useless forever?"

"It be no business to you. He my nephew, my slave, I do with him what I will," came the curt, cruel reply.

"No, let us think about this. I ask humanely. This whipping be cruel, you kill the lad."

"No big loss, he useless like his dead father. Now be gone, or I take the whip to you."

"You give me reason to fight you, if you do." Karl, his spirit charged from his successful jousting with the knights, drew his long sword, waved it threateningly in the angry

Viking's face. Aksel and Ingvar nearby, walked up behind Karl as do several others who saw the cruel beating given to the young lad.

The Viking angered even more, roared as he raised his whip to strike at Karl. Aksel moved to one side and grabbed the boy from the Viking's grasp and Ingvar came in front of Karl with his sword to divert the whip as it fell. As Karl stepped aside, however, the whip fell uselessly to the ground. The angry Viking, thrown off balance by the thrust, also fell to the ground. Several other Vikings moved in and subdued the brute, pelted him hard with their fists and said, "He torture that lad too long." Another said, "He need feel the whip himself," and promptly grabbed it up and used it on him - thrashing his back. Then another took it from the first, added a few more lashes. The beaten uncle lay on the ground, moaning as Aksel led the young lad, sobbing uncontrollably, away to their quarters.

Aksel did his best to soothe the lad's welts with a cool wet cloth and recalled the lass who soothed the welts he had placed on the wizard's shoulder, it was so long ago. He dwelled on the thought and felt shame in the memory of his own brutal actions.

The next morning when all was quiet, they talked with the lad who told them, "My name be Kiev. My sire, a Viking be killed in the war against Boru's army many years gone. My marm be Irish. My Uncle Skorre say she a tart. What be a tart?" he asked in innocence. "My uncle make me slave as punishment to my father who wed an Irish." He paused then asked again, "What be a tart? Be it bad?"

"It not a nice name to call a lady, your uncle be the bad one," Ingvar consoled him. Kiev stayed with them. Knowledgeable of both languages and local customs, the young lad became a valuable aide and enjoyed being with them, learned from them and helped them.

Aksel relaxed among the Vikings in Dublin who aided the local Baron to control his realm of stubborn Irish who wanted the Vikings gone from their land. "I enjoy the peaceful weeks here, we visit many villages and see the churches built to their one God, met King Brian Boru. The people be friendly, intelligent, live well and prosper," Aksel admitted to his companions.

"Ya," Ingvar agreed. "Observing, talk to and learn from them, I find much to impress me. I find the Celts just as ferocious as we."

"Indeed," Karl agreed. "They stand firm in their beliefs, are staunch fighters, live and work hard with much love and enjoyment of life."

"And love of women." Aksel added laughing, "Don't forget the lovers we be."

"Well, when did you decide loving women be important?" they laughed with him.

- - - - -

The Irish broke the peace and stormed the stronghold full of drunken Vikings at the end of their evening of heavy carousing. The fighting being vicious, the three decided not to join the Irish cause or the fight and retreated cautiously to the rear of the fort.

"We best to leave this place. They think naught to kill us. Follow me, leave all behind. There be a break in the wall near the west gate, the river beyond. Come fast!" Kiev said, out of breadth from the effort.

They pounded on the opening to make it larger in order to get through the wall as it was not a large break. Kiev found a small skiff at the riverside, motioned them to climb in, pointed the skiff west and they rowed toward Kiev's home in a small settlement several miles downriver. They traveled cautiously in the dim moonlight, hid in growths of reeds when they saw the roving brigands along the shore. At daybreak they went ashore at a small village where Kiev inquired for food from a nearby farmer's lady.

"I can give travelers eggs and bread to ease hunger and mugs of milk for thirst," offered the gracious woman to Kiev's inquiry.

"We thankful and grateful," Aksel said. "I give you coins to pay for food, so you can replenish and not do without food for your family. You have beautiful children to care for, my lady."

Kiev translated Aksel's words of thanks and inquired, "You know distance to village near lake at end of River Liffey? My Marm live there, await me to come home. Be it two days travel?"

She responded with a nod and gave even more bread and smoked meat to ease their hunger along the way. They left the next morn to get to Kiev's village by nightfall.

Angelica happily greeted her son when they arrived. "My son, my lad, how you have grown! I not remember the look of you. Where your uncle be? Who be these men you bring? How I miss you, my dear son." She cried, engulfed him in a loving hug, ran her fingers through his unshorn locks and took in the look of him from head to toe.

Kiev fought tears, not wanting to appear weak before his friends. He had not seen his mother, had not touched her, or kissed her for more than two years and missed her much.

"I see my uncle killed as we leave the fort this past week. The Irish fighters attack to rid the Vikings of this land. These men be Vikings, but not of the fort, and save me from Uncle Skorre who beat me." He sobbed, took a deep breadth and then introduced the waiting men.

"Beat you?" She looked in horror at the three explaining, "Skorre say he would raise the boy, teach him to be strong Viking as I not able do. He beat you!" she repeated incredulously, took him in her arms again. I be glad he dead, so I not need kill him." She turned to the three as Kiev continued to translate, "I thankful to you, Prince Aksel, Cousin Karl and Knight Ingvar. You be welcome in this village as long as you need to stay."

Karl whispered to the other two, "This be a tart?" They shook their heads in agreement, she was not a tart.

They lingered longer in Kiev's small village, enjoyed the hospitality given them. The word passed among the villagers that they had befriended their young lad and the friendly people welcomed and accepted them.

The three soon felt the need to leave the land of the Celts as there was much conflict among them and they feared to be caught up in it again.

Angelica aided them, "I have neighbor who show you the path to ports east. Let me find him for you."

"Sires," the neighbor informed them, "the traveling merchant leave the morrow, in that direction, to replenish his stores from the port. He will carry you there for a price, if you need."

Ingvar asked, "What type conveyance does he travel in, not behind an ass I pray?"

"I think he use two work horses, they be stronger and faster," the neighbor answered.

"A horse-drawn sledge?" Ingvar asked, recalling the Celtic vehicles they saw throughout the countryside.

"Ya, a large sledge to transport passengers, with benches to accommodate them inside. Come, I show you, we speak with him."

The discomforting look of the sledge and many assigned passengers did not please Ingvar. They decided to follow on steeds along side the merchant for direction. Aksel agreed and the merchant supplied horses for them to use on the journey.

They bid Kiev and Angelica farewell, gave the lad both a manly hug and handshake. "This be the Viking way," Aksel told him and turned to his mother. "We be grateful to the lad for his assistance. We save him from cruel uncle and he save us from warring Vikings and Celts. He earn silver for his work, see he use it well. He be a fine lad, my lady, and will grow to be a fine man." He paused, looked at her a moment, than took her in his arms for a loving hug.

"Farewell. May the loving God of heaven be with you." She looked at them with grateful love in her eyes; they had returned her son safely home.

The three journeyed several days, slowly riding on roads of dirt and stones through the countryside. They saw an occasional brigade who found no reason to accost the peaceable merchant wagon and escort.

After an uneventful trip to the port, Ingvar arranged for a ship to the Britains. "We need wait till the weather clears of the high winds and rough seas. It short journey across channel, but the captain be cautious to not lose the stores entrusted to him. May God give us calm seas and strong winds to take us on our journey," Ingvar prayed. Thinking of his family in Heborg, he added, "May he give us God Speed, this our last stop afore home."

CHAPTER SIX

BRITAIN

The boat arrived toward evening on the west coast of Britain and followed the Bristol Bay up the Severn River sheathed in a wet, cold fog. The men watch while the captain, with considerable concern and trouble, navigated slowly, carefully to avoid the funnel shaped, brushwood weirs, used by local fishermen to trap fish. He brought his ship in slowly to a proper landing on shore at Bristol, despite the poor visibility. The three travelers exited onto the land where lanterns peered through the dense fog from the entrance of a nearby alehouse.

"Gentlemen of the north," a tall lad called to them from shore as they disembarked, "can I be of service to you on this glorious foggy eve? Many items of use be available for fine gentlemen that I can sell you or find comfortable accommodations befitting men of station."

"Be gone," Ingvar interrupted him. "We need not your services or merchandise."

"Perhaps you need an escort? I speak Danish language as you do - speak also the English and Celt. I be knowledgeable of the countryside wherever you plan to travel through the Isle." He followed alongside as they tried to evade him, to escape his company.

Aksel ignored him and said to Ingvar, "Here be an alehouse, we replenish and refresh ourselves and inquire for accommodations this night."

"No, no sires," the lad insisted, "This not the alehouse for refined gentlemen, this be alehouse for seamen seeking tarts and diversions! There be fights every night! Let me take you away from the dock to pleasant, acceptable accommodations. I show you. If you not pleased I direct you back here."

As he spoke, the door opened, a noisy melody emanated as a painted lady exited the alehouse and gestured toward the group inviting them in. "Whoa," said Ingvar, "the lad be right. It not pleasant accommodation. Let us see where our tall lad will take us."

Karl turned to the other two and spoke softly, "Be careful, he may lead us to an ambush where we get trounced upon, to awaken in the street the morn, shorn of all."

Aksel agreed and they followed the lad with trepidation, not knowing where they were going, not able to see where they were going as the night and the dense fog closed in on them. "What be your name?" Aksel asked the lad as they followed close behind.

"Wulf, sir, my name be Wulf, my sire be Irish."

"Perhaps," Karl spoke again to the two quietly, "we can test the lad, feed him ale to loosen his tongue, thus discover if he be one to trust." They nodded in agreement.

They agreed that the pleasant alehouse they soon approached was quality. They followed Wulf inside to fine seats in a corner where they would not be disturbed or interrupted.

"Wulf, you do well," Aksel told him. "Since you know all, what do they serve best to satisfy our hunger?"

"The prized fowl they grow from the countryside nearby. Slaughter them fresh each morn, two women roast them and I eat them," he jested with an engaging smile. "If it be ale you desire with food, they brew the best." He ordered for them and soon they feasted. Wulf indulged himself of the food and ale, smiled with happiness a glow in his eyes as he proceeded to eat his fill.

"Why you be here in the Isles, if you Irish?" Karl asked.

"I captured as a babe into slavery by the Vikings with many others. I work my way from bondage and now work for small wage touting goods for merchants and services for visiting travelers. I yet to save sufficient to pay my way back to Ireland." He paused to drink more ale and then refilled all their tankers, being certain to save more for himself. The three glanced among themselves as Wulf stuffed himself like a starved animal and answered their questions without hesitation or deception.

Aksel inquired, "If you be a babe when you taken from Ireland, how you know you be Irish? How you know your sire or even family?"

"Six years I be. I see the look of my Marm every night and my Aunt Jamie. I speak the language, remember my home in Limerick. I need get passage on boat, but earn only enough to keep body and soul

together, touting for merchants who not appreciate my service. Now all I desire be to find my family in Ireland. There be no status here, even as a freeman."

"How know your status with the Celts?" Karl asked.

"My sire has status," he assured them with a firm nod of his head. "I remember - he has status."

Karl smiled knowingly at Aksel thinking the lad storied them.

They allowed Wulf to help find quarters and he escorted them to different areas, sights and places of interest for the next few days. The lad became indispensable and endearing as they traveled throughout the nearby Bristol coastline.

Ingvar found him to be like his own young son and craved more to return home but advised, "Use caution still, he may not be trustworthy and make trouble for us."

"Yes," Aksel agreed. "He useful and he understand the English language. We need find a place to settle the winter, can we trust him thus?" he asked his companions.

Wulf directed them east to the industrial city of Winchester, southwest of London. "This be a busy burb with a strong wall all around to protect from enemies who storm and pillage. Has much trade. Cattle be herded in one street, penned up in next street, slaughtered and smoked in the third, their hides made into leather goods in the next where craftsmen make into sale items of cloths, implements and containers for travel and work. There many businesses throughout the commercial streets of town: hosier, shoemaker, soap maker who sell wares to visitors and citizens, many meeting halls where prosperous citizens feast and drink. Sheep are shorn, their wool woven into warm cloth and dyed many pretty colors to sell. There be a mint where the king make

fine silver coins to trade many things, here and in countries afar. Make even trinkets for ladies and gentlemen of prestige and importance."

The men spent several weeks in Winchester. Aksel checked his purse, decided he had sufficient coins to see them home and to purchase gifts to take back to Norway, gifts for family and for a newly wedded wife.

"What say you, Ingvar, what gift a young lady like. What be proper for marm and sire?" Ingvar and Karl selected gifts for their women also, and Ingvar for his son.

Wulf looked on while they bought and Aksel asked him, "You have someone to buy gift for?"

"Have marm, sire and sister, but not know what they like, what they need. Not know if ever get home to see again."

"You see them again," Aksel assured him. "You earn enough coins to buy passage to Ireland, you see them again."

"That be enough gift for me, for them, Prince Aksel. I not need gift of trinket." Wulf spoke with sincerity, appreciation and a lilt of happiness in his manner.

Aksel smiled at him in understanding. *We didn't appreciate the Irish tout before*, he thought, *I now know he be good of heart. He just desires dearly to return to Irish family and homeland.*

For several weeks they lived among the English, observed the commerce in this planned city, spoke with many men of business who looked of knowledge and wealth.

They plan to ride further east to the village of Danelaw, the settlement of Normans. "We come upon the village of London by nightfall where we find accommodations to please a king," Wulf is quick to advise and found clean accommodations behind a pleasant alehouse up the river.

They slept sound the night. They woke late the next morning and Wulf is nowhere to be seen. "Where the tout? Are we rid of him now? Did he lighten our purse?" Karl asked, quick to accuse.

Aksel looked after his coins. Ingvar found his sword and possessions secure. "All be well, he not far," Ingvar assured them.

The three look to the owner, request food to eat and warm water to refresh their bodies. As they sat outside enjoying the warmth of the sun, Wulf returned humming a joyous melody. "That be the song from the ale house the night we come ashore on the river," Karl said. "Where you hear it? How you know it well enough to sing?"

"The song be known over the Isles, all sing it," Wulf defended himself. "I hunger, there be food for me to eat?"

"Look to the kitchen, we ride shortly," Karl informed him.

They took lodgings when they arrived in London, as none come forward with hospitality. They traveled about the large area for a few weeks and compared the tradesmen with those in Winchester and with the farmers selling their wares. "London will grow and expand with trade, a fine place to make a business and live a good life," Ingvar predicted.

"It better in Heborg," Aksel told him. "Do you not like our country? Does not my father support you well?"

Ingvar smiled at his prince. "Yes, sire, very well, but a freeman often yearns to be on his own, with allegiance to his own skills."

"Yes, I feel the burden of duty and responsibility, as freemen do also." Aksel pointed out to him.

They moved south toward the pleasant countryside of farms and small villages. With no Viking forts in the area to welcome them, Aksel decided, "We sojourn the winter in Danelaw. It be like Heborg, they speak our language and we understand what they do."

They introduced themselves to a local Baron who answered their questions on how he ruled, the hierarchy, the laws they observed and their acceptance of Christianity. The Baron was pleased to direct them to the local church to learn more of this new religion and even attended services with them on God's day. It was a pleasant experience.

They met the local Friar Mac, a charming, very right-eous Irishman who spoke the Norse language well. "Ye be Vikings from Norway and inquire of the Christian faith. Glory to God!" he exclaimed. "Ye come to the proper place, teaching the faith be what we do. You must join us for service every day or best on God's day." Over many days they became friends and spent many hours speaking and learning more of the Christian faith.

The Friar read stories of Jesus, son of God on earth. "He did much to help man live good lives, to show men how to live together in peace. You follow your father to rule your kingdom. Christianity teach you to have an un-derstanding heart to judge your people and distinguish right from wrong. This be good thing for our young prince to learn."

The three listened intently to his words, became en-thralled with the written word and Friar Mac gave them in-structions every day on how to read the words in the book. The three Norsemen stumbled through the lessons, tried hard to learn all the words. It was slow and tedious. "I give you this book to keep, so can practice often to learn well".

"I teach you Jesus prayer. 'Jesus, Son of God, have mercy on me, a sinner.' This a simple prayer, say it often, God will hear and help you have faith," and Friar Mac re-peated it for them, listened to them repeat it many times until they learned it well. They learned to read and listen to the stories of Jesus.

Friar Mac also taught them that, "Vikings plagued the coast of Britain for centuries, made it not possible for peo-ple to live peaceably for fear of their annual raids. The British suffered much from these past invasions. One rea-son Vikings keep to their settlements, because they are not always welcomed among the British. They not always friendly," Friar Mac informed them.

Aksel agreed and said, "Our countrymen wrought much havoc on the Icelanders, Celts and Brits these many centuries. The Christian concept of 'loving thy fellowman' be a fine one to live by." He paused, looked at his companions, "How you feel to accept this new Christianity we learn in Ireland and now in Britain, to be baptized and become one with them?" The three decided to convert and Wulf joins them also as he was Christian when in Ireland and the Celts' island was very strong with Christianity. The group became regular attendees at the small church in the nearby village and Aksel wonders what his father will say of this.

One fine day as they journeyed around the countryside of Danelaw, they came upon a young maiden who struggled with a cart full of garden vegetables attached to a donkey who refused to move. She struggled and enticed the animal with a carrot and still the animal did not cooperate. As the men passed her on the path she looked up at them beseechingly. Wulf stirred them on, "Don't be involved with it, Sires. She will make you pull the wagon and the donkey. We be not slaves to an animal."

Aksel and Ingvar stared hard at Wulf with displeasure of his uncaring manner while Karl looked at the lass with a gleam in his eye. "You find her pleasing, cousin?" Aksel asked.

"Ya, that I do," Karl answered. He slowed and turned his steed toward her. He threw her one end of a leather strap, "Take hold the strap, lass, and tie it tight to the donkey's harness. We pull enough - teach him to do his work."

She did as he said, but the strap did not hold. Karl dismounted and tied it more securely to the harness. Aksel returned to help, "Let me take hold the strap and secure it to my saddle." He then prompted his steed to move forward, to pull hard. The animal balked, neighed and even kicked, but pulled back on the rope and did not move forward. Aksel paused, thought to say a prayer, and silently repeated the Jesus prayer. Once, twice and the third time beseechingly pleading for help, giving the rope a strong pull as he urged his steed forward. The donkey moved reluctantly, still fighting the rope and Aksel smiled to himself, the Jesus prayer really worked!

"He moved," Karl shouted, as they continued to move slowly on to her destination. The ass took off without further assistance when they came closer to the farm and he recognized his home.

"Thank you, sires," the lass gratefully bowed. A man laboring in the field alongside the dwelling walked up. "Father, these gentlemen helped to make Burakki move. The ass refused to pull the full load so they towed him," she explained.

"We grateful to you, sires. This animal be stubborn as only an ass can be. I am beholden to you," he graciously said.

"No need," Aksel replied in like manner. "Tis naught. It be our pleasure to aid a maiden in distress," and with a friendly wave turned to go on his way.

Karl dallied behind to smile and bow to the maiden. She shyly smiled and curtsied in return. "I be Karl of Heborg, Norway," he introduced himself to the father.

"I be Harald Ringnes and this be my daughter, Gerda," the farmer introduced himself and his daughter. "We come from Norway, many years ago."

- - - - -

They attended the Christian service the next day and were pleased to see the maiden, her parents and siblings there also. "Good morn, Sire Ringnes and Lady Gerda. It a fair day for Christian service," Karl greeted them with an engaging smile to Gerda.

They were introduced to Lady Ringnes and a younger sister and brother after the service. The friendship became more intense as Karl showed more interest in Gerda. Her father preferred his daughter take an interest in Aksel, 'since he be a prince.'

Aksel, very flattered, gave Gerda a pleasurable smile. He took her hand to his lips and said, "I be promised a princess, my fair maiden, and claim her when we return to Norway." Karl glowed with happiness, now he could pursue her for himself and Gerda also smiled with pleasure.

"I not favor this maiden for myself, cousin, she for you," Aksel spoke aside. "Her father be ambitious on her behalf. Her status be much like yours, cousin to royalty. Pleasant to look upon, sweet of voice and manner, she will be a good wife for you. Be there another who awaits your return in Norway?"

"No," Karl admitted. "None want me," he jested. "I pursue Gerda, perhaps she be the one."

"Will she return to Norway with you? Will she leave her family here?" Ingvar asked, doubt in his voice.

"If she love me, she will come," Karl reassured Ingvar. "Perhaps I stay here. Will you find your path home without me?" he jested. There was happiness about him as Karl stopped often to visit at the cottage of Harald Ringness. He sat beside Gerda in church, even worked by her side on the farm. They all went to labor with him. It kept them occupied. The men learned to live among the Norsemen in

Britain, learned how to work in the fields and make things grow as their bodies also grew and developed in strength.

Wulf worked also, but complained about it. "This not the work I do," he let them know.

"You eat like a horse, if you work hard you will grow a strong body and become a strong man, like Ingvar. It best we all work. I prince, I work hard in field," Aksel told him with encouragement. He let Wulf understand, "Look at you. When first we saw, you be a tall, skinny lad. You now heavier, stronger, have more the look of a man. Work help make you strong like it did for me when row the longboat across the sea. It be good for the body, the soul. It not kill you!"

Ingvar listened with pride at his prince who was teaching the young tout to mature in body and mind, and looked at Aksel with approval.

Aksel and Ingvar found ways to fun Karl in his wooing of Gerda, as he continued pursuit. "She be my lady," he kept saying. Ingvar as older protector of his young charges, arranged with Gerda's father for her hand in marriage. Aksel gave Karl many coins for the groom's price, as be the old Norman custom, but Harald Ringness decided as this be a Christian wedding, there be no need to follow the heathen practice. Karl and Gerda were happily wed in the Christian faith in the warmth of spring. Aksel purchased a full carcass to roast for the wedding feast and all from the church are invited. They sang and danced into the night, drank ale and then slept. It was a happy occasion.

Aksel envied Karl's happiness and felt sad at his own lack of wedded bliss. As time passed well into spring it became time to return to Heborg. They had been gone for more than three years - three long years. Aksel thought of his father and wondered if he would greet him with favor.

Ingvar looked forward to their last journey across the channel north to Norway and yearned to join his family. Karl and Gerda decide they also would like to start their new life together in Norway. Yes, it was time to return home to Norway.

Wulf prepared to leave them, traveling on a merchant longboat to return to his Limerick home in Ireland with the money Aksel paid him for his service. He was speechless with emotion, could not believe he was really boarding a longboat to his home. With a round of strong hand shakes, a manly hug and pat on the back, they wished him, "God Speed and a safe journey home." He waved a joyous farewell and turned to gaze wistfully to the west toward Ireland.

Karl and Gerda looked at each other with love in their eyes. Ingvar gazed to the northeast toward his spouse and son. Prince Aksel looked to his thoughts of the curly-haired lass who struck him and called him animal. He wondered if another had claimed her.

CHAPTER SEVEN

(RETURN TO HEBORG)

Upon landing at Kaupang, Aksel asked Karl and Gerda, "Do you desire to see this large, prosperous village of Kaupang or perhaps travel north to see your village of birth?"

"She be just a babe when father took her to the Isles." Karl agreed, "It will be good for her to see where she born."

"Yes, can we see both?" Gerda happily agreed with a cheerful smile.

"Sire," Ingvar interrupted with urgency in his voice, "I leave now, go home to Heborg, to my family who wait for me – we be gone more than three years. You be safe now back home in Norway."

"Yes, Ingvar, go. You be a good companion and protector to me and Karl these many years. Tend to your family. Tell my sire and marm all be well, Karl and I return home soon." They gave Ingvar a hearty hand shake and wished him God Speed as he mounted his steed at the crack of dawn the next morning.

Ingvar rode hard to reach his spouse and son in Heborg. It rained the afternoon as he climbed the mountain area between Kaupang and Heborg. He rested his steed at a wayside shelter and waited for the rain to stop. When it waned somewhat he went on slowly in the soft drizzle. It was well after dark when he arrived in Heborg, sopping wet, not sure of the path as it looked unfamiliar. More thatched roofs greeted him than he remembered before.

He approached one that did have a familiar look and called out, "Hallo inside, be anyone home?"

In a moment, the door opened slightly as a lantern was held out to see who called. He dismounted and approached slowly, "I come in peace, I Ingvar, Knight to King Gregors, returned from sea this day. My spouse be here, but I see not her cottage for the darkness and the many strange cottages about. Can you direct me?" he queried.

The door flew open, "Ingvar!" shouted Asmund, his neighbor. "We thought you dead, you be gone so long. Welcome home! Lady Dagmar live down two cottages, next to wall as afore. Let me take you," he started to come out, but Ingvar waylaid him.

"No, I will find, not need you come out in rain. I see you the morrow!" He hurried off with just a strong quick hand shake, did not remount, just pulled the steed behind him as he splashed along the path in the mud. He knocked at the door of the cottage which he recognized as he came up on it, and could hardly wait to hear the lock-bar rise.

The door opened and a young lad looked out at him. "Who be there?" the lad asked meekly, seeing a soaked, wild looking man in a cloak standing in front of him.

Ingvar slowly entered, water dripping from his cloak onto the floor, and knelt to his son's size, "I be your sire, Erik. Do you not remember me? You be half grown, almost a man." They looked at each other a long moment. Ingvar removed his wet cloak, gently took his son in his arms and held him close, fighting the tears of joy.

Erik looked up at him, "Ya, I remember, you gone long time ago. Where you be so long?"

"Our King sent me away on mission many years, I come home now for you. Where be your marm, she not about?"

"She be at castle, she care for king who ill. She not return home 'til the morn. I take you to her," he said and held tightly to his hand so as not to lose him.

"It wet outside, you have cover?" Ingvar asked. He felt protective of his son and took hold of him again, hugging him in a close embrace. "God in heaven, I miss you both. Be your mother well?"

Erik nodded while gathering his cover, "Yes, she be well. She not cry anymore now you be home."

Erik led his father to the castle as Ingvar held a lantern to lighten the path. A heavy mist chilled their bones as the fog rolled in making it difficult to see.

They were challenged at the castle by the guards who took a few minutes to recognize their old friend in arms. "This be my sire!" Erik shouted at them, "My marm be with My Lady, we come to get her."

Dagmar was on the stairs when she heard her son shout at the doorway. She paused. Did she hear him rightly, his sire? She returned down the stairs, rushed to the entrance, and saw the guards greet him. "Ingvar," she said softly. "Ingvar!" she said louder and again even louder. She ran to him, threw herself on him, tears of joy poured down her face as she clung to him. He enveloped her in a strong embrace, lifted her up off the floor, as the guards smiled at them. Sobbing with all her heart she reached up, touched his wet face, hair, his wet beard and tried to talk between the sobs, "My love, my liege, be it really you?"

Ingvar stood back, looked into her happy eyes, "It better be me you kiss, My Lady or I will need to trounce whoever else it may be," he laughed with joy. He held her tight, slowly rocked her back and forth, oblivious of all near by. "Just the look of you is all I need for the moment," he whispered in her ear as he kissed her again and again. Ingvar felt the touch of his son at his side and took him into their circle of embrace. He was home – he was content! Thanks to the loving God, he was home!

- - - - -

Back at Kaupang, Aksel, Karl and Gerda enjoyed the activity in Kaupang and rested in the small ale house along side the ocean. Karl and Gerda strolled along the sandy beach hand in hand. They enjoyed the peaceful quiet. They watched the seagulls come and go, fight over a morsel of fish or a crumb of bread Gerda threw to them. Aksel dozed in a chair nearby enjoying the warm sunshine, the sound of the seagulls shrieking, calling to each other, and the smell of the sea as the waves crashed upon the shore.

Later the three rode a wagon up the path to view an old fort built by Norsemen of old. The walls were still standing though worn by wind and rain, a farmer's small cottage was within the wall to secure his cottage and livestock from intruders - a vivid vision of the past.

They slowly strolled along the vendor's area at the port and visited many shops with their home-made merchandise displayed on tables to entice the buyer. Aksel and Karl kept watch for Verner, the merchant from their sail to Ireland. Aksel saw a merchant's stand with the smoked meat available to purchase and inquired if this was Verner's shop. The shop keeper directed them to another area away from the port. They ventured out to locate it, without success.

The trio traveled inland the next morn to the village where Gerda was born and located an old neighbor who remembered her as a babe as well as her mother and father. It was a pleasant visit with the older couple and they were invited to spend the night in the small cottage. It was very discomforting, the odor strong, as a goat and her kid were also in residence the night.

The three returned to Kaupang the next day and sat outside the alehouse where they replenished themselves and were startled to hear someone call their names. "Yes, it be me," Verner said. "I be told you asked for me by name and where I live. I look to find you at the alehouses for hungry travelers." Verner was happy to see them; they greeted each other with hearty handshakes. He was pleased to meet Gerda, gave them his best wishes, "May the God of Love bless you with much happiness and babies to love. I give hug to beautiful bride of young knight." He delighted in the newly wedded couple and joined them on the bench just chatting away.

"There be reason I seek you, not only to renew acquaintance," Verner began. "Ingvar seek you, he returned to Kaupang two days gone to look for you. He found me, asked me give a message to the wayward son who does not return to the home of his father."

Aksel looked at him under shielded eyes, "He sent me away, now he want me return?"

"Ingvar say your marm want you return home. Your father be ill with consumption, has not much time to live. He calls for you, wants to see the man you be now," Verner added.

Aksel bowed his head in sadness, "Ya, I leave with the sun."

"You be sad," Karl comforted him softly, placed his hand on Aksel's shoulder.

Aksel nodded and looked up at him. "He will want to see me wed before he die. We be gone too long, What I do?"

Karl and Verner exchanged glances, "You claim your promised bride on your way," Verner cheerfully suggested. "It not be far from the path to Heborg. Come to my cottage now, meet my spouse, she prepare food to eat, ale to drink. You sleep the night to rest, than rise early in the morn. My neighbor has steed you can buy and you be on your way."

Verner's spouse, Gudrum, was delighted to meet the recently returned wanderers. She fed them well and enjoyed their company in pleasant conversation the whole evening. She especially enjoyed talking with Gerda about life in England, about her impressions of her birthplace here in Norway and her hopes for the future.

Nothing was said of her niece, Kaja, other than plans for Aksel to stop to claim her. Verner did not want to influence the prince one way or another; it had to be a decision of his own making. "I be sure you make the proper decision," was all the encouragement he gave.

Karl, was more explicit, "Who else can you wed, you know another? Kaja will be a lovely maiden now, learned by a wizard. You like a saucy lass, a beautiful green-eyed vixen. You give love to her, she give love to you. In time make a happy life for both. You do well, a happy prince and princess, someday king and queen."

Aksel slept that night thinking of his father dying and his desire to see his son. *Ingvar said he called for me. He want to see the man I be now, not the willful prince. He sent me to see the world, to learn, to make me a man, a judicious king. Is this not a father's duty? He doesn't hate me. No, he doesn't hate me and I don't hate him!*

Aksel rose early before the sun. Verner gave him the directions where to turn off from the path to Heborg to ride to Alfhild. Aksel rode hard as the sun slowly rose above the tree line lighting the way. His mind churned with questions: *Do I want to claim her now, before I see my sire? Do I truly want to claim her ever? How does Verner know which road to direct me, we never say where she live?* He rested his steed at the path that turned to Alfhild and wondered what he should do. He remembered again in his thoughts the picture of a young lass jousting with her brother, the lass who struck him to protest him striking her wise man. He remembered the aura of love and respect from her father as he spoke of his daughter and the older wise man. It was not always so in his father's castle. He admired the saucy lass, much as he denied it. She would be a good queen, a judicious queen, like his father wanted him to be - a judicious king.

Prince Aksel had sought knowledge on his journey, how other kings controlled and ruled their kingdoms their thralls and serfs. He learned how they made laws for the common good, how they judge right from wrong, showed regard and appreciation of those who were about them. He observed where justice was equal among the people, there was contentment among the people and they were respectful and supportive of their liege in return. He remembered the Althing, where judgment was made by the people and that fared well. That was what his sire sent him out to learn. This was the kind of kingdom he wanted to rule, the kind of king he wanted to be.

Aksel wondered how she looked now, full grown. *Her sister was beautiful, her mother too. Karl said she do well. As Verner said; she be lovely to behold and learned, be all*

*a man wants or needs. She be the kind of queen needed to
sit next to a judicious king.*

He wondered again, how Verner knew where she
lived? He mounted his horse to travel the path to Alfhild.
"Ya, it be the right path," he spoke aloud to his steed as he
urged the obliging horse forward.

———   ———   ———   ———   ———

Queen Alva sat with her ladies in the hall at Alphild,
embroidering cloth to make clothes for the children to wear
in the coming winter. Her attendant scurried in to tell her
the young Prince Aksel had arrived and requested to speak
to King Ivar. She rose to go quickly to him. She was surprised to see him rather disheveled and scruffy, somewhat
nervous and agitated, but bigger and stronger, more a man.
He stated his case, his desire to make claim to his promised
lady. She listened and hesitated a moment, "King Ivar say
you wait too long. He travel another realm to visit, perhaps
arrange a very young prince for Kaja. This prince be just
twelve years, but Kaja be not content with that."

Prince Aksel pleaded, "Please, My Lady, I come back
to Norway to claim my maiden. She be my promised lady!
I away at sea these many years, now need tend my dying
father. You all come, will be welcome in my father's castle
for as long as need, so we can be wed." He paused to consider what needed to be done. "It be not too long a journey
- the snow will hold another month or more. Ya, it best
you come to my father's castle in Heborg."

Queen Alva sighed, paused as she thought a moment.
"Ya, you be promised, though it too long. I will tell sire
you have been gone away at sea, now come home to
claim." She looked up at him, into his eyes shining azure
in the sunlight. She saw the insistence, the need. Her heart

melted, he be much more a man. *Be there regard and love in his eyes? He be much different, more grown, well spoken, polite, more man than the willful prince afore. Will he be well for her Kaja?* she questioned to herself and smiled with pleasure at him. He smiled back and took her hand, held it to his lips graciously, politely. She be charmed by him.

"Be your wise man about? May he come attend my father's needs and ease his pain? I send a coach with driver to show the path to Heborg, carry you all and your wise man," Aksel planned aloud.

"He be with King Ivar and Kaja, I send him when they return," she agreed. He bowed, kissed her hand again, smiled a farewell and turned to leave. She trailed behind him a few steps and followed him with her eyes as he returned to the courtyard.

Aksel recognized Kaja's brother, Jorgan, in the courtyard and repeated to him the plans made with his mother. "Be your sister well, still the saucy young maiden of memory, with the spirit of a colt and love of knowledge and people?"

Jordan did not know what to say, was this the willful prince who was promised to Kaja? "She be a lady, Ya. She be a lovely lady with shiny hair of golden ringlets, sweet of manner, sings melody like an angel, smiles all the time. I look for a maiden just like her, to wed when I am grown. She speak much, too much perhaps, but speaks true," he chided.

Prince Aksel smiled in pleasure, gave Jorgan a strong handshake and mounted his steed to leave. He wished the days to pass quickly as he headed home to his ailing father, home to Heborg.

It was late the next evening before he arrived at his father's castle in Heborg. His old withered steed was worn down, could hardly carry him. Aksel was afraid he would go lame, so stopped often, rested him and eased his pace. He entered the courtyard slowly when he arrived and greeted the guard on watch at the road. The guard did not recognize Aksel and commanded him, "Hold! I not know you, Sir Knight."

"I be Prince Aksel, son of your liege, King Gregors, arrived from Kaupang. Be Ingvar about? Torbin, or Alf? They know who I be."

He heard his father's voice roar from inside the castle. His sire had called his name, paused and roared his name again. He passed by the young guard and rushed inside where others accosted him. He pushed them all aside, as they recognized him. "It be Prince Aksel! It Aksel, he here!"

He was halfway up the stairs when his mother greeted him from the top. She had heard the commotion below and her son's name addressed. She rushed into his arms and broke into tears. "My son, be it really you? It be so good to behold you. Let me look upon you, touch you. You be bigger, stronger, more a man. We thought you be dead you gone so long."

Aksel could not speak, choked up with emotion, but hugged her close, kissed her face and lips. He walked her back into the chamber where his father lay in bed still calling his name. Ingvar, held the king down in bed trying to comfort him as Gregors struggled to rise up. He wanted to see his son who had returned from the sea.

Aksel attended him. He sat on the edge of the bed and took his sire into his arms, cried into his father's hair as he held his emaciated body close to him. The king looked into his son's face, saw that it was him. He saw the tears in Aksel's eyes, the look of love and concern in them, the look of a grown man. He reached out to touch him, to feel the nearness, it be really him. He had feared that he sent him out into the world to his doom, but all would be well now, he relaxed with a sigh, his son was home, - home, with the look of a judicious man!

His odyssey fulfilled! Aksel, his son, his judicious son, was home! He could thank his loving God. He could now depart this life in peace.

A VIKING AGE TRILOGY
PART TWO – KAJA'S ANGST

A LASS IN QUANDRY,
ANGST, MATURITY AND SUBMISSION

CHAPTER ONE

ALPHILD

A large log burned in the open fire pit and warmed the long hall comfortably on this cold winter day. Many villagers worked about at various duties, children played and ladies sewed or were busy with needle work as they socialized with one another. A large slab of wild venison roasted on the spit, the chamber filled with its delightful aroma. A cauldron with cabbage, carrots and onions stewed above the fire hanging from a tripod next to the meat. Barley bread baked in a pan above the fire. Munk and Punk, the hunting dogs who lay in the warmth of the hearth, eyed the juicy meat and licked their chops in anticipation of the feast to come.

Kaja sat at the table with two young friends from the village, Segrid and Thora. Kaja's mother, Queen Alva, and her sister, Aunt Gudrun, who was visiting from Kaupang, instructed them in the fine art of needlework and sewing. They spent many hours by the warmth of the fire all winter long just knitting and embroidering as they learned the new stitches and patterns directed by the ladies.

"Ever since that prince came last summer when Margrethe died of the fever, they train me to become a queen. I not desire to be a queen, especially for that nasty prince," Kaja told her friends. "I do enjoy embroidering except on summer days that call me outside to play or joust with the young lads."

"Goodness Kaja," Thora said. "Will you ever not act like a lad? You after all, be a lovely maiden with shinny, yellow ringlets all over your head, will someday be a queen. Can you not put aside the games of lads?"

"Must I?" Kaja appealed. "I enjoy competing with them, especially when I win!" she grinned with pleasure at the thought of besting the young lads at their games.

Every day the three young maidens worked together during the long cold months. Sigred said, "I like to knit wooly scarves to cover my head and neck and keep me warm on winter days."

Thora replied, "Embroidering fancy designs on table covers or to decorate the walls be artful. It make the halls look pretty." They stitched their names into the hems or designs to identify their work, it became their trademark.

"Can I do some embroidery work?" Sigred asked.

"Ya," Thora encouraged, "and I will try to knit, perhaps a sweater."

"I like to knit something also," Kaja decided.

Queen Alva spoke to the wizard, Frode. "I am concerned for her non-acceptance, can you address Kaja and convince her of her place in life, she must be prepared for her place."

Frode took Kaja aside and explained to her as they strolled through the village streets one chilly, sunny afternoon, "You will be a queen, learned or not, but you will be a better queen if intelligently educated in the things a queen has need to know."

"But, Frode," she interrupted. He raised his hand and would not listen.

"You may not feel that way now, as you be still a young lass, but as you grow a mature maiden you will need be learned to instruct others in what your needs and that of your liege may require. Ya, many will serve you, but you need learn how to serve them. Just as your mother do," he emphasized. "Do your marm not do a complete job of tending to the needs of her castle, her people?"

"Ya, that she do, but Frode . . . "

"Do you admire and appreciate her skill?"

"Ya, I do, - but, but" she tried again to interrupt him.

"Do you want to become like your mother?"

"I think so." She responded hesitantly, meekly. He did not let her speak in her own behalf. She felt annoyance at her wise man, he will not let her speak. She felt resentment, he would not listen to her thoughts.

"What other can you do? You cannot be a knight, you cannot work hard in the stable or fields. Your lot in life, to be a wife, mother, and see to the needs and comfort of those about you, to assist your liege in whatever he may need of you. If you are properly prepared, learned and with experience, you will become a very able assistant, a valuable advisor to whatever brave king weds you. You can be sure, if he any kind of man, he will value the tender advice and intelligence of the lady at his side."

Kaja, respectfully accepted the reproachful words of Frode and resigned herself to go about her duties, however reluctantly. *I still don't want to be queen to that willful, nasty prince,* she stubbornly insisted to herself.

The realm was busy with work as spring approached. Kaja and Jorgan's assignment is the care of young village children to allow parents to work in the fields, tend animals and other duties. "See Jorgan," Kaja told her brother, "the work of bathing little children be fun, they squeal, scream and splash in pan of warm soapy water. Then giggle and cuddle when bundled up in warm cloth to dry."

Jorgan said "No, I would like play with older ones, help them learn to walk, run and play games. That be fun. When they fall, hurt their knees and cry, I can give them kiss and hug to make it better. They like me give them a kiss and hug."

"Come, let us walk to see the animals by the barn," Kaja called to several of her charges, "while the little ones are napping. We watch how the pigs root and snort in their muddy denizen."

Fridley, the young herder, talked to the children and explained all about the pigs. "They eat mush from the furrow and gobble it up in a noisy, messy manner. Do you eat like pig?" he joked with them.

The children laughed at him, shouting "No! No! We not eat like pig!"

Fridley approached Kaja, put his arm around her shoulder, "Will the maiden like a kiss?" he asked as he reached out to peck her cheek.

"This maiden no like a kiss," she asserted and gave him a strong shove, which knocked him off balance and he slipped and slid, arms flailing, down into the pig pen.

Fridley looked up at her from the muddy depths, an expression of surprise on his face, gasped in horror at his muddy clothes and the animals snorting at him. Kaja quickly gathered the laughing children about her and returned to the large hall. She did not dare to look back.

As summer wore on, Frode helped to keep the children's interest, "Come," he said, "let us set up learning sessions to teach reading and writing. You older children will help." The younger ones seemed to enjoy the attention and progressed slowly, but rather well. Frode was pleased with their interest the summer long. He, also, told stories about wild animals and knights in combat to keep them happy.

Aunt Gudrun needed to travel to the seacoast at Kaupang to inquire after her spouse. He traveled often to foreign ports, traded local wares for foreign goods. He was long overdue from the northwest.

Kaja asked her parents "May I accompany Aunt Gudrun? Sigred and Thora too? We will take our scarves and embroideries to sell among the vendors at the port." After some thought and discussion with the other parents, it was agreed. Two knights, Esben and Vig, were assigned to escort and protect the four ladies and see to their safety.

"I will join them and take advantage of this opportunity to find spices and rare herbs from foreign vendors," Frode decided when he heard of the upcoming voyage.

The castle was a buzz of activity as they prepared for the trip; the young maiden's excitement soared in anticipation of the adventure. Finally, all preparations were made and all were ready, the last farewells were heard. "Bye Marm, bye Sire," the young travelers waved to their parents from the coach,

"We will be careful." Their parents waved back and called after them, "Ya, take care, have a safe journey. Heed Esben and Vig."

They left at dawn on the tedious three day trip by coach, the two knights in attendance followed on horseback. They were made welcome along their route and accepted the hospitality of the neighborly families of two realms.

The maidens listened in amazement as Frode expounded of the many wonders of the countryside they passed through. He pointed to young rabbits running among the underbrush along the road, while a larger parent scurried them away from the danger of the horse's hoofs and coach

wheels. A large elk bounded across their path which startled the horses, made them rear up on their hind quarters,
almost tipping the carriage over. The lassies screamed in
fright! Frode identified a hedgehog running away from
them in the underbrush as they passed. "There must be water beyond the trees of the forest, see the grebes flying
about, even a covey of gulls. There be black coots slowly
flying overhead - all like to live by water. Some dive from
above when they see fish in water to snatch." He was in
awe of nature and saw beyond the obvious therein. They
all listened to and enjoyed his observations.

The first day at port, they followed behind Aunt Gudrun wide-eyed at the strange, new surroundings to be seen
at the busy port. They gazed in wonder at their first view
of the sea with waves rolling in, crashing up on the sand in
rhythmic succession. They ran down to the water's edge
and scurried back to escape as each wave rolled up the
shore. Frode tried to explain how this movement of water
happened, but was not as knowledgeable of the science of
the earth. "Not sure what make it so, but know it be the
nature of the sea."

Aunt Gudrun spoke to many merchant men and seamen, "Do you know where Captain Sune be? He sailed
many months ago, to Iceland, Verner Eskild be with him.
Have you seen him, have they returned?"

"Iceland, you say?" one seafaring sailor asked. "That
be long journey, maybe take two years lest you sail the
winter. That be dangerous, foolish to attempt."

There were none who know of him or the seaman he
sailed with. Gudrum was sad and concerned for his welfare.

The maidens were successful in selling their wares,
even to foreign traders whose words they could not under-

stand.   Happily they counted their coins and split them among themselves. Aunt Gudrun walked with them to find cloths, colored silk threads and beads to decorate their embroideries for the next winter. They looked at all the vendors wares, shop by shop, discussed what to purchase, even delighted at choosing which sweets they would acquire to take back home to share with those awaiting their return.

The young knights watched their charges faithfully and silently observed as two street urchins approached the shoppers from behind. Suddenly they made a move toward the lassies, grabbed their purses and turned to run. The two young knights, Esben and Vig blocked their path, each grabbed one by the scruff of the neck lifting them up off their feet.

"Aha!" Vig shouted to them. "You think coins belong to you, do you?"

"We see you steal them from the fair lassies, do you want we tie you to back of carriage and drag you away?" Esben threatened.

"No, No, Sire," they screamed. "We be hungry, have sick marm and little sisters to feed."

"Oh now, that be pretty story. Your sire be dead?" Vig asked.

"He gone at sea many years. I tell you true!" he insisted.

Aunt Gudrun, nearby, listened. "You show me where sick mother and sisters be. I see, I believe. Maybe help, bring food. Where they be? They be far?" she demanded.

The urchins looked at each other than at Aunt Gudrun and led them away from the dock area. It was true indeed, a small humble shelter with a woman lying on the dirt floor and two young lassies sitting nearby in unkempt squalor. Aunt Gudrun did not know what to do first. "Find Frode," she directed Vig, "bring him here with milk, food. We tidy, sweep dirt, find water to wash all. They have the look of hunger. We need find someone to help poor lady, poor children. It not good to let them starve while sire away at sea."

Frode did find help for them. The lassies prepared bread and milk and made them all eat slowly to gain strength. Frode spoke with a neighbor who helped them find a home to take the family where they all could work in a large garden and assist in caring for young children in return for food and a small neat shelter to protect themselves from the elements.

The next day, after they are settled in their shelter, the poor mother spoke, "We be grateful for help, for clean clothes and sustenance to comfort our innards. We work hard to earn all." She gave Aunt Gudrun a big hug and God speed. She hugged Frode also as he wished her well. Her young lads stood by, "We will work with marm and help. Not need steal, we work to earn coins now," they told Frode. They watched the three girls as they waved a pleasant good-by and returned to the vendors' area along side the sea.

The girls purchased their selected necessities, the fine silk cloth and threads they chose from distant lands and, also, the many sweets to share with their families at home.

Frode talked with a seaman who came from distant lands. They had round, brown seeds used to make a dark drink. The seaman said, "It comes from land where sun shines hot, with much rain. They not grow in ice and snow, they do grow in warm garden sun, grow in cottage the winter. You buy some now and try to grow? Then crush berries to fine powder, make a drink with goats milk, perhaps some honey." Frode purchased some, he would experiment and try to make them grow and produce.

The girls sat on a low wall along the beach to watch the waves rolling up on the sand until they were mesmerized. They watched the people walking, going about their business for the day. Sigred laughed at a man with a small animal on his shoulder with a long tail, it made a funny squeaky sound. Thora was frightened of a large spotted cat, penned in a cage, who stared intently at her as she passed by. It gave her a scary feeling inside. Kaja listened as minstrels strummed on a lyre, blew on a bone flute, pan-pipes and a cow horn trumpet as they strolled down the street. They enjoyed the music, it made them feel like singing and dancing. A pair of jugglers strolled by throwing balls into the air and catching them, over and over again. Aunt Gudrum threw them a coin and they stopped and entertained the three young ladies fancily for a few minutes. They saw many unusual things, were filled with wonder, thrilled at new experiences and tasted foods never eaten before. It was an exciting learning experience. They had many interesting things to tell their parents when they returned home. They rested a day in Aunt Gudrum's cottage beyond the shore area before returning to Alfhild - it was such an exciting trip.

They were still filled with the wonder of it all when they arrived home. "We saw a strange sea creature trapped in a large enclosure on the edge of the sea," Kaja told her King and Queen. "They called it octopus, with its long arms called tentacles coming from a large head and little body." She demonstrated with a flourish of her hands.

Thora said, "We ate little pink sea creatures with thin shells, a head and tail. We needed to peel off the thin shells so can eat them. They be very tasty; but not taste like fish," she explained in wonder.

Sigred excitedly spoke, "We traveled on board a longboat with a big flapping sail, just a short distance out on this large lake, called the sea! The waves rolled our boat up and down, make us so dizzy we hang on the side so not fall in water."

-- - -

The village activity slowly settled down for the approaching winter, as the summer has almost passed. Kaja, Jorgan along with other lads and lassies were sent to pick wild berries and edible vegetation in outlying fields. They helped wash the fruit to cook and preserve with honey in large clay jugs for future use. It would sweeten their bread all winter long. They washed the greens, but did not enjoy the eating of the tart bitter leaves. Their marm said, "It make you grow strong! Look how strong cows be, they eat many greens from the fields. We cook, with piece of pork fat to flavor and a sprinkle of salt and spices."

They all agreed, "Ya, this taste better."

Kaja and Jorgan watched the men slaughter the livestock, then clean and treat the hides to make covers, sacs to carry things, thick soles for their shoes, and much more. The bones were fashioned to make tools, skates to strap on their feet to ride across the ice in winter. The meat was preserved with salt to last the winter. They watched the men prepare grain to age into ale, and collected honey from the beehives to sweeten their bread and to make mead, the strong sweet drink the men enjoyed. Their sire, King Ivar, walked with them to oversee what the men do. He had the workers explain why they do these things this way, how they cooked and prepared the ale and mead. Kaja and Jordan watched with wide eyes and listened intently to what was said.

Jorgan, along with studying, was taught to use a battle axe, joust with a sword of steel, ride a stallion and to care for animals. He showed fear of the huge beasts, but admired their strength and learned to control them with care and sensitivity. "Why must I learn all these things? I will be king; others will do this work."

His father made him understand, "How can you know what to instruct them to do, if you don't understand what need be done?"

Jorgan countered, "Be they not wise, they not know what need be done?"

"Ya, but perhaps it not what need be done at the time, which happen. This spring, the farmers want to divert from the lakes all the rain water from the hills above to sodden the dry fields below. Think of this - the small lakes aside the fields to handle the overflow of water, become dry, because the quantity of spring rain be not enough to fill them. Frode advise half the water be directed to the lakes, should the quantity of summer rain not be sufficient to last through fall. It worked well, the fields watered and the lakes sufficiently filled. Otherwise, the overflow of water from fields would drain to the river below and be wasted. Such things like this we must be wary of, oft the workers do not know to look ahead."

Jorgan listened carefully, paused in thought a minute or two and then asked his father, "Why we not make the fields drain to the lakes, than the river?"

"Think," he paused, "rain water come from hills, to lakes, to field, to river, in natural order. The lakes be above level of fields which make it difficult to get water to flow up. That be a question to ask our wizard, he will think on it. Perhaps a young mind can help find a way." Ivar smiled at his son. He took pride in both his children, they demonstrated inquisitive intelligence, for which he credited Frode.

As Kaja grew toward womanhood she was given an attendant, an older lady named Hega, who remained constantly at her side. She watched over Kaja every day and scolded her when she got too friendly with the young lads. "You must be cautious of them, they have strong need of maiden's body and will try to defile you in many ways. Must keep pure and save self to give to husband only after you wed."

"Why I give my body to husband? I not need keep it for myself? Why give body to him, what he do with two bodies?" Kaja was aghast of Hega's words. Hega reported to Queen Alva of Kaja's inquisitiveness yet apparent ignorance of nature.

When winter returned, with all outside work completed, Queen Alva and Aunt Kudrun decide, "Is time."

"Is time for what Marm?" Kaja asked.

"Is time to instruct you to care for yourself, Kaja, your person." Queen Alva replied.

"After I work the summer washing babies, picking berries, scrambling after little ones, making them mind and sit in class, now I need sit and be a delicate flower. This be wearisome," she complained with a shake of her head. "as it be."

"More reason to do what be needful to be ladylike. Someday you be full of gratitude you take time and make effort so it be second nature." Queen Alva informed her firmly, "Be of belief, dear Kaja, you be thankful. You mature to a fine young lady and it a fine lady you want to be."

They made it a point to take Kaja aside, to explain the future functions of her body as a mature woman, of a woman's body in relation to that of a man's in procreation.

Kaja was bewildered, she had not heard of this before. She had known animals birthed baby animals, knew there were many babies around in the village, but never knew, never thought of where they came from. She sat and just looked at her mother and did not say a word, did not know what to say.

Days later, Queen Alva took Kaja and Jorgan by the hand, all were bundled in warm animal skin caftans against the cold wind and walked them to the farmers shed where a pig was about to give birth to a litter of piglets. Kaja looked at her mother with a big question in her eyes as the sow squealed in pain. Alva explained, "This be the way piglets born. They start from seed, just as a flower or tree, grow to baby size piglet in mother's womb, come time to birth, the body push it out through place near her belly. She have litter of many little pigs to feed from milk made in her body. They suck it from nipples and grow to be big pigs. This be the way for all animals born, so also the way for man and woman. The need be for one male and one female in act of love to make baby." Alva did not say more, she let them dwell on the ways and means of birth. She knew the other questions would come later and prepared in her thoughts the proper words to explain to them the "strong need of man for a woman's body."

Kaja gave her mother an endearing hug and then, also, her Aunt Gudrun. "I not be stubborn, stupid," she hesitated. "I not grown yet, desire to be lass with no duties, no responsibilities."

"I feel same when your age, Kaja," Aunt Gudrun confessed and smiled, as Kaja shyly blushed. "A year or so and you feel and think different, will need to know all. There be suitors to fill the hall, look to woo, to win you," she predicted.

Kaja blushed even more and thought to herself, *Just so it not that haughty, mean, willful prince.*

CHAPTER TWO

(ALFHILD)

Aunt Gudrum's spouse, Uncle Verner, finally returned to Norway from his journey to foreign lands, bringing gifts for his spouse's family in Alphild. For the realm he brought a pair of furry little creatures in a cage. "They be called 'sables' and have a thick, warm coat of fur. You release them to live in the wild. Let them breed 'til you have many, many animals in a year or two. Then you trap them in a cage, skin them for their fur to make beautiful warm coats. Ladies of quality enjoy wearing them not only for their beauty, but for the warmth in cold winters. For my spouse, Gudrum, and Lady Alva I bring sable fur hats so they can gaze on the beauty of the animal's fur and wear them to test their warmth in the cold of winter."

Alva and Gudrum admired the hats and felt the smoothness of the texture as they passed their hands over the soft fur. They looked at each other and smiled with pleasure as Kaja and Jorgan enjoyed the touch of them also. Then they passed them around to others nearby to let them delight in the pleasant sensation.

"It be important to be careful of the animals because they can be fierce with sharp teeth," Verner explained. "They catch and eat rodents, hares, grouse, even squirrels. They eat most anything they can find when in the wild, even berries."

King Ivar asked, "You say we let them loose to live in the wild? Are they hard to tame so cannot live as pets among us? Perhaps we can build a closed area for them? They will dig tunnel to get out? They freeze in winter?" he asked questions as fast as he thought of them. In the back of his mind was the idea of raising them to supply warm clothes for the people and perhaps to eventually sell to others.

"You be right, sire, they dig," Verner agreed. "We look for place to keep them in forest nearby so they can build a den, away from village where it be safe, for the sables and the people. They not freeze, have warmth in their den, have thick fur to keep warm. They function well by themselves and know to care for themselves.

"You want pet to keep in castle?" Verner questioned and brought out another container with two little animals in it. "See, I bring docile little pigs to play with and rub backs. They like lads and lassies to hold them, it make them happy. Keep in small area where they can hide and play. Feed them small amounts two times every day. Best keep male and female separate so not have too many pups, lest there be no room in castle for you," he laughed. "You like, Kaja, Jorgan?" he asked as they took the guinea pigs from him and carried them off to sit down and hold on their laps. The guinea pigs squirmed and sniffed at them and made them laugh.

As the lads and lassies played with the guinea pigs, Verner took King Ivor aside. "They can be eaten, are favored in foreign lands. So if you have too many, harvest them, clean them, cook them. You not tell all what they eat, lest they not favor to eat a pet," he jested.

"I bring smoked meat I learn to prepare in Iceland. Better than salt to preserve meat, it last longer, taste better. You taste, see yourself. Last, I bring harp from the Britons for King Ivar, as you request."

Ivar held the harp, inspected it, his eyes aglow, plucked at the strings with his fingers and told all with a delighted smile, "I play this instrument when just a lad, pleasure to hear again the lovely song it sings."

"I will be content to assist you, Sire," Verner told him. "I too played this instrument many years gone, with enjoyment, look forward to play it again." They practiced on the instrument in the morning, sometimes in the afternoon outside in the courtyard for hours at a time, 'til everyone within hearing was weary of it and ready to take the sword to them. They not play well.

A feast be prepared and all the citizens welcomed Verner and the many things he brought from foreign shores. They tasted the smoked meat he brought from foreign lands. Frode had Kaja scribe the words as they listened to Verner explain the manner of preserving the meat with the new method. After tasting the smoked meat all are eager to use this new method to preserve their meat to store away for the winter.

"There be one more thing I bring from the isles," Verner told Ivar after the feast, as they sat and watched the young people dance around the courtyard. "There be the one God of Heaven the people thrive on in most lands I travel. The Irish for many years have belief in Jesus, son of God, who come to earth and teach all to live in peace and harmony among each other. It be in Iceland now and Britian, too. Be there any here among the Norsemen who believe in the peaceful way of life? Be there any priest who teach you to pray, tell stories of Jesus' life and crucifixion here on earth?"

"Ya, I hear young lad, who return from Kaupang many months, speak of the One God. We not have priest here to teach," Ivar told him.

"We have a Friar in Kaupang now, who be a fine man, he speaks well and true. He trains other young men, the teachings and the way of Jesus, so they can spread throughout our land. I hear even our High King Olaf accept Christianity. Soon you have a Friar come to Alphild, listen to him, learn from him, you too will like and accept this peaceful way of life," Verner was very convincing. "I bring a cross to hang on your wall. It be the symbol of Christianity."

Ivar listened and took note, *a peaceful way of life among our barbaric Norsemen*, he mused. *He doubted his people, so deeply rooted in the many gods of old, would accept it.*

Uncle Verner and Aunt Gudrun, soon took their leave to return home to Kaupang, where his business awaited him. Gudrun sadly spoke her farewells, "It be a joy living among you while Verner gone at sea, I feel sad to leave you dear Kaja and Jorgan. I pray you be happy as I be, now my spouse home again."

"You grow into delightful maiden, Kaja, I see in your future a prince who prepares himself to be a judicious king. He will come for you afore long, be patient, my lady." Verner held her close, bade her farewell and gave her a sweet kiss on the cheek.

Kaja was speechless, "He tell my future?" she questioned her mother.

They found an area in the distant woods to encourage a habitat and a den in the hollow trunk of a large old tree for the two young sables. They watched them from a distance. The sables prepared the den for comfort in the winter as they frolicked about and investigated their new home. The children of the realm made it a game to see how many small rodents, squirrels and grouse they could trap and release into the dens area and watched the sables chase and catch them to eat. They wagered which sable would be first to snatch a mouse, and decided the male, whose fur was slightly lighter than the female's, was the better hunter of the two. However, they did not like to watch them rip the small animals apart with their sharp teeth and would run from them.

Kaja picked up the harp one afternoon as she passed in the hall, held it as her father held it, stroked the strings to make them hum. She tried one string then another. It pleased her, the melodious sound, except when she strummed two strings together. She carried it outside to the courtyard so as not to disturb others. She strummed it and tried to sing along with it, but became frustrated – she did not know how.

"That not the way to play the harp," a voice behind her announced.

"Oh, and you know the way?" she questioned as she turned to see the owner of the voice.

"Sweet maiden," he smiled at her, "I do know the way, I learn this past winter. It be easy. Will you allow me to show you?"

"Perhaps ya, perhaps nah," Kaja said, not recognizing the young man coming up behind her. "What be your name, where you come from?"

"I be Godvin, the blacksmith's son. I crossed the wooden sword with you many an afternoon." He paused while Kaja studied him and searched for memory of him.

"You not have the look of the skinny lad I knew be Godvin."

"You not look the wily lass I cross swords with," he countered. "Lad's and lassie's do grow, you a lovely maiden and hopefully me more a man. Be this not in proper order?"

"Proper order, true," she paused, "I have no memory of you, where you go?"

"To Kaupang for two years, I be with uncle to learn the blacksmith trade and, also the delicate craft of fancy gold and silver articles that ladies and men of rank and wealth enjoy to wear and behold."

"Also learn the harp," Kaja added, "or did you not say it, perhaps on purpose? You not learn well, therefore hesitate to demonstrate your talent?"

Godvin smiled at her, "You a saucy maiden still, My Lady. When think of you I remember the many times you give sharp words to make joust better, harder and you still joust better than we. You still use the sword?"

"Only when marm not look, I be maiden now, learn ladylike things. I wonder, playing the harp be an acceptable ladylike activity?"

"Many ladies of quality play in Kaupang. It be accepted there," Godvin nodded his head.

Kaja learned to play the harp with much practice. Godvin attended her every afternoon for a quiet hour or so, taught her how to match the different strings that sound well together and pluck them properly. She sang with it and he joined her on occasion. Queen Alva heard them and made it an afternoon diversion to listen and enjoy the young voices and music.

King Ivar returned from a visit to a neighboring realm and hunting trip, bearing two carcasses on an ass. "Another carcass, a large bear, be traded to a farmer for his ass. The ass is old and useless, won't last another year. We fear lest it not see us home with the game on his back," he jested.

Queen Alva laughed with him, happiness in her heart that he had returned in time for his birthday feast. The butchers prepared one carcass to smoke, the way Verner had instructed them to preserve, for another feast. The larger elk of the two, they prepared to roast over the fire, to cook the night long, before the birthday feast. "Kaja," her mother spoke aside to her, "We surprise your sire. You and Godvin sing, play the harp, at the feast tomorrow, perhaps from behind curtain. It be test, see if he remember your voice." Kaja be pleased and gave her mother a hug as they schemed together for the surprise.

And what a surprise it becomes! King Ivar feels high of spirits, "More ale, more meat," he roared. "Does not the entertainment begin?" They played and sang, first Kaja than Godvin, then together.

Ivar sat in silence, glumly hunched looking down with a frown on his face, then raised up and roared, "Who play my harp?" Ivar did not sound pleased.

"Queen Alva hurried to his side, "We perform entertainment for you, sire, do you not enjoy the music?"

"Who play my harp?" he roared again, trying to rise from his chair.

"By the Gods above," Alva waylaid him with her hand, "We found a learned music man and lady to play proper for you. Be silent and listen." She whispered sharply in his ear.

With anger, he gave his wife a long, hard stare, the ale stirred in his veins. Alva directed her servant, "Tell Godvin leave quickly out through the cooking chamber, the king be not happy they play his harp. Tell Kaja continue, sing sweet, play his favorite story ballad of conquest to divert his attention."

King Ivar calmed with the familiar, sweet music and singing and fell fast asleep. An attendant placed a bear rug on the floor and the king spent the night snoring by the fire.

Kaja found Godvin the next morning and they laughed of the evenings events. "That be the first time I hear my father roar of the ale. He always laugh with the ale. I must tell him of our learning sessions, but not know if he show anger. Perhaps if I sing another song when he wakens, it will soften his heart."

"I will stay far from him 'til he shows no anger," Godvin decided. "I plan to stay and work beside my sire for many years; not want our king to banish me afar." He paused a moment, "I made gift of brooch for my king for his birthday, with the gripping beast upon it. Do you think he will like it? It will appease him perhaps? I also made a gift for my lady, Queen Alva. Will she like delicate jewelry of Borre filigree? It be an exquisite brooch, many ladies of quality wear in Kaupaug."

Kaja looked at the gifts and then at Godvin in amazement. "You make these?" and when he nodded, she said, "Ya she like! She like it much, they be beautiful. You make one for me? I pay you coins," she quickly commissioned.

Godvin was pleased and agreed to make her one, also.

She smiled, returned to the hall, strumming softly, where her father was sitting at the table only half awake. "Stop that music," he growled.

Kaja stopped playing, attended him, brought him food. "Take away, I want no food."

"Did you enjoy your feast last evening, Father?" Kaja asked softly, knelt at his feet up close to him.

He looked at her from lids shielding the sun's glare, "My head hurts, I not remember last night. I want naught to eat, want naught to drink. Go from me, my head hurt."

Kaja quietly left him, told her mother and everyone what he said. Relieved, she hoped he would not remember his anger on the morrow when his head cleared. She gave her Marm the gifts, "Godvin made gift of gold for our sire's birthday and one for you. I commission him to make one for me. They be beautiful, he has wondrous talent to make fancy jewelry."

Queen Alva was amazed and very pleased and gave Godvin many thanks and compliments when next he came to the castle.

Kaja enjoyed the attention of the junior knights in the court and they enjoy little flirtations with her. Queen Alva cautioned her, "Do not greet them too well, they be not of suitable station, you must wait for a prince."

Another winter arrived with snow and ice on the land. "Shall we ski down the snow this day? The path on the knoll over the mountain be smooth and safe," invited Sir Jacob.

They screamed as they skied. "I like to fly down the knoll, the cold air freeze my face," Kaja screamed as they landed into a soft bank of snow. She rose up laughed and brushed the snow from her heavy coat, her cheeks all pink from the cold.

"Does my lady enjoy skating on ice? The pond be frozen solid; it be of ease to skate, perhaps this noon when the sun warms?" Jacob asked.

That afternoon Kaja was ready. "We hold your hand so you won't fall on the hard ice," invited Sir Poul, another knight. "Shall we go faster?" they offered.

"Ya, hold my hand firm, lest I tumble," she shrieked with glee.

They covered the frozen length and width of the irrigation pond on their bone skates as her lady attendant, Hega, shivered near the edge, watched intently and wondered why they enjoyed skating and freezing in the icy cold air. But then, she remembered skating on the ice when a young lass herself. She had fallen repeatedly many times and decided not to skate any more.

Kaja invited, "Come to the hall after dark. I play the harp, we sing by the fire and roast chestnuts." Also invited were many friends so it was a social, rather than a courting encounter. Thora and Sigred happily obliged, as do several other lads and lasses yet unwed and willing to join them to socialize the winter evening in the hall. Godvin also joined them to play the harp and sing.

"Come Kaja, come My Lord and My Lady, Thora called from the doorway when she arrived. "See the lights in the sky frolic about. Put your heavy fur caftan over your smock. It be cold as ice, but beautiful lights from the Gods make your head swim, make feel soft and warm inside." They all followed Thora out to the courtyard where the northern lights kept them spellbound with awe until their hands and toes froze with the cold winter breeze.

Frode followed them out to see the wonder. "I not know what cause this phenomenon," he admitted. "Some say it be a bridge built by the gods from earth to heaven. But I say this not true, it be beautiful lights in the sky. Light come from the sun. Not know where this light come from? Reflected light perhaps? But reflection on what?" The young observers are disappointed, had hoped Frode would be able to explain what made the beautiful flashing, colored lights float across the night sky, but he is not knowledgeable of earth science.

They return to the hall, danced around the fire to warm their blood and sang songs to warm their hearts. They danced the ring dance, swayed back and forth, tangled through and under each others arms. Even Queen Alva and King Ivor joined them for a short time.

"These young people tire an old man, I retire to my table and sit. Anyone want to crack chestnuts for their King?" Ivor invited. All sat, cracked and ate the warm chestnuts and sang songs, while Godvin played the harp, content that the king did not remember the incident from his birthday feast. The King sat by the fire with the little guinea pig in his lap and petted it 'til it fell asleep. Even the guinea pigs enjoyed the music, the youthful exuberance and the pleasant evenings by the fire, most winter evenings long.

"It too many years we wait for the prince we promised Kaja. She be past fifteen summers, ready to wed. The young men about are not of status suitable for a princess. I not let her go, lest there be no other prince," King Ivar spoke to his spouse.

"She be young, can wait another year or two. She happy here with many activities to interest her, not need to rush. Verner see prince in her future, he say not to fret for her," Alva explained.

"Ya! He can see her future?" He responded incredulously with a flourish of his hands. "Ya, she be a delightful maiden, keep me happy with her quick wit and the sound of an angel with song. She has the look of her marm, Frode teach her well as does her marm. Frode say she do well to instruct the young lads and lasses and two promising young lads with great intelligence to develop. Sir Knud be amazed how well the young lads she instruct with the wooden stick progress with the sword of steel. Ya, she be a prize; we not let her wed without status," he insisted with sincerity.

Even Jorgan, who trained with her when a lad, easily became an expert with the sword of steel. "Now I be almost grown, sister, I soon joust better than you a mere maiden."

"Ha!" She joked in reply, "I not wager on that, little brother, I still swing a strong stick." They fun each other - Jorgan was mature enough to realize that his sister was a fine lady to respect, admire and he watched diligently as young men flocked about her. He even let it be known to them, "Don't speak disrespectful of Kaja and other maidens, as men we must hold them in regard and protect them!"

"Cannot she protect herself?" one jested, being familiar with her skill.

"I say she can whip one weak as you," Jorgan responded harshly. "If not, I trounce you." There was an agreeing nod from others and the offender took his leave, not wanting to feed anger among the group.

King Ivar, planned a journey to a neighboring realm to consider a union with a younger prince. "The lad be not yet twelve," Kaja argued, "younger than my own brother! He not grown enough to take wife for many years. Then I be too old for him. He will desire a younger maiden. Father!" she pleaded. "There many young knights among our realm I fancy - can be happy with. Is not that of importance? I see much happiness among our people and others of note. I care little to be a queen."

King Ivar considered her words, "We think on it, my dear Kaja. No need for concern. Ya, we consider it."

CHAPTER THREE

ALFHILD AND HEBORG

Queen Alva slowly followed Prince Aksel from the long hall and watched as he left. She had been surprised to see him, hardly recognized him for he had grown and matured, was so much more a man. He told her he had been away at sea these many years, now he needed to rush home to his father who was on his death bed. He had come to claim Kaja so his sire could see them wed before he died. After all the years they had waited, Kaja did not desire him for her spouse, did not desire to wait for the other young prince to grow older, prefered a handsome knight or two among the men of court. Alva could understand her angst.

She hesitated, *But this Prince be not the willful lad from years hence. He be grown, be pleasant, a gentleman,* she sighed wistfully, still seeing those eyes. *His azure eyes, just begging for his promised lady to come to him. Was there a need, was it even a desire for her? Must tell Kaja – must insist, she need look again at willful young prince, now a grown, discerning man.*

Jorgan and Queen Alva spoke long and intense of the prince. Jorgan agreed, "He be changed, grown up, tolerant, intelligent. I see him much more a man. Kaja would best wed with the Prince than wait for the younger boy to grow. I ride to tell her, tell sire not to promise her to young lad. Her prince returned from the sea, to claim his promised lady."

The next morning, Jorgan mounted his steed and with a young knight to accompany him, rode to the neighboring realm to alert his father of Prince Aksel's return to claim his promised bride. As there was no moon to shed light on the path, they stopped at a wayside shelter for the night and arrived the next mid-day.

Jorgan spoke first to his father and then with Kaja. He told his sister, "The Prince be very anxious

to have you, asked if you still the lovely, spirited, intelligent young lady of memory. He fancies his lady saucy," he jested and she gave him a nasty sisterly look.

She looked to her father for some sort of sign. "I not know," she thought aloud, "I not like his mean manner of old. I be more learned than he ever. He be willful, haughty. Because he be prince, not make him a good king. Even a king must do well for his people, not make them full of fear or enslaved," she complained of his negative traits.

"You be promised to him," King Ivar, reminded her, "Jorgan say he be more a man, he speak with respect. Ya, it be many years he not claim, but he has first promise. We tell King Havard we give no promise now to his young son. If you find Prince Aksel unsuited when you look on him, we will consider elsewhere. You can refuse him, if you so desire."

"Thus, I choose my own knight, there are many who suit me," she persisted.

King Ivar looked at his daughter and smiled, "You be most independent, my young lady."

"And who made me so?" she smiled teasingly at him. He just loved this maiden and wanted her to be happy.

They arrived home late the next day and received the same message again from her mother. "He send a coach and messenger, take us to his castle. He much more mature, manly, speaks well with knowledge, intelligence, with respect and graciousness in his manner and an urgency to be beside his sire before he dies, if not already. He pray you be available to come so his sire can see him wed, and settled with wife, before he dies."

The old memory of him whipping her Frode, does not leave her. Even though Frode explained the Prince's actions logically and with empathy, she credited that to the wise man's love of human beings and knowledge of her future. He was often known to "see" things no other could see. She wondered if the prince really had matured to become a judicious man?

Her mother resolutely continued, "He requested Frode come to aid his father, bring herbs and cures to save him or ease pain. We need to prepare for travel to Heborg," she ordered.

Kaja sat with her mother, didn't know what to do. Go meekly to the barbarian? She discussed her plight with her father, he too was dubious of the barbarian's change. "We go and look on him, Kaja. You see him, talk with him. We return if you not convinced," King Ivar proclaimed again. "It be your decision."

With no other recourse available, Kaja went to her promised prince when the coach arrived from Heborg. Her parents, brother and Frode accompanied her with a small entourage, which carried the wedding clothes and the usual bride's gifts for the marital ceremony. It was a three day journey as the two coaches traveled slowly to accommodate Queen Alva's ailing body,

The Prince watched from the small balcony as the travelers received greetings from his mother Queen Hulda, with cousin Karl and Gerda also in attendance. The Prince was pleased with his first look of her and stepped down to greet them as they entered the main hall. He walked toward them, politely bowed, greeted and welcomed the King and Queen, then turned to Kaja. She was startled by his composure, his presence and the manner in which he seems to consume her with his eyes. Gently, he took her arm and walked away from the others to talk privately.

"Do you remember me?" he inquired lightly.

"Ya, I do, you have changed, I not recognize the brash, lad Prince I challenged years ago."

"I'm also called 'animal' if you remember?" he added with a side glance at her.

"Surely, a magnificent stallion!" she responded with a quick smile, glanced at him from the corner of her eyes.

"I'm told you be saucy, green-eyed vixen."

She paused, "Do you find favor with that name?" she asked sweetly meeting his eyes straight on.

He looked down into her face and softly said, "I am addressed as 'Sire', if you will be so gracious."

" I, Sire, am addressed 'My Lady'." She returned with just the trace of a smile.

He paused as they strolled slowly, "Do you always have the last word?"

"Depend on the subject and circumstance, My Liege." She spoke as softly to him as he had to her, emphasizing the title, so he would know she did not use the one he chose. She kept her eyes down to avoid his direct gaze, realizing he had a sly smile on his face.

"Still the wily, spirited filly, I see."

"My Lord, I be schooled to act the lady - at times I find that be difficult."

"So there be war of wills between us?' he suggested.

"That be an ugly word," she countered, somewhat furrowing her brow. "Can there not be peaceful talk, discussion to compromise, viewpoint to investigate as my parents do so successfully.

"Be this how he rules his realm," Prince Aksel asked, "by talk and compromise?"

"Ya, it be so, each has a say in dispute, he do his best to rule judiciously. Only one time he loose patience, when a third man come to counter with a similar complaint to the man who had grievance against another for the same affront. It be quite a problem," she shook her head slightly in emphasis.

"My Lady, be your mother happy with this arrangement, with her husband king?"

"They very content, Sire," she smiled mischievously

"I have my duty to keep you the lady and loving wife."

She paused just a moment, turned to him. "You find, Sire, a lady respond loving, readily when respect and love be given," she looked up at him with sincerity in her eyes. He held her eyes a moment, paused a moment, looked back at the other people in the room and then down at her, "Will you attend me tomorrow here in this court and vow to be my wedded wife to love, honor and obey?"

"I will, Sire, if you be prepared to do same," She said softly, respectfully and with a tiny smile, looking again into his eyes.

"Ya, my work be ahead of me." He acknowledged with a slight nod.

Kaja gave him a big smile and whispered, "I look forward to it," she paused and added, "Sire," with just a little tilt to her head.

The Prince paused as they returned to the group who were waiting for them, he hesitated, took her by the shoulders turned her to face him and looked down at her. She looked at him with a question in her eyes as he slowly bent down and kissed her lips gently. "I have the last word?" he questioned softly with a sneaky smile.

"If that your desire."

"It be my desire. Cannot you say, Ya, my sire?" he questioned.

She paused, just a second, smiled with a slight nod of her head and said sweetly, "Ya, my Sire." Kaja was pleased with him, enjoyed the flirtation as he seemed to, also. Perhaps, this will be well, she thought, he much more a man. He excites me.

Aksel, also pleased, turned to her parents and welcomed them again with a pleasant demeanor, gave orders to his servant to see to their comfort and tend to any needs they may have. As he mounted the stairway he turned back to look at them as Kaja, also, turned to look after him, their eyes met again for a moment. *Ya, much more a man.* She be smiling in her heart. *He stirs my senses.*

King Ivar did not need to get verbal acceptance from his daughter, she glowed with a light he had not seen in her for many moons. Their eyes met and she smiled graciously at him. He was pleased and returned the smile with a gentle nod.

That afternoon after a short rest and a light repast, the men convened in King Gregers chamber to conclude the contract for Kaja. "We not speak of marriage contract for Kaja afore. We use the contract agreed for Margrethe?" King Ivar questioned. Gregors agreed, coughed hard into a cloth and breathed hard with a wheezing sound.

The exchange of gifts provided for the brides' portion and the grooms' portion, usually given and received, took place in the Kings chamber where he lay in bed, periodically coughing. Knight Ingvar, Cousin Karl and Prince Jorgan witnessed the agreement and exchange. Purses of silver and gold coins were the groom's portion; jeweled silver pieces, linens and household sundries were the bride's portion.

"Be there a priest of Christianity in your realm?" King Ivar asked. "Is your realm of Christian faith or still the Gods of old?"

"There be Friar Kristoffer of the Christian faith to perform the marriage.   There be some still cling to the Gods of old," Aksel informed him.   "Many adopt the Christian faith as did I on my journeys. It be more peaceful a manner to live among men."

The banns of marriage were read that evening in the courtyard before the citizens of the village. No reason was found that the couple could not wed and Friar Kristoffer dispensed with the necessity of the second and third readings to facilitate the wedding the next day to favor the ailing King. Friar Kristoffer announced the wedding ceremony would be held the next morning and all the villagers were invited to attend the ceremony and join the festivities after. The Friar spoke with Kaja and her parents to see if they were content with the arrangements made for the wedding ceremony in the courtyard the next day.

Queen Alva was concerned about weather, "What we do if rain come?"

"It not a problem, the hall be large to accommodate most all who attend.   Should be clear weather." Friar Kristoffer assured them. "Good fall weather for wedding and feasting all day long. All be happy to see the young prince wed and prepared to be the new King when need." The villagers prepared for the ceremony and food for the feast to celebrate afterwards. The castle was swept, the courtyard decorated with wild fall flowers growing from along side the ponds and music played until late in the evening by light from the large harvest moon and oil lamps that hung from the walls. Two large hunting dogs pranced around the courtyard, excited with the activity and getting in everyone's way, until a guard called them off and secured them behind the castle wall.

The citizens passed by to courtesy and bow before their new princess and her family. Kaja was pleased with their welcome and friendliness and responded in kind, talked with the ladies, reached out to the children. One little girl came to her and hugged her legs. The mother hurriedly came to retrieve her, but Kaja bent down, embraced the beautiful child in a hug before letting her return to the mother. She met the mother's eyes and they smiled in understanding.

Kaja remembered and recognized the tall, strong knight and young cousin who accompanied her prince many years ago. They greeted her and she found comfort in seeing their familiar faces.

Cousin Karl introduced, "This my wife, Gerda, My Lady, I find her in the Britians among the Norsemen there. She tired of the British countryside and beg me take her home to her land of birth," he jested.

Gerda laughed happily and gave Kaja a soft hug, "Welcome, my lady, we pray you be happy here in your new life, as I be," she graciously said.

Ingvar also introduced his spouse, Dagmar, "I hear from my man the wonders of the young maiden who be our future Queen. We pray all be well for you," and she held Kaja's hand and looked into her eyes with kindness. Kaja was delighted, *Dagmar be a lovely woman, no wonder Ingvar such a fine man,'* she mused. *I pray I be that way too.*

"This my young son, Erik, he almost forget his sire, I be gone away so long with your prince," Ingvar told her.

Kaja reached down to hold Erik's hand, "You have brave Sire, my lad, who did wondrous thing to care for our prince. We be grateful. You have the look of a strong knight when you grow, also."

"My Lady, I be a wise man like your Frode, he teach me many wondrous things," Erik's response surprised her.

"That be a wonder. Ya, he taught me many things when a lass. Listen to him and you learn more than I," she encouraged.

Erik glowed with pride. *He could be a knight like his sire and wise man also.'* These were his thoughts.

Kaja, Jorgan and their parents mingled with the people the evening long, enjoyed the feeling of welcome and harmony. The pleasant warmth of the evening breeze was delightful as the musicians played their horns and flutes. They joined them in the Ring-Dance singing to the Ormen Lange.

"Glad sounds of song fill the hall, as we dance and sing."

"The King, he said he'd have a ship all built upon the strand

'Ormen Lange' – the biggest ship ever built in Norway's lands."

They danced to the beat of the music holding hands, the leader led them stepping under each others arms and back around again, knotting the dancers into a tangle till no one could move while rampant flirting was carried on. Kaja received a kiss on the cheek a time or two and even Jorgan is smiled upon sweetly by several young lasses. He was tempted to sneak a kiss but was shy, not knowing any of them. One little lass looked at him fetchingly and reached up to peck him on the cheek, making Jorgan blush. He followed her with his eyes as the dancing step was reversed and the long line of dancers were going in the opposite direction until they became untangled. The little lass coyly passed him closely the second time and Jorgan reached down, kissed her cheek and gave her a flirtatious grin.

Kaja and Jorgan enjoyed dancing until they tired of the exertion and retired for the night. It had been a long, tiring trip the last three days and Queen Alva was exhausted. Sleep was welcomed by all. A few of the citizens danced on into the night, however, and enjoyed a mug of ale and the aroma of meat roasting on the open fire. They looked forward to the wedding ceremony of their prince in the morning and afterwards the day-long celebration and feast.

CHAPTER FOUR

HEBORG

The sun rose clear and bright that morning and all was ready. Kaja wed her prince wearing the pagan bridle crown her mother and grandmother wore before her. They made the exchange of ancestral swords handed down to wives of sons and husbands of daughters, to pass in turn to spouses of their children to signify continuation of the blood line and power of guardianship and protection. They said their promise to each other in words spoken to them by Friar Kristoffer in the Christian faith of the one God, received the holy bread of life and exchanged rings one to the other as witnessed by their families and the community. Though they wed in the Christian faith of the one God they continued some of the ceremonial customs of old. Kaja served a drink of mead to her new husband in a vessel with handles on both sides and spoke of health and strength to the drinker. Aksel made a toast to the one God, took a sip and passed the cup back to Kaja. Kaja made a toast to the Mother of God and drank a sip. This ritual drink made them one in the eyes of the law and God, confirming their wedded status. All the people in the village who came to see their prince wed, welcomed and spoke with respect to their lovely new princess and enjoyed the feast and gaiety past nightfall.

They paid homage to their ailing King who insisted he would stay at the banquet and sat in a large lounging chair among them with his old companion dog, Alf, alongside him, sometimes napping and sometimes dully watching the gaiety of the people throughout the day. Kaja bowed before him, accepted his blessing, sat along side him, held his hand in comfort and reached out to pet the old dog beside him. She barely remembered him from years gone when he made the contract for her sister.

He was pleased to speak to her, "You a pleasure to look upon, a strong young lady. When last I saw you, you be skinny lass. Aksel grown now, not a willful prince as before, he be a good king and husband." He paused to take a deep breadth, coughed, took another deep breadth and his voice croaked as he continued, "I pray you be happy, have many babies and much love. God be with you both." He wished her well, laid back in his chair, took another long, slow, deep breath and motioned with his hand to Aksel. "Why you not dance with her, want to see you dance, be happy, she your wedded wife!" He closed his eyes, rested for a long moment and when next he looked, was happy to see them doing the kissing dance with other young people.

Aksel enjoyed dancing with Kaja, delighted in looking at her, being close to her while keeping her across from him at arms length, his hands on her shoulders to follow the music and the dance. She delighted in his nearness, his strength and felt shy with him. They were in line, stepped side to side, the men sang their song verses boastfully. The women replied scornfully till the last stanza, when they eagerly invited the men to "come over" and then ran from them. The men were to chase the women and catch one to kiss, but Aksel does not let Kaja run from him with the other women. He held her to him and engulfed her in a close warm hug and kissed her lovingly. He didn't want others kissing his wedded wife. She responded willingly and they lovingly gaze at each other, learning the look of each other, until Karl came up behind him and chided him for not being a sport.

"Ah, my prince, I see you not willing for others to kiss your lady. Me thinks you delighted in kissing my Gerda in Britian when we be wed. You be still the willful prince?" he laughed.

Aksel smugly looked at him. "She not skinny lass of years ago, she my lady, my lovely maiden, my wedded wife - mine! I protect her from lustful barbarians." Kaja cuddled close to her sire, Karl laughed and gave Kaja a quick kiss on her cheek, turned and joined the others still chasing and kissing women. Kaja was pleased and followed him with her eyes smiling.

Many stories were told by the guests about famous people, romance and the supernatural to keep all amused that afternoon while the young children sat among them to listen. They enjoyed listening to the stories of ancient Norsemen and clustered around the ailing king's chair to keep him interested and hear his comments.

Aksel remembered the sagas Unne Arason, Gregor's old companion in Iceland, told them and reveled in telling his father of them and their visits with all the people they met in Iceland. Gregor's spirit rose to hear about his old friend and listened to the gruesome story of the outlaw Gish who hid in cliffs and valleys near his spouse's farm.

Ingvar spoke of the worst blood feud started by Hrutur and Unnur. Their divorce after Hrutur became lover to aging Queen Mother Gunnhildr, then to his beautiful niece, Hallgerour, who married twice. Both husbands were killed by her doting foster-father. Hrutur avenged their deaths.

Karl chipped in, "Then Gunnar, a man of outstanding physical prowess, and Njal, a man of lawful judgment, are introduced and become friends. Gunnar be obliged to revive Unnur's dowry claim against her divorced husband, Hrutur, and wins with Njal's legal assistance.

Gunnar returned with much honor from Scandinavia, attended the Althing in splendor, met the lovely Hallgerdor and became betrothed despite warnings and misgivings about her character. The misgivings were proven right when Hallgerour clashed with Njal's wife, Bergpora, and Hallgerour charmed a number of dubious characters to kill members of Njal's household. The spirited Bergpora demanded blood revenge and their husbands made financial weregild after several killings.

The story continued -- Hallgerour used one of her followers to burgle the home of a churlish man named Otkel and Gunnar immediately sought to make amends, his offers were not accepted. A lawsuit started against Gunnar and again Njal and his legal expertise helped him win. He gained great honor.

Gunnar disputed with Hallgerour about a burglary and slapped her, followed by Otkell accidentally wounding Gunnar. Insult followed injury and Gunner avenged himself with help from his brother and killed Otkell and his companions."

Aksel added, "Gunnar's reputation grew. Njal warn him 'this be the start of your killing career.' Gunnar accepted a challenge to horse-fight. His opponents cheated and Gunnar be in a new quarrel. Njal tried to mediate, but it not accepted. On journey with his two brothers, Gunnar be ambushed by his opponents, fourteen attackers, and Gunnar's brother be killed."

Ingvar picked up on the story, "Unnur's son, Morour, envied and hated Gunnar, bring about attack on Gunnar. Again Gunnar won, he killed a second man in the family. The settlement required both Gunnar and his brother,

Kolskeggur, leave Iceland for three years. He resolved not to leave Iceland, his beautiful homeland, thereby became an outlaw.

"Morour and other enemies seek revenge, Gunnar defend himself in his home until his bowstring be cut. Hallgerour not give him strands of her long hair to restring his bow, in revenge for the slap he once gave her."

Karl continued, "It be most exciting battle of saga - the Njalssons with Kari prepare to ambush Prainn and followers. Skarpheoinn overtook his brothers, leapt over river, slid on ice past Prainn, beheaded him as he passed and killed four men. Morour knew Hoskuldur be such a proper chief, his own chieftaincy declined, so set Njalssons against Hoskuldur who be murdered as his field be planted. Hoskuldur be killed for less than no reason."

A legal fight resulted, arbitrators chosen, Snorri proposed a weregild of three times the normal compensation for Hoskuldur to be paid by arbitrators and Althing contributors. The settlement broke down when Njal added a gift of a fancy cloak and Flosi claimed insult at the offer of a unisex garment. Karl ridiculed in jest of the telling.

"All left the Althing, prepared for a showdown," Ingvar continued. "A hundred descended on Njal's home which be defended by just thirty. Flosi and his men set fire to building. The innocent be free to escape but Njal, Bergpora and grandson Porour die with the guilty, eleven die. Kari escaped, plan vengeance for to burn."

Aksel added, "At Althing, sides gathered, took action against the burners, legal jousting occurred. Porhall, Njal's foster-son trained by him in the law, fought. When legal action failed, several were killed, also Ljotur, Flosi's brother-in-law."

"Ljotur's father, Hallur of Sioa, appealed for peace, sought no compensation for his son, as change from Viking to Christian thinking. Thusly burners be exiled."

"Kari attacked Sigfussons afore they reached home and the rest of saga described vengeance for the burning," Karl added.

"It be after a pilgrimage to Rome, Flosi return to Iceland, Kari follow, be shipwrecked near Flosi's home. He go to Flosi for help where be arranged a final peace and Kari married widow of Hoskuldur. In end there be a full reconciliation, - blood feud be over." Ingvar told the end of the story with a shake of his head, a flourish of his hands.

King Gregors be amazed at stories told by old friend. "Blood feud be the way of Thor, Odin and the gods of old," he roared. "Be better the forgiving nature and goodness of the one Loving God," he breathed deep, closed his eyes. "I tired now," he whispered. His faithful old dog, Alf, followed slowly behind as Ingvar and another strong knight helped Gregor return to his bed as he coughed and struggled to breath.

Other story tellers wouldn't be outdone, which started them telling sagas they knew of old, each additional storyteller trying to outdo the last with a more incredible story. The celebration continued till well after sundown, the dancing started up again for a short while and they all retired to their cottages content with happiness and ale.

Kaja, assisted by her attendants, prepared for bed as was done before Christianity. When Aksel entered with his witnesses, they were put to bed according to the old custom, and all the attendants left with joking and hilarity, taking one torch light with them. The two were left alone to consummate the marriage.

They smiled at each other, Aksel held her close as he lay beside her, listening to be sure all were gone, but heard the voice of his father calling him. The sound echoed throughout the hall, ringing in his ears, he bowed his head in her hair, nuzzled her neck, reached up to cover his ears. "Dear God, I hear him call, how can I love my newly wed-ded wife, how can I sleep?" He shook his head, looked at Kaja apologetically, "I be needed to attend father the night, I not be husband to you now. I come to you soon." He looked long into her eyes, kissed her lips soundly held her close, caressed her cheek with his hand, gave a long sigh, rose from their bed and left her. She sat up, followed him with her eyes as he walked away and seemed to disappear in the darkened room. Then slowly lay back in bed. *What I do now?* She asked herself. *He leave me, his father be first? This be marriage? I have a wedded husband, but sleep alone, without my husband.*

Her attendants assisted dressing her the following morning, prepared her to receive the morning gift. Her hair was braided and coiffed as reserved for a married woman, with a long snow-white finely pleated linen cloth covering her head as a badge of honor, a token of her new status as wife in the household. Her blonde curly hair was hidden, just a wisp showing out the top.

Aksel came to give her a gift of a necklace and keys to the locks of all the doors to the household, as was the cus-tom, making her the head of the house. He spoke gracious-ly to all and left again to tend his father when he heard his Sire's call echo again through the castle.

King Ivar and Queen Alva rested for a few days among the people in the realm. Seeing her daughter wed had been good for Alva, she was content that Aksel was the proper prince for her. They returned to Alfhild before the cold weather set in.

Kaja did not tell her mother about non-consummation of her marriage, that her newly-wedded husband did not sleep with her. Alva returned to Alfhild thinking her daughter be happy with a good husband and went about her duties with a song in her heart.

Kaja had the chamber next to her husband's in the castle where she slept alone for the next couple weeks. Her husband too busy tending his ailing father and duties of the castle and could give her little time. She rarely saw him, but walked among the villagers, met them, and talked with them and found things to maintain her attention.

This castle stood on propriety, in some respects, to a greater degree than in her father's castle. She was assigned a young maiden, named Jannike, as befitted the future queen. The young maiden, was somewhat overwhelmed, but Kaja put her at ease, worked beside her to fulfill their duties. They worked together to place Kaja's clothes and linens in proper order, her personal articles too. They cleaned her chamber and that of her sire, aired out the bedding, laying it out in the sunshine on the balcony to freshen, removed weevils and other vermin that may have housed themselves among the tufts and refilled the bedding to a firm consistency with the fresh straws sowed from the harvest. They washed dirty bed covers and clothes that lay about, her sire was not a fastidious prince.

In moving about her sire's chamber, she discovered an opening along the back wall and wondered what it was for – where it went. She hesitated to investigate. It dwelled on her so she asked, "Jannike, do you know where this door will lead us?"

"My lady, it takes one to the King's bedchamber, the Queen Mother can hear her babes call in the night." Kaja acknowledged the information with a smile.

Together they prepared a small domicile for a pair of guinea pigs Kaja had carried from Alphild, kin of the pair that Verner had brought from his travels. They had mated readily when first they arrived in Norway, King Ivar soon discovered what Verner meant when he laughingly warned to be cautious "lest they fill the castle".

Jannike worked with Kaja and the carpenter, in preparing an open wooden cage for the guinea pigs to live in together. They prepared a second cage to house the male pig after the female had her first litter. It was necessary to separate them to control the population.

They carried the cages out to the courtyard on many pleasant days so the children could see them, play with them and learn how to care for them. The little pigs became quite the curiosity and everyone enjoyed to pet them and watch them frolic about. Kaja felt it would be easy to find homes for them among the families with young children, as new piglets arrived.

King Gregors rallied for a time. The wizard, Frode, was still in attendance and Kaja heard the Prince roar at him in his old barbaric fashion on occasion, but he did not strike him. Frode kept Kaja abreast of the Kings' health status and brought her little messages from Aksel.

Frode said, "I have told your prince there not be much I do. He must understand there be nothing to repair damage his sire's lungs suffer from consumption. King Gregors not likely survive the severe winter coming. Prince do well, he take advantage of sire's lucidity when can, asks questions and be given instructions and history that be of use to him as king. I scribe this for him in journal for future."

With the Prince involved with his father and other serious things, Kaja was called upon to settle a minor infraction among the serfs. "My Lady," Ostman the head gardener came to complain, "this young lad be guilty, he destroy garden plants afore they be ready for harvest."

Kaja was flabbergasted. "This be a bad sin?" She asked him. "What punishment do we give? Tie to whipping post to flog him?" She saw his mother gasp. "Where be this damage? Come my young lad, we see and talk." She motioned the gardener to follow, "Come, show the damage, we not be long, mother can stay here." She took the young boy's hand and walked with him out of the courtyard as he led her to the garden where the pulled plants lay on the ground near the edge of the path. As they walked along, Kaja talked to the young boy, "I grew up with a young brother, he be always in trouble. He be willful and someday be king of father's castle." When they arrived on the scene, she knelt down to his size and kindly looked at him face to face. "Tell me how this came to be. It not look like a thing a big lad, like you would do. Tell me true; more likely get punishment for a story than true words, be they bad."

The boy hung his head and started muttering indistinguishably.

"Speak clear, I not understand," she implored.

"I to watch my brother, he not yet has third birthday," he spoke loud and clear.

"How many birthdays have you?"

"I five birthdays, my lady."

"How be you called and your brother?"

"I be Gaius, my brother be Jorunn. I not watch him well, when I turn to him, he pull up most a whole row of plants. I put back in dirt but gardener Ostman see me, scold me and take to you for punishment. He said they not grow anymore, they lost."

"Ah, you not destroy garden plants, little brother, Jorunn do. You be guilty not of pulling plants, but be guilty of not watching young brother as mother assign you."

She turned to the gardener, "Be there a way to plant again so they grow again?"

The gardener was quite sure, "They be lost, My Lady, but we try. Growing season soon be over, there not be time to mature before the freeze."

Kaja believed it worth a try and asked the gardener, "Show you the young lad to properly replant, water them each day to grow. We see, perhaps some mature. If not, it be a lesson learned, he will remember." she turned to Gaius. "They be your responsibility, Gaius, we watch, see how you do. You work hard and they not mature, we know you tried and next time you will watch your little brother better so he not pull plants from ground afore they ready. You do that?"

The young man looked at her, eagerly nodded his head, "Ya, My Lady, ya!" and smiled happily.

"Be sure when work in garden, you not bring Jorunn. You not watch him well and attend your work at same time. Next spring you work with Ostman, the gardener, learn how to be a real planter."

"Ya, My Lady, ya!" He bowed to her repeatedly and smiled broadly. He seemed to like that idea. Ostman, however, raised his eyes to the heavens in a silent appeal to the Almighty.

Kaja saw this and smiled at Ostman. "He be good helper as he grow a big lad and be good farmer full grown." She tried to convince him.

Gaius stayed and replanted the pulled plants under Ostman's direction. Kaja walked back to the castle where his mother waited and explained to her what was to be, so she would know. She was in awe of Kaja, finally controlled herself, knelt at her feet and kissed her hand. "No, no," Kaja insisted, "that not be necessary. He learn lesson. Must keep other little dangerous lad from garden 'til he be older and learn not pull plants." She laughed as the brown haired little lad reached for her. She lifted him up and gave him a soft hug and kiss on the cheek, talked casually with them for awhile and returned to the castle.

The story of Kaja's justice was told around the realm and the people gazed on her in admiration. Where did that mean Prince find this lovely jewel. Will he appreciate her? They were not aware he had learned well and matured through his travels. They could still hear him roaring in the castle as from days long gone.

The people greeted Kaja pleasantly as she moved about the village. She spoke to all, asked questions of their methods, positions and showed real interest in becoming a part of the life of the community. "I be learned in birthing animals, helped my marm birth a baby a half year ago," she told the weaver's pregnant wife and the farmer with a herd of cows and pigs. "I will help when need."

She felt torment with the sadness in her heart, she felt alone as a stranger in a strange land. She be wed, but her husband be a stranger, she not know him. The people be friendly, responsive and accept her as she walked among them and talked to them, but when will her prince come to her?

CHAPTER FIVE

HEBORG

King Gregors slept fitfully the night, breathed hard, erratically and coughed intermittently for a long time. He softly called the name of his spouse, called the name of his son, and his daughter, then breathed again a rattle deep in his chest, a long slow exhale and he ceased breathing. The Prince dozing along side his bed, did not hear him call his mother's name, his own name and then his sister's name. Did not know he no longer breathed till he turned over in his restless sleep, heard the eerie silence and lifted himself up to look at his sire.. He no longer moved, no longer gasped for breath, his sire was dead. He knelt beside his bed and took his hand held it to his face, gazed upon the wizened, bearded man he both hated and loved all his life. Sadness overtook him as he laid his head on the bed next to his father's and trembled inside. He reached up to stir Alf who lay beside him, but Alf did not move. His body lay inert, his head lying on his master's leg. Alf had died along side his master.

In grief of his father's death, he went to his chamber found his wife in the darkness and without a word, took her to his bed in an unpleasant, demanding fashion. She is not receptive of him, trying to say something, but distraught with grief, the need so strong, he would not listen, told her to be quiet and afterwards, fell into a deep all-consuming sleep. He did not even hear her silently weeping beside him.

The next morning, the Prince still slept way past sun-up, Kaja returned from the home of Joseph the Weaver where she assisted in the delivery of their infant son. She had spent the night with the mother through labor. She is greeted by Jannike, who had been asleep on the kitchen hearth and wakened when she entered. With head bowed and eyes red from crying, Jannike did look directly at her and pulled her aside. "My Lady," she whispered still weeping, "the king died, the prince came to his chamber the night, he took me for you, it be dark, he not let me speak, command me be quiet, drag me to his chamber and to his bed. My Lady, oh my Lady" and she continued to cry more openly. "He thought I be you! I left his bed as soon I could, he still sleep."

Kaja looked distraught at her maiden with eyes wide open, took her arm and walked upstairs to her chamber where they sit and quietly talk. "You speak this to anyone?" she whispered.

"Oh no, my lady, I be afraid to."

"I sorry for the mistake, dear Jannike, did he hurt you?"

"No, my lady," she confessed, "it not the first for me. I have a lover, we plan to wed soon."

"Oh my, what we do? We tell Aksel? He not know what he do?" She wondered.

"I tell my betrothed he will be angry, there will be court gossip, scandal, perhaps it be wise not tell them, oh dear." Jannika said.

They hesitated, talked quietly and finally decided "Ya, it best not let your betrothed or Prince Aksel know what happen, let my sire believe it me, his wife in his bed."

Suddenly the adjoining door from the prince's chamber flew open. Jannike rose quickly, curtseyed to her lady and left. Kaja turned from him in an attempt to control her inner emotions. He walked slowly to her wrapping his shirt around him to cover his nakedness. "My Lady," contriteness oozed from his voice. "I owe you apology for last night. I be brutal, ugly when all I need was comfort and relief. This not how I want to be with you our first time together. I prove myself a barbarian still. I will make it better." He took a few steps toward her, bent down on his knee and took her hand up to his lips, kissed it tenderly and held it to his bearded cheek. He paused for a minute. "My father, the King, died last night". The Prince did not go to Kaja for several days.

The funeral service for the king was held in the nearby mound which had been prepared according to custom. Friar Kristoffer gave the last blessing for the deceased. The King was buried in splendid robes, his crown upon his head, his gilded sword along side him all wrapped in a large tapestry of conquest. His old companion, Alf, who had lain by his side these many months, was also put to rest with him. He had been a judicious ruler, his people paid their respects to their deceased king, their condolences to his spouse, Queen Hulda and son, Prince Aksel.

The following day in the courtyard, the Prince and his Lady were crowned King and Queen of Heborg with a small degree of ceremony. Friar Kristoffer read the decree to all and placed the crowns on their heads. A short blast of horns from the wall announced the crowning as the citizens again respectfully bowed to acknowledge their young King and Queen of Heborg. A cold blast of air from the north announced the approach of winter as the sun was slowly obliterated by heavy snow-laden clouds.

The Queen Mother took to her bed in grief and Kaja cared for her. "My Queen Mother, you must not stay in bed constant, it make you weak. You be a vibrant lady, healthy with much love to give and much happiness for all." Mother Hulda did rise from her bed the next day. She loved children and joined Kaja who cared for the castle's children while the mothers helped the men work to complete the harvest before the snow and freeze set in.

On an evening, Kaja tried to communicate with her sire, but he asked to be excused, he dwelled on the loss of his father. Mother Hulda called him to her to give him her thoughts as Kaja had to her. "You are young, strong, now have responsibility of King of this realm. Your father sent you away to grow to a man, to learn to lead your people. Your wedded wife needs you, the people need you - now be not the time to hide away in your chamber. Put aside sorrow, live as I do, as Kaja say do."

Aksel left his mother's chamber, his head hanging and walked out into the fields at a fast pace for a long time. When he retraced his steps back to the castle, he stopped a young lad who was pushing a cart with dirt in it. "Young lad", he called, "run to castle, tell Queen Kaja to come to me above the garden."

"Ya, Sire, Ya," Gaius bowed and happily ran off to the castle.

When Kaja arrived, Aksel was lying on his back among the wild flowers, sheltered from the cold wind, his head rested on his arms, eyes closed to the sunlight.

"You summon me, Sire?" Kaja asked quietly, so as not to disturb him, if he be asleep. She pulled her shawl around her to shield herself from the gusts of cold north wind.

"Come, sit by to me, so we talk." Propping up on his elbow, he noticed the young lad, his messenger, did not leave. "Does the lad not know his way back to castle?"

"Ya, Gaius think you call me to come, to kiss me. He watch to see if this be true. Perhaps, if do, he leave us be," she suggested sitting next to him.

"This be your thought, or his?"

"His," she affirmed and smiled. "I not object."

He put his arm about her shoulder looked into her face and eyes, and kissed her lightly. When he looked up he saw Gaius happily skipping and running away. "That content him."

"Ya. It contents me also, for a time," she agreed.

"Come, let us walk." He took her hand to help her rise from the grass, held her close to him, looked deep into her eyes, paused a moment and then kissed her soundly. She happily responded. "I desire to give my thoughts to you," he paused, "not know how to say, what to say." He paused a moment. "You be my wife now. Many times I think of you, the little lass who struck me and called me animal." They walked slowly, he held her arm to steady her in the uneven terrain, the cold wind gusting from the north, pulling at their clothes. "When I return from your castle many years ago, Ingvar report to my King the circumstance of your sister, how you struck me, called me animal for whipping your wise man. Sire sent me away. My sire be shamed by my actions, sent me away to learn of people in different lands, instructed Ingvar to make me learn the way others live, how they govern and rule, to think not of myself but of others, prepare me to be king, a good king to help the people here in my realm, not misuse them.

"I not want go. He took me to the sea, put me on a merchant longboat, with Karl and Ingvar, order to see the islands west. Not return 'til I grow a man, no longer the blemish of a young willful prince who fancy all his way. I hate him." Aksel had spoken fast, now paused and kept walking, "I not like him afore, I hate him shoddier after send me away. My father do that to me," he emphasized.

"We saw Iceland, Ireland the land of Celts, the British Isles - and a land beyond Iceland that we not know name of - where strange people live. More than three years we travel the ocean, the world. We see many people, strange people and fair," he asserted. "Many wars to run away from, much injustice done to innocent people. Vikings in all lands we go, warring, pillaging. Many fine things we see, good people work together, realms of contentment to make a king proud. I learn the rules and laws they use to be just among each other. I remember the peace I feel when at your castle and feel in far away places, much the same. The Icelander's no have King, rule themselves, the 'Althing' be their government; Celts have Christianity to guide them. It be a loving religion, better than the Gods of old. Even the English believe in the one God, as we now do.

"I see a young lad beat by uncle who slave him for sin of his father. The sin of father? He married a Celt woman. We see uncle killed in battle and take lad home. His mother happy he be back. I tend the welts of lad from uncles beating. Remember young lass who sooth welts of the wise wizard I whipped, I have shame by my actions." Aksel paused a moment and turns to her, "It hurt in my heart, the shame, I never feel shame before. I hear words you spoke. I be animal, no less than uncle who whip Kiev. I long to see you, tell you of my shame, I say it now." He hung his head a moment, looked up at her and continued.

"Another lad be stolen and forced into slavery. He work the way free for many years, work more to earn money to return home in Ireland. We not give him trust at first, he give friendship and help, be our speech in England.

Afore we take leave of Isles, we put him on longboat to Ireland with handsome purse to start life anew in home land.

"Ingvar left us when return to Norway, has wife and young lad need him in Heborg. Karl and Gerda, his wedded wife he find in England, travel with me to see where she born and compare Norseman with the Brits, Celts and Icelanders. It be much the same, some be good people and some be bad, always good realms protecting theirs from the warring realms." He kept walking, thinking for a moment. They had reached the top of the hillside adjoining the castle and he motioned her to sit in the grass with him.

"On ship from Iceland, we speak to merchant who be much like your wise man, Frode. Had rough weather for many days, make me sick, I still sick to think of it. Karl laugh at my discomfort. I be never sick afore, not ashamed afore, not listen to wise man afore, not think of young lass afore. Now," he paused and quietly continued, "I not hate my sire, he be wise man, send me away, make me grow a man.

"We land in Kaupang, where live Verner, the merchant from Iceland ship. We inquire where he live, but not find him - he find us. He pleased see us again.

Ingvar when go home to Heborg, returned to Kaupang to find Verner and leave word for me. My father, the King, be very ill, dying. Marm want me return home, my father calling for his son.

"We stay the night with Verner and spouse, a lovely lady, I leave at next dawn. Verner show sorrow of my father's illness, I talk my heart again to him. I talk to him and thoughts come. I know what I must do and tell him. He not advise yes, he not advise no, to what I say. He say, 'If this be your destiny, do it.' On Iceland ship he advise not to look afar for lady of status, look again at young lass who grown, now a learned maiden. He think Sire want to see me wed before he die, agreed it be wise stop in Alfhild on path home, claim my promised bride."

Aksel stopped again and turned to Kaja, "I tell this so you know what I do, why I gone so long, why I come for you and why I feel the need of you. You be learned, from a peaceful realm, strong willed and, Ya, a saucy lady still. You be a good wife for any king, you be a good wife for me. I have shame for bad manners, not come to you when wed, then act like barbarian. We be good together? You speak of how you feel of me? Do you come to me only because your father promise me?"

Kaja be awed of him, looked at him, rose from the grass and slowly walked pulling him with her. "You give me much to think on, Sire, I need some time to . . ," she hesitated, looked again at him and sat on the knoll overlooking the valley below, the wide expanse of freshly harvested fields, the distant mountains beyond, a panorama of nature's bounty and promise. He gave her time to think, walked from her, came back, sat with his back to her and pulled up the tall grass nearby glancing at her.

"I not like you when first I see you. You use your whip on my wizard, then I hate you, as you hate your father. I fear you come to claim me. After many years pass, you not come, my sire take me to distant realm for a prince of status. He think to promise me to a lad younger than my brother, though I beg him not. I favor a knight or two before I favor a lad. Jorgan come with message from my marm that you had come to claim. Your father dying, you need attend to him. Marm send my brother to tell me you be different, grown up, not the willful young prince from before. Jorgan say the same. I come to see if my mother and brother did well in judgment of you. Father say we give you leave." She paused looked thoughtful a moment, turned up to him. "You say <u>Verner</u> advise to look again at lass? This be Verner Askild? Verner from Kaupang? Verner the merchant from Kaupang?"

Aksel nodded, "Ya."

"How you know him?"

"He travel on longboat from Iceland, we talk, he much, like father."

"He wed to my Aunt Kudrum, she come live with us while he be away on journey. When he return he advise me wait for young prince that learn to be judicious, he come for me soon. He spoke of you?" she asked somewhat in-credulously.

Aksel hesitated, thought, took her shoulders, looked in-to her eyes, "I not know if he the same." His mind thinking, slowly reasoning aloud, "He hear Karl say your name, hear your sister die of fever, he know path to Alfhild - tell me which path to take to Alfhild, I not tell him your castle in Alfhild. I think, Ya, he be the same man. Why he not tell me?"

She turned to look at him, thinking, "Perhaps he think it best not? Want you decide with your own thoughts? That not be bad thing."

"Not a bad thing, he want me to make my own thoughts," he repeated, still musing of the mystery. He gave a shake of his head, smiled at her and she spoke.

"Here we be. We now wed. You be more a man. I pray, Sire, I be wife sufficient for you. We do well, with much work and love. I pray we do well together."

He turned to her, looked deep into her eyes and slowly touched her lips in a gentle kiss of promise for the future. "Ya, we do well." He looked again into her eyes, smiled broadly as did she in return. He cupped her face in his hands, kissed her lightly, "You be my wife, I wait many years to have wife," then he enveloped her in his arms as they embraced clinging to each other with desire.

When they returned to the castle, his mother said to Kaja, "Marriage good for him, he be more man, less willful child."

Shortly after dinner, the young king rose from the table, to retire to his chamber. "My lady will come with me," he asked softly.

"Ya, Sire. I have one chore, I come shortly." She bowed respectfully.

He looked at her for a short moment with beseeching eyes, "I wait for you," paused a moment, "My Lady."

She hurried to her quarters, changed into her night garment and was about to tap on his door, when he entered from his side. She went to him as she shook her hair from its wrap and he took her into his arms tilting her chin up to look into her eyes. "You be beautiful, My Lady, I chose wisely. Let me be lover to you, not just a barbarian?" Kaja smiled bashfully, closed her eyes as she received his kiss. He lifted her in his arms, carried her to his bed, made love to her gently and they fell asleep wrapped in each others arms.

She was no longer a maiden, no longer a wedded wife without a husband and no longer in angst. She was completely content in her happiness!

A VIKING AGE TRILOGY
PART THREE: A LIFE OF HARMONY AND
TRIBULATION

ACCEPTANCE AND CHRISTIANITY
STRUGGLE OF LABOR AND LOVE
A LIFE OF HARMONY AND TRIBULATION

CHAPTER ONE

HEBORG

Kaja woke the next morning and gazed at the man lying next to her - her sire. He could feel her eyes on him, opened just one eye and smiled mischievously at her. "You be indeed a lover, My Lord, a great lover," she said softly, lovingly.

He grinned again, "You compare me with other conquests, My Lady?

"Oh no, Sire, there be none to compare you with, but I feel now like I am loved, fully and completely. Will it be ever thus?"

"We will make it ever thus," he agreed. She smiled joyously and clung close to him, tempting him with a kiss.

She arose from bed, wrapped her night dress around her frame. "You hiding yourself from me," he exclaimed.

"It be not easy for me, Sire," she stammered.

"In time, you be as one with me. Must you leave? Come back to bed with me, there no urgency, come," he softly asked her and she obeyed as he wrapped his arms around her. "This the way I with you in my thoughts," he whispered in her ear and gently kissed her again. She was content as he played with the ringlets of her long, blond hair, lying loose in an array of swirls and curls on the bed next to him.

Rain lightly sprinkled over the land on this God's Day and Kaja was concerned about where Friar Kristoffer would hold the service this morn. "Aksel, it be raining. We hold Christian service inside the hall this morning? There be no other building of size to hold all who come."

"I not know where they hold service when rain, always see all gather in courtyard and sit in the sun. We ask Mother Hulda, she know." Aksel answered, looked after her as she rose again, "You leave me again. You not like to lay aside me in bed?"

"You sleep all day 'til rain stops. There be service in the hall. We need prepare feast for all to eat?" she questioned, chatted on, and worried to know what to do on a rainy God's Day. All Aksel wanted to do was to lay in a warm bed cuddling his warm wife. *Maybe that be a good thing to do on a rainy day,* she mused and found herself going back to his bed to lay with him and turned to him with a giggle as he cuddled her close again.

When Kaja finally rose from her sire's side, she descended into the long hall to find the people arriving, bearing stools and benches to sit on. The table was at one end across the long room so it faced everyone and there Friar Kristoffer would address the worshippers.

Kaja was pleased to see a harp on the table and asked, "Good Morning to you Friar Kristoffer. Who plays harp?"

"There be one freeman among us who can strum it so we know what tone to sing. Do you know how to play?" he asked.

"Ya, I know how. I try?" she questioned. Friar Kristoffer graciously nodded and offered her the harp. She plucked one string, frowned somewhat and tightened the cord, plucked another and had to tighten that one also, until all were tightened and the harp had a melodious sound, it blended well. She sat and placed it on her lap and ran her fingers across the strings for a full flowing chord which caught the attention of people waiting around and talking.

"We sing songs with the morning service?" she asked the Friar.

"We sing, but not well. You play the proper notes, we know better how to sing. My Lady attend us?"

Kaja nodded, happy to oblige. "Ya, but your freeman be unhappy with that? I not want to take his task from him."

"He not fret, My Lady, he be pleased to hear your lovely music." The Friar looked about the hall for a lad, spotted Erik and called him to come to him.

"You summoned me, Friar?" he responded.

"You a strong lad, have strong arm to carry bells to the courtyard and ring them hard for all to hear. All will know it be time for Christian service to begin. Direct them here where we be sheltered from rain and be warm by the fire."

Erik was quick to obey and the distant sound of bells added to the music as Kaja played and sang a melody. The hall filled with cold, wet people and they huddled around the fire in the center of the room as others joined in the singing. Aksel and Mother Hulda entered, the Friar raised his hand for the music to stop so the service could begin. Everyone took to their seats.

"Welcome all on this rainy God's Day," the Friar greeted them." We pray for the soul of our departed King who joined the angels in Heaven, we pray for new young king, his new young queen and our Queen Mother. We welcome the weavers' new babe, Gustav. We pray for all who are ailing or grieving, and our healthy hard-working citizens as well. Our new young queen has discovered our harp and will accompany us as we sing. All will please rise and greet our neighbors next to us."

Aksel turned to give his mother a light kiss on the cheek, turned to Kaja and gave her one on the lips. He turned to those nearby and grasped the hands of the men and brought the ladies' hands to his lips, touching them with a light kiss, exciting them with the courtesy. Soon others were doing the same. Aksel noticed and smiled with favor that they followed his lead. He caught his cousin's eye, who also was pleased and smiled his approval. His Gerda sat beside him, happy with the child she nurtured. Yes, Karl would soon become a father.

A lass who Kaja had spoken with in her journeys about the village, approached her after service was finished. "My Lady, you show me how to strum the harp to make pretty music?"

"I can try teach you, Magda, sit here beside me, I can show you how to pluck the strings." They spent a pleasant hour trying to make music and Magda showed promise. Several other people gathered about them and listened to the instruction and tried to pluck the strings to make them sing. Later, when the cold of winter allowed them free time, they would spend many hours by the fire learning to play the harp. Others brought a hornpipe and a cow horn to add a variety of sounds. God's Day services soon became a community singing service for all to learn and enjoy.

Friar Kristoffer spoke aside to Aksel after the service, "My Liege, be it time we have a church in our village to hold service? Can we address the congregation? Ask if all will assist to work together to build a church, perhaps on the rise west of the path to Kaupang? Do you have thoughts on this?"

Aksel paused to look at the Friar, "Nay, I not have thoughts of church. First have care and attend to my dying father, a new wife and need to make acquaintance of all in village. We think on it, Ya, it be necessary. We build a church with a cross on top so all can see we be Christian.

This be good thing. Need find a good place to build, ask about for thoughts of others so we can decide where it best to build and how to build."

Friar Kristoffer was pleased his young King agreed and went out happily to approach the villagers for their thoughts.

The new young King enjoyed his wife, his new position as King, was learning the responsibilities of his office and got out among the people. He made it a point to speak with all of them so they could know him and so he could get to know them. He had been gone for many years and wanted the citizens to know he was now a grown man and hoped to rule well, even better than his sire.

"This be Gustav, my new born son." Joseph the weaver told him. "Your wife, Queen Kaja deliver him. She be a true lady, sire. He be born the night your sire, the King died, I thought to name him Gregor, but my wife favored one we chose before, Gustav."

Aksel made note of that in his thoughts. As he returned to the castle, he thought back, remembered that his wife had accommodated him the night his father died; he had literally forced himself on her in his need. How could she have been there to assist with the birth of this babe? He remembered more. She was overly sensitive and shy to him later, in many ways. He questioned this in his mind and called her on it after the evening sustenance. "My lady assisted in birthing a baby on the night my father died. Josef said so. This be true?"

"Sire, I know not what you want of me, I beg you, discuss this in chamber, not make it a court issue."

"What be so horrible for you to say that the court cannot hear? You admit you do wrong?"

"No, My Lord, I not do wrong," Kaja was firm. "It not of my sin I would speak of, but transgressions of others and sensitivities of innocent others. If you require this be known by all, I gladly tell, but after you alone hear, judge and approve. I beg you on my knees, if you wish."

"No, I do not wish." He paused, frowned at her, at her insistence, "What you think I say to these transgressions?"

She thought a moment, stood in front of him, unabashed but trembling inside, looked up at

him and in a hushed voice, said, "My liege, the barbarian, he laugh, loud and brash at what I tell him. My liege, the man I have come to know and love, he consider the sensitivities of others and be more to forgive any sins and omissions."

He paused a moment, looked at her, took her by the arm to lead her away. "My Lord, there no need to force me," she tugged at him, "I come willing." He turned to go to his chamber as she meekly followed, did not look right or left and breathed a sigh of relief.

He closed the door behind her as she passed through; stood tall in front of her looking down at her with his arms crossed over his chest. "Can my liege be more exact, what you want to know?" she softly questioned in a sweet voice.

"I want to know where you be the night my father, the King, died?"

"My Sire, I be in cottage of Josef, the weaver, and his wife to help deliver new born son. When I return to castle early next morning I found my maiden asleep on the cooking hearth, her eyes red from crying. I took her to my chamber where we be alone. She confessed the night before, she be mistaken for me in the dark and taken to your bed. You not let her speak. You took her and then sleep. She left your side soon as she could easily slip away.

"I asked if she be hurt, she said not. She be promised to the Squire's son, Thomas, and they have since wed. She feared, wanted no one be aware of it, afraid of how her promised sire would react to know, perhaps challenge you and be banned, or fight you and be killed. Or perhaps in anger, not wed her. She be distraught. I not know how you would feel of this, not being wife to you or even talk to you. We decided to leave you believe it be I that night."

"You expect me to believe this?" he said in harsh whisper. "I took your maiden to bed, not you that night?" He paced the floor in front of her, looked at her wide eyed, she nodded affirmation. He paced again, looked at her with a deep frown, she nodded again. Then as she predicted, he let out a loud boisterous laugh and turned to her. "So you want me to forgive this?" still spoken in a hushed whisper.

"It your transgression, My Lord. You be comfortable whole court know what you do? What purpose it serve? Make you look more regal? I think it not make you look just, perhaps, make you look foolish and barbaric?" She slowly shook her head for emphasis.

The young King, thought, "How do you feel of this?" he asked softly, apologetically.

"It be an honest mistake, you apologize for brutal way you, - -" she hesitated, left it unsaid. "I spoke your apology to Jannike. We now come together with love, understanding." She motioned with her hands from him to herself. "We let this pass, perhaps upon occasion enjoy a quiet smile at the thought - someday make it story we tell grandchildren?" He acknowledged with a smile and nod.

She remained in front of him with her head bowed, and he sensed she had more to say. " There be more?"

"Yes, Sire, much more. I sure you soon remember; it weighed on me." She paused, geared up to confess her sin of omission. "I almost thankful for what happened, because, Sire, as a young lass I be very active and one day I bled after jumping on the pony that be my jousting companion. My mother explain what happen but I fearful you not believe me. That be my sin, Sire, my sin of omission."

He smiled at her, took her shoulders, looked down into her eyes, "My Lady, I know, I hear this twice afore. Your wise man and your sire, both tell the exact story."

She clung to him as he held her close. "You believe me, if they not tell you?"

"I think so. Ya," He nodded. "You told me there be no others I believe you then."

Holding him tight to her, she said, "There be more, my liege, it many weeks since my body last cleanse, I always feel hunger and many times dizzy."

"I know," he said, "and what that mean?" He coyly asked as he looked down at her.

"I be with child?"

"Yes, I know."

"Do you always know all?"

"I not know it not you that first time."

She giggled, "What we do about that, shall I confess?"

"No, I think it best left unsaid, I make story of the wise woman I wed. I did laugh at what she say and being the sensitive man she knows and loves, agree it not of consequence to the court and best left to the sensitivities of the innocent. Will that make you content?"

"Yes, My Lord. And will you announce our heir?"

"Not now, we wait more weeks 'til we sure, perhaps the new year?"

Later that evening when they retired, he held her close and asked, "Be you with happiness here?"

She pulled back from him and looked up into his eyes. "Happiness be many things, Sire. I grow to enjoy and love your people and take them as my own, as they accept me."

"What of us?" he countered.

"We can talk of that?" she asked. He nodded. "Well consider me at 12, an innocent young lass be told she be promised to wed a barbarian prince when she be grown. Consider this young lass see this willful prince trounce her favorite wise man and teacher with his riding crop because wise man raised his hand to waylay him not to whip his steed. This same barbarian prince leave without say a word. We not see or hear from him for many years. The King, father of this lass groomed to be a Queen, confers for another younger prince to wait 'til he grow up to wed. Then comes the barbarian Prince demand his spoken-for lady and want her to immediately attend him at his dying father's bedside. She does attend him, she be rather pleased with this now older prince, they attract one another. Then this prince be too busy for many days to even speak to his wedded wife. She by herself and moves about to meet and know his people. Suddenly he there, demands her, but it not his wife he takes. He leaves her again for several days before he takes her to his bed in a loving manner. She not sure what he wants of her, not spoken enough to him to know his mind, his thoughts, his needs," she paused and looked up at him. "Happiness? Yes, it be coming, sire."

"What can I do to make it easier, so we can be as one?"

She paused, "There one thing I think of, *sire*." She emphasized the 'sire.' "If we be as one, why '*Sire*' and '*My Lady*' needed when we alone together? My mother and father have much regard for each other and use title address in court; but in private they have many loving names known only for them."

"And what can I call you?" he asked softly.

"My name, Kaja, always acceptable. My brother calls me Kaj, you called me vixen on many occasions, be there no other name you know?"

"Yes, 'wife.' I like call you my wife, my very own wedded wife. I find alarm in my thoughts, I feel so close to you, have never desired or needed to be so close to anyone afore. When away from you I feel something be amiss. What be this?" He asked caressing her face softly with his hand.

"Love? Be what you feel Love? Can it be you never felt this close emotion for someone before? You clung to your father on his death bed, it not from love?"

"Not like this. I hate him most my life, think of him a brutal barbarian. Not 'til I travel the seas, visit and observe many kingdoms that I understood what it mean to be responsible for the safety and care of others. What it like to be a father, a King. I know need help, less I do worse than my father. That be why I come for you. You be learned from your family and wise man to sit beside me and help me, as you do. We learn many things from you, compassion be one."

"Be it only need for my help that brought you to get me?" she inquired sweetly.

"No, you vixen, I never forgot the young lass jousting with her brother, hollering like a fishwife, goading him to do better, to slay you. I want take that little lass and tame her. Then you struck at me in rage and I not sure I want a lass who would fight me. When I saw you again, it be with pleasure. The saucy young lass be still there with a pleasant manner to entice me. I be occupied with care of my father, Ya, but raged with the desire and need of you."

"Now that I yours, the rage be gone, replaced with a strong love you never know before?"

"Perhaps," he acquiesced. "This love, it make me weak?"

"No, not weak my love, love make us be strong, strong beyond belief. We learn to use love for the benefit of those we care for." She paused and hugged him close, "There be one small matter to mention while we speak of love."

"What this?" he asked when she didn't explain.

"I desire to feel the soft tenderness of your lips when I kiss you; there be this prickly beard in the way." She paused a moment. "I see many men with beards trimmed to leave place for proper kissing," she added softly.

He looked down at her, "You want a barbarian to shave the beard that makes him a barbarian? All will surely then know that I weak."

"No, not weak my love - just in love and harmony with your wife, your wedded wife," she teased with a happy smile.

That evening, after sustenance, when all had retired to their cottages, he looked at her with love or perhaps it was lechery. Taking her hand he reached over to their bed and lifted a soft quilt as he led her to the wall, pushed through the door section and walked through. It was the same wall opening Kaja had previously found. "Where we go, love?"

"Out on the hill above , behind the castle. It be bright with the full moon out. I want to love my wedded wife under the sky. I have always wanted to make love under the moon-lit sky with many stars looking down on me - on us, together."

Kaja followed behind him slowly, unsure of the footing. "I found this door when I first clean the chamber, Jannika say it be a back passage to Mother Hulda's chamber. I fearful to investigate. Now I know it be an escape to the hill outside of castle."

"Yes, escape, also place to sit quiet when in need of peace and quiet - day or night. Also place for love on moon-lit night in comfort on the grass with a soft, warm quilt about us."

"Can others see us up here?" Kaja looked about to see how private it was, if any could see them.

"No, none can see, less they climb the steep hill from the other side. In daylight, I show you how to find passage to the far side if there be need to escape from invaders. I play here with my sister many times - run from her and hide. She would have anger with me, she feared to climb down the steep hill. It be dangerous. Up here be pleasant, quiet, even sleep on hot summer night, except insects find me and make it miserable," he laughed at the memory. "Now soon have new memory to remember, love my wife in night under the stars." He held her close as they bundled in the quilt together and made love. "You a skinny lass," he said softly.

"You compare me to other conquest my lord?" she imitated him sweetly.

"Not compare you love." He chuckled, looked at her with love, "Always look on ladies, see young lassies be skinny, grow to be pleasant then plump maidens - they marry and be with child, then grow more round, more pleasant to love."

"Like Dagmar?" she asked sweetly.

"Ah, Ingvar be fortunate man, has beautiful, plump, loving wife." He paused, gazed at her, "as I do also. But you be still skinny, you will grow more round, more pleasure to love." He chuckled with contentment and slept the night with great happiness and satisfaction of his wedded wife.

CHAPTER TWO

WINTER IN THE ELEVATIONS

A small group of warrior Norsemen came through the realm. Aksel gave them hospitality as expected - this being one of the Nine Noble Virtues. He spoke aside to Ingvar, "These be barbaric Norseman, have allegiance to no one, want only to make war and pillage wherever they go. Do you see them in that way?"

"Yes sire, I do."

"Put all on alert, watch they not become too friendly among our peace loving people. Be cautious and quiet of it."

Ingvar agreed, "Our men be trained to protect the village, sire, we be eager to have this opportunity to test their worth with small group of supposed marauders. I be certain we can handle their trouble."

Broder, their leader, drinking ale and talking with the young King, sensed his discomfort at their presence and had the mind to challenge him on the matter.

Aksel introduced Kaja when she entered the room. "This be my saucy green-eyed vixen who make me happy," he looked at her, smiled, and turned again to his visitor with pride. Kaja did not like what he said and rose to leave. "Kaja!" he called and followed after her. "Why do you leave?"

"I be a green-eyed vixen for you, not for all in court. You fun me in front of all," she whispered.

"No, no, my love. I let them know we have much love for each other, I not fun you. Come stay with me," he reached for her hand and brought her back to sit beside him.

"Is this the young Queen who can joust well?" Broder asked, viewing Kaja with lecherous eyes.

"When a lass, Ya. My wife now a refined and learned lady, no longer a lass who jousts." Aksel stated emphatically.

"No, I hear she shows young lads to hold stick, take position, attack, defend. She still know how to joust. I not see a lady do this, would like to watch, perhaps laugh or regard well," he added somewhat unbelieving. "What say you, a demonstration?"

Aksel turned to Kaja who looked back at him, eyes shielded and shook her head lightly.

"My Lady, say no, she not demonstrate," Aksel told him, looked straight at him eye to eye.

Having had enough ale to loosen his resolve, Aksel was disappointed Kaja would not demonstrate her skill and make him proud. He waif his ale, turned to try to convince her, "My Lady will you join me in demonstration so these Norsemen from the north can see how strong ladies of the south be?"

"No!" she stood up, faced him and shouted for all to hear. "I not joust with you sire, I will not!" then sat down and turned away from him.

Aksel observed her and knew she wouldn't, there was no use to order her. He turned and met Ingvars' eyes from across the hall.

Ingvar approached, "Sire, perhaps My Lady demonstrate her skills with me, as when we teach lads to use sword in training. Perhaps that will content these men."

Kaja turned to him in agitation prepared to shout "No" but was stopped by the warning look in Ingvars' eyes that she alone could see as he faced toward her, away from the visiting Norsemen.

She turned to Aksel still stubborn of face. He slowly removed his sword from its sheath and handed it to her, raising his eyebrows. "Will my lady demonstrate for our visitors with Sir Ingvar?"

Kaja rose slowly took the sword from him, the tip dropped to the floor as it was too heavy for her. She raised it with two hands, tried to swing it gracefully, as she was met by Eric, Ingvar's son from the training group, with a lighter sword for her use. They made the exchange and the lad returned the heavier sword to his King. Reluctantly, Kaja faced Ingvar with a beseeching expression on her face and they spared off facing each other with routine moves. Slowly they assumed the different positions of attack and defend. Ingvar gradually escalated the forcefulness to make her defend with more power and strength. She became agitated with him, then angry, vented her rage and attacked him vigorously enough to force his retreat.

He locked swords and stayed her hand, giving her an appreciative smile. "My Lady, that be enough demonstration to satisfy these gentlemen." He took her hand and led her to her chair next to Aksel who reached out to assist. Ingvar ignored him and knelt before Kaja and kissed the hand he still held. He stood before her, "You be a worthy demonstrator, My Lady."

"And you be a strong gentleman, Sir Ingvar." Still breathing heavy from the exertion, she looked at him with a loving look of appreciation as he turned, bowed to his Liege, ignored the barbarians who stared at them in awe and returned to his tasks. After a moment of quiet, Kaja turned to Aksel, breaking the silence in the hall. "The entertainment complete, I leave now. I have no desire to partake in your drunkenness." She rose, left without so much as a bow or a look at the visiting men and sought Eric on her way out to return his sword.

She did not see him but heard a whispered, "My Lady, over here." Eric was hiding beside the stairs. "I hear the men in the yard who wait for their leader, speak of pillage in the night when all be asleep. Be not my sire about? Can you have him come out so I can tell him what I hear?"

"Ya, stay here, I can have him come to you." She paused, turned to him, "Be your marm at home?" He nodded. "Perhaps it best if I tell him his son say Marm needs him at home quick. When he leaves, you meet him outside." Kaja turned toward the revelers, scanned the long room for Ingvar and tried to catch his attention. He was engrossed in conversation with one of the barbarians and did not notice her. She slowly walked around to where he stood, interrupted their conversation, spoke quietly to him and he left hurriedly out toward the door.

As Kaja left the hall, Broder was in deep discussion with Aksel about the design on the handle of his sword which was lying across the table between them. She glanced back to where the others were sitting and drinking and watched momentarily - the two men still engrossed with the sword between them. She armed herself with a small sharp knife from the rack on the nearby wall, covered it within her skirt and turned toward the table where the two men still spoke. She stood alongside the visiting barbarian and listened. He was unaware of Kaja's presence nearby and was cockily challenging Aksel, "Your realm too peaceful, sire, it would be with ease for just a few men as I have to seize your castle and kill all your young knights.

Where you be without them? Could you fight alone, against all of us?" he questioned.

Kaja came in close, the sharp knife pointing into his side, "Have your men stand back or you will be a dead man," she warned.

Broder laughed at her, reached for the sword on the table, as Aksel moving swiftly, intercepted the sword and held it to Broder's chest. Kaja spiked the knife into his side hard enough to draw blood and harshly said, "Do as you be ordered or I dig further, if my sire does not get you in the throat first."

He tried to laugh it off, "I jest to show you how vulnerable you be in your peaceful way of life."

"But we be not vulnerable, we be prepared always for strange barbarians who come to visit and expect hospitality. Not all be of peaceful mind," Aksel said. "Tell me, what be in your mind? Why you be here? What you expect we do, sit here, let you kill and pillage? Ingvar great warrior, know all tricks and methods of war. He fought when a lad with my sire who taught him well. You tell your men to lay back, drop their swords or you never leave our castle alive. May not leave alive anyway, kill you so others know we are not weak as you say."

Ingvar had returned with another of his men, collected their swords and other weapons they had. They were housed in a shelter aside from the castle for the night and Kaja went to her bed with a knife nearby, prepared, if needed, to defend herself against the barbarians. Aksel reassured her that all was fine, but she dreamt in the night, waking him with her restlessness and fought at him. Her dream was frightening - the marauders had killed everyone and came after her.

"No, Kaja, they be secure in the locked armory with posted guards on duty." Aksel spoke softly to calm her, allayed her fears and held her close for comfort. After she relaxed and returned to sleep, he quietly left her and checked the men on guard to be certain all was secure.

Broder and his Norsemen left in the morning. "We desire not to confront a realm where the hospitality be good, but the men stand guard against pillaging barbarians and the lady of the kingdom be prepared to fight all - if not with the sword, with sharp words and knives."

Aksel was right, however. There are among those Norsemen some who feel the young King be weak, easy, not strong and forceful as his father had been. That he was preoccupied with a new wife, peaceful living and they schemed to show his weakness. Broder and his men left that morning but one of his men, Ramgerd, returned with his own crew at his first opportunity to watch the castle from a nearby elevation. One morning they saw Aksel and a small hunting crew leave the castle before the snows. "Now be the time," Ramgerd observed, "he go to hunt wild game to feed the people and not be back soon."

Ramgerd sent one of his men to enter the courtyard and inquire, "Will my lady come help care for a wound my man suffered. He fell hard, has much bleeding from a cut which needs cleansing. He be in the path nearby, so weak can not ride further." Kaja followed him with a young lad to carry water, soap and a clean cloth to use. When they were beyond the point where they could be seen from the castle, Ramgerd forcefully lifted her up on a horse behind one of his men, bound her hands around his waist so she could not fall or jump off and headed west to a small village where they had made previous arrangements for the night.

They left the young lad who ran back to the castle to alert the guard, Torben, of the kidnapping. Torbin climbed the wall, saw their dust on the path to the west and ran to alert Ingvar. "You say three men took Queen Kaja away on a horse?" he asked the lad. "Do you know who they be?"

"By name sire, no, but they be here with the barbarian Norsemen. I saw them, heard them, they not speak well of our king. Say he too peaceful, it be easy to steal and pillage."

"Quick," Ingvar ordered Torben, "waylay Aksel in the heights, blow the horn of need, tell him the Norsemen barbarians kidnapped our Queen, be headed on the path west. We follow them, meet on road, there be just two villages to look in the west. Hurry!"

Kaja was distraught. They rode hard the whole day. When they pulled her down from the horse, her legs went out from under her. "You beasts," she screamed at them. "Who you be? What your names? Why you take me, it hurts to ride so hard, so long without rest."

Ramgerd sneered at her with his vicious smile, but did not say a word. She was secured in a small chamber in the stone building. They brought her sustenance and proceed to drink ale and revel in their success.

The men found a place to rest for the night, but Ramgerd, entered the room where Kaja lay on a cot. She was on guard, had hidden the sharp knife from sustenance in her skirt to defend herself, if needed. She backed away when he came at her with fowl breath, attempting to grab her and she fought him. He ripped her smock in an attempt to tear it off. She cut his exposed private and he jumped and yowled in pain, bleeding profusely. He attacked her ferociously. She screamed, ran from him, swung the knife at him at every turn. He was pitifully drunk and just floundered around. She escaped the chamber and ran to the hall for help - there was just one old night attendant asleep near the door. She hid behind a large chair to catch her breadth.

Aksel with a couple of his men had entered the small village center, their steeds snorting and prancing from the long run. They rushed past the sleeping guard, came into the darkened room with just one torch on the wall to cast some light. They drew their swords and looked around.

Kaja recognized them and ran to Aksel's arms with a cry of relief. "Are you alright?" he asked.

"Ya, Ya, I be fine." she gasped.

"Did he defile you?"

"No, Love, I defiled him. I cut him with the knife from sustenance."

"Where be that drunken pig?" he asked, looking up to see Ramgerd crouched, approaching them holding his wounded private part, blood oozing over his clothes. Aksel reached for the drunk, struck him forcibly several times until Ramgerd lay on the floor senseless, mumbling.

The men tended to Ramgerd's wound. His bleeding contained, he lay in a drunken stupor and snored loudly. As it was late, dark and freezing with light snow falling outside, they were given accommodations for the night. The drunken, sleeping men involved in the kidnaping were locked in the chamber where Kaja had previously been sequestered.

The next morning a thin layer of snow was on the ground as Aksel stood before the perpetrators to make judgment. "Ramgerd, you blemish of a man, I should kill you. My wife defiled you to protect herself, will this be punishment enough? No! I kill you." He paused, stepped toward Ramgerd, threatened him, then turned away, paused, returned with his sword drawn. Kaja, nearby, turned away, she did not want to see her sire kill. Ramgerd raised his arm to shield himself from the blow that never came. Aksel sheathed his sword, turned, took Kaja by the arm and left quickly unless he changed his mind.

The perpetrator was angered beyond reason, thoroughly convinced the Prince was really weak to let him live. He would plan another attempt at the weak king or at her for cutting him.

Kaja was bleeding heavily before they arrived home in Heborg at the end of the day. She went straight to her bed, weeping and in pain. The lengthy, rough ride on horseback for two days had done its damage. She lost her pregnancy and became saddened and depressed.

Ramgerd, still not convinced of Aksel's strength, returned, attacked a herd of cattle on the outskirts of Heborg, set the farmer's barn on fire, also his cottage, and then fled to the far north. Aksel tracked him as snow continued to fall and found Ramgerd in a shelter in the elevations and called him out, "You coward, you attack a peaceful farmer's herd, burn his barn and home and then ran like the weakling pig you be. I let you live once, now kill you sure. Protect yourself, I cut more than Kaja."

Ramgerd raised his arms over his head, "I not be armed, you would kill an unarmed man?" He jeered, "All will then know *you* be the coward!" He laughed loud, raucous and escaped out the door.

Following him, Aksel directed Alf his knight to "Throw him a sword," but Ramgerd let it fall to the ground.

"The choice be yours, take up the sword now or I kill you without," Aksel demanded.

Ramgerd laughed even louder, ran fast and hard straight for the cliff's edge, jumped long over the crevasse, but did not reach far enough to step onto the other side. He grabbed the rocky edge as he came down, which crumbled under his weight. He struggled to grab a firmer hold, as the others watched in desperation, unable to help him. He fell along with the rocks he clung to, into the chasm many leagues below, his voice echoed all the way down the hollow shaft. They heard his voice eerily ringing in their ears for a time afterwards as the sound ricocheted off the walls.

Ramgerd's followers in horror of the incident, feared for their own lives and in terror, declared, "We not want to fight and pillage, as Ramgerd did. We want life of peace with good people."

"You not story me? We be a peaceful realm, but let no one make war on it. We fight to the death to protect it and our people in it. We learned there a better way to live, enough hard work and problems just to survive, no need to war on neighbors. We can accomplish more by trade, help each another, share knowledge and work together." They nodded in agreement, so Aksel said, "We watch you close to see if you be true."

The cold winter weather had set in. The next morning a foot of snow was on the ground the blizzard was still raging strong, the winds howled, the snow swirled and the visibility was impossible. The small shelter was meager for them, the extended barn too small for the horses to be comfortable. There was no supply of food for themselves or the animals. It would be fatal to attempt to travel as the perilous passages were blocked and covered by mounds of drifted snow and slippery ice.

The storm finally eased after a couple days and they ventured out to hunt for game and firewood. Fortunately, Ernst came upon an almost frozen elk which he killed and they hauled it back to the shelter.

Bue and Ernst, skinned the animal and cleaned and cut it in pieces to cook on the open pit. The sun was pleasant, the wind had abated so they were able to work outside for short periods at a time. Aksel's men, Alf and Edmond, stretched the elk skin to dry as best they could - it would make a warm cover. Aksel and Torbin scrounged small amounts of wood from nearby snow-covered trees whose branches are above the level of the drifted snow. This would keep the fire going. They spent the night talking on many subjects as they waited for the meat to cook, a jug of melted snow to quench their thirst and a crock of warm melted snow to wash their hands of the blood from the slaughtered elk. When a few of the smaller pieces of meat were cooked enough to eat, they feasted on it like a pack of starved scavengers.

"There not be sufficient wood for the fire to cook the meat, we need search the forest for wood to harvest before it snows again. The nights here be long and cold, the heat insufficient." Bue told them, "There be warm caves below where people live in comfort. They store their needs to last the months of ice, slaughter many animals to smoke the winter days on the hearth that heats the air even more."

Aksel's ears perked up, "Where be these caves, why not we go there so we not freeze the winter here?" he demanded.

"Oh, Sire, I not know how to find cave in the snow. It hard to find when there be no snow. We freeze before we find the entrance," Ernst shook his head.

Aksel mused, "There must be a way - we must find a way. We not last the month here." They slept on the rim of the fire box to take advantage of what little heat was available.

The next morning, Ernst directed them, "We walk carefully on the snow to trees seen above the snow, their naked bark shines in the sun. We cut thin trees for ease of transport, push and drag down to cottage and hack to size for fire." All the men worked hard all that day, they felled the tops of many trees protruding above the snow and drug them down to the shelter and carried a large supply inside to dry out and prepare to burn. It was stacked so high there was little room to move inside the small shelter.

"Hail below! This be Skjold," a voice called from above. "Bue, be that you?"

"Ya, welcome Skjold, you come from cave shelter?" A few minutes later two men appear on the path above them.

"Be you well? Heard a scream, did someone fall the chasm? Heard trees fall to the ground, know you be up here," Skjold explained their presence.

"That be Ramgerd fall the chasm. He try to fight with King Aksel, he lost, now be gone."

"Gone? He be with the Gods? Perhaps they teach that scoundrel to live well?" Skjold questioned.

"We cut wood to heat the small cottage. Not know how to find the cave covered in snow where you live the winter. We fear to get lost and frozen, so prepare to live here the winter." Bue explained.

"We stay the night and take you to cave the morrow. We take the meat you have, and trees to burn, never have enough," he explained. They happily agreed. Ernst introduced Aksel and his men to Skjold and Asbjorn, their companions from the cave.

The six men with help from the two from the cave, used the horses to drag the logs to an elevation above the path where they then slide them downward to the top opening of the cave entrance. Some logs missed direction and slid off the ledge into the chasm below. They worked the rest of the day until the sun sat below the mountains and the icy cold set in. They slept that night in discomfort from lack of space and accommodations in the hut. They were able to eat the cooked meat left from the elk before dark and carried the remaining carcass to the cave the next day. It was a perilous transfer of food, fire wood, horses and men.

The horses were happy to be able to move about in their portion of the extensive underground cave and to eat some oats. They were getting very week, it had been several days for them without sustenance.

Aksel was in awe of the cave, the extent of it deep into the depths, the availability of warm water and heat rising from the center of the earth below. The darkness was dreary, but in time their eyes adjusted to the dingy light. They became bored with the lack of activity and join the people in games of chance, games of thought to challenge one another and to occupy the long hours. They had some music, they did not play the harp and horns well, but it was a light-hearted attempt. Some lads and lassies sang sweetly, Aksel tried to sing along with them, but he did not sing well and they frowned at him.

The women kept busy, they sewed, embroidered, washed clothes, cleaned the living areas and cooked meals from the stored vegetables. The men helped prepare the slaughtered sides of meat brought in from icy storage and set upon the fire to roast the day long. The roasting meat filled the cave with an enticing aroma which did not mix well with the odors from animal and human waste.

Aksel and his men helped where they could, came to know the people in this colony of freemen and admired their fortitude and fabrication. He was happy to learn they had survived many winters in the cave, had kept to themselves, independently until Ramgerd, the pillaging barbarian joined them. Skjold confessed to them, "I be glad Ramgerd gone to Valhalla, he be more trouble than worth. We have much work to stay alive in winter, he expect we treat him like king. He be a barbarian! He be a villain!" he declared. "None here took pleasure in him – he not our king! We not need a king. We be freemen! We be beholden to you and your men who rid us of this vermin! Bue and Ernst be welcome to live in peace among us, they also be freemen."

They spent the next few months in the cave, Aksel looked about him, looked at all around him with 'eyes like Frode' and wondered what the wise man knew of this phenomenon. "This a wondrous thing," he told Skjold "a large cave, natural heat come from below the earth, water to wash and drink, house young animals inside. Slaughter game and beef, let freeze outside in ice until need, then roast on fire to eat. You store grain for the animals, food for the people, even sow seeds to start growth before the spring."

"Yes," Skjold agreed. "We have many problems to live here in the elevations. There not enough land to grow food. Have only a short season to grow, the ice and cold of winter be with us too many moons. The darkness not good, many get weary and sick. Vermin from the animals be troublesome, get in hair, clothes, on body. We wash, but they come right back. When spring comes, we shave off our hair, wash with strong soap, burn clothes and start anew. Sometimes we even need to walk about naked until make more clothes," he jested with a chuckle.

They came to understand what Skjold meant after a couple of months of long, dark, dreary days, the monotony of the daily routine, the awful stench throughout. Aksel was sad, dispirited, his heart full of trepidation. He dreamt of the good life among his people, dreamt of his wedded wife, his love of her, the comfort and warmth of her body next to him. He worked with the freemen the day long, exercised with them often just to feel fit, slept much, tried hard not to think of Heborg, of Kaja and Marm.

CHAPTER THREE

HEBORG

The winter was unusually hard in Heborg that year, the snow excessive, the people in their thatched cottages could not keep warm. In Aksel's absence Queen Hulda, Kaja, Karl and Ingvar had as many as possible move into the castle hall and kept it well heated for comfort. It was a strange winter, too many children, too many couples in need of privacy, too many pets to separate. They kept abreast of it and managed well to keep a modicum of comfort and privacy among themselves. It was one large busy community learning, playing and really getting to know everyone closely, very closely - too closely.

Kaja was sad and ailing from the loss of her babe, her husband gone in the frozen elevations. She had no interest in the world about her. She listlessly sat and played quietly with the small children the winter long, worked with them to keep busy and stayed inside in the warmth of the open fireplace.

Karl and Gerda moved into Aksel's chamber and Kaja kept to her own small chamber. Early in spring, before the warmth returned, Gerda's babe was born and Kaja helped and comforted her during the long labor. Karl was proud, he sired a beautiful son, his wife gave him a beautiful sun. They named him after his grandsire, Lodin.

When spring weather did arrive, the people were relieved to venture back to their own cottages, mend the needed repairs from the winter mayhem, prepare the fields for seeding and take up their lives in the aftermath of a hard winter, putting the cold and misery behind them. When the work became tedious and things got difficult, they would stop and think of the winters' discomfort and turn a happy face.

Spring in Heborg was well advanced before Aksel was able to leave the higher elevations, where the cold and ice lingered. He and his men, Alf, Torbin and Edmund, finally straggled into the village on a gloomy, rainy day, when all were in the comfort of their cottages. Kaja laid listlessly on a couch, did not pay attention to anything about her, until she saw a wild looking man walk in with a head of bushy hair, full beard, smelly clothes, a sword dragging at his side. She screamed, "A barbarian! Call Ingvar, we be invaded by barbarians!"

Aksel tried to calm her, "I not a barbarian, Kaja, I be Aksel, your spouse, your wedded husband,"

"No! No! You be barbarian. My Aksel dead in the ice, like my babe be dead. Be gone! I say."

Aksel left her, she was upset and would not listen to him. He convinced his servant he really was Aksel, and ordered him to "Heat water and bring soap to wash and a sharp knife to cut hair and shave beard. I have need to make myself clean so Kaja recognize me." He decided not to wait for water to heat, went to the water reservoir alongside the fields with his men and stripped himself of his vermin-infested clothes as did the others. His servant lifted them with sticks to carry and burned them in the smelters fireplace. Aksel jumped into the reservoir's cold water with the soap and scrubbed himself head to toe. The others followed him. Frode heard the commotion, went out to investigate and fetched salt to rub in their hair and skin. A blanket awaited the men when they came from the pond shivering - mercilessly cold. His servant prepared him a mug of mead to help warm his blood as the sunshine broke through the clouds above. Aksel called for food and it was there at his side along with a barber who shaved his head and beard, examined his ears, nose, every crevice of his body where vermin could hide, as not all died or drowned with the salt and water.

They also burned all the hair and clothes from Alf, Torbin and Edmond who were being cleansed alongside him from a winter in the higher elevations with unusual underground accommodations. Living among animals was desperate, especially from the standpoint of vermin-free cleanliness. "Sire, do we too get some mead to warm the blood?" Edmond asked, his teeth chattering from the cold water so he could barely talk. The pitcher was passed to them.

When Aksel was finally cleansed, shorn of hair, vermin and dressed in clean clothes, he approached Kaja again. She was still not sure it was him, "First you look like a wild barbarian - now you have no hair. You not my Aksel."

He felt guilty that he was gone the winter, not there for her with the loss of their babe and sat himself cross-legged on the floor in front of her, spoke softly to convince her. She sat quietly across from him, her eyes on him. He looked at her and smiled and was happy to see her smile slightly in return. "You my vixen, my saucy, green-eyed vixen who trounced me when just a lass, who wait too many years for me to claim her, who say I took her maiden to bed, not her that first time."

"How you know that?" she startled at his knowledge of it.

"You told me. We keep story to tell our grandchildren someday and smile the memory. Remember?"

"You my Aksel?" she said softly, he called me vixen, "You my sire?" He be pale, his hair shorn, his face drawn and thin. "You be my Aksel?" He said I be his wedded wife, shared stories known only to us. She rose from her chair, walked to him slowly as he rose to his feet, "You my Aksel? You my sire?" she repeated, reached out to touch his face, tears filled her eyes as he reached out and took her close. "In my thoughts you be dead as my babe. Aksel?" she questioned as she put her arms around him, her head on his chest, their tears flowed as they slowly collapsed to the floor in each others arms.

"Yes, I your Aksel, you be my wife. We still love, Kaja. We make more babies, that will make happiness, yes?" He spoke softly to her, loving the touch of her, caressing her face, hair and holding her close as she cuddled in the comfort of his embrace.

"This be what she needs," said Mother Hulda who having heard Aksel's voice came to see if her ears heard true. She knelt to the floor next to them and Aksel looked up at her and gently touched her hand. "She be sad all time you gone, feared you be dead as her babe." Mother Hulda told him.

Soon they picked up their lives, the horrors of the winter forgotten. They enjoyed the sunshine as young children played in the courtyard and village paths. The fields abounded with the grains they planted, their gardens produced food for their tables, the citizens worked hard to keep the animals fed and themselves healthy.

Kaja and Aksel feel alive again, the sadness slowly left them. Aksel's hair grew with time , he kept his chin cleanly shaved to give her the pleasure of his kisses and the love they both needed to heal. She sang with happiness in her heart, they joined the people in working, praying and playing and soon she is with child again. She reveled in her expectancy and ventured out to tell Dagmar and Gerda. Gerda's young babe was squalling and Kaja picked him up to hold close and comfort him. "Don't cry little Lodin," she sang as she rocked him slowly. "Marm come soon to feed you." They sat and happily talked of things to come while Lodin fed until he was full and fell asleep.

Aksel spoke with Frode at length of the warm cave where he'd lived in the elevations. Aksel was amazed, "You know of this?"

"Come, I show you a natural cave in the hills beyond the castle. It receives a warm flow of water from the center of earth which keeps the cave at a median temperature, even in the cold ice of winter." He instructed Aksel on how the hot water heated the large extensive cave, not only to keep the animals to live in during the winter months, but could be used by people as well, just as those in the elevations. "The hot, clean water be pure and safe for humans as well as the animals. It, too, can also adapt to the planting of young seedlings to start growth for an early crop."

Aksel observed this cave was larger, more extensive than that in the elevations, but lacked the height in many areas.

The wizard suggested, "A way may be found to transport the water to the village for use by the citizens, a continuous natural supply of warm water or even a man-made bath for all to use. The iron the men use from the nearby hills to make tools and arms can also be used to build strong supports for living quarters nearby the cave and divert the natural flow of heat from the hot water cave for smoke-free warmth." The wizard spoke at great length and Aksel asked him to stay with them even longer to instruct and direct the construction of an underground habitat. Frode was eager to attempt the project and started making plans in his mind.

Aksel had discussed among his neighboring realms, the method of governing he saw the Icelanders use in his travels. Many kings deemed it a good method to use for the betterment of all. Several of the kingdoms in the area agreed to call a conference to discuss a similar, peaceful organization of realms to share knowledge, encourage the trade of goods and be prepared to defend themselves against the roving barbarians, if needed. Aksel prepared to attend the conference with Frode as his advisor.

Kaja wanted to go with him, but her sire was resolute and strongly spoke, "You not travel now, you with child. You not want to lose this babe." She abhors the thought of him being gone from her again and begs to go. "Kaja, my love." He took her by the shoulders, looked deep into her eyes, "I must attend this conference of Kings, all realms be represented. The road be not easy to travel by coach, will take many days. It only two days journey by steed, one week, maybe two to talk and plan, then ride back again. I not want to be away from you, but you must not travel now. Even Frode say it be dangerous, your body weak, susceptible. Please, my love, I not want to hear you weep again. I return to you soon. This be of great importance to all of us."

She meekly clung to him and shook her head. "I know you be right, my love, I miss you so much when afar."

The sun rose early the next morning. As Aksel left the castle, he asked her to kiss him "good-by" in the courtyard so that his mother could also tell him goodbye as he mounted his horse, as she did for his father for many years.

Kaja understood his request and held him close as they quietly looked into each others eyes. He kissed her long and tenderly. "I come to love my green eyed vixen even more. I miss you already, my love." She fought tears as he turned from her, gave his mother a loving hug and mounted his steed. Kaja followed him to the entrance and when he turned to gaze upon her, she curtseyed deep and bowed to him. He looked long at her and then turned his steed to go to her, bent down low to reach for her hand, and drew her up so he could kiss it and gaze into her tear-filled eyes again. After he crossed the bridge and headed toward the path he turned and saw the two women walk together back into the courtyard. He was grateful his mother was there for her.

"I sense you have found much happiness with my son," Mother Hulda said. "Do not fear for him, he return soon, they arrange for peaceful relations among the kingdoms. We prosper many years so your young prince will have a wholesome life to live in peaceful realm." Mother sensed her condition and was happy for her. Kaja glowed with contentment and new life.

The conference went well with agreements on many things, primarily trading among themselves to share the bounty of their lands and labor. Too often one realm had abundance while another was lean - trades are feasible. Frode devised a method of keeping track of the flow of goods from one realm to another and trained enough learned men to scribe and figure from year to year so one realm did not excessively benefit more than another. There would be mistakes and problems, but all felt it well to try and show patience and concern of one to another.

Late the following winter, Aksel heard Kaja cry out and moan in pain – it was her time to give birth to their babe. He worried to hear her groan and entered the chamber where she lay, with Mother Hulda, Jannika and a birthing lady from the village hovering by. He sat along side her bed where she lay in agony, took her hand kissed it and held it close to his face, "Kaja, my love, pray to our God like Friar Magnussen taught me in Ireland."

She turned to him, "It hurt Aksel, it hurt bad, make it go away."

"Look at me," he said softly. "Say 'Jesus, son of God.' Say it, Kaja. Say it, 'Jesus son of God.'"

"Jesus, son of God." she groaned.

"Have mercy on me,' say it," he insisted.

"Have mercy on me," she repeated.

"a sinner."

"a sinner."

"Now say again, 'Jesus, son of God'"

"Jesus, son of God,' it hurts again," she groaned.

"'Have mercy on me,' say it"

"Have mercy on me, a sinner." She completed the prayer.

"Say again, over and over, I say with you, come. 'Jesus, son of God, have mercy on me a sinner.'" Kaja repeated it with him and moaned with every pain that started. Together they said the prayer, over and over again, for what seemed hours. She sweated with the agony, he showed strain just watching her. The praying did have the effect of calming her, she even closed her eyes and relaxed between the pains as they slowly grew in intensity with the hours.

"Jesus, son of God, have mercy on me, a sinner. Jesus, son of God, have mercy on me, a sinner." The words became frantic until she could no longer say them as she strained, bearing down hard with all her might as she pulled on Aksel's arms for leverage. She screamed, cried out in pain and prayed loudly, "Jesus, son of God, have mercy on me, a sinner." She breathed deep a few times, turned her head aside, closed her eyes to rest. She mumbled quietly, repeated "my babe, my babe" as Aksel caressed her face, lay his head next to hers and silently wept with her in happiness.

It had only been a minute or so until Kaja stirred with relief that the pains were over. She heard the squalls of her babe, opened her eyes to see Aksel looking at her. "It a boy Kaja. Hear him holler, he be strong boy. You pain more?" he asked.

"No, I be fine, still hurt, but I be fine." She tried to smile, but didn't quite make it. "Where my babe? I not see him."

"Mother Hulda cleanse him, have him ready soon, wrap in warm quilt. You cold, too?" he asked as her body shivered. He covered her with a goose-down quilt and hugged her gently. He gazed into her eyes as Mother Hulda placed the washed, wrapped infant next to her. Kaja look at her baby, then look at Aksel. He still gazed at her intently, gently touching her face. He bent down and kissed her lips saying softly, "I have great love for my wedded wife who give me a beautiful son." He paused, "I love you, Kaja. I sorry the pain be so fierce, not know the pain be so fierce."

She smiled happily at him, touched his face, touched the face of her infant lying next to her. "This be my babe, he beautiful babe." She looked at Aksel again. "You his sire, he be your babe, too." He watched her close her eyes as she quietly said, "We make beautiful son together, you help ease my pain. Ya, we do well together."

Mother Hulda said, "Yes, pain of birth be fierce the first time, next time not so fierce. I see some who after many babies, birth them with ease. Woman's body be accustomed in time."

They had a beautiful, healthy baby prince with a wisp of blond curly hair like his marm and eyes of blue like his sire, the pride of his father and Kaja was more beautiful than ever, in Aksel's eyes. They considered many names for their son; even asked among the people in the village for suggestions. They could not choose which one to pick. "Bjorn," Kaja finally said. "Let him be named Bjorn." Aksel smiled, nodded his head in agreement and was content, for a time. Soon he was heard roaring about his son. "He pee on me, my son pee on my face, He not know I be King? I his sire?"

Queen Hulda looked at him and laughed, "No, he not know you be King, his sire. He have need to pee, he pee. You not put your face down close. Have cloth to cover his nakedness, then he not pee on you. When you be a babe, you do same to me. Your sire laugh, now my turn, I laugh." She turned away so he did not see her smile. Kaja laughed, wiped his face with a clean cloth and soothed him with soft words and a light kiss. It was a story Queen Hulda delighted in telling everyone in the village, with a chuckle.

The summer was upon them again, the gardens growing fast. Bjorn babbled in contentment among other babies of the court, the realm was a hive of activity. Aksel looked out on all that was good. "The farmers work very hard, I too, work with them."

"I can watch babies, Jannika has a young child to watch. We all help so more work be done and then all have time later to play together," Kaja said.

"You can help, but be of mind to be careful, must not work too hard to do yourself harm." Aksel was concerned for her recovery. He was tired when he came home after a day's work, had need of rest, had need of her and need to love and play with his son who grew fast with mother's milk.

There was a Lady Eirene, who visited the realm. She had become enchanted with the young king and attempted to seduce him in many sly, coy ways and manners. Aksel became aware of this, which distressed him. He discussed the ladies devious manner with Kaja.

"Perhaps we let her know, in little ways, that she not needed. My Liege be well loved and cared for. She come to court this evening and dallies longer than proper, I appear in my night dress and seduce you from top of stairway, you come away from her, you come to me." she gestured with her hands.

"You do that? You want do that?" he got excited.

"Perhaps I disappear and leave you to her graces?" she teased.

He looked at her with that glint in his eyes, "Still the spirited colt, I see. Why would you subject me to less than I have become accustomed, my love, I want no other, need no other."

Kaja smiled sweetly. "Yes, Sire."

Aksel and cousin Karl, were in conversation on the subject of Lady Eirene. Karl mentioned, "She has look of a tart we played with when we were young scoundrels." They both thought about it and recalled the incident. "She and another tart seduced us, served us much ale then took us to bed for love."

"Yes," Aksel agreed, "We slept soundly the night with ale, they stole the coins from our purse, even stole our weapons and heavy furs. When we wake the morn, the tarts were gone along with our coins and clothes."

"The inn-keeper storied us, pled ignorance of the ladies thievery," Karl added.

"He filled our bellies with food, gave us coats for warmth and sent us away," Aksel finished the story.

"I remember a mole on her neck, even made mention of it. She wore a wrap about her neck for warmth so we could not see the mole well." Karl paused again, looked at Aksel. "I must find a way to see her neck." When next she came, he approached her pleasantly and she responded in like manner. He saw the proof he needed when he assisted her with a cloak in gentlemanly fashion and reported to Aksel.

They discussed ways to quietly make her leave, "Perhaps it be best to insult her privately so she leave of her own will with no gossip for the court," Askell decided. So it was just a night or two later that the lady in question dallied at court after dark and spoke to the king in conversation alone. "It be a pleasant night for diversion, my liege. Be you in need?"

"Ya, I be always in need of diversion," Aksel said, looked at the lady with the mole and then up the stairway toward his chamber, where Kaja waited, enticing him in her night dress, still full of bosom from nursing Bjorn. "If you will excuse me my lady, my diversion be in attendance." He turned, climbed the stairs to Kaja, his eyes solely on her. At the top he loving took Kaja in his arms, turned and told Eirene in a pleasant voice, "There be many men in the realm who enjoy a night of diversion. Mine be ready for me any time I desire and need no other.

This not content you? I see you escorted to your cottage at your earliest convenience."

Insulted, she gave him a strong look, turned abruptly and left the hall.

Two months pass and Eirene requested an audience to speak to the King and Queen in private to make her confession. They looked at each other and agreed to talk with her. They had heard from others of her alliance with Josef the weaver and his young son.

"My Lord, My Lady," she addressed them. May I have time to explain what happen since I left your castle two moons past, how I still here, why I still here?" Aksel nodded and she continued.

"I be angry when I leave here. So much anger I lost my direction, took a wrong path and was surprised to see a young lad sitting in front of Josef, the weaver's, cottage. I look to see if there be someone in charge as it be late and dark, the lad need to be in bed. When I saw no one about, I pick him up, held him close. He so beautiful it made me cry to remember years afore when I held my own little lass. I carry the lad inside the cottage, found the weaver asleep with his head on the table, a mug of ale beside him. I shook his shoulder to waken him, but he be sound asleep - drunk. He reeked of the stale smell of ale. I let him sleep, carry the babe to another chamber, found a bed for him there. Fed him milk from a cup on the table, hugged him close a little, which make him content, lay him on the bed and sing a quiet song 'til he be asleep.

"I woke in the morn, stiff, I fallen asleep on the floor next to his bed. I not remember where I be. The child still lay asleep. His father, I find outside, distraught, waking himself with cold water on face.

"He questioned who I be, not sure he seeing what he saw. I tell him 'I be Lady Eirene. I find your son sitting outside the door last eve when I return to my cottage. He in need of care; you be at table asleep with ale. I put child to bed, sang him a melody my daughter enjoy. We both fell asleep.' I ask him, 'He do this all the time?' He said, 'No, he sleep well and sound. I thank you for take care of him. Would you like some nourishment to ease your fast?'"

"I say, 'That be nice, yes. May I assist you?' I ask him 'where the lads' mother be'? Does she not tend to him?'"

"He said, 'His mother died of fever two months after he be born. His grandmother care of him for a year; but now she in need of care herself and be with her daughter, his sister.' He struggle alone with young son much time now," she paused.

"I find myself help him, care for his child, prepare food, tend his house. Josef cleaned himself, not drink too much ale, work hard - all for me! We find regard, one for the other, then love of each other, love of son, we now be wed. It be like before my spouse die in fire, my babe die too, I have a new life. I pray you not condemn me for past misdeeds so I can live in peace among your realm where all live in peace. I be happy, content now and expect a babe of my own this winter."

Aksel and Kaja looked at each other, nod, and Kaja went to her. She looked Eirene eye to eye and gave her a little hug, "You say there be love between you, and regard?" Eirene nodded lightly. "You love his son?" Kaja smiled when she nodded again, "I help his mother in delivery when first I came to this realm, he a beautiful boy in much need of loving mother. You be well for them both, welcome to our realm, may you be one of us and live in happiness among us," Kaja blessed her.

Eirene smiled in gratitude of her welcome, and gave Kaja a hug in return. She bowed to her sire and to his lady and they all walked side by side out through the courtyard to the street, so all see them together in harmony.

CHAPTER FOUR

AKSEL DISCOVERS A DAUGHTER

Friar Kristoffer was happy – the realm was about to build a church. They had discussed the where and how among the citizens and Aksel was gratified the people were excited with anticipation. They had waited many years for this, his sire, their old, ailing king, could not tend to the challenge before his death. Aksel spoke to them one God's Day after service and had them speak their thoughts on the issue. Where should they build it, how large to build it, to build it of stone, as the castle, or perhaps wood and turf as most of the cottages are built.

Ostman, the gardener suggested, "The rise before the garden area be not large enough to plant, it on higher ground so be above the village level. A church there with a steeple and a cross high on top would be seen from all over the realm."

Friar Kristoffer said, "I see the church built on the path to the castle so all who arrive to our village see the church first and know we be Christian."

"But that be the place where barbarians raid first when they come to our realm," Ingvar pointed out. "Best not make it their ease to pillage. The rise be within the village. All can walk there with ease and the stone quarry be nearby to supply good stone for a strong church and a strong stone path and steps to climb the rise." They looked at each other and then turned to look at Aksel.

"We look at the rise near the garden and at the path to castle, then we think on it. Perhaps look at the rise behind the castle. That a nice area also except it be a steep climb uphill which cause difficulty for many. Be there enough stone in the quarry to build a church?" Aksel asked.

"There much stone, Sire, can build two churches." Ostman smiled, "Even build another castle," he joked.

"We not need another castle, but can build stronger cottages for our people in the village, you think?" The people looked at Aksel with disbelief. "A stone cottage to make comfort in the cold of winter be wonderful, yes? We can also plan for that?"

It was something for them all to think about and the Friar thought about the size of the church, which direction to face it, should there be an opening from the east to catch the morning sun - another opening on the west also for the afternoon light? Would a stone table for services be appropriate? There was some pleasant colored stone in the quarry to make a special altar for services. Have long benches for the people to sit on, so they wouldn't need to carry seats from their cottages and a solid stone floor above the dirt level with clay to secure it for ease to walk? Would there be a room for him to live? His mind was rampant with plans and ideas. "How long it take to build? Will we have it finished in time for winter?" he asked.

Sten, the builder, told the Friar, "To have it built by winter be not realistic – it take much work just to prepare stone, just chipping it from the quarry will take many months. The men work only when not needed in the fields and winter snow will slow our work. We do best we can." He took the measure of the hill and had men level the dirt on top to firm it to lay the stone floor.

Farmer Vitolf told them, "I have a pile of clay set aside. It not do well to grow grain, but it do well to compact ground and secure stone in place." Yes, Friar Kristoffer saw that they planned and prepared well and soon the church would be built. It was a happy project for the whole village to plan and work toward – something to look forward to in the next year or two.

Aksel had considered the topic of slavery among the Christians, to him it was against the teaching of Jesus. He had individually spoken to the freemen in his realm for their thoughts and found some who agreed and others who dissented. He tried to get their reasons, so he could prepare rebuttals in his mind. It was not easy. Most dissenters had no reason, that's just the way it was, slaves were bought and sold, used in any way the owner needed.

He discussed it with Frode, who agreed, "Slavery be not a humane thing. If a man owed someone, he should be allowed to work off his debt without being owned body and soul, without being considered property. In that manner, if he not happy to work for the man he owed, he could leave when his debt be paid. It be a happier way of life for all."

Aksel took count of the number of slaves in his realm, even spoke to some he knew who had been many years among them and worked hard. These were content, their owners were fair and just to them, allowed them to own possessions and raise families. This was as it should be, he thought.

Aksel and Frode left to attend the Alliance of Realms meeting, with Knights Alf and Edmond in attendance. It was still just a business meeting as there were none who could accommodate many families for several days, therefore, Kaja did not attend. She was content to remain in Heborg with her young babe.

Aksel did submit his thoughts on slavery and found resistance from some in the group. "They want freedom, they earn it by harder work and earn money or credits," one king spoke up. This was the attitude among most.

"How many slaves you free this way?" Aksel wanted to know,

"There be few," he responded. "Slaves not know they can do this. I have some long-time trells I free for their faithful work. They stay and work more, but work better now they be freemen. Two brothers travel back to where they lived afore and returned. They find it better to work as free man among our realm, even brought back wife to live with them. You be right, freeman be better citizens and workers than enslaved men." After much discussion, it was agreed that thralls and trells could repay their owners with hard work for five to ten years, depending on the price spent for them and then be freemen to leave or work for compensation with their past masters or work elsewhere.

On the return trip from the Alliance meeting, Frode, with Knight Edmond, traveled to Alphild to spend time there with his first sire, King Ivar, and spouse Lady Alva and be of assistance, if needed. Aksel with Knight Alf hunted in the hills on their return journey and sojourned a night in the castle of an old friend from his youth, Hjordis.

Hjordis' wedded wife, Slovene, was heavy with child. Having experienced one child with Kaja, Aksel was joyous for him, "You must be happy! I want meet your wife with child, see my friend's good fortune."

"Good fortune? To look at her, look my fat wife?" Hjordis replied with aversion.

"A woman never be more beautiful as when with child." Aksel began. "It be my great pleasure sit next to my wife, gently massage her belly which rouse the babe within.

I delight to feel the movement. My son, our son!" he beamed. "Have you ever felt your babe move?" he challenged.

Hjordis shook his head, made a disgusted look at the thought, as they entered his castle and Slovene moved slowly toward them to greet them. "Come," Aksel urged him, "sit next your woman and gently rub her belly." Hjordis hesitated, but moved close, hesitated again. Aksel asked permission of Slovene, "May I show him?" She nodded in agreement, not sure how to react to this spontaneous, vibrant, young king. "Feel that hard belly," he told Hjordis. Aksel took Hjordis hand, spread his fingers for him, "Now gently massage, gently. In there be an infant, your babe, your heir. He feel the warmth of your hand and will move maybe even kick you."

Hjordis continued to move his hand over Slovene's belly and she took his hand and placed it on another part of her belly where she felt the fetus move. Hjordis was startled, "I feel it," he said, quickly removing his hand and then placing it back on the same spot to feel movement again. Slovene moved his hand to another spot. He smiled, even laughed. Slovene was happy with his response, her face glowed with a big smile.

"See," Askel told him, "it make her happy to have you content with her big belly, your babe, her eyes shine with love of you." He turned to Slovene, "I be Aksel of Heborg, my lady; your man need to learn this to make him content."

"You be kind, Sir Aksel of Heborg, you always be welcome in our household."

"You not tell I do such a thing," Hjordis warned Aksel, "lest mine enemies think me weak."

"I know what you mean; old Ramgerd thought I be weak. I so happy and content in comfort after I wed."

"Oh, he fought you?" Hjordis asked.

"No, he not fight me. He stole my wedded wife and took her to a neighbor's shelter, drank too much ale and tried to defile her. Well, Kaja be prepared, she be quite the saucy vixen and fighter – that what attracted me to her when she be just a young lass. She cut him and run from him, he yowled like a banshee. God be with us. We found them in time and save her. We stopped the flow of his blood. She defiled him for his misdeed, I let him live, he be punished and learned lesson not to scheme against me and mine. Well no, this fix in his mind that I really be weak since I let him live. He came back to my realm, set fire to a farmer's house and barn and run like the pig he be. We rode after him, followed three days north to his realm where we made war on him. I told him he made a big mistake when he believed we be weak. I let him live because Kaja punished him, but he attack my realm and that be the end of him. He jump across a crevasse to escape me, but not reach the other side and fell the chasm below. It now be known that any who mistaken me as weak will face the same. We have no more barbarians fight us. Kaja lost the babe she carried; it be early in her time. Now we have another, a beautiful male child. Bjorn now one year. I hurry home, she again with child. I be there to rub her belly and gaze upon her beautiful face, the face of my wedded wife who taught me to love. She say, 'Love make us strong.' We be in Alliance with many realms, we have treaties, trade agreements, share knowledge and give support to each other in times of siege."

"Alliance of realms?" Hjordis aroused with interest asked, "Do many come? How I join this alliance?"

"We meet every year, talk of many things, we trade among us, have problems to solve, help in need. You come next year when we meet, ask if we make you welcome."

Before Aksel left in the morn, Hjordis took him aside for a walk in the village to talk. "It many years past we be brash young princes. We enjoy the entertainment of young ladies who give themselves for sport and compensation." Hjordis said, "One of my people, a farmer by trade, claim his wedded wife give birth to a female babe seven months after they wed. It be not his child. The wife would not confess any wrong, until she lay dying of fever. She name you, the sire of her babe. Farmer not know who 'Aksel' be, it the name his dying wife give him. I never say to anyone about the child or that I know Aksel of Heborg. The farmer told me this when he himself in decline with some malady and feared for the welfare of this beautiful lass his wedded wife gave him. He now be dead.

"The little lass be more than four years now. She be attended with love. Thought you want to help in some way- perhaps, to cast your eyes on her."

Aksel looked at his friend, thought on this, and looked again. "You not story me friend? This be truth you say?"

"Ya," he confirmed nodding his head, "The lady in question be one I remember you dally with when you here many years gone. If you want to look at child from afar, we approach the cottage of the neighbor who care for her, gives her the necessities to keep body and soul together. I see her sitting by the doorstep with a stick, playing in the dirt with the look of a wretched urchin."

Aksel looked in the direction Hjordis indicated, a little lass was humming a ditty while she played in the dirt. He walked slowly to see her up close, can this be his child? He kneeled in front of her, she startled and looked up at him, a touch of fear in her little eyes. "Little maiden," Aksel said softly, "what be your name? Do you know what your name be, can you tell me?"

A woman came from the cottage and challenged him. "What you want from this little lass, my lord? She disturb you?" Her voice softened as she realized this was a very regal looking man and she didn't desire to offend. He was also with her Lord Hjordis, sire of her village.

"No, the little maiden not offend or disturb, I only speak with her a moment, if I may, my good woman." Aksel said politely, not sure what to do about this. If indeed she was his progeny could he leave her? Could he take her to Kaja? How would Kaja feel about this? What would mother say?

"My name be Birgitta," Her little voice spoke from his knees. "What be your name?" she asked in return.

"I, Aksel of Heborg," he replied, enjoying the sound of her sweet little voice. She looked at him with a steady gaze.

"I know you?" she asked quietly.

"No," he replied honestly. "I be told that we be kin."

"What be kin?" she hesitated.

"It means we be of the same blood. You understand?" She nodded her head hesitantly.

"You come take me away to your castle?" she asked.

"I not know. I need be sure. Your mother say anything that prove we kin?"

"She gave me jewel to keep. She said it be my sires who left her."

"You have the jewel?"

"No sire, my lady, Berit, take from me."

The woman listened to this exchange of information and volunteered, "Ya, sire. I have it from her, she play with it and I fear it be lost. It look of much value for a child's play thing."

"You still have it?" Aksel asked. Berit scurried into the cottage and returned momentarily with a jeweled brooch and handed it to him. Aksel took it in his hand, recalled the young maiden he had given it to several years before. After two days and nights of pleasure he had felt obliged to gift the delightful lady with the golden brooch.

He rose and turned to Hjordis, still examining the brooch. "Well friend, does this tell you true?" Hjordis asked him quietly.

Aksel nodded his head. "So what I do now? Take the little lass with me? Will this upset my home, my mother, my wife?"

"Your mother not the one to be concern, your wife be who would throw you both out of the castle" he chuckled under his breadth.

"Kaja very understanding and forgiving, this before we wed when I be a wild scoundrel. She love the child and accept her. My mother scold, make me feel the fool, but show love. Birgitta be a likeable lass as her mother, I be taken to her already." He paused, gazed again at the little lass, "As King Hjordis of this realm, do I have your permission to take her with me? There be another to speak for her?"

Hjordis spoke with Berit and discovered there was the farmer's sister, who didn't want to take the child. She had many to feed and care for and cannot take another. So Hjordis gave his permission, "There be no reason you not take the little lass to your castle, under your protection where she need to be."

Aksel looked down at Birgitta, she stood at his feet and looked up at him. "How you feel about this, you come to live with me in my castle? You have a mother to love and a little brother to play with."

"You be there?" she asked.

"Ya, I be there. You come now, ride with me on my big stallion to Heborg, where we live."

Birgitta went to Berit, hugged her skirts to tell her goodbye and Berit bent down to respond in kind. "I will miss the little imp, she a good lass." Aksel felt obliged to give the woman a couple coins for her attention to his daughter and she gratefully curtseyed to him as they left hand in hand. Birgetta, between the two men, proudly looked up first at one and then the other, then looked back to smile and wave at Berit. She is proud, she is going to live with her sire, with her new sire.

It was a full day's journey back to Heborg and they started late with the delay. Birgitta was cleansed and dressed fresh before they left. A supply of nourishment was prepared for her. It would turn cold late in the day so a woolen cloak was also supplied. Their hunted game has been shared with Hjordis and a pack horse supplied for their own large share of meat. Aksel sat the little lass with him on his steed and Alf led the pack horse out to the road east to Heborg. Birgetta, had never been on a horse before and feared of falling. She wept softly, holding tight to Aksel her face hidden in his cloak. He spoke to her in comfort, slowed the pace to make it smoother for her and she dozed off for a short while. They stopped to rest and refresh themselves, Birgitta did not want to remount his steed.

"You want stay here in this wooded place by yourself? At night the animals come out to graze and might harm you. There be none here to feed or comfort you. I take you to my castle where you have care, comfort, new mother and a little brother, even a grand mother who will come to love you. Come, Birgetta, I shelter you."

Reluctantly, she let Alf lift her up to him and they started off on their journey once more. As it was getting dark and the path hard to see in the mountains, they took the lower road where the full moon was bright and they continued slowly through to Heborg.

The night watch called the arrival of travelers and a lantern was brought to the gate to guide them in safely. Kaja heard the call and rose up from her bed to see if it was Aksel. She dressed in a warm cloak and swiftly descended to greet him in the court yard. She saw him hand a bundle down to Alf. He dismounted, came to her slowly, took her by the shoulders and hugged her close. "I sorry Kaja, I bring a surprise that was given me. I pray it not upset you, upset us. You want see her now, or wait for the morn?"

"Her?" she questioned. "Shall we go inside?" The sleeping bundle was laid on the couch in front of the smoldering fire and Kaja gazed down on her. She looked at Aksel, back to the lass and then at Alf who accompanied him. "Who she be, or perhaps I need not ask? Do she have a name?"

"Her name be Birgitta, daughter of a lady I make love many years past. Her marm die of the fever last year. I stopped with Hjordis the night after our hunt and he told me this. The lady told her husband before she died, 'Aksel be her sire." The husband told Hjordis they were wed seven months when she be born. He took ill and died also. I could not leave her, Kaja, I just could not leave her." He repeated slowly his head bowed. "You object, I make other arrangements for her. Shall we think on it and rest now? I be weary." He looked at her, longing to hold her in his arms. Yes he was weary, his heart heavy with trepidation.

"This be enough to prove?" she questioned, "She have the look of you?" Kaja gazed at the sleeping lass. "Perhaps it best we rest. We talk the morrow." She turned to leave and hesitated. "Will she do well the night in front the fire? Perhaps take her upstairs to my chamber with Bjorn?" Aksel lifted Birgetta and carried her up the stairs. Kaja opened the door for him and he gently laid her on the small bed next to Bjorn's.

CHAPTER FIVE

ACCEPTANCE

Kaja heard quiet weeping just before sun up and rose quietly so not to disturb Aksel. She looked to babe Bjorn, who was sound asleep, then remembered the young lass from the night. She was not on the bed. She heard a sob come from the corner and found her there. Kaja comforted her, spoke softly to her, showed her the chamber pot to use, gave her water to drink, a crust of bread to eat, spoke softly some more and held her close for comfort. "Are you better now, little Birgetta?" The child looked up at her, gave a weak smile and nodded her head, "We sleep more now, 'til the sun wakens us?" Birgetta nods again and lay down on the bed. Yes, she a sweet lass, Kaja acknowledged to herself.

Kaja wakened at sunrise, Aksel was not at her side, she left her bed and saw him below in the hall. Memory of the young lass the night before came to mind and she went to the chamber to view the child, who was still asleep. She looked at her long, what to do? She turned to leave - Aksel was there beside her and took her in his arms.

"I not know about this lass before, Kaja," he spoke softly, and repeated the story Hjordis told him the day before. "She a fair, sweet child. We keep her, if you like, or we find other home for her. Do not hate me, not have anger. I could not leave her. She be yours, could you leave her?" He paused, "I have older sister when a lad, she be married to Danish King many years now. Remember her well, love her well, it be nice our son has older sister as did I."

Kaja looked into his eyes, saw a compassion there she had not seen before. "Don't know how I feel of this, my love, best we see how she fares among us? Then decide."

Aksel wrapped his arms around her, gratified she was willing to help him in the decision and did not condemn him. "I talk now to mother, so it not be a shock for her anger."

Kaja took the wakened Bjorn from the chamber so the sleeping Birgetta was not disturbed.

A few minutes later Queen Mother Hulda charged in, Kaja alerted her to silence as she walked in to gaze on the sleeping lass. Bjorn, in Kaja's arms reached up to his mother's face demanding his share of attention.

They went into the bedchamber where Kaja placed the baby on the table to wash and change him. "How you feel of this lass?" Queen Hulda asked of Kaja.

She considered a moment, looked at Hulda while tending Bjorn's needs. "He said he not know of her. He said he not leave her there, will find new home here, if we not want to keep her. She not a threat to Bjorn or other male child of King, she a sweet lass, can we not try and see how she be among us?" she paused, "We accept her here where we can watch and welcome her, it no problem. She be away, he need always leave to look after her, no?" she questioned. "He become attached to the sweet lass. I, too, find her acceptable and loving when she wake the night sobbing with fear, not know where she be."

Aksel entered the room, Kaja handed his son to him and Bjorn chattered and bubbled all over his sire in pleasure to see him. Aksel hugged him and carried him into the chamber where Birgetta lay awake in her cot, not sure what to do. "Well good morn to you, little lass, you sleep the whole day?" he cheerfully asked.

Birgetta rose, looked up at him not certain he was the same sire who carried her last night.

"You my sire?" she asked softly.

"That I be, or so Sir Hjordis tells me. Are you hungry to break fast?"

"Yes sire, my lady gave me water and bread the night, she your lady, too?"

"Be it the lady with the curly golden hair?" he asked her.

"I not know, it dark the night. I cried, not know where I be, need to pee, not know where find chamber pot. My lady come, speak soft and help me, give me drink and bread. She be my new Marm?"

"We give her time to know you, love you, then ask if she will be your new Marm. It be strange to her, a surprise. We need give her time." He took Birgetta's hand and head down the steps to the main chamber, the fire warming the air, the smell of pork rinds cooking over the fire. "This be your brother, Bjorn, I carry, he still a babe, but will grow fast and then you can play with him. There many lads and lassies in the village to know and play. We eat now."

As they approached the table, the two hunting dogs, Stak and Pank sensed a different smell and charged noisily. Birgetta cringed and held on to Aksel. "Hold there now Stak, this a little lass to play. Come Pank, come and smell the sweetness of her, she be friend." They do sniff and lick and Birgetta hid her face in Aksel's tunic as they moved forward to the table, the dogs followed close. Before the meal was completed, she was sitting on the floor, petting the big dogs, rubbing their ears as they lay contentedly at her side enjoying the attention.

Later as the sun warmed the air outside, Aksel took Bjorn in his arms and Birgetta by the hand to walk in the village among the people. He introduced her to them, "This a daughter I found in a nearby realm and brought her home to live among us. We welcome Birgetta," he told all with a touch of pride in his voice. He saw Dagmar and Eric and introduced them to her. Eric although shy of girls, talked freely with her and she with him. They become instant friends.

"Your name be Erk?" she questioned.

"No, Err ic." He pronounced more clearly, and she repeated it emphasizing the rr's. Eric laughted with her and was mesmerized by the sound of her tinkling laughter. As they walked on, she looked back at him and waved. "Sire," she looked up to him, "Be he a nice lad?"

"He a fine lad, his sire a strong, good man, who help me grow be a man," he emphasized. She was pleased with his answer and smiled inside her thoughts.

As they walked into the workers area, Birgetta looked up at her sire quizzically, "I hear baby cry, scream hard."

Aksel heard it also and realized it had a dire sound, "We look and see what be wrong." They approached the cottage of a trell nearby where the screaming came from within and Aksel called out! "Hallo, inside, be anyone there? We hear a baby cry, you in need of help?"

A thin woman came out with the screaming infant in her arms looking pitiful. She recognized her Sire and bowed to him, her head tilted in shame. "I have not milk for my babe, she hungry, but I have no milk. Not know what do, have not goat or cow to get milk for her. My sire left to find milk and not returned."

Aksel looked at the sad woman, who must be new in the realm, he did not recognize her. He reached to look upon the infant wrapped in a crude blanket, his thoughts in a quandary. 'Kaja has much milk, Bjorn a fat little babe. Can she feed your starving little babe?' He looked down at Birgetta. "Can you find the way back to castle? Tell My Lady Kaja come quick need her help to feed a starving baby. Tell her come to end of the path near wall. You do that?"

"Ya, Sire, castle straight up there, we come back down this same path. You wait for me here?" She turned and ran up the path while Aksel spoke gently with the frustrated lady. The infant screamed even louder.

In a few minutes he saw Kaja scurrying toward them, Birgetta pulling her hand to hurry her on. "What you say, a starving infant?" She looked at Aksel unbelieving, turned to see the thin woman holding the squalling babe. The mother was fighting tears of despair.

"You feed babe?" Aksel asked her. "You have much milk, Bjorn share with tiny hungry babe?"

Kaja looked at the mother, "You let me feed your babe?"

"Oh My Lady, I have not milk, I shame to have others feed her."

"No, not have shame you have no milk. It shame to let babe starve, cry with hunger when others have plenty to give. Let me take her." Kaja took the infant into her arms and lifted her smock to take the baby to breast. The infant latched onto the nipple sucking hard so that Kaja frowned until the babe relaxed her hold as her little belly filled. They sat on a bench nearby and held the babe up straight to rest and burp. With a full belly she nodded and dozed and it wasn't but a few minutes she was nuzzling for more.

Bjorn in his sire's arms reached for his mother wondered why she had another taking his milk. "He thinks he lost favor with his marm," Aksel said joking. Birgetta laughed at him and hugged her little brother.

"We take babe to castle so I can feed her 'til mother can find milk? Perhaps I can feed her longer, while I have much milk. Bjorn soon eat other food and not need me." Kaja turned to Aksel for his reaction.

"That a good thing. Will mother let you?"

"We ask her."

The mother cried with thankful words to have someone to feed her babe. "Yes, I be grateful, but also sorrowful to loose my daughter."

"You not lose daughter, you come to castle, we find room for you both. You care for her, she be your babe - I feed her when hungry. What your name?" Kaja asked.

"I be Helge, my baby Janne, our sire be Rolf - he look to find milk."

They take the mother and child to the castle, Aksel alerted a young lad to help carry the few things needed for the babe and mother. "You watch for Rolf, when he return tell him babe and mother be in castle. He come there to find them," He instructed the lad.

Aksel accepted Rolf, when he came to the castle to inquire for his wife and babe. He had been bartered as a new slave from a neighboring realm and Farmer Vitolf had not properly assigned him duties or supplies to care for them. Even the meager cottage he lived in was not suited. Vitolf was reprimanded for the oversight and Rolf was vindicated, reassigned a better cottage, sufficient supplies and work assignments.

Birgetta became known and accepted in the realm and joined in the children's activities. She hadn't been taught as the others had, and felt inferior to her new friends. Frode told her, "You not inferior, little lass, just not learned. Stay and listen to what we teach and you too, will become learned. It not take a day, not two days, maybe many days and even years, but you will become learned as they."

"Who be you?" Birgetta asked.

"I be teacher, I teach My Lady Kaja when she just a lass, she be much learned lady now. She help me teach young lads and lasses when she can."

Birgetta wasn't sure of this, when next she's near her new Marm alone, she asked, "You be learned and teach young lads and lassies?"

"My teacher, Frode, train me when just a lass as you, now I help him to teach the young lads and lassies. All in castle learn to read letters, make words, do numbers and learn well."

"When I grown will I be learned - teach young lads?"

"If you do well, Ya, Frode always need help to teach. I even teach older lads in some things, even to joust!" she emphasized. Birgetta looked at her in awe, not sure if she believed. Kaja smiled, saw young Eric at the door and told Birgetta to watch Bjorn play on the floor. She retrieved two swords from the wall rack nearby, handed one to Eric and said, "Come Eric, we demonstrate, show Birgetta how we train with swords among the lads of our realm."

Eric looked at my Lady with surprise, but took the sword and spared with her for a few minutes, going through the training lessons she had taught him. "Now you believe?" she asked Birgetta who just sat in awe to watch them, looked first at Kaja, then Eric. "You spar with lady?" she said to Eric.

"She be my teacher, she say demonstrate, I demonstrate. She a great lady, can do all!" Eric was quick to explain with pride and a big smile.

Birgetta followed Kaja, watched as she cared for Bjorn, fed him, played with him, put him on the floor so he could move around and learn to crawl. "You teach Bjorn to crawl?"

"Baby learn how to crawl as grow stronger, sometimes I help a little, he rock on knee, now move on knee, soon he crawl all over and we need to watch him carefully so he not hurt himself. You learn to watch baby? Help his marm?" Birgetta beamed and nodded her head. Kaja took her in her arms with Bjorn and they hugged together as babbling Bjorn reached out to Brigetta and looked up at his marm.

Eric still waiting nearby told his lady, "Sire, request you come to field and see the large crop they harvest."

They rose to hurry out to the lower garden as Kaja called, "Mother Hulda, come along to the fields with us and see. Aksel proud to show the work they do, the grain they planted and now harvest. It make much flour for bread." All the barns were full and there was need of more, so they built two more barns. The people prospered - there was sufficient food for all the winter. The people were happy with their new young king and planed a feast on the Lord's Day to give thanks to their God.

The service was held in the courtyard outdoors in the fresh coolness of fall as the aroma of roasting venison filled the air. Friar Kristoffer announced, "It a pleasant seasonal day to have a feast to celebrate a full harvest. We have a full harvest of babies among us also, it a good day to have a baptism so we celebrate two harvests, the fruits of our land and labor and the fruits of our loins and labors. We go to the lake, we wash Original sin from the infants, children and adults we have amongst us who be prepared become Christian."

Birgetta watched as the little babes cried when dunked in the cold water after prayers of Baptism are said for them. Baby Janne, with her mother and father, were baptized together. The cold water shocked her and she cried hard as her mother took her from the Friar, held her closely wrapped in a warm cloth to sooth and comfort. Lodin and Bjorn were older, had been in the water before and enjoyed splashing. They were prepared to play, but were disappointed when not allowed to as their fathers snatched them up to strip their wet, white robes from them and rub them dry with soft cloths.

Aksel had prepared Birgetta to be baptized, she was willing, but, "I be feared of cold water, it scares me," she cried.

"I have nice warm cloth here to wrap you as Bjorn be, he not afraid," Aksel convinced her. Soon there were many crying or shivering babes, lads and lassies as well as some uncomfortable adults trying to get warm. Friar Kristoffer was the most uncomfortable of them all – his feet were numb. He had been in the water for a long time, as there were many newly baptized Christians that day, both adults and young infants.

A stag had been caught, slaughtered and cooked the night over hot coals. The citizens were eager for the feast, ready for the thanksgiving meal. Friar Kristoffer prayed. "Jesus, son of God, we thank you for this abundant crop. Bless the farmers, who planted, bless all who worked the fields and harvest, bless the archer who slew the stag. Bless our newly baptized families, may they live good Christian lives, good health to our king, queen and little prince and princess, and all our people in the realm. Amen."

The head of the stag with a huge rack of antlers was hanging from the wall for all to admire. The new farmer, Rolf, who shot him was proudly bragging his kill – he was adept with the bow and arrow, a skill he learned when just a lad.

Then the feast began! All brought dishes of vegetables, breads, and some sweet cakes. A dish of food was brought first to Aksel and Kaja to test if it was well cooked and ready to eat. Kaja tasted a small piece and offered the plate to her sire. He looked at her, took the plate and set it on the table before him, gave her a big smile as he turned and smiled at the citizens, raised his arms in conquest, held a tyne in one hand, a sharp knife in the other. "It be done, it be good. Time to feast," he declared.

Musicians came forward to entertain, Kaja joined them with the harp for a time 'til Helge brought little Janne to her, she was hungry. Helga looked refreshed and healthy and Janne didn't cry except when she was hungry or cold from the baptismal water. Even Rolf was happier to see his family content. He had been worried, having no status in the realm, worried he would not be able to care for his family.

Yes, the people were happy to join in the feast as carved meat was passed to all. Bowls of cooked cabbage and onions, stewed greens and potatoes, loaves of dark bread slathered with honey and fruit compote were also passed to all. The musicians took turns to play for the enjoyment of all and to eat their share of the feast. The citizens started to dance among themselves to celebrate their successful harvest and happiness.

Birgetta sat aside and watched the happy people about her. She ate a portion for herself and even fed some soft mashed vegetables to her baby brother, who opened his mouth wide and blabbered at her, blowing his food all over himself. She wiped him, chastised him and returned to the open fire pit, to refill her plate with more. A big man was standing there holding a stick in the fire, she did not know him, had not seen his face before. He left carrying the hot stick of fire, walked away toward the garden where the freshly sowed grain was stored. Birgetta followed, wondered what he would do. From the top of the hill she watched and saw him go to the new barn, put the fire stick into the bottom of the stack of freshly harvested grain. Birgetta saw smoke come up from the grain, then fire. She turned, ran to Kaja and Aksel. "Marm, Sire", she shouted on the way. "Man put a hot stick of fire in the barn, hurry, it burns with fire."

"What you say?" a guard nearby heard her as she ran past.

"A man burn barn, hurry!" and continued to run through the courtyard festivities.

Aksel listened to her story, "Who be this man?"

"I not know, no see before. He put stick in fire then carry it to the barn - put hot stick in straw. It burn, *SEE!*" she shouted, pointing to the garden area. "Smoke rise in air!"

Aksel rose, looked about for his men, shouted, "Sound the alarm, all head to the barn. Get buckets, carry water from the pond to fire – all move fast." They all dropped the festivities and ran as the bell tolled for the emergency. "Ingvar!" he called. "Move fast, find a man who moves away, he be the one who set fire to our grain." Turning, he called, "Birgetta, which way he go, after he set fire stick in straw?"

"Sire, he go down away this way," she turned toward the burning shed and pointed with her arm outstretched to the right. Ingvar and Edmond followed her direction and moved out fast, jumped bare back on horses outside the gate to make a wild dash.

The grain being freshly sowed was not dry enough to enflame fast. It was smoldering and smoking, with little burning. They were able to douse it with more damage from the water than the fire and smoke. Just a very minor part of the harvest was affected. Birgetta won the hearts and praise of all for being alert to a stranger doing damage to their crop.

She smiled when Eric came to her and bowed low before her. "You did great deed, My Lady Birgetta." She was thrilled, blushed and shyly accepted his thanks with a little bow. Kaja, who was sitting nearby nursing Janne, witnessed the exchange, smiled and called Aksel's attention to it.

"Shall I promise her at this young, tender age? They be well suited for one another," Aksel teased Kaja who just smiled coyly at him.

The strange man wasn't found, he completely disappeared in the fields to the west. Aksel pondered, *Who would do that? Who want to destroy fruits of our labor, the food we work hard to feed us the winter?"*

After the fire was secured and all returned to the feast in the courtyard, Toras, a farmer from near by, sought to speak with the King, "I have a brother, Sire, who be a troublesome man; where he go - there be trouble. He come to see me, spend a day to visit, ask permission to stay and be part of family, then try to bed my wife the night. I sent him away this morn, he angered with me and left. Do the little lass remember the look of him, what he wore? If it be him, I try find where he go so we try him for punishment."

Birgetta and Toras spoke at length of the man, she tried to describe him, "Remember only that he be big man, like Ingvar, full beard of dark hair and wear plain clothes."

Toras said, "That's the sound of him, he big with dark hair and full beard."

They searched the countryside, without success. Toras' brother never returned again to Heborg to disturb the peaceful harmony of the realm.

CHAPTER SIX

UNEXPECTED RELATIVES ARRIVE

The castle was busy with their usual tasks as winter came to a close and the warmth of spring prepared all for planting and enjoying living outside. A small covered coach entered the village and the driver led the pair of horses to the front of the castle entrance beyond the court-yard.

Mother Hulda heard the noisy coach come to a halt and rose to investigate who had arrived. Two women disem-barked, looked about the courtyard and the castle as they slowly approached the entranceway. They completely ig-nored the noisy dogs who did not accost or approach them, just stood off and furiously barked at them as they slowly walked by.

Mother Hulda was surprised. What manner of women are these that Stak and Pank allowed them to pass with lit-tle more than fierce barking? She did not recognize them, did not know who they were. "What be your names? Do I know you?" she asked as they approached her at the door-way. They barely glanced at her, just walked past into the hall, looked about at the children sitting at the foot of a pregnant woman, others were sewing, doing needlework and socializing with each other. Still others continued on with their work barely noticing the two as they stood tall and insolent of manner in their observation of all. The old-er woman turned toward Hulda, "Yes, Hulda, you know me. We grew up in the same realm when young. Your sire be King and you be Princess. You not remember? I be daughter to cousin of your father. He work in your realm, work hard, care of serfs and doctor to animals. You not make us welcome?" she indignantly asked.

Hulda looked upon them as strangers, she did not remember. "I be just a child when your sire left our realm, you old enough to remember. I be a younger lass. not know you. You older and not know me. I remember doctor well, remembered he put ointment on burn that made it sting more. I have mark on arm where healed. No, not remember you. Come, come in castle. You know my name, but I not know yours?" she prompted them.

They ignored her inquiry and continued to look about the large chamber active with daily activities. The dogs lay down beside Kaja who was large with child content in her comfortable chair reading a story to Bjorn, Birgetta and many children in her care sprawled over the floor. She saw the women enter, they did not acknowledge her and she ignored them since Mother Hulda spoke to them. She continued with the children.

The haughty one walked to her, slowly but purposefully one large measured step at a time and watched, listened, and finally spoke up loud. "Who be you? You not greet visitors to the realm? We traveled many days, be tired, hungry and require assistance. You sit there telling silly stories to children who don't understand what you say."

Kaja looked up at the woman. "I know who I be, my lady, who be you that you demand time and attention when I busy with assigned task?" Kaja spoke to her in the same tone of voice. The lady was taken aback. "I ask who you be. This my home, my realm. I welcome guests here, but I know you not. Not like your manner, your demands, your lack to consider. You expect me attend you? I ask again, who you be?" She paused and looked direct at the woman.

Mother Hulda from the doorway considered what should she do? She does not know what to do. The lady was somewhat subdued by Kaja. "I be second cousin to King Gregors, I live here when young, I come to visit – this be his realm, be it not?"

"It be his realm two-three years ago, King Gregors dead of consumption these many years. You not answer my question. I wait a short time more, then ask you to leave." Kaja said.

The lady straightened up with a huff and proclaimed, "My name be Queen Clausette, this my daughter Dorte."

"You be queen? Where your realm? Why you come to our realm?"

"There be no realm, my brother take the throne and send me afar. He find me disruptive," she boldly stated. "I speak truth to him, he not like truth. Be you the same?"

"My dear lady, we a peaceful village, all work to keep peace and make plenty. Not need anyone to take control, we all know our work, do our work. I be Queen Kaja, wife of King Aksel, who be hunting for game to feed our people. I care for young children, read to them, teach them to read – not need for stranger who disrupt us. You be third cousin to my spouse, you be welcome to visit. We find accommodations for you in the village."

"In village? I be accustomed to chamber in castle."

"Castle has accommodation only for King, his spouse, children and mother. Servants have room below, you join them?"

"Live among the servants?" she straightened up tall - was livid.

"Quarters in village be comfortable, do as suit your manner, Lady Clausette. My children become restless, we read now." She turned to the children, had them settle down and continued to read the story and show pictures of little animals they drew from the story. They laughed and called, "More, Lady Kaja, more!" Bjorn laughed and clapped with them.

The guests were escorted to a cottage in the village, water and bread with fruit preserves was served to assuage their hunger. They were ushered into the evening meal at the castle and joined the family at table. Friar Kristoffer, Frode, cousin Carl and Gerda attended also and were introduced to the cousins. Aksel had not returned from his hunt in the wilds.

Lady Clausette was visibly upset to see the frocked clergyman sitting at the table and to hear him say a prayer before the meal was eaten. "You have a Christian man here? He said prayer to A Christian God? May Thor strike you dead!" she pointedly declared.

Mother Hulda, bolstered by Kaja's earlier stance against the disruptive uninvited relative, indignantly answered. "He be our Friar, the minister of religion for our realm. We accept peaceful Christianity here, not the rule of warring thunder gods of the past. This disturb My Lady?" she paused, expected Clausette to respond – which she didn't. "There be some among us who cling to old gods, you may join them and not fret our ways."

Frode who had been silent until now asked, "Does My Lady pray to the gods of old? Do they answer your prayers? Our realm prospers well now, have good health, pray and play together. We pray to the white god of Christianity, the God of peace."

This silenced the outspoken, uninvited relative. She looked at the food, tasted a little, ate more and helped herself to a second helping from the bowl. She liked the food prayed for by Christianity. Kaja silently smiled at her fervor.

Aksel arrived home the next day from his hunting trip leading an oxen laden with a boar and a stag. There would be a feast on God's Day to enjoy the fresh meat. He sat at the dinner table and welcomed his third and fourth cousins. Clausette swooned when she saw him and took him aside to speak soft and sweet. "You be a fine King, provide well for your people and work hard among them. Your wife cares for you well? I have daughter who be a fine companion."

Aksel smiled at this strange older cousin, "My wedded wife cares for me well, too well, make many babies to love and not need more."

This did not stop her. She sat next to Axel at the dinner table before Kaja arrived with Bjorn and Birgetta. "You have my place, Lady Clausette, guest sit on other side." Kaja spoke to her, the request was ignored. Clausette did not even acknowledge her. Kaja placed Bjorn on his father's lap, left the room and returned shortly. Four strong guards followed behind. They lifted Lady Clausette in her chair and moved her to the other side of the table. She was caught off guard, surprised, clutched the arm of her chair so as not to fall from it. The guards placed a chair for Kaja next to her spouse, where she belonged. Aksel watched with surprise, Kaja usually did not act with discourtesy. He did not say anything to her until later, "You did right, that Lady needed to know who be queen here." He smiled and gave his big-bellied wife a big hug and kiss.

After dinner, Aksel played with Bjorn on the floor. Bjorn climbed all over him squealing and having fun while the dogs jumped and barked about. Birgetta sat nearby, her ears covered with her hands. Lady Clausette took offense, Aksel ignored her and she sat along side his mother, Hulda, who did not know what to say to this disruptively boisterous cousin. Clausette finally left in a huff, unescorted, to the accommodations given for her use. Dorte stayed to speak with Frode and the Friar and enjoyed the pleasure of watching the King play with his son and daughter. She thought how pleasant it must be to have a good husband, a lovely family and a peaceful community in which to work and live. She enjoyed the pleasant company until Kaja took her children to bed. As it was late, Frode escorted Dorte to her cottage. "This realm be always peaceful?" she asked Frode.

"We have problem two years gone, marauders say we be weak. Aksel and his men fight them, the leader be killed, proved to all that we not weak. Have no trouble now. Make peaceful agreement with realms to teach, trade, protect – which be well. All work hard, work together, play together, it be a good life." They walk in silence awhile, "Are you learned?" he asked.

"I read some, Ya, not do numbers, try hard but not remember well." She shrugged her shoulders.

"You be welcome to join our class in the morn, we help you learn more. All children come to hall, learn to read words and do sums with numbers."

"I will come to hall in the morn," she smiled at him in pleasure with a polite courtesy.

Kaja awakened the morning with the early pain of childbirth. She tried to care for Bjorn, but sent Birgetta to fetch Mother Hulda to help. Kaja was surprised when

Dorte came in the door. "My Lady, I be happy to help. I birth many babes for many years." Many hours pass and the men leave the castle. They don't want to listen to the painful cry of a mother birthing her baby. Aksel dallied as he looked up toward their chamber where she labored, a sober expression on his face. Afterwards Aksel was proud, he had a second yowling son and Kaja did not have as much pain as the first born. She remembered the Jesus prayer Aksel taught her and she used it again as she had used it many times in need.

Mother Hulda silently spoke a request to her son. He passed the request to spouse, Kaja, who asked the request of her infant asleep in her arms. The infant stretched, yawned and smiled with acceptance and contentment. The infant was named Gregors like his grandsire before him at his grandmother's request.

Dorte became a help in the castle, Janneke was busy with her own babes and no longer able to serve Kaja full time as before. In time, Dorte became the queen's lady and helper and did a remarkable job. She insisted on living in the cottage they were originally housed, but to really be of assistance, she needed to be available day and night for the newborn and the children so she accommodated them the best she could.

Clausette was livid, "You work as servant in cousin's castle?"

"All work here. Even king and queen work. I be baby tender to future kings, perhaps even a queen. I now have my own life, with work I can do, not need mother to care for me as before. They welcome me. This be nice comfortable home, a realm of care and love," she made her mother understand. "I feel much love and comfort here. I be at ease."

Frode continued to welcome her in his class of students, and soon she is among the most advanced group, even assisted with teaching the smaller children. Kaja watched them one day from the stairs as the children studied below and told Aksel that evening after all had gone to bed, "Frode favor the Lady Dorte."

Aksel laughed, "Frode and Dorte?" he questioned and chuckled again harder.

Kaja be right! A fortnight later, Frode spoke aside to Aksel, "Sire, need speak for marriage to Dorte. We wed soon. Need approval of her sire? Be there some one to speak for her? Do we have your approval as king of this realm? Can we talk with Friar Kristoffer to read the announcement bans to all?"

Kaja smiled at her sire with her wise face and big smile. Aksel looked close at her, kissed the lady with the wise face, a big smile and young infant in her arms.

Lady Clausette was not happy with her daughter's decision. "You must wait for a prince! You be of royal blood. To marry any other be not proper," she discouraged. She was ambitious for her daughter!

"I an older lady now, not wait longer for husband. A prince desires a young maiden, not older lady. I love the wise man who regards me well, who all respect for his wisdom. All here hold me in regard also now that I be learned and help Kaja with the young children."

Frode had his young assistant clean out his part of the cottage and move himself to other accommodations so Frode and his wedded wife could live alone together as it should be.

There be a day of feast and song when Frode and Dorte made their promise to each other before God, Friar Kristoffer and all in the village. Frode was aglow with happiness of his lady, now his wife. There were many smiles and much love between them and all wished them well. Kaja was all smiles also, happy for her teacher and was convinced Dorte would make a wonderful wife for her wise man.

Kaja cared for her babe in the night as needed, but Dorte insisted she would remain in attendance during the day to lighten the load for Kaja until she completely re-gained her strength. Dorte also continued helping Frode with the children's studies as well. This did not last long, however, as it was just a few months before Dorte and Frode were smiling with news of their own expectations. Kaja was pleased, couldn't believe her teacher would be a father soon. Lady Clausette was non-committal, did not approve and said naught. The expectant pair be housed in the castle during the cold winter. Mother Hulda shared a portion of her chambers with them, she had all that extra room and the winter weather was very severe. So severe that two other pregnant women sought refuge in the castle hall where a divider was set up to allow a small degree of privacy for them and their mates. It was very noisy when the other active children expressed the need to move, play and be exuberant in the restricted quarters. It was a chal-lenge to keep all occupied, actively quiet with peace among them.

Late in the winter as the temperature became less se-vere, the men were able to work during the warmer part of the day chipping stones for the church building. They had prepared the location on the crest of the small rise and placed steps to the top on two sides with the least degree of rise for ease of climb. The main quarry was a short dis-tance away from the village and they had chipped out dif-ferent sized stones for the walls, pathways, columns and even some thinner slabs of pretty colored stone for the altar table. It was carried to the building site by ox-cart and stacked for ease of accessibility when needed.

The building progress slackened in the spring when all were busy preparing for the planting. Growing areas were extended beyond those of the previous years as more citizens need to be accommodated with food and work. Aksel was concerned they should not increase their citizenship too extensively. The realms in the alliance were being inundated with peaceful loving freemen who were willing to work in a caring cooperative village.

Frode, however, felt that the extended growing area could easily accommodate many more citizens. The land could be refurbished with the residue of previous plantings to add nutrients to the soil for the following year along with the sulfate found along the bottoms for fertilizer.

There was one area that did not produce well the previous year, Gardner Ostman had observed. He suggested to Frode, "It best we not plant this area for a season to rest it and spread the aged manure accumulated from the animals over the winter. I have seen the manure method work productively when plowed into the soil and allowed to revitalize for a year." The farmers were skeptical but listened to his words and since Frode agreed they were instructed to plow it under, even a second time during the middle of summer to eliminate some of the strong stench of decomposition. The following year would prove the viability of this method.

A tall, strong Norseman came to the realm with an ox-wagon and two young lads, seeking to live and work among them. He asked to speak with the king of the realm who was busy working in the fields so the guard led him to where the king was. Aksel came to the path and the strong

Norseman bowed to him and addressed him politely, hesi-tantly. He hadn't thought to find a king working in the fields along with slaves and freemen. "Sire, I told you be King Aksel of this realm, I travel with you on longboat from land of ice beyond the sea many moons ago. Evoch be my name. I bring little lad with me from land of ice, you remember?"

Aksel paused, looked at him, searched in his memory for the Norseman they rescued. "Yes, remember you and little lad you carry back to Norway, welcome to our realm. We be of assistance to you? You be alone, you bring lad with you?"

"Ya sire, brought the lad with me and another. Have need to find home where we can live and work in peace, in company of others, share in labor and reap benefit to keep body and soul together. I speak with trader in Kaupang who send me to your peaceful realm where I find ac-ceptance to live among you and work to become a member of your village."

"What trader you speak to?" Aksel asked.

He be Verner Eskild, who on longboat with us. He help me in Kaupang. I no longer needed there. Need leave port and go to countryside, find work on farm, perhaps buy piece of land nearby to plant and be a farmer as I be when a young man. Sire Verner recommend your realm, has great praise for your realm, a village of Christianity and love of the one God." Evoch paused, "He speak true?

"Ya, he speak true, I think he be prejudiced - he be un-cle to my wife by marriage and favors her." Aksel gave a pleasant laugh, came up to the Norseman and shook his hand looking at his full height and girth. "You be welcome here in our realm, we find work for strong man like you be. You say you be a farmer?"

"Ya, sire, I plant and sow. I build with stone and wood, build wagons, even fight with sword, if need, be ferocious against enemy."

"You be a man of many skills, that good. Your lads be with you?"

"Yes, two lads of strength here and a spouse and daughter in Kaupang. They live and work with Lady Gudrum, Verner's spouse. Will bring them here when have a cottage and security for them. My spouse be not strong, our daughter cares for her well. "

Evoch was given a cottage to house his two lads, supplies to get them settled and they were put to work in the fields. Aksel told Kaja of the "Norseman we found at sea and returned him to Norway, he be now a new citizen in our village. Verner, the merchant from our trip to Ireland and your Aunt Gudrum give them much assistance with family in Kaupang."

Kaja addressed them at the next God's day service and was surprised to discover the older lad was one of those they had accosted when they went to Kaupang with their Aunt many moons ago.

The young lad, Agge, recognized her. "You have the golden curly locks and green eyes of the lass who help us with Lady Gudrum many moons ago," and told her of their pain for many moons until their sire retuned. "One brother and sister died afore sire return from sea. Mother still be not well, has much congestion. Sister be now a maiden, she care for our marm in Kaupang with Lady Gudrum. Kyush who my father bring from far away at sea be different, but a fine strong, healthy lad, like him well. He learn speak our language, learn how to work with us and likes this land better than the frozen land he lived afore. He be very young lad when first arrived here." Kaja welcomed them and spoke with them often. They became an integral part of the community and soon Evoch returned to Kaupang to bring his spouse and daughter to join them.

Spring had started with an over-abundance of rain which then slacked to almost no rain. The water level was so low, they found themselves carrying water jugs from the reservoir by ox cart to water the young seedlings. Even young lads and lassies were assigned rows to carry the jugs of water to feed the individual dry plants, being cautioned not to trample the tall shoots as they walked the paths between rows. After a month or more, the drought ended and the wind blew in a glorious heavy shower that startled the young water bearers in the fields. They danced about washing the sweat off their brows and dirt from their clothes and bodies. Eric and Birgetta laughed and danced among the others. Even the men who worked in the quarry joined in the cool romp in the rain, taking a respite from their heavy work.

The warmth of another summer was upon them and this time it was Dorte who was bringing a new life into the world. She was still living in Mother Hulda's quarters and Kaja and a birthing lady from the village were in attendance. Kaja had, since her first baby was born, encouraged birthing mothers to use the simple prayer that Aksel taught her. She remembered how it helped her to relax and gave relief from the pain, it was comforting. Dorte was saying the prayer, Frode was pacing the hall below and fretted whenever he heard her moan and cry out. He, too, said the Jesus prayer "to help his wife relax," he said. It went long into the night and Aksel sat along side him and tried to get him interested in playing a game of numbers to take his attention.

"This be your first babe?" Aksel hesitated to ask.

"No, had one afore, she died of the fever as did her mother. It be many years ago," he admitted.

"How many years you be?" Aksel inquired, "You have much knowledge, must be old man."

"Sire, I look an old man, have almost 40 years. Always look to learn from all about me. I learn much from a scholar who taught me well for many years. Have the words he said when I was learning. I scribe all I hear and see. I try remember all I see. This be a big world full of mystery and wonder. Always questions of what happen, why happen, what to do, how to fix."

They were quiet for a time and both lay their heads back and dozed.

Mother Hulda shook Aksel, called Frode. "Your wife in pain, have your babe and you sleep? Wake Up!" She raised her voice so they wakened. "You want to see your son? Be that all you men do now, make sons? Who be wives for them when they grown?"

Frode startled and rose, "All be well? Dorte well? Babe well? Can go see her now? I go," he said without further ado and swiftly, for an old man, climbed the stairs.

Aksel stood up and stretched with a big yawn, smiled at his mother, "He a happy man, has a son now. I be tired - go to sleep." He hugged his mother and went toward his chamber.

Kaja was not there, Gregor woke calling for his marm. Aksel comforted him, gave him a hug, rocked him for a minute and laid him back down. "Sleep now babe, time to rest."

Frode was at Dorte's bedside, looking down at her. He was overwhelmed with his son, Svend, he wanted to laugh and cry. It be his father's name and Dorte liked it also. He looked to be a healthy babe. She looked tired, she tried to smile and he caressed her cheek tenderly with his hand. "You make me very happy, sleep my lady, rest now."

The door opened rather suddenly and Clausette charged in, stopped at the look of her daughter with a babe between her and the wise man she married. She was without words, struck speechless, tears filled her eyes. Frode went to her side and took her in an embrace. "You have a grandson, Mother Clausette, he a beautiful babe with the look of you." Frode wasn't sure the babe did look like her, but knew it would make her proud, for all her obstinacy.

Aksel decided to see where his wife was and greet the wise man's newborn son. He gazed down on the drowsy Dorte and recalled Kaja after her deliveries. He bent down, gave her a light kiss on the forehead and touched the babe's dark hair. He had the look of Frode. Would he also have the intelligence of his sire? Aksel hoped so. The need for intelligent people throughout the realm was of great importance for all.

CHAPTER SEVEN

DISHONOR AND FORGIVENESS,
HEBORG AND ALFHILD

Kaja was expecting her third child after more than five years of marriage, Bjorn had his third birthday two months ago and Gregor was soon to have his second. Aksel felt denied, Kaja could not abide bedding him during her final weeks of pregnancy – it was discomforting for her, to say the least.

Aksel walked through the village as he often did talking to those who were available, to see that all was well. Birgetta walked with him and stopped off to play with her young friends in the village while Aksel headed out to the fields.

He spoke with Farmer Vitolf, greeted him and inquired, "Are Rolf and his family faring well? We have not seen them since Kaja no longer nurse their babe."

"They be fine, work hard. Their babe be a happy little babe, growing well," he replied.

"They have sufficient food to eat, a cottage to suit their needs? The little shelter they live in afore not be worthy - even for an animal."

"Yes Sire, much food, a bigger, better cottage, swept it clean added fresh straw to sleep in comfort and it be secure for the winter cold." He paused a moment and added, "Sire, I have brewed a beverage of great strength. It has been stewed for many seasons with added ingredients to make you gasp with the taste and strength."

"What grain you use for this beverage?" Aksel inquired cautiously, not wanting to try something unknown.

"First it be just rye, add later some barley, corn mash and water to lessen the strength. You come and taste, see if you like it?" he invited, leading him to a small, nearby barn, expounding on the strength and glorious euphoria received from the drink.

Aksel took the mug offered him, smelled the aroma of it and pulled away from the strong surge into his nostrils. He held his breath, tried a very small sip and took a deep open-mouthed breath to ease the burn and tried a second small sip a moment later. "It be strong!" his voice croaked, hardly able to talk. Vitolf laughed and sipped right along with him.

The farmer's young niece came into the barn and was introduced to Aksel. He was struck by the look of her which reminded him of Kaja when first he saw her as a lass. He took yet another sip and felt no pain from the strong beverage, stronger than the usual ale. He tasted and sang while the birds flew overhead squawking loudly, buzzing in his ears and enjoyed to talk and jest with Khora - the sweet little lass. He took a shine to her and bedded her that afternoon.

He brought her to his castle for the evening meal and seated her on his right at the table. When Kaja entered and saw the lass in her chair next to Aksel, she paused in wonder of who she was. Aksel talked to her and laughed openly with familiarity, gaiety and put his arm around her and kissed her with abandon. Kaja saw all this and turned away to leave. Aksel called to her, she ignored him and he went after her. "Why you leave? Come sit at table."

She told him, "I not sit at table with your tart. I will not!" She turned from him to leave. He grabbed her arm, swung her around firmly as she raised her hand up which soundly slapped his face.

He was shocked, "You strike me!"

"Ja, I strike my willful prince again!" He took her arm again as she faced him, horrified by his fowl breath, repeated in a loud voice for all to hear, "I not sit at table with your tart!" Her expression pained, she grabbed for her belly, cringed, turned toward the stairs and slowly pulled herself up them.

Mother Hulda, who had been sitting aside quietly, angered and perturbed at her son, rose and followed Kaja. As she passed the still stunned Aksel, she said to him, "I decide I also not sit at table, I tend to my daughter." She left to help Kaja who was obviously hurting and struggling to make the stairs.

Karl and Gerda had watched in silence. Karl rose, paused as he passed, spoke softly as Aksel angrily eyed his mother going up the stairs. "What you do? You hurt your wife, make her sad – she with your child and you taunt her with tart? In front of her direct?" he accused incredulously, backed off from Aksel, his hand shielding his face from the smell of his breath. "What horrible thing you drink to make such a foul smell?"

Kaja paused half way up the stairs as Karl rushed to her aid beside Mother Hilda and Gerda quickly followed. The three of them helped Kaja, practically lifting her up, to her chamber and took her to bed. Kaja was obviously in labor, her water had broken.

Aksel oblivious of this was angry at Kaja for not joining them. He apparently saw nothing wrong with bringing the lass to his table. He drank down a large goblet of mead, looked about the empty table, the empty room and turned to the puzzled lass at his side. Without saying a word, took her by the arm and led her from the castle back to her uncle's cottage and spent the night with her.

The next morning, he returned to his hall and found it empty, he heard an infant squalling. His head was hurting, he felt sick to his stomach. He sat and pondered his plight, his aching head.

Frode came in and said, "Sire, come with me, it be important. The farmer's niece be very ill."

Aksel said, "I know, she drank too much ale as did I."

"No" Frode told him, "she has spots of the fever coming out all over her face and neck, – soon all over her body. You must not go to your babes. you carry the germ and will pass it to them."

Aksel groaned, held his head and told him, "I have spotted fever when just a lad and recovered well. Does not that make me protected of it?"

"Many times it that way, yes, but," he stressed further, "you carry it on your clothes, skin, - you slept with the lass!" he emphatically stated, trying not to raise his voice. "We heat hot water, fill tub and scrub with soap, wash clothes and clean all others who she was with in the cottage. If you give germs to your babes now, they could die, they be too young to fight the fever! It be very severe. You stay away from your family, from all people for two-three weeks, 'til we be certain you not have the fever. All who came near her must stay away from others. If feel sick, cough, runny nose and eyes - this fever can blind you, make you sick in the head, even kill you. Do you want to do this harm to your lads?"

Aksel was quarantined, banished from his castle, could not even look upon his newborn babe. He felt sick in the head with grief. What he do? He let a tart into his life and this happened? God punished him? He wanted to talk to

Kaja, to beg her forgiveness, to gaze upon her and his sons, his new babe. He followed Frod's directions for cleansing and moved into an improvised cottage to be away from all. Farmer Vitolf, even Birgetta and several others who were in close proximity to Khora had done the same. Khora was sequestered in her uncle's cottage raging with the fever. They kept watch on each other over the next few weeks to check if any had symptoms. Frode was kept busy and worried about his own wife and son contracting it through him. He partially quarantined himself and thoroughly washed frequently.

Kaja was surprised to see Sir Ebsen, a knight from Alphild, arrive on horseback one evening. He brought word that her mother, Queen Alva, was very ill and dying.

"I prepare my babies, we leave for Alphild to visit my marm. She never see her grandsons, perhaps it help her get well, or make her happy to see them afore she die." She told this to Mother Hulda, so she would understand her need to leave.

Frode decided, "I travel with you. Perhaps can be of assistance to my Lady Alva. You think it will make her happy to see my wife and son, to share my happiness?"

It was ten days into the quarantine and Frode and Kaja decided that it was best not to tell Aksel they were leaving lest he get angry and break his quarantine."

Kaja was not fully recovered from childbirth and was very uncomfortable making the trip. She brought two soft quilts to soften the jarring on the hard coach seat. A two-day coach ride on rough paths with three active lads and one infant was very exhausting. They ran out of stories to tell. The water spilled from their leather drinking pouch and they stopped to find more along the way. The lads slept on the floor when they tired and Kaja shared her quilts to ease the bumpy ride. They were offered hospitality at a neighboring realm for the night and left again early in the morning. It was with a sigh of relief that they arrived at Alphild with Sir Ebsen leading their way.

Although Queen Mother Alva was invigorated by their visit, she did not recover. She enjoyed watching the children play actively. It was a pleasure to hold her grandchildren and love them. Ivar and Jorgan helped her rise from her bed and walk outdoors where she could sit in the warm sunshine, look at the clouds above, the flowers that bloomed in the nearby gardens and the trees bending with the wind in the distant fields. Bjorn would come to her and reach up to give her a hug which she favored. Gregor tried to speak to her, but his words were unclear. He did follow Bjorn's lead in hugging and kissing though. Unne, the infant who Aksel had named after his father's friend in Iceland, looked at his grandmother with the vacant stare from eyes that did not see well. She held him close and sang to him little songs she had sung to her own children. "When he grows older, you tell him his grandmother held him close and loved him when he was just a babe."

Kaja tearfully told her mother, "I surely tell him."

Jorgan, well past his 20th year, decided he would wed his promised maiden, Alexandra, so his mother could see them wed – much as Aksel had done for his father. The lass was somewhat learned, of sweet disposition, and lovely to look at. Alva and Kaja delighted in her presence and Frode and Dorte were pleased to know and visit with her.

The wedding was to be held in the courtyard a week after Kaja arrived and she helped them prepare for the event in small ways as she still had not recovered completely. Her strength was drained with nursing Unne who was a glutton, a happy little glutton. They all shared in spoiling him.

The wedding day dawned with a heavy mist enveloping the area in the early morning and becoming heavier through the day. The ceremony had to be held indoors in the hall and the citizens of Alphild celebrated the usual festive occasion with song and dance. Godvin and Kaja played the harp and sang together as of old. Kaja's spirits were lifted with the gaiety. She saw her childhood friends again, shared in their present lives, saw her brother married and enjoyed his newly wedded wife. "It be wonderful to have a sister once again!" she told her marm.

Alva joined the party after the wedding, even did a quiet dance with her sire who literally held her up and tight to him as they stepped slowly to the soft music. It brought tears to Kaja's eyes just watching them. Toward evening, Frode carefully listened to Alva's heart. "It be not a good beat. It uneven, not regular as be proper. She grow weaker every day, not know how long she live," he told them sadly. Dorte was at her side to help and her little babe, Sven, also played along side her on the lounge chair. Alva enjoyed watching them all play and especially to hold babe Unne.

Ivar talked with his dying wife, fed her the stew the cook fixed for her daily. Alva ate slowly, well, and looked at her sire with love. He sat and looked at her and quietly wept as she slept. He adored his lady, Kaja thought to herself. She was sad thinking of her own thwarted love. - Aksel had dishonored her, insulted her. Could she ever feel that way about him as her father felt for her mother?

Alva withered slowly and eventually perished, closed her eyes to nap one afternoon and never opened them again. They had been in Alphild for almost five weeks, her mother would be buried the next day, her grave was prepared.

Bjorn saw his mother cry and was sad. "You cry for grandmother?" he asked and climbed into her lap, looked into her eyes and put his arms around her neck to cry with her.

"Ya, I sad. My marm be gone from us, but she be happy in heaven with Jesus to watch over her," she explained to comfort him.

At the burial the next day, Aksel rode up on his stallion. As he approached, he saw Kaja beyond the castle standing close to her father and brother among the mourners. Frode and Dorte were also nearby and the citizens of Alphild who paid respect to their deceased Queen. He dismounted and walked up behind her, startled her and looked on her somewhat stern. He bent down to whisper in her ear, "I come to take you home."

She looked up at him, tears were in her eyes from the burial still in progress. Could he not wait until after? Show respect for the dead, she thought. "Soon, not now." She carried his new babe and gently he took him from her, held him close and enjoyed the first look of him, touched his cheek and the feel of his fine yellow hair.

He squatted down to his other two who are at Kaja's feet. They crawl to him and whispered quietly while Kaja was engrossed with the funeral proceedings as the Friar spoke the prayers for the dead. "Where you gone so long, Sire?" Bjorn whispered and Gregor tried to imitate him, repeating the question.

Aksel was joyous to see his lads again and touch them and tousle their hair holding them close to him one at a time with his free arm. Little Unne woke and stretched, yawned, squeaked and tried to see. "Your brother awaken to look at his sire," he whispered to them and they smiled at the babe and their sire. Aksal stood up to watch the proceedings as the lads clung to his legs. He looked down at them and smiled as they looked up. He looked at Kaja standing in front of him, her blonde, curly hair wrapped in an unruly bun. He yearned to hold her close. He looked down at his sons and the infant again, it felt so good to look at them, to have them near, to hold them.

Later, they walked the path up the hill away from the castle – the same path Aksel rode many years ago when he first saw her jousting with her brother. He asked her, "Do you leave me?"

"I be thinking of it," she spoke softly. "You not need me, you have tart to satisfy your lust."

"She be dead from the spotted fever."

Kaja looked at him with shielded eyes, paused, "So you miss her and now have need of me?"

"No, I not miss her. I have sorrow for young lass, not miss her. Miss my wedded wife, my saucy green-eyed vixen."

"You sinned," she accused quietly.

"I speak my sin to the Friar."

"I not hear your words of sorrow for sin," she replied. He doesn't seem to understand that she wants an apology, an explanation, the promise he won't do it again, will keep fidelity to wife sacred. Perhaps he is afraid to make a promise, afraid he can't keep it? She also wants an apology for expecting her to accept his tart, to sit at table with her.

He tries to placate her, "She mean nothing. I be drunk, raged with the need of you. She be there, she accommodate me."

She angers with him. "You think me fool. You take lover, bring to my table, try make me sit aside her - accept her. If I did that, bring a young handsome man to your table, expect you to greet him pleasant, what you do?"

He paused, looked at her a moment from shielded eyes, "Kill him," he said softly.

"You expect I not do the same?" she spoke with an irritated, raised voice.

"You talk to me like I be child," he told her, "scold me like I be a little boy."

"No!" she hollers. "You talk to me like I be a simple little lass, not care what you do, you just smile and I fall to your will? No!"

He thought a moment and asked, "What we do about this, what do you want to do?"

"You to tell me true what happened with tart, how it happen, what I do that make you seek another elsewhere. You not do that afore?" she questioned.

"It not important, she be nothing," Aksel tried to make light of it again.

She angers. "No, not make cute story. You look at me, look in my eyes and speak true. Look in my eyes," she repeated heatedly pushing her face into his, "so I see if it be story or true."

He realized she was serious, "I not want to talk about it, I not want to think about this."

"You think and you talk, you tell me all and look to me straight." She demanded again steadfast.

"Kaja, I not remember much. Remember farmer Vitolf ask me taste beverage he make from rye, it be strong, he said. I look, smell, taste a little. He say it soak for many seasons, he add barley and mashed corn, soak more seasons. It had a smell so strong to take my breath away. He added more water; soaked and cooked it more seasons. He taste. It choke him, burn his mouth. I taste again. it burn my mouth and burn hot in my stomach. He said need add more water, make it weak so can drink. Farmer have a little lass visit him, she taste drink also and shout with burning mouth. I feel heat crawl up to my head, make it spin. No, not think more, not remember. Oh God help me" He hid his face in his hands, "Hear farmer laugh - he went away, left lass with me, we, , , we," Aksel hung his head in his hands, moaned in pain, slowly shook his head. "I not know what happen. Remember we be in hall, laugh, sit at table. There be food to eat and ale. Remember I saw you, talk to you, you holler at me, not sit with me, I not know why. You leave, Mother, Karl and Gerda go with you. I anger, be dizzy, drank more ale and not remember any more. I sleep, remember waking in farmer's cottage with lass next to me. She be naked with no cover. I put my clothes on, go to find you. Frode come for me, took me away to cottage where I stay for many days. Feel sick of the farmer's ale, throw up, not eat. Feel more sick than when at sea from Iceland." He groaned with the memory. "Frode tell me lass have spotted fever, very contagious I cannot go to my castle, to you, to babes, they could die from fever. I cried inside, sick inside, just want to sleep. Two days I sleep, maybe more. Frode come to see me, bring me hot liquid to drink, to ease stomach. He told me others have the illness, I must stay alone in cottage away from every one for many days. Karl come, talk to me from distance, he not come close. He told me, 'All be well in castle, you have a new baby boy.'" Aksel paused and looked at her, "I cannot look on my new babe, danger from fever. Need stay away longer. When next I go to castle, you be gone, boys be gone. Mother Hulda and Birgetta tell me messenger come from Alphild, your mother, Alva, be sick, will soon die. You take boys to her. I waited for you to come home, many weeks pass. I miss my Kaja, what did I do to lose my wedded wife? Spotted fever be almost gone – lass die, farmer die, others die. I leave Karl and Ingvar in charge of village, I leave to find my wedded wife and sons and bring them home. You come with me?" he paused, looked at her and beseeched, "Kaja, you come back to Heborg with me?"

"You drink strong liquid, it made you senseless. You not think with your head or your heart. You forget everything but that thing that hangs between your legs – you think with that, like an animal. You ask God's forgiveness for broken promise of fidelity, but not ask forgiveness from wife. You think if say sweet words she come, like simple lass who knows naught." She turned, walked away and left him standing in the lane.

He watched her go and called after her, "I need to bring you home, my mother not favor me without my wife, I not favor me without my wedded wife. I love you, cannot live without you, without sons you give me. I try not to look on others, will stay away from strong drink that make me loose resolve. Will work hard so I not lose control," he pleaded.

He still hadn't apologized. She turned again to leave and he followed swiftly. "Not leave me – Kaja, I need you." He took her into his arms, held her close for a long moment, nuzzled her neck and embraced her. She cannot pull away, he is too strong. "You want apology? I be sorry I act like a barbarian. I sorry I take another though I not remember. I sorry when you need me, I not there for you. I do better. Come back with me."

"I think about it," she quietly acquiesced. "I think on it." She had looked into his eyes, saw they were true. He was drunk, didn't know what he was doing, doesn't remember. He spoke words of apology, words of love and need. "I hurt in my heart, need time to forget, to heal," she told him, her eyes brimming with tears as she lay comfortably in his arms, her head on his chest.

They stayed a few days longer in Alphild. Ivar was in need of comfort. Jorgan was preoccupied with his new wife. After they wed, they moved to a small, comfortable cottage near the back wall to be alone. With Alva ill and dying, and with Kaja and Frode with their families occupied in the castle, there was no room for privacy. The newlyweds joined the family for meals, assisted when needed in the care of Mother Alva, but spent much time alone, getting to know one another.

Kaja had concern for her brother, he had not been sure he wanted to wed the young lady his father had promised to him. Like Kaja, he favored another not of royal blood. They had spoken of it when she first arrived and he asked her thoughts. Kaja told him of her own wedded bliss, "We have great love, satisfaction and happiness with each other and became as one, even though I favored others before." She liked the young princess, Alexandra, whom he wed, she was learned and pleasant to be with and a beauty to behold. Kaja did not want to tell Jorgan or her father of the problem she had now. It would only create another agony in a time of sorrow.

After the funeral Kaja sang for her father, played the harp for him and others who were still about. Aksel watched her from nearby, slowly came to sit on the floor in front of her so she would have to look at him and sing to him. His sons followed and sat with him to watch their marm. They enjoyed the sound of her voice, she smiled at them and played for them until Unne protested his hunger.

She spent an afternoon in conversation with her father; it seemed to comfort him to just talk about her mother. He confessed his experiences as a young man, "I traveled far when just a young man, all over our country. Just as your young king traveled the world to help him become judicious, I traveled our world to learn more of our laws and people. I met and loved many ladies in my time but wed your mother and loved her most of all. Just once I strayed from her, when I went to fight the Britons. We be gone for more than a year and I be weak. I shamed of my actions but she forgave me when I confessed. She sad, but soon her spirit rose when she be with child and we became happy. We had much love for one another, much love of our children. We be as one, she be a good wife, a good woman." He bowed his head his eyes filled with tears, "I have great sorrow she gone – my Alva be gone."

CHAPTER EIGHT

HEBORG

Kaja and her sons had been in Alphild for six weeks. They arrived home in Heborg toward dusk and the dogs barked and the little guinea pigs frolicked and jumped with excitement, which announced their arrival to Birgetta and Mother Hulda.

Birgetta came running, hugged her two little brothers and her Sire and Marm. "I missed you, you gone so long. I be tired of playing with others. Mother Hulda not let me see many of my friends because some had fever. I never got fever." She chattered on, looked with awe on her new little brother for the first time and gave him a little kiss on his cheek. "He tried to eat me." she exclaimed as he had turned to her with his mouth wide open.

Kaja laughed, "He thought you were his marm who needs to nurse him." she reached down to engulf Birgetta in a big hug and kiss. "I missed my big daughter, I glad you not get the fever, little Birgetta. Be you a good lass while we gone?"

"Grandmarm Hulda say I good," she reported.

They sat at table and ate a hearty dinner. Kaja fed her infant and watched her sire who fussed with his sons. 'They must have lost their manners when away at Alfhild, or perhaps he just enjoyed having them near by at home again to fuss with. Ya, it feel good to be back home with all her loved ones,' she mused.

The chldren did not object to being sent to bed after sustenance, went willingly, even spoke a little prayer for their grandmother who died and went to heaven, at least Bjorn spoke the prayer, Gregor still tried to emulate his brother, he was slowly improving.

Kaja prepared herself for bed, cared for Unne, fed him again and placed him in his small bed next to hers, where, content with a full stomach, he fell asleep. She sat on the edge of the bed she shared with her sire. He was still in the hall, talking with Ingvar, Karl and several others catching up on the realm to hear of happenings while he was gone. She looked below but could not make out what was being said, so returned to her chamber and being weary went to her own familiar bed and fell soundly asleep.

Unbeknown to her, the boys slipped in along side her as they had done while in Alphild. That was how they were comforted being in a strange place and they automatically continued now they were home, it was like being in another strange place.

When Aksel entered their chamber, quietly slipped in beside her, softly called her name and asked, "Be there still pain in your heart? Can we talk of our love?"

Kaja wakened, turned to him, upsetting the comfort of the boys who whined of being disturbed. "What happen here? Do not you boys have a bed of comfort of your own? Marm need her own bed, she sleep with me, her sire," Aksel gently scolded and removed them to their chamber one at a time where they closed their eyes, rolled over and slept.

Kaja opened her arms to him in welcome, "I still be hurt my love, ya, but I forgive you so we can be as one again."

He trembled with the closeness of her, embraced her, made passionate love to her and they fell asleep in each others' arms, with the happiness of forgiveness.

Aksel was worried about himself and spoke aside to Frode the morning after they returned from Alfild. "I still have a pain in my stomach and then when I loved my wife there was another pain I never felt afore."

"What manner of ale did the Farmer brew?" Frode asked. "How much did you drink? I brought you a drink of healing to ease your stomach when you were sick. Even now after many weeks you still have pain?"

Aksel told him what he remembered Farmer Vitolf gave as the list of ingredients and method of brewing. Frode shook his head. "That sounds strong enough to kill! Is there more of this ale about? We can look at it and see."

They walked to the dead farmers barn where the keg of ale had been kept and found it with a leather cover to protect it. Frode took a mug from a nearby table to dip some and was amazed at the strong stench when Aksel lifted the cover. He hesitated to bring it closer to his nose. "This has the stench of a compound I saw many years gone. It be used to clean tarnish and rust from metal and gold. It be strong enough to eat a hole in your stomach and even kill you. I not wonder your stomach and other parts of body hurt. This must be what killed Farmer Vitolf. He died before the lass with spotted fever. He die a week after she had spots and he did not have spots. He raged in pain and madness, fought with all who tried to help, then dropped to the ground. He quivered and twitched all over the ground, his eyes stared wild and then moved no more. He just stared straight with unseeing eyes. He smelled strong like this beverage. How much he drink? How often he drink this poison?"

"We spill it to the ground to be rid of it." Aksel looked at Frode. "We not keep it about to tempt any of our people. It taste strong, but made me want more. I drank many mouth full and went back for more. How many days I be sick?" he questioned trying to remember how long he suffered. "We tell others of the illness, pain and death this ale has caused, so we not have many crazed men in our realm."

Frode considered, "No, not spill to the ground. It be used to clean much equipment with ease. We tell men of what it does to iron and gold and will do same to their innards if they drink it. It work well to clean our plows and other tools, but not as beverage for pleasure. It beverage to kill, make you have much pain."

Aksel bowed his head thinking, "Ya, we talk to all at feast on God's Day, in thanks the spotted fever be finished. I tell them of the bad thing I did. Tell them of the poison brew. Make them listen, make law this beverage be not for drink."

He was aware of a distance among the people toward him since he returned; they did not address him easily as they had done before, with respect and a common sentiment. They tended to avoid him. He wondered what gossip they had spoken of him, what stories they said among them. He asked Frode who reported, "I not hear what they say, but I feel they speak against your actions. You do well to tell them, so all know what happen and that now all be well between you and your wedded wife." Frode was anxious to have him vindicated.

When God's Day dawned bright and sunny, Aksel attended services with all in the church. Yes, the church walls were up in place and well braced to stand tall, the floor secured. The roof was not complete, the seats not complete, even the altar was not there, but they took pride in having a church almost built and used it for God's Day services.

The people did not receive him well that morning. Aksel would have to confess his sin to them, yes, to all of them. After the service Friar Kristoffer asked all to stay, "Our King needs to make a new law and to make a confession."

The people were astonished, what law, what confession? Our King will make a confession?

Aksel ascended the step to the altar platform and faced his people, wasn't sure how to start. He heard his babe squall, looked at his Mother Hulda, Kaja and his sons and daughter. "It be many weeks we not see each other to talk together, many weeks we fear the fever, many long weeks for me without the look of my wife and babes about me. It started one day when Farmer Vitolf invite me to taste a beverage he make, a brew of many grains he work on for many seasons.

"I taste one mouth full of this strong ale. It be not a pleasant taste, it be so strong to take my breath away, but it make me want more and Vitolf be pleased I try again and taste more. He had young lass visit with him, she came to barn, talk and taste the drink with us. She be a pleasant lass." He hesitated a moment and frowned

"I drink more, ya, not remember how much more, not remember all that happened. My head spin, I fell pleasure surge all over my body. Remember I speak to my spouse, she struck me, I took the little lass and left. I woke in the morning with the naked wench beside me, still not remember all I do." He shook his head, bowed his head in shame.

"I sick in heart, I dishonored my wedded wife who I love, who gives me healthy babes, who gives me her love and always cares for me. Frode took me to cottage away from castle, away from my sons, my wife. I not look upon my newborn babe. I bedded a lass with spotted fever and must not pass it to my babes. My head hurt, I sick, dizzy, not remember all I do, not even know where I be.

"I sinned. Sinned against my wife, my vow of fidelity, defiled a young lass, sinned against my God who punishes me now. I be sick many days. Many weeks gone, many die of the fever. When I go to castle, they all gone, no wife no family. Mother Hulda tell me messenger arrived from Alfild. Kaja's mother dying with faint heart. She took our babes to show her marm afore she die. Frode go with her to help ease her pain as he did for my sire.

"I wait many weeks, sick in heart, not know if my wife leave me, if she come back to me. I have need to talk with her, have need of her, have much love of her. I say my confession to Friar Kristoffer, to God. He be a forgiving God. When I talk to Kaja I say my confession to her – that not easy. She crucify me. She want to know what happen, why I sin against her. She want apology, I give apology, beg her come home with me. She hurt in her heart, I give her time so she heal the pain. We be together again in love and forgiveness, but still need to heal, it take much time.

"I still hurt from poison Farmer Vitolf brewed, the beverage he asked me to taste. Ya, it be poison to drink. Frode look on this brew, it be strong enough to clean rust from metal with ease, strong enough to polish gold and make it shine. It strong to burn skin on hands, burn inside your stomach and make it pain hard, it even hurt to make love to my wife. I want to pour this brew into earth and be rid of it, but Frode say it has good purpose - to clean metal. Use it for metal but not to drink.

"Vitolf die, he die before the lass with spotted fever. He die from drinking too much of the poison. He went mad, Frode said he be raving mad. This not good. We make a new law, this liquid be to clean metal not to drink. Vitolf not know it poison, now he be dead. I not know it be poison, I not dead but still have much pain. *We all know now it be poison, we not drink.*" He emphasized strongly and looked sternly to all in the church.

"We have much to thank God for today, the fever be gone from us. We lost two grown men, three lads and one lass, it could be many more. There much work needs be done, but we rest this God's Day. I thankful all be well. I pray my people forgive my weakness, my sin so we can live and work together as before, in peace, in harmony."

"Sire," Ostman the gardener rose to speak, "Many moons ago, Farmer Vitolf invited me to taste this brew he made. I smell it, not like the smell, he said again to try just a little. I put my finger in and licked, it choked me so bad I coughed for many minutes and told him, 'I not like this ale,' and l went from him. I know how strong this beverage be, it not good. I think Vitolf drank it often, I have seen him stumble around drunk, he forgot his work, not tend his work in proper manner. I not surprised it kill him. I pray my Sire will heal from his pain soon."

Aksel thought on what Ostman said and nodded his head in gratitude, "Did any others taste of this brew? Do any have pain from this brew? Frode has a healing drink to ease the pain, it help my stomach well." As none come forward he said, "Let us go feast and dance in good health to all. We have good harvest soon." He stepped down and went to Kaja, looked at her with love, took her to him, gave her a loving hug and they walked out to the courtyard together. The children scurried after them, Birgetta took Gregor by the hand as Bjorn scampered ahead. The citizens hurried by to reach the feast first.

Friar Kristoffer blessed the food cooking on the spit and added, "I pray the next feast will be to celebrate the completion of the church before the cold of winter. We need a name for our church, all will think on it so we have many names to make choice."

The butcher sliced the side of beef, the women brought food to accompany the meat and platters for their families to eat from and the feasting began in earnest.

Aksel was gratified many of them came up to him with a word of cheer or forgiveness, even a word or two about a similar experience in the past. Some even topped his story with vivid descriptions of their misdeeds without the consumption of poison brew to blame it on.

Kaja stood along side, listened to the stories and agreed in her mind that men are animals. After a few minutes, she took her babe from his sire saying, "Ya, men be animals. Perhaps even worse, you gloat and brag of your misdeeds. I take my babe away so he not hear the wickedness about him, - he will grow up to be an honorable man."

Aksel smiled at her as did the other men about. "She still the saucy lass."

The villagers soon relaxed of the threat of the spotted fever and the unfortunate lass who brought it and died from it was also forgotten from memory.

Late the evening the horn of alarm sounded from the main gate. It was the first time in many months it be heard. Since the peaceful organization of realms was created, none who were not peaceful dared enter the area for fear of annihilation. Aksel went out to see who was coming, his men were on guard and Ingvar was there to accost the barbarous looking group of men approaching.

He heard their leader call, "Hail, King Aksel of Heborg. I be Broder, I come in peace."

Aksel walked out of the courtyard and saw that it was indeed Broder. "What you do here in Heborg, did not we trounce you enough when last you come? Want us to trounce you again?"

Broder dismounted his stallion and approached Aksel, held out his hand in a gesture of friendship. Aksel was not sure of this, but met his hand in greeting. "I not come to fight with your peaceful realm. I came to visit like a friend and taste the strong ale I hear tell about."

"Who told you of strong ale? It not good to drink, it be poison to the stomach and whole body. It kill the man who brewed it. We make law against drinking it, use only to clean rust off tools and to shine gold and silver trinkets." Aksel was firm in his message.

"I hear from man who pass through here and share a drink with farmer who made it. It made him drunk, he drink it in Heborg. I like to taste this beverage, you not share?"

"You not listen what I say. It kill the man who made it, he be dead! He die with convulsions, his whole body shake 'til he die. This be what you want? You be a mad man?"

"You make story, I like to try," he insisted."

Frode who stood aside, observed the interchange of talk, stepped in to assuage the barbarian and support Aksel's stance. "Sir Broder, you do not want drink this beverage, it be not good to drink. Aksel be sick many days after he tried, still has pain, cannot even love wife without pain. You want this? That be foolish. We serve good ale brewed in proper manner that will not harm. We not want to have another dead body to bury."

"Who be this old man," Broder looked with disdain at Frode.

"He be a *wise man*," Aksel was quick to correct him with emphasis. "You best listen to his words, lest you die from the strong poison."

Broder laughed, "No, not believe you. Desire to taste, judge for myself if it be good or harm."

Aksel looked at him slowly shook his head, "No, I not give it you."

"Ya, I want a taste, see for myself!" Broder insisted.

Aksel looked hard at him, looked at Frode, looked at Ingvar who shrugged his shoulders, looked at Karl who remarked brashly for all to hear. "He want to taste, let him taste, give him all of it. It kill him too and we be done with him."

Aksel bowed his head a moment and then looked up at all around him and at Broder's men. "You hear what I say, it be poison, not for drinking. You hear what Broder say, he want taste, judge for himself. He think I story him. I not story him." He shook his head and motioned Broder to follow him, "You smell the strength this poison have and you know it bad – you taste, it chokes you. Then you know I not story you."

Broder followed Aksel with one of his men to accompany him. He would stand guard of his sire or perhaps to taste also? With a smug look of satisfaction on his face, Broder took the small amount of ale Aksel dipped into a mug for him. As if the odor in the barn wasn't strong enough, he put it to his nose and inhaled almost choking himself. He couldn't talk for a minute, could not even take a breath, cleared his throat several times before he let out a croaky, "Wow, you be right, that be strong!"

His companion took the mug from him and smelled from a distance, then held his breath while he sipped it. He didn't say anything but discomfort showed in his face as he swallowed it and took a long, deep breath of air. "He be right, that be poison," his voice rasped.

"You like a weak woman," Broder took the mug and drank a good mouthful of the ale. His expression changed, but he took another mouthful and was about to take a third, when Aksel interrupted.

"Broder, that enough, you have your taste, that be enough! We know you be a strong man, you not need to taste more. Even your man here, who bigger and stronger than you, say it be poison. Enough!"

Broder laughed at him and drank what was left in the mug. Thankfully, it wasn't too much and his companion was able to hold him away from the keg before he could help himself to more. With a shake of his head and a distraught look at Aksel, he was able to pull Broder from the barn and take him out to the courtyard. Half way there, Broders' legs were hardly holding him up and he was assisted to make it back to his horse. His body stood and weaved along side his horse as he tried to mount it from the wrong side with the wrong leg and plopped down to the ground in a heap.

"You believe me now?" Aksel asked the inert man on the ground.

Frode approached him with a pitcher of liquid and asked his companion to hold Broder up and tried to force the drink slowly down his throat to ease his stomach of the ale, or even make him throw it up – which he did, all over himself. A bucket of water and a cloth was brought to wash him off and wash away the mess in the courtyard.

Frode looked on Broder then at Aksel, "The beverage be even stronger than before, best we use it, clean our implements and be rid of the rest. It be a danger to keep about."

Broder lay there the whole night and woke early before the dawn, wondering where he was. "I not feel well, where we be?" he inquired, but no one was around to answer him. No one awake, that is. His men had camped the night out of sight of the courtyard. Broder had been placed on a bear skin where he had collapsed in the courtyard, his companion rested nearby not having tasted enough of the poison to effect him, except for a headache. When Broder realized what must have happened, he woke his men and they were gone before the sun came above the horizon. His head was hurting, his stomach was hurting, he was in a fowl disposition and didn't want to talk to anyone. Ya, he told himself, it be a strong poison. He felt shamed, he would never return to Heborg again.

Aksel spoke to Friar Kristoffer, "Do you have many names to use for our church? Have any come forward with a name?"

"No sire, none have come foreword. It be possible they not know names of saints. I not know of many."

"What say we name it 'Jesus, Son of God,' which be name taught to me by friar in the Britains who taught us with the stories of Jesus. It an easy name, that all will remember." Aksel suggested.

The Friar nodded with a smile, "It good name for our church. We speak to all after service on God's Day. See if all agree or perhaps have other names to suggest. Ya, 'Church of Jesus, Son of God' be a good name."

The congregation was in agreement. It was the only name suggested, Friar Kristoffer did not divulge who suggested it so not to intimidate any others who might offer another name. "There be time, so if other names come to mind, submit them to us to think on and consider," he concluded, to leave it open for more suggestions.

With the harvest completed the citizens were able to work in earnest to complete their large church building of stone with a high steeple and cross seen above the homes in the village. The citizens were in awe of the steeple rising into the sky, it brought a smile of accomplishment to their hearts. They looked up at the cross every morning, it was the first thing they saw each day.

The roof was secured before the first snow with thatch on top of the limbs and beams to hold in the heat. The fire pit in the center was prepared for use. Many would come to live during the freezing winter in the simple comfort of stone floors and walls, using their bearskins and woven woolen blankets filled with straw and tuffs of cotton to keep warm. The church name would be carved in the stone above the door come the warmth of spring.

CHURCH OF JESUS, SON OF GOD

CHAPTER NINE

HEBORG

Aksel had a young admirer who enjoyed following him around as he walked about the village. She was a very young lass and he tried to be pleasant to her, not wanting to traumatize her by scaring her away. She was waiting for him as he left the courtyard and spoke pleasantly to him, "Pleasant morn to you, Sire. We walk together this day?"

"Have you no other task to perform? Perhaps your marm needs help?" he suggested.

"No, Sire, she assigned me to walk with you and talk pleasant."

Aksel acknowledged that with a small grunt and doubtful nod of approval. He had business to address with Friar Kristoffer and others and didn't want a young lass to follow him about. He turned to pick up his pace when he heard Kaja call him. She was holding Bjorn's hand, pulling him along with their pet guinea pig snuggled in her other hand. Little Stig was wiggling and struggling to get away from her and she was struggling to hang on to him tight.

Taking Stig from her, "What be the problem, this little pig being bad?"

"No, it not Stig who be bad; it be Bjorn who not behave. He almost choke little pig. He did choke him on purpose - he say he not like him, he say so. He not listen me what I say, he need his sire to enforce discipline. He need you tell him not choke poor defenseless animal. He a pet, a play thing, not to kill," she scolded at Bjorn again as she explained to his sire. Bjorn pouted and held his gaze on the ground.

"You do this?" Aksel asked his son in an entreating voice. "Why you choke poor little pig, what he do to you?"

"I not like him sit on me. He want me rub his back, I tell him go – leave me be. He not go," Bjorn pouted his eyes still fastened to the ground.

Aksel squatted to his size, took his face in his free hand and tilted it up so he could see his eyes, looked into them while Kaja still scolded. "He a willful prince as his sire was; I not like willful prince. I spank, it not hurt him, it hurt me!" she complained.

"What happened that you not like Stig? He be your playmate for much time, now you not like? You chase him away?"

"He bite me," Bjorn told his father.

"Ya, he bite you after you choke him. He defend himself," Kaja told him.

"Well, we take Stig to another lad to play with him. You have two brothers and many other lads to play with. It bad to hurt animal because you not like him. We find another friend for Stig and he not sit on your lap again. You not have any little pets to play with, just big dogs who bite if you hurt them." Aksel thought how to teach lesson, to teach him not be cruel? "Come with me, you tell Friar Kristoffer you try to kill Stig, he give penance for sin. Do penance well, I not spank. Say sorrow you were hurtful, I not spank. You choke him again, then I spank – hard," he emphasized. Aksel stood up and looked at Kaja a moment, stepped up to her, gazed into her eyes and she returned his gaze with an inquisitive look. "Fret not, my lady," he took her face with his free hand while Stig tried to climb up his other arm. "He grow, be a fine lad." He slowly met her lips in a long endearing kiss and gave her a tender smile.

As the two walked away hand in hand, Kaja watched them for a moment with love in her heart for the willful prince she wed. She just didn't want her son to become a willful lad as his father had been. She noticed the young lass staring at her. "I not know you, what your name?" she asked the young lass.

"My name be Sara, who be you?" she asked hesitantly in return.

"My name Kaja, spouse to King Aksel, marm of Prince Bjorn. It a pleasure to meet a lovely lass. You new here in Heborg, not see you afore. Who be your sire and marm?" she questioned

"My sire be Vagn, my marm assign me to be pleasant to our king."

"Your marm, . . ." Kaja hesitated, then spoke politely, "King a busy man, has many important duties to perform. He no have time to talk pleasant with little lass. You best stay with marm and learn how to cook, sew and tend to children. When grow to be a maiden you know how to do all these things. This be what I did when a lass."

"You learned to cook and sew when a lass?" Sara asked in disbelief.

"Ya, my marm and Aunt Gudrum teach me, now I be a marm. I care for my lads every day. My king, my sire, help me care for them, this you see." Kaja smiled at Sara, hoped she was able to influence her toward learning how to live well, not to be a tart for king or any man. Sara gave her a little bow, smiled back at Kaja as she turned to return home to her cottage. She needed to tell her marm what the queen said, "I learn to sew, cook and tend babies as she did when a lass." She repeated this all the way to her cottage.

Kaja recalled that back at Alphild her marm and Aunt Gudrum taught the young lassies during the cold of winter to do these things. She resolved to speak with Mother Hulda, to teach the lassies when next winter came.

- - - -

"There be a need to speak of indentured slaves among the freemen of our realm," Aksel spoke to Friar Kristoffer, "The Alliance of Realms declared that slavery be eliminated soon ." After some discussion they agreed that, "It should be made known among the indentured slaves that they can earn their freedom after they have worked their designated number of years of labor," Friar Kristoffer summarized.

The subject was brought up to all the citizens after God's Day service, Aksel announced, "The Alliance of Realms declared slavery will be abolished among us. With Friar Kristoffer, we plan a legitimate manner to relieve men of their debt, end their time of indenture, they become master of their own fate and future. This be welcomed by most, a progressive measure, that be in line with the Christian way of life. We ask all indentured men come forward, register with the realm, the name of the man they owe, the debt they owe, the years worked under the indenture and the balance of years to work. It be best the freeman who own these indentures, register with them. There be no mistake or misunderstanding between the two. Frode and our Queen Kaja scribe what needs be paid, we keep records of all."

Rolf was especially anxious to clarify his position since Vetolf died. He had continued to work on the section of land Farmer Vitolf had plowed. Working it mostly by himself, except for harvest time, when all combine to get the crops secure before winter. "Agreement with Vitolf to work five years, to repay him for my price . I worked almost two, the crops do well. There be enough to care for my family from my share. Cottage be secure - not when ice be present, now we be allowed in warmth of the new church."

Aksel thought a moment and considered Rolf as well as the others, "Ya, you do well, work hard, all work hard. Continue work til' paid off your price then talk to arrange how you work as freemen among us. Other realms speak well of free workers where their share be fair. We do the same – try be fair, so all work in harmony, have good life and none lack for necessities." Rolf was pleased with what was decided as are the other indentured servants.

A feast was planned to celebrate the completion of the new church. It was secured against the winter's cold with a good supply of cut logs for the fire and sufficient room to accommodate several families with a modicum of privacy. "It be difficult to hold services for all in church during winter while families live there," Friar Kristoffer announced at the feast. "Our king approve to hold service in church for those who can attend there and a second service in the castle hall to accommodate the people there. It also serve to give me needed diversion, to leave the church and walk for exercise, even in the icy cold," he jested and the congregation laughed with him. "I think to ask Ingvar and another large, strong man to walk with me so the wind not blow me away," he added, with a smile.

Work went forward on the preparation of stones to continue building solid homes and other structures as long as quarry rock was available. Aksel announced, "We decide the senior freemen to be first to build cottage of stone and then others, 'til all families have a proper, permanent habitat."

"There be need to plan where to place these permanent cottages to accommodate living among the fields, paths, gardens, castle and church. What need to be built and where to build them need serious consideration," Frode pointed out to the group. "Plan where to put cottages, so they not be in way of one another, so they be not far apart to aid and protect one another. Not to obstruct the flow of water from hills in spring and be alee the winter wind for comfort. There be other considerations?"

Gardner Ostman was quick to suggest. "There a problem when drive wagons on paths that be narrow. We often struggle to drive through with full load of harvested grains. Need to keep paths clear and wide for ease of passage."

"That a good thought," Frode agreed, "any other thoughts to ease our way? For the time being, there are no other suggestions.

"We have the winter to dwell on this plan, will mark the wall in the castle with soft white rock we find in quarry, make a diagram of our realm." Aksel planned. There was a smile of agreement among the congregation.

"Who draw this picture?" Karl asked with a mischievous grin, "Surely not sire?"

"Perhaps, we assign you do the job," Aksel was quick to jest as others laughed in agreement. "Ya, draw picture on wall to show castle, church on hill, where water reservoirs and fields be, where paths lie so can decide where it best to build cottages to serve and protect families.

"Sire," Farmer Toras spoke, "I see many cottages built in open area where they be exposed to much cold wind, have need of many strong walls. I see many cottages built into side of hill or along side a wall to use as one wall of cottage. It work well, it make for more warmth and comfort in winter. There be several hills about and the walls can make many strong quarters for our knights and guards."

"Ya, I have seen this also. You know how to build cottage like this?" Aksel asked.

"I help to build cottage in a large hill. Ya, sire. I work on this." He offered.

Aksel smiled, "It make me content to see all willing to work and share knowledge. We do well together. We build a well-planned realm. Perhaps, first cottage built in a hill be by church so our Friar has cottage nearby," the Friar smiled with acceptance and the congregation accepted this plan.

Late one afternoon, the horn of alarm sounded. A contingent of armed men came marching through the countryside astride their steeds and were stopped at the gate by Ingvar's guards. The man in the lead pronounced, "I be Auslaug, evangelist of the one true God, come to spread his word among all Norsemen in the land. Do you receive us with hospitality and piety?"

"You be a religious man?" Ingvar asked incredulously, "You travel with band of armed soldiers to spread the word of God? I not see this before. Why you need an army to preach the word of Jesus?"

"There be many who abide by Thor and Odin in the land. Need to convince them of the love of the one God of Christianity."

"With arms, by force?" Karl asked as he came up behind Ingvar to listen. "Be that the proper way to spread the Christianity of the one God of love? We have both here in this realm, we abide our own faith and not fret the other — as they do also."

"The great king of Franca traveled with his army, baptize heathens in far reaches all over the land as we do," he announced and proceeded to enter the courtyard into the village to make himself at home.

They found a space to camp, even set up a tent of skins to protect their leader, parade about the village with pride as the citizens shy away from the fierce looking men. Aksel spoke with Ingvar who wasn't sure what to do about them. He was concerned that the many men were larger and stronger than his crew and was hesitant to start anything. Aksel instructed Ingvar to send a knight covertly to Degfinn, the nearby realm that was also a member of the Alliance of Realms, to alert them of this problem and ask for a contingent of armed men to assist.

Aksel approached the evangelist along with Friar Kristoffer. "Good day to you gentlemen, I King Aksel of this realm, and this be Friar Kristoffer, our Christian Friar. We welcome men of God to visit us. You tell us who you be? Where you from? We not see a Christian army afore."

The evangelist remained seated, stared up at the king of this realm, gave a grunt and said in a strong voice to be heard by all, "I be Saint Aslaug come to baptize heathens in the land."

"You saint? That be strange." Aksel said softly.

"Why? Why you say this be strange, you not know the look of saint when you see one?" Aslaug replied in an irate voice.

"It be strange. The church make a holy man a saint after he die, when he go to heaven after he has lived a holy life, not before," he answered.

"God made me saint to baptize heathens. He made me saint, now, before I die," he insisted and rose to his full height in front of Aksel, who did not back down.

"We be Christian people here, already baptized," Friar Kristoffer ventured to inform him.

"Who make you Friar to baptize Christians?" Auslaug shouted at the top of his voice. "God send me here. He say there be heathens in Borheg. Go baptize them."

"This Heborg, not Borheg, you in the wrong realm, not know where Borheg be," the Friar replied, not intimidated in the least by his bold reply.

"You be welcome, stay for religious service in morning, join in song and prayer. We prepare feast to share with Christian army before you go on your way," Aksel invited him.

"He not a saint," Friar Kristoffer told Aksel aside. "As you say, church make man a saint after dead, after he live a good life, a good Christian life. He not living a good Christian life," he emphasized.

"Ya," Aksel agreed. "I know. Sent to Degfinn for help, we wait 'til they arrive afore we make barbarians leave - unless they make trouble and harm our people."

The armed men joined the congregation for an outdoor service in the morning as it was a glorious fall day and the additional men from the army would not all fit in church. Friar Kristoffer invited the 'saint' to assist in the service and, to even speak to the people, to give them his evangelical spiel. Which he did, he ranted and raved passages from the bible in a manner that made no sense to them. Joseph the weaver, who had learned much of the bible, rose to confront Aslaug's translation. Friar Kristoffer signaled him not to become negative against the invading Christian soldiers. Joseph was stilled, but felt something was wrong.

Later, Karl told him, "There be need to wait, we send for help from a neighbor to rid us of these vermin. Know he be a false prophet who not know what he speak about.

They strong barbarians, need more help to rid them from our land, not want to loose any peaceful citizens."

Joseph looked at him, "Farmer Rolf, use a bow and arrow, he help. He taught many young lads to use with skill to hunt deer. Line up on wall above, they fire down on barbarians, kill them all. Barbarians not reach with axe and sword from below."

Karl looked at Joseph, nodded his head in understanding with an enlightened grin on his face, his eyes wide with glee. "When he train these lads? I speak with him, let Ingvar know of this. Perhaps we prepare them to fight from the wall." Karl happily left to find Rolf and Ingvar with the welcome information.

The barbarians did not leave in the morning, they continued to stay, accepting the hospitality of the realm. The realm was busy with the harvest, but the visitors do not help with the work, just idly pass the day moving about and talking.

Kaja made it a point to tell the evangelist, "All citizens in realm work, all share in the fruits of realm when work in the realm. Visitors are welcome, Ya. They stay our realm many suns, they share in work, earn their food and shelter," she explained.

The evangelist was insulted, "We be armed men of God," he ranted indignantly and again raised up to his full height. "We be soldiers of God, need sustenance and shelter to spread

Christianity to all, spread the word of God."

Kaja rose to her full height to him in return.

Aksel was concerned to feed the many huge appetites of these strong religious marauders. Their crop was good, but they were to trade excess to another realm of the organization in need not to keep useless men with gluttonous appetites fed through the winter. Ingvar and many of the freemen sat in conference to discuss the pros and cons of keeping and feeding them through the winter or asking them to leave or even forcing them to go on their way.

Ingvar told them, "They be many large, strong men, I fear they do harm to young knights and warriors even though they be trained well. Can wait for assistance from Degfinn, it take two days or more to arrive. It be better to wait for their help."

Kaja was assigned to speak to them again, to tell them politely in no uncertain terms. "I do this Sire, must first take care to protect Friar Kristoffer from them. Fear he not be secure among the barbarians, they kill him, say we have need of them here."

"My lady has good thought." Ingvar agreed, "Keep Friar among us, protect him 'til we rid our realm of these barbarians."

Kaja bundled herself in a warm cloak against the cold evening air to go among Aslaug's men to talk. A few knights stood nearby to watch for her safety. "Saint Aslaug, there be no work for you in this realm, we be Christians, have own Friar and church. All have much love of Jesus. It be best you move to place where there be worship of the gods of old, your work be needed there."

Aslaug looked at her with disdain, "You, my lady, have the authority to speak this?"

"I speak pleasant as Queen of this realm," she responded. "I say in pleasant manner, so it be a departure of friendship between us. All give you hospitality for many days, it be time you go on your way. Sire say it be time you leave. Not keep all your men the winter, where we put you? Have not accommodation for so many - have not food for so many. You become not guest, but thief of gracious hospitality given at great sacrifice. This be not fair to people who work hard to keep a good life among our realm. We not need to support evangelist we not need. You be men of God you say, we have own man of God, he work well with us. I ask you, leave our realm in the morn, find others who welcome the need of you." She held Aslaug's hard stare for a long moment, gave him a slight courtesy and solemnly turned to leave.

Aksel heard revelry from the courtyard after dark. He investigated, found the militaristic evangelists had become unruly from ale, they were drunk. "Where they find ale to drink?" Aksel asked. "Our supply be diminished, wait for more grain to brew, it not be ready for many moons."

Frode entered the hall seeking Aksel, "Sire, they discovered the remains of the old poison brew, I not destroy it! Hid it in my cottage, to use for many things about! Many barbarians drink it, it be even stronger than afore. We let them drink all?"

Aksel looked at Frode, a sneaky smile spread across his face. "You think they let us take it from them?" he responded smugly. "Let them drink all. We can watch what happen?" They strolled out beyond the courtyard where the revelry was in full swing. The men floundered about and raucously shouted and demanded more ale.

Aksel cornered Ingvar and told him of Frode's deed. "Watch, see they not leave area to reap havoc on our peaceful citizens. They be useless before long, get sick perhaps and sleep. Have lads with bow and arrows watch the night as Karl say, take turns to rest. I also watch and not fear to kill if they act with danger."

Ingvar nodded in agreement and suggested futher, "They not in condition to be danger to us. We load them in wagons when fall asleep drunk, transport to far side of mountain beyond lake, leave there with steeds. When they wake in morn, they not know where they be. We see they come our way again, shoot with arrows from the wall. Not let them come in the courtyard."

"Ya, do that. That be good," Aksel agreed whole-heartedly and gave him a broad grin. "Not tell Friar Kristoffer, he say that not be Christian way. They be not true Christians, they be barbarians, not believe in one God. How many men you need for this? Best not let all citizens know what we do, be quiet of it."

Ingvar chuckled at his sire and left to arrange the transfer of men and horses.

Aksel told Kaja he was leaving for awhile, wrapped himself in a warm cloak and left. He did not even give her the opportunity to ask where he was going. She prepared for bed. Everything seemed to have gotten very quiet. She looked down from the balcony and saw movement beyond the courtyard, it was dark. She heard a wagon move about, horses being herded and decided the barbarians must be leaving.

The next morning the militaristic evangelists were gone. Ingvar claimed no knowledge of them. "I look for them, they have slip away the night. That be good! We no need of them." He let all know and Friar Kristoffer led them in a silent prayer of thanksgiving that they were gone.

Late in the afternoon the horn of alarm sounded again and Ingar and Karl rushed to the wall to see who arrived. Aksel came up behind them and was relieved that it was their young knight returning with a contingent of men from Degfinn.

Aksel welcomed Emanuel, their leader, into the hall and explained what had happened and how they were able to take them away, drunk from ale, in the night. He didn't say that it was the poison brew they drank for fear of being accused of poisoning them on purpose.

"You be fortunate, they stay at our realm in Degfinn many more moons. We sent away when realize they be barbarians, not evangelist. They try fight, we have large contingent of farmers who want to fight, love to fight. They use pitchforks and chopping axe, kill two of them before barbarians find their swords. We laugh at them, anger them," Emanuel bragged with a big smile. "Need to train farmers, be fighters so can help in time of need. They be strong, can fight well."

Aksel considered his advice, thinking, "We build our new church, now complete. Be busy with many plans, to build stone cottages for our freemen. Our people work hard to do this, chip more stone from quarry, plan where to build new cottages to make a fine realm. This we do, work, not fight, not want to fight, have no need to fight. There be many roving evangelists about? We need prepare for others who come?" Aksel asked and prayed there weren't.

The roving evangelist did not return to Heborg.

CHAPTER TEN

HEBORG and FRANCA

Birgetta was approaching thirteen years of age and had blossomed into a lovely, petite young maiden. Aksel was concerned to find a proper mate for her. It was felt she and Eric would make a good couple, but Eric, a tall, strong young man with intelligence, realized, "She be royalty, I not a proper man to wed her. She be lovely little lady and of good will, Ya, but I grown taller than my sire, need a young maiden more my size. In Degfinn I see a lass who has the look of my marm. I favor her well and desire to speak for her to be my spouse," he smiled happily as he let his sire and king know. "This be acceptable?" he politely asked.

Aksel standing along side him looked up at the tall lad who was taller than his sire, looked to Ingvar who was non-committal and the king nodded to Eric in agreement, "Ya, you best wed to tall lady, Birgetta be small for a large man like you. We look elsewhere for young prince who eligible, perhaps."

Birgetta was not full blooded royalty, therefore not eligible to wed a prince who was first in the hierarchy to become king. Kaja recalled the young lad her father almost promised her, before Aksel came to claim, and informed him about the younger brothers the lad had who would be able to marry one not of full royal blood.

Aksel knew King Havard from the Alliance and made it a point to approach him at the next meeting. Havard had his two younger sons, Edvard and Georg, with him, just as Bjorn was with his father. Bjorn had nine birthdays and reveled in the Alliance gatherings, meeting other young lads from nearby realms. To the young lads it was a learning time as well as a fun time with many friends to make. After the Alliance had adjourned for the year, King Havard accepted Aksel's invitation to travel to Heborg to meet the lass and consider a match between the two young people.

The lads were excited and curious to behold the lovely lass. Edvard had a promised maiden whom he would soon wed and teased his brother about the maiden who was not full born royalty. "She be homely as well as not of full royal blood?" he questioned and jested.

"No," Aksel answered his question, having overhead their conversation. "Birgetta be lovely maiden with silken hair down her shoulders, pink skin with the look of smooth alabaster, slender and delicate of body, with pleasant disposition and tinkling laughter to make heart sing with joy." He added further, "She be a prize for any prince, a pleasure to know. You see and you will love her."

Georg was pleased with Aksel's description and smiled smugly at his older brother. "My maiden be even lovelier than your princess," he challenged.

Kaja made certain that Birgetta was washed and dressed in her best gown when the lads arrived late the evening from the Alliance, she looked lovely. Birgetta looked on the young men, Georg the younger, who would be her promised lad, and his older brother. "The older prince be manlier, I favor him more," she told her marm.

"The younger grow manly before you wed," Kaja convinced her, "and more striking to behold. He has strong, prominent face like his sire."

Birgetta had spoken to him bashfully, pleasantly and they were allowed to visit and walk in the village for a spell. "Yes, he be a strong young lad, will grow a man soon," she agreed wholeheartedly and smiled with happiness at her marm.

Kaja thought back to the years when she saw them as very young lads and had fretted at the thought to wait many years for the oldest before he would be old enough to wed. Then her Aksel claimed her and now she be the marm of four sons, she mused while nursing her infant, Arne. She contemplated with happiness in her heart. She had four beautiful sons and lovely Birgetta and was not yet 29 birthdays, her Aksel almost 35.

- -   - -   -

Mother Hulda was aging and not feeling very well. She spent considerable time in her chamber, not getting out among the people as she had been accustomed in years gone by. She spent the winter mostly in her bed becoming weaker and weaker with a deep congested cough that was not healed or comforted by the potions Frode brought her. Aksel, Kaja and the boys spent her last days in the room with her to cheer her and urged her to rise from bed and join them.

The boys had fallen asleep near the fire, or in the chair, babe Arne slept on the foot of her bed as their parents tended to Hulda in her last struggle with life. The young children were completely unaware of this and the silence that followed. Mother Hulda died in the night. The boys wakened in the morning to find her bed empty. She was wrapped in a leather burial shroud, her remains were placed alongside her sires on the frozen earth that day and covered with heavy stones to protect her remains from the ravages of hungry wild animals in winter. The Friar spoke prayers for the dead and words of comfort for the citizens as they passed by to bid their Queen Mother farewell. Then they returned quickly to the comfort of the castle or church to escape the icy wind. She would be buried below ground next to her sire with the spring thaw. She had been much loved.

Several of the inhabitants from the elevations came to Heborbg early in the spring as the growing season was underway. They did not enter the village. They requested to speak to King Aksel and waited for him to come to them. "Sire, no come close," Ernst addressed him. "We ask you accept us as citizens in your realm. Conditions now be unbearable in the elevations. A winter plague destroy all citizens but these few here. Livestock dead, fear to enter caves again. Fear the plague still be there. There not be enough of us left to work, to supply our meager needs."

Frode who saw them arrive, was concerned about them. "What manner of plague be this, you know? Be it fever? Be it from animals or vermin in cave? Do any have symptoms of this malady still? We cannot permit you mingle with our citizens 'til we study and decide it be safe, else the plague take away our people. You understand?" he asked with concern.

"Ya, understand you be concern. We go wherever want us to, stay away from your people for appropriate time, 'til sure it be safe. We not want sicken your village."

Aksel talked with Ernst, asked questions while Frode listened and also asked questions. From what they could gather, it seemed the stench from their waste and the animals that had accumulated over many years, set up an unhealthy atmosphere which carried germs, perhaps contaminated the air and water.

The survivors were supplied with food, shelter, hot water and soap to clean their bodies of vermin and disease. They spent most of the summer in quarantine and kept themselves occupied building shelters away from the village to house themselves. The men who worked the quarry during the growing season brought wagonloads of stones for their use.

The new quarry diggings disclosed an area of beautiful white stone with colored patterns. Alsel and the Friar were alerted and decided the stone would make a beautiful altar for the church, better than the one they had. It also made beautiful tables for the castle, even the citizens used it for tables and furniture in their cottages. One craftsman designed a beautiful chair for his king to sit in. Aksel asked him to build another, large enough to hold both he and his queen together. Beautiful as the chairs were, they were uncomfortably hard to sit on. Kaja worked with a seamstress to make four delightful leather encased cushions to ease the discomfort for their seats and backs and enclosed them in beautiful embroidered casings. "They adorn the hall so well," she told Aksel, "I order more tables, place along side wall for decoration, be used to make long table when guest come for sustenance . You give craftsman many coins for his work?" she asked. Aksel nodded in favor of that.

As none became ill and died among the new citizens from the elevations, they were eventually allowed to join the citizens of Heborg. Frode said, "We be happy we now have people with knowledge to assist to build waterway from the distant caves to accommodate our citizens in the village." His vision would soon be served. Ernst climbed with Frode in the nearby mountains to investigate the where and how. They marked water levels and access on the walls of the cave, studied the area and planned the method to transport water to the village.

- - - - -

The Alliance had an urgent call to assist one of their realms with an unusual problem. Aksel was obliged to send some of his men to assist a team who needed to travel a far distance to save their men from slavery, a village of strong women who enslaved their men to work the grapa orchards and fruit presses at their will. They were held in bondage by drinking a strong beverage called vinum. Kaja looked at Aksel who turned to Karl and Ingvar with the memory of Vitolfs poison ale. "This beverage holds men in bondage? Vitolfs ale be poison, held man's body to ale, not to bondage."

Aksel looked at his men, "Do any know of this beverage?"

Ingvar said, "Soldier who came from afar speak of beverage that make men lose resolve, keep him happy to work and be enslaved to the will of their master."

"Bring him here, we talk and learn more. Perhaps he go with our men to rescue those enslaved."

Giedde was alarmed when Karl called him out and asked him to speak with the king. "I be freeman Giedde, sire, how I serve you?"

"I be told you know of beverage named vinum? Used in village to south to enslave men to work the will of their master. You hear of this name?" Aksel asked him.

"Ya sire, I hear the name, it make man loose senses, work as slave for more beverage. See men craze for this beverage, kill for it. It be an evil thing," he emphasized.

"You go this village with company of armed men, rescue soldiers kept in slavery? Help get free of bondage and bring back to the Alliance? Can you direct the path?" he questioned.

"Ya, sire, I lead the way. I go with your army to bring men back to the Alliance, I have young brother caught in this bondage, bring him back to Heborg. It take many moons, it be long distance away from Norway. When we leave? I have crops need be harvested soon. You care my family while I be gone?" Giedde, was concerned.

"Not fret the work or care of family. People will attend the work and family while you be gone," Aksel assured him.

Ingvar and Karl spoke more with Giedde, "Need to know how well that realm be protected - with walls, many soldiers or other means of armament. Need prepare defend our men and whatever may happen," Karl declared.

"There be no protection, no wall. Women controll farm and men who work. Feed them well, give vinum to sleep the night, even have tarts to keep them happy.

Aksel, Karl and Ingvar look at one another. "This not be a war of arms and manpower," Aksel observed out loud. "This be war on women who use vinum and female wiles, seduce men to stay and work for them. How we fight this?"

Ingvar organized a group of his experienced men along with well trained younger men to make the distant journey south with enough equipment and supplies to last them for many moons and coins to replenish the supplies as needed.

Aksel spoke aside with Ingvar, "I not want you go with the army, need you here to protect our people. We have Karl lead the men, he has much experience, can do the task well."

"Say you, I be too old to fight, Sire?" Ingvar was quick to defend himself. "I not old, still strong to whip most men in service."

Aksel smiled at him, "Ya, you be strong, can whip all, but feel you need be here to protect people. If others know we send men south, they attack realm to plunder, no can leave realm undefended. Karl be a strong leader, he do well with small army, return with much glory for our realm. You stay with us," he beseeched.

Ingvar bowed to his sire in acceptance of his will. Later he told his spouse, "Sire thinks I be too old to fight war, want me stay here, protect our village. Send Karl to make war against the realm who use vinum." He paused and looked at Dagmar, "Ya, I stay in village, stay with wife. I not be too old to fight, but lack the vigor. Desire not - be gone from my loved wife for many moons." He looked at Dagmar, love shone from his eyes and Dagmar returned his smile. She gave him a loving hug and thanked their king in her heart for keeping him at her side.

It was a long journey to the south, the men sailed from Kaupang to the coast of Franca. There they purchased steeds. The mounted army with a wagon loaded with supplies made its way through the pleasant countryside in the coolness of early fall. Giddie led them through the countryside of Franca, even spoke enough of the language with the natives that they willingly gave him the directions he often asked for, to be certain they traveled in the right direction. As they traveled the men spoke of ways to join or attack these people, many came up with ideas.

"We attack early in morn before know we be there, surprise them," one warrior suggested.

"No, it best to join them, watch how they keep men enslaved, just not drink vinum." Giddie suggested.

"Ya, we pretend to drink, pretend to get drunk, sleep with all. In the dark of night carry drunken men to our wagon, leave long before the sunrise. This be how we rid our realm of unwanted missionary barbarians, it work well," Karl told them.

Giedde agreed, "We try join them - see how it be. Pretend to drink the vinum, pretend to be drunk the night. Ya, that fare well."

They arrived in the area and Giedde described the layout as he remembered it. "It be larger than before," he recalled, "they now grow more grapa and more grain."

They put their arms and martial trappings away in the wagon as they peacefully marched up to the large building that housed the women. They were needed and welcomed to work in the fields of fruit and the harvest in progress. Karl watched the workers get drunk on vinum every evening for a week, while his men pretended to drink and acted drunk. They scouted about the farm, located another wagon on the far side from the women's large cottage. One of the men checked to see that it was in good condition to easily carry half the many drunken, sleeping men. As all was in place, they plan to do their deed the next week when the new moon appeared in the night to lighten their path.

Giedde spoke aside to those who understood him in the Norse or Franca language, to see which men from the Alliance needed to be rescued. Those he spoke to did not want to leave, were content to work hard, drink vinum, eat good food and enjoy the tarts. They didn't want to return to the Alliance or to Norway. They liked the moderate weather of Franca and the vinum that warmed the blood. They did not desire to return to the icy Norwegian winters. "No," they said.

Giedde did not locate his brother, did not see him any-where. He asked some of the workers if they knew him, what happened to him? They didn't know. He spoke pleasantly to one of the women who were in charge and ventured to ask her, "You know lad named Sunesen, large lad who be a friend. He leave Norway many moons ago, seek adventure in warm south. His sire never hear of him again. His sire asked to inquire, find him and see if he be well. You know of him?

The woman looked at him, but did not answer. Slow-ly, she turned from him and walked away. The next day toward evening, the woman signaled Giedde to follow her. Karl nearby saw the interaction and followed behind a short distance. She led Giedde to a shed behind their large cot-tage and took him inside where it was quite dark. Karl fol-lowed behind and was stunned , the room had several mats on the floor where men lay semi-comatose or jerking and blabbering nonsense.

"These men drink too much vinum, they go mad, can-not work, cannot speak. We not know what do for them. All they want be more vinum, this make them worse." The woman spoke in Franca, Karl could not understand her, but Giedde did and shrunk away in horror when he recognized the large lad who was his brother.

"Sunesen," he spoke to him softly in Norse, "Sunesen, hear me?" The lad did not acknowledge him, just lay in a stupor. Giedde turned to the woman and asked her, "What happen to him, what cause this? Surely he not drink much vinum to make him crazed."

"Ya," she said softly, "Some drink much, some not drink well, do them harm. He be a nice lad I not give him more vinum, made him stop drinking. He grow silent, not eat, not sleep, not even drink water. I not know what do for him."

"I take back to Norway, father care for him. Giedde said. Among family he be well. Leave when harvest complete." Giedde went to his brother several times a day, coaxed him to drink water, some milk, even to eat some meal mush. The men worked the rest of the week in the orchard, picked the fruit, even turned the wheels to press the grapa to prepare the juice for fermenting, then pretended to drink the wine and be drunk the night. The harvesting was almost complete.

On the day they planned to leave, they filled their wagon with hay from the grain fields beyond the vineyards, enough for two wagons. That evening, as dark was upon them, they procured the second wagon from the orchard, placed it behind the worker's shelter along side their wagon and transferred half the hay. The sleeping, drunken men were carried from their sleep quarters to the wagons. They just plopped down in the hay completely oblivious of where they were. They count forty-six men, including those from the cottage where Sunesen lay. He had revived enough to request his friends be taken also, which Giedde did.

Their horses were saddled and led quietly to the shelter. They had greased the wheels earlier that morning to quiet the noise as the wagons slowly left the orchard. The clouds covered the new moon so there was little light and one soldier led the way with a lantern, following the path he had marked with posts the previous day to take them to the north.

By dawn they were several miles from the vinum village, two wagons loaded with men suffering from hangovers. The men were provided with buckets of spring water to take the dry fire from their throats. Some of them threw up and stumbled back to the wagon to fall in the hay and groan with the misery and called for vinum.

They stopped at a farm along the way and bought bread from the farmer's wife to feed the men. She had an abundance of smoked pork, more than she needed and was happy to sell it and have coins to buy other necessities at the market. She could never depend on what the merchants would pay her for the pork. She pleasantly waved to them as they left.

It took many weeks to find their way back to the coast. They didn't know where they would find vessels sufficient to transport them across the sea. They traveled along the coast stopping at every port, but seamen didn't want to attempt the dangerous sea voyage at the approach of winter. There were sixty-eight men and twenty-two horses. Karl decided it was best they sell the horses, find quarters perhaps where they could earn their keep till the warmth of spring, then seek transport to the port of Kaupang. Three large longboats would be required.

"You work for sustenance and shelter the winter?" a local merchant asked. "What work you do?"

Giedde told him, "We do farm work, some can build with stone, wood, what need be done. You have work for many men?"

"A local man need to build path across his land. It be over grown, many hills. He want make level to transport wagons and livestock to market and need much help. You be strong men. You work hard, he feed you well and give warm place to sleep. Get path built fast."

"He have proper tools to level ground?" Giedde asked. "Cannot do with hands alone."

"Have many diggers, levelers, wagons to move dirt and stone. Can use your wagons and horses to work," the merchant offered.

"These not be work horses, they saddle horses of much value for use by men and warriors."

Karl and Giedde spoke at length with the landowner and made a contract to work for several months till the warmth of spring. The food was sufficient, it filled their bellies. They were sheltered the nights in sod longhouses along the route. They were far enough south where it didn't freeze as in the glacial north.

Karl looked back at the months in the sod longhouses with the group of smelly men they had rescued from slavery and vinum. After they had rid their bodies of the effects of too much vinum, he spoke to them about the experience and was amazed that few of them did not remember very much about it. Even Sunesen who had been practically dead when his brother, Giedde, found him, hardly remembered what had happened to him.

Karl took it upon himself to tell them what had happened to them. "You be enslaved by these farming women to work their fields, pick the grapa and press into juice to ferment into vinum. Vinum be like ale, only stronger." He told them of farmer Vitolf who brewed ale of many grains that was so strong it killed him. "This vinum be strong like Vitolf's ale of many grains, stronger than ale we brew in Heborg. Vinum make you forget all, except to want more vinum. You work in slavery to have vinum at night after work, then sleep. Some, it make sick, almost kill. Some it make loose resolve, not think with good thoughts, only want more vinum. You work as slave in the vineyard to drink more. When first came, we tell you want to take you back to Norway. You all say "no!". You want stay here, you like here, like vinum, like tarts. You think that way now the vinum be gone from body?"

One man spoke up, "You say tarts? I not remember tarts, remember work and vinum. Not remember tarts!" he insisted.

"It be as I said," Karl said with urgency "You loose resolve, loose memory of home, loose memory of tarts, loose memory of everything. Become almost dead as Sunesen be, as his two friends be. You want us take you back the orchard? Work all day in vineyard? Drink vinum then sleep the night, wake up next morn, do the same. Never see family, not live life with the wife you love. Stay here 'til die of vinum or go crazy. Be this you want? You want we take you back?"

They looked at him, some lowered their heads in thought, some looked at others about them. They didn't know what to say or think.

The work kept them so busy it flushed the venum from their systems and the need for venum from their minds. Time went by and soon spring was upon them and they looked forward to heading home to Norway. Giedde went to the coast and contracted for three longboats for the men which would be available in a week.

The work was complete enough that they could travel on the path they had completed. In one area that was built up to make it level, the first rain that came along threatened to wash it down. They shored it up with stones and mortar and replaced the soil with a foundation of clay. The land-owner was pleased with the new path, with the work the men had done over the winter. He gave them the means to take a warm bath, to clean their bodies and their clothes, and to each man he gave a coin. He carried them to the coast in their wagons and was able to see them off the next morning.

Karl gave him a strong handshake and appreciative thanks for having kept them occupied through the winter as well as for the food and housing. The other men hailed him as well, except for a few who had a grievance that no one would listen to – they wanted vinum.

CHAPTER ELEVEN

HEBORG

Several years passed, Bjorn is now a young man of sixteen, he grew tall and stronger with every year, was well trained in the defensive arts and archery and had proven a worthy adversary with lads even older than he. Aksel had his sons work with the farmers and tradesmen of the realm to learn many skills to keep them strong and healthy. They were not always happy about the fieldwork, but eventually they felt the growing strength in their bodies and realized the worth of the physical activity.

Gregors told his brothers, "Even our sire be strong with the muscles of a man, he work hard in fields. I want to be like him when I be grown."

Unne countered with, "Knight Ingvar be bigger, stronger. I want be like him when I be grown."

Even young Arne was showing his muscle to his older, bigger brothers and made them laugh as they tousled their young brother's hair. "You need grow more years to be big and strong," Gregors told him.

"It good to be strong," Bjorn agreed, "but I want be like Frode and know many, many things – to be wise man makes us strong also."

"I be intelligent for a young lad. Frode say I be," Arne bragged.

Frode continued to teach the young students, even his own son had learned far beyond the expectations of his parents, he would surely be another 'wise man.

Aksel answered the call of a realm in the Alliance and had gone off with a company of men to help a neighbor ward off an invader from the sea. A fleet of boats was camped along the shore and the invaders created havoc among the peaceful villagers in the area. They preyed on the farmers, stole their livestock for food, as well as pillaged the gardens and fields of grains and corn. Many realms of the Alliance answered the call for help and many of the invaders were annihilated. Before additional reserves arrived to help stem the flow of the powerful invaders, Aksel was seriously wounded in a very fierce battle. He was swiftly carried back to Heborg in a small horse-drawn wagon, supposedly dying.

Karl explained to Kaja and Ingvar when he arrived back in Heborg. "I suspect foul play, He be attacked by men from realm in the Alliance, I *see them attack him*," he emphasized. "Had him surrounded and cordoned off from others short distance from where we be fighting. I broke from those I fight with, call Torben and Alf to follow, rode over to them, put sword through one, the others turn and run. Had slashed Aksel with a sword – he has a bad gash in shoulder and arm. The sword be aimed at neck to behead him. He bent down, be knocked off steed and trampled with their horse's hooves. We be able stop the flow of blood, took wagon from people there, made bed of straw for comfort and travel fast most of two days and nights, not stop all the way to Heborg. I fear he dead, My Lady." The words caught in his throat as he looked toward Aksel, tried hard not to cry, his cousin dying - maybe already dead?

Kaja looked closely at her sire as they lifted his lifeless looking form from the wagon, decided to tell everyone he was dead, perhaps those who committed the crime would come forward with some reason or devious plan in mind.

"Take to my chamber, we prepare him for burial." She gave a knowing nod to Karl. Kaja in the meantime, gave the deliverers a tongue lashing, "Why not just throw his body in the ocean. Why bring him home dead?" This was a ruse, she realized the murderers, whoever they may be, expected he would not live long – if at all.

Frode went to the inert body lying on the bed, put his ear down to Aksal's chest and

listened to his heart. "My Lady, he not dead. Heart be weak yes, but not dead." Frode and Dort worked diligently on him, cleansed his wounds, used herbal powders to seal his cuts and stop the flow of blood and bound his broken arm so it would heal properly.

They faked a funeral the next day. A slaughtered pig was enclosed in a shroud, laid on a pyre over an open grave. Friar Kristoffer said the prayers for the dead and blessed the body in the grave. Kaja put the torch to the straw and sticks, watched it consume the 'body", with her weeping sons and the citizens along side - all are sad and mourn the loss of their young king.

Well after dark, the partially cooked animal was retrieved from the ashes, stealthily, by her sons under the light of the quarter moon. It was taken to an area aside from the village where it was placed on a spit and slowly roasted for the next day's mourning ceremony and feast. They filled the burial plot and covered it over with soil. Plants were transplanted to the grave early the following morning as directed by Kaja. She was there at the crack of dawn to watch and direct the work, unsmiling with a pained, mourning face. When they were through, she sat on the grass along side for several minutes and silently wept, her face bowed on her hands folded in prayer.

Gregor and Unne knelt along side praying with her and helped her rise to return slowly to the castle.

Aksel lay in semi-consciousness as they nursed him in secret from the citizens. They urged him to sip the healthy broths cooked for him, potions to give him strength, sips of water and goats milk for nutrition.

Birgitta, now 20 and wed to Prince Georg came to spend time with Kaja to help her in her sorrow after the death of her father and when she found him still alive in secret, stayed many weeks to help care for him. Prince Georg followed her after a few weeks - not only to give his condolences to Kaja, but to take his wedded wife back home, much as Aksel had done many years before when her Queen Mother Alva had died.

"My wedded wife needs come with me now. I miss her, she has left me for too long." Georg held her close and looked at her. Birgetta touched his face gently, softly whispered in his ear, "I now with child, my love," and he smiled and enveloped her in a loving embrace. Kaja was happy for them and wished them well on their journey home.

Kaja put on a strong front, led the realm with the help of Frode, Ingvar, Karl and the freemen – even her sons sat at her side.

The citizens were still unaware that Aksel actually did not die. He was still sequestered in chamber to mend from his many wounds which kept him primarily lying in bed. As he lay for several months, he reconstructed in his mind, the events of that fatal day when he was almost killed. He remembered several things and people who must have participated in the attempt to slaughter him. His voice was barely audible, it hurt him to talk. He had not healed after being stomped by the horse's hooves; but he tried, in a croaking whisper, to pass these remembrances and thoughts to Kaja to pass on to Karl & Ingvar to investigate what they could.

He spoke to Kaja with his eyes, followed her around the room and he would motion her to lie next to him. She obeyed his wishes, lay alongside with her arm across his chest, cuddled him close and kissed his lips often. It seemed to make him content for a time until he healed more thoroughly. Gradually, his demands became more that of a robust husband.

They waited, watched and were on the alert for any action that might bear evidence of those who were guilty of the misdeed. They watched for any who might try to interfere in the work of the realm, lest they have reason to take it over. They were prepared to flaunt any take-over attempt.

Aksel gradually healed enough to rise more frequently from his bed with help from his sons. He spent much time in the quiet place on the hill above the castle, when he was able to climb the steep, rough steps, where he basked in the sun, moved about undetected, worked his injured muscles and broken arm to strengthen them. Eventually, after five months he was getting up and about with ease, though still clumsy. His mended arm did not have the strength it had before and did not function well – it was very stiff. His voice was rough and deep. His scars from the slash across his back and arm healed well. He wanted urgently to join the realm and the work, but agreed to wait longer to see if the devious schemers showed their hand.

Kaja, who had lost considerable weight after Arne was born, had put on weight and was looking very pregnant. There was whispering among the citizens, gossip was flying, was she expecting - how could this be? Who could the father be?

Visitors arrived at the realm, a company of armed men, headed by a man not known to Karl, Bjorn and Gregors or others who were at the seaside invasion. Aksel watched from the balcony where he could not be seen and recognized one man as the one who had attacked him after the invaders retreated. He spoke with Karl, Ingvar and his sons who were there. "Ya," Unne finally agreed. "I see him, he be there. He bump my horse, nearly knock us over, I remember now."

The others thought hard and recalled the man also, but had seen him mainly from a distance. Karl welcomed the visitors and addressed the man, the others had recognized, and told him. "I see you afore, you fight invaders at sea when we be there many moons gone. I be Knight Karl of Heborg," he introduced himself and put out his hand for a similar response.

"I be Sir Borghild, cousin to King Esben of Dagny. Hear your king be killed in fight with invaders at sea." Karl nodded sadly, "You do well without him, have the look of industrious realm."

"We work hard in our realm, all have responsibility and perform duty well. Even our king worked well among us, now his sons, his spouse. Yes, we be industrious people." He paused a moment, looked about at the men who accompanied him. "What be your need? You have a mission to perform?

"We have mission to west, we stop to see if you have need, perhaps we be of service, give assistance," He spoke politely.

Ingvar smiled graciously, "As you see, all be well among us. You be welcome to join us at sustenance this night," he invited. They sat at table with a mug of ale and conversed pleasantly about many things which include the confrontation with foreign barbarians at the seaside.

Sir Borghild was able to fill them in on the results of the conflict at sea. "More warriors arrive in time, kill off the invaders, and many be taken as slaves." He took delight in describing the funeral at sea for the many men who lay dead from the slaughter along the shore. They spoke on about other battles and incidents. Borghild was quite the braggart and consistently boasted of his accomplishments of war. Ingvar was amazed at the many fabrications of the events he spoke of – not at all as he remembered.

Kaja joined them that evening in time for sustenance and sat in Aksel's large chair which she had shared with him, and introduced herself, "I be Queen Kaja of Heborg. Welcome to our realm."

"You sit in King's chair, you rule the realm?" Sir Borghild asked in surprise.

Kaja nodded slightly, not saying a word.

The man looked at Karl, Ingvar and her sons sitting nearby. "All these strong men be here and a lady, a Queen, rule the realm? Why this? Be not any man among you strong enough to take the reins?"

"You think I be weak?" Kaja asked and looked at him straight on with a smirk of a smile on her face. "I be strong enough. The citizens of the realm honor me as queen. The freemen, tradesmen, knights, all work together to see we be safe, secure in our village. None come to pillage, none *dare* come to pillage," she emphasized the word strongly and glared at them. "You think we not fight to secure peaceful life, if some come, to do us harm? You think thus, Sir Borghild? You come, do us harm?"

He was taken back, surprised at her verbal attack, her blunt accusation, didn't know what to say. "No, my lady, thoughts be not to harm, perhaps join you and help secure realm from raiding barbarians. Perhaps even to become king of your realm."

"You a barbarian become king of peaceful realm? You not be happy in peaceful realm as we. We not be happy with a barbarian king as you. We do well without king – we have strong queen for now. Soon Aksel's son have years enough to take reign, be wise enough to become judicious king. We not see barbarians come to realm, we be strong to defend our realm against raiders." She shook her head to enforce her words. "We not ask for help of others, have many strong men, trained and armed, prepared to fight to the death. Every citizen be trained in defense against invasion. No need you concern self with our welfare." She was adamant and abrupt in her final refusal of his help and turned to invite Friar Kristoffer to say the blessing before meals as all stood and bowed their heads.

"You pray to the one God? You defile our gods of old?"

"We pray to the one God, Ya!" she responded with enthusiasm. "Build our church to the one God and live in peace and harmony with our God of Love. You be of different mind? There some among us who pray to Thor and Odin, you may leave us and join them."

Borghild glared at the Friar as he spoke the blessing and then sustenance was served. All ate in silence inside. The bulk of the visiting men noisily ate in the courtyard.

The visitors went willingly to the shelter provided for them for the night. They were watched through the wall the night long, guards on duty have there bows and arrows at the ready and were prepared to blow the horn of need if they see anything amiss.

Aksel descended to the hall early the next morning and walked out among the citizens beyond the courtyard. His appearance scared them - was this their king? Perhaps a ghost? They could not believe their eyes – they thought he was dead. He did look different. Could this really be their sire? He nodded to many he knew and continued to walk to where the visitors were sheltered.

He stopped in front of Sir Borghild and spoke with the rasping voice that was not fully recovered, "Remember you. Remember what happen at sea when I be struck. Remember face of man who attack me. Not know who he be, but remember face." The visitor was startled, stunned, and stepped back as Aksel advanced and continued recounting the events. "Your company of men charge to the shore where we fought invaders. You join us and we killed some invaders and others took leave, return to sea. You turn on me, three surrounded and slashed at me. I remember the face of the man who tried behead me with swing charge of long blade. I duck below arc and blade of another, a second face I remember, struck across shoulder and arm. Another struck with flattened sword, knock me from steed, his horse trample me. Remember not face, but cut of head, brash color of hair, bulk of body. He, I see yesterday when look on you from balcony. Other two be standing here in front of all. The first one be you!" he asserted.

Sir Borghild was speechless. He looked about at his men, his eyes passed across the courtyard and the walls surrounding it. He was startled to see it manned by young men who had appeared with bows and arrows at the ready.

"You be mistaken, who you be?" he asked somewhat nervously.

"You know who I be, I be King Aksel of Heborg, be-long to Alliance of Realms, as do you." He paused briefly and ordered, "*You* leave our realm *now!* I see you at Alli-ance council soon, I make complaint against you – you try kill me. Best you prepare words of defense for your actions for all to hear," Aksel threatened, looked at Sir Borghild for a long moment, turned slowly to the others in the contin-gent of men, paused and stared at the second face he recog-nized and then the third man with brash colored hair and large body. "Ya, you best prepare defense. You leave now and never return my realm. You be not welcome here!" he spoke in a firm voice. He watched as they quickly gathered their belongings, mounted their steeds and retreated from the courtyard. Aksel stood by and watched them leave, then followed behind a short distance as they rode away.

The men on the wall also watched them leave, fol-lowed them with their eyes until they were beyond the hills and no longer seen. Rolf had been assigned as a forward guard along with a few men carrying their bows and arrows on a hill located in a perfect watching post to see if the men left the area completely or stopped to plan an attack. Aksel went up the wall to observe, saw the signal from Rolf on the hill that the men had continued on past him. They waited for a second signal that the men were seen at the second post, but the signal never came.

"Sire," Ingvar spoke, "they see our men on the first hill, wait, come back under cover of dark, attack when our bowmen be relieved of duty, when we be more vulnerable, when they have upper hand. Rolf be on the hill with his bowmen. They kill them first. We send Rolf a signal, re-turn to village through hidden path, watch for enemy attack from here. I go, meet and help if there be need. We keep men on wall, thus their swordsmen not attack our men one at a time. Want us come to them, we not leave cover of wall, they come to us, we slay before get too close."

When Ingvar returned several days later, he reported that Sir Borghild and his men had finally left the area, headed back to their own realm. All the men at post were safe and would return after tracking the supposed invaders a while longer.

Two months later when Aksel returned from the meeting of the Alliance, he was heavy with anger and brooding silently. He had many strange, quiet moods since his recovery and Kaja was worried about him. He had made quite a scene at the Alliance, all thought he was dead, many could hardly believe the accusations he made. He proved it with the scars on his body, his crusty voice, his weak arm and the confirmation of Karl who attended the meeting with him.

Aksel told Kaja, "The offenders were chastised at the Alliance, declared outlaw, must make retribution. But offenders not attend Alliance, not pay penalty. Borhild's cousin be told to give message to him. He required attend the Alliance meeting next year to make retribution and pay weregild or he become exiled from our country for life."

"This be just," Kaja agreed quietly, "He be gone from our land, cannot come back. He does, I kill him," she asserted softly. "He try kill my sire, did him damage, make him unhappy. I try keep him well, but he has much hate in heart. He not be man of love I know afore. What I do now make my sire happy?"

Aksel reached for her hand, pulled her down next to him on their bed and hugged her close. "I love my wedded wife, my green-eyed vixen who make me happy. No fret my moods, Kaja. I need forget, forgive, give attention and love to family, all my people who need me." He kissed her gently, turned her toward him and looked deep into her eyes, "You be well with our babe? He kick you hard?"

"No, *he* not kick me hard," she responded emphasizing the 'he.' "She kick me hard," and smiled up at him.

"Oh? You think I let you have girl this time?" he questioned.

"Ya, I think *we* have girl this time," she answered again with emphasis and her 'knowing' face.

"I rub belly, she kick my hand?"

Kaja laughed, "Ya, rub belly, she like you rub her. Name her Alva or perhaps Hulda."

Aksel thought a moment, "Perhaps name her Halva, or Hulva, or Vulda. Think you?"

Kaja looked at him and laughed. "Have the plumpness of a woman, now, after many babies." She pat her plump belly, "I plump like Dagmar, the way you like?"

Aksel smiled at her, "No, I love Dagmar when I be a babe. My marm be delicate for many years after I be born. Dagmar be just a lass when assigned duty to care for me when a lad. Many years she be like mother to me and I love her like I loved my marm. You not be plump, I love my lady with big belly, who never be more beautiful as when with child."

They named their daughter Margrethe after Kaja's deceased sister.

- - - - -

Hjordis, Aksel's old friend, came through the realm and stopped to visit with his friend from his youth. Aksel welcomed him, "Hail frend Hjordis, you travel far from your realm, it be many years since I set eyes on you. You get fat in your peaceful castle. You not bring Slovene?"

Hjordis slowly shook his head, "My wife die in child-birth many years gone, she give me two sons and one daughter and then another ailing babe that had problem. Babe die, Slovene die. I miss her, but have young tart to satisfy needs." He called to her, "This be Ulrika, my lady."

Ulrica bowed deeply to Aksel and gave him a knowing smile. "Welcome Ulrika, you be welcome to our castle, the lady of my friend, Hjordis, be welcome." And Aksel ushered them inside to sit at table.

Hjordis gives Aksel a mischievous grin, "Be your wife about? Be she still the saucy, spirited lady?"

"Kaja be still my saucy green-eyed vixen, ya, she be with our babe daughter. After four sons, I let her have daughter," he jested. "She come soon."

"Where be daughter you took from my realm many years gone? She surely be a maiden now, ready to wed?"

"Birgetta be wed to youngest son of King Havard, she have small babe, too. She a lovely lady, make spouse happy as her marm make me happy," he bragged as they sat and wafted a mug of ale.

"Kaja be spirited lady, not like other ladies take her place at table. What she do we let Ulrika sit in her place at table?" Hjordis asked with a sly smile at his old friend. "We play game, see she anger. Tell her you want Ulrika sit next to you."

"I not like to anger my wedded wife, she be good woman. Have much love of her, desire

only to keep her happy as she care for me well," Aksel was adamant and poured another mug of ale for them.

Hjordis had his lady sit at Aksel's side in the large marble chair, which Aksel did not appear happy about. Hjordis continued to speak, egged him on, and when Kaja arrived with her young daughter he greeted her graciously as though nothing were wrong.

"Sir Hjordis, your lady sit in my chair," she let him know.

"Aksel ask her to sit next to him, he like my lady, want her sit next to him," he replied.

Kaja looked at Aksel who was non-committal. "My sire want your lady sit beside him. She must be lady of castle, must do the work of lady of castle, take care of the babe of castle, feed when hungry, clean mess she make. You do this?" Kaja asked Ulrika as she placed her babe in Ulrika's lap.

Ulrika looked at Kaja with disbelief, "Feed her? What do I feed her?" she demanded, not knowing what to do with the wriggling infant.

"Babe drink milk, mother's milk – you have big breast, not have milk?" she asked incredulously as she poked the woman's breast with one finger. She turned to Aksel, "What good his woman, have big breast but no milk," Kaja giggled and walked away.

Aksel looked at his old friend, chuckled silently at his expression and with a wide grin, followed Kaja with his eyes as she left the hall. He wondered what she would have to say to him later.

Ulrika did not have to tend little Margrethe for very long. Margrethe's brother, Unne, came by and took her, returned the infant to his mother who smiled mischievously at her son. She put her babe to bed and rejoined the others below. She did not say a word of the annoying incident, just sat in her chair next to Aksel – the chair that Ulrika had relinquished. She gave her sire a sweet smile and joined them in a mug of ale. "It help to make milk for babe," she proclaimed with her wise face.

CHAPTER TWELVE

HEBORG

(17 years later)

Why I just lay here in the warm sun while all work so hard? Where my young daughter gone, she no longer tend me? She look like her marm, so much like her marm. Wish she be her Marm. Cry in heart for her marm, why God take from me? Why not he take me too? I sit in warm sun while all work about me. I not like to live without her, without work to do, without my people to serve and to serve me.

They now serve my son, their young King Bjorn. He serve them well. He learn well as young lad. His marm taught well, he not be a willful prince as I be. "Kaja, where be you? Why not you sit next to me?" *She no can sit next to me, she be dead, he killed her, he killed my wedded wife that I loved. I dead, too, in my heart, no can find another love, not want another love, want my Kaja. Son tell me to forget her, she be dead. He forget her, not think of her, live life without her. He have spouse to love. I not have spouse to love. No want any other spouse.*

I see my daughter, my daughter Kaja. I name her for her marm when marm die. I be sick in body, sick in mind, sick in heart.' "Kaja! Where be you? Come to me, need to look on you. Look upon my – no, no, she gone, dead, she not be here. Need to look on daughter, she be here."

'There she come to me now, bring me sustenance, feed me like a babe. I not want to eat, want to die – be with wedded wife, with Jesus in heaven. She my beautiful maiden who care for her father well.

"Sire, you have good rest? You enjoy peace and quiet here above the castle? I bring you stew of vegetables and venison to satisfy hunger. Come, sit yourself up to eat. You need get up from chair, move about to make muscles strong, make body active. You like what I cook for you?" she encouraged while feeding him.

"Beautiful Kaja who look like her marm with curly yellow hair all over head." He reached out to caress her hair and mused. *Just to watch her be a joy, I not taste what I eat –I eat, her with my eyes as did with my Kaja, her marm. She not love me like my Kaja did, she be my daughter. Love her as my daughter, she love me as her sire. I cry in heart, she not my wedded wife. This I think now, think only of the past. I not be like king any more. Not know how to act like king. I look on my daughter a long time.'* He turned to her and asked, "How many birthdays you be?"

"I be twelve birthdays now, my sire. It twelve years since your Kaja died. I not ever see my Marm, she die right after I born, you tell me. She not see me, not hold me or kiss me. You not tell me how she die, why she die after I be born. Tell me now? Why you not speak of how she die, I not need to know?"

"No, no can speak of it. Hurts in my heart to tell how she die, hurt in my mind to see her lay there dead. Ya, there be need to tell you all how she die. Her babes have need to hear of it from me before I die. I not allow others to talk of it, hurts to hear others, have them know how she die. I sleep now, I tired."

Aksel dreamt in his sleep, reliving that horrible scene once again, wrenching his heart to make him weep. When he wakened from his nap, he called for Kaja, called for his sons and paced the quiet place above the castle till they came to his side.

"I tell you of your marm." He paused, rubbed his head, his full bushy beard and sat down in his soft chair as his sons and daughter came to him. "After the barbarian almost kill me in battle beside the sea, Borghild be his name, I be almost dead, my men carry me home in wagon from battle. They almost kill me. Frode, Dorte and your marm care for me well, I heal, still week, but move about. All going well in realm, people be happy, work hard, crops grow well, young people learn well.

"Your marm, Karl, Ingvar and my sons told all the people that I be dead and perform burial service for me for all to see. Burned pig in funeral pyre, not me. After dark they took pig away, finish cook in the fireplace for feast. Make mound in graveyard, plant flowers, mark grave with stone – I be buried.

"They sequester me in chamber many months 'til all my injuries heal. Borghild come to our realm with small contingent of men, be friendly, accepted hospitality, pretend to act gracious. He suggest to Kaja and my sons that he be king for our realm, since there be no King. He not understand, Kaja be our Queen, a good Queen. Kaja tell him 'NO!' Next morn I walk to courtyard where greet citizens of realm I not speak for many moons. They thought I be a ghost, they thought I dead. I spoke to Borghild, who not believe what he see. I convince him I be Aksel who he thought dead. I make him leave. He not welcome in my realm. They left, yes, but he scheme against me, against my realm, against my wedded wife.

"After many years we forget Borghild, he a bad memory. It time for Kaja to have sixth babe, she ready for birthing, they prepare for your birthing. Margrethe your sister have five birthdays now, she look much like her Grandmother Hulda, my mother, who be gone. I favor her, my beautiful little lass, who now wed to a prince in realm far north.

Borghild return to our realm the day you be born, surprise us with army of strong barbarians, big strong men. Guards see them, blow horn of alarm, and close the gate. Ingvar called men to arms, sent men to their post on the wall with bow and arrows, knights with swords be ready. Borghild be prepared with his men with bow and arrows, strike many of our lads on wall before they know what happened. Ingvar ordered men to get down on walkway inside the wall and shoot from cover, they be able to hold them back.

"Borghild had men circle around outside the wall to fields where crops growing. They came into village that back way and surprised us, they be behind us, many soldiers with long swords. Our swordsmen fought them hard, held them off at the courtyard where we made a stand. Not want them in castle, Kaja be birthing her baby in chamber, no let them disturb her.

"Ingvar be surrounded by many men, they kill him, ya, they kill him too. Karl and many other men be wounded as barbarians swarm into courtyard. They protect the stairway to chamber where women busy with Kaja. My sons and swordsmen come along side and from behind, give them good fight. Unne be injured, he just a lad. I raged in anger, fiercely struck at Borghild. His men moved to protect him and Borghild be able to circle me, climb the stairs to Kaja and her ladies in chamber. Borghild stopped in shock at what he see, startled to find he walk into room in middle of birthing. Bjorn ran up stairs, accosted him, I come up behind him.

"Borghild fight us for few minutes, he switched to my side where bad arm be, knocked me to floor in Bjorn's path, blocked him. Borghild leapt over me to bed as Kaja be bearing down, babe's head appearing in last thrust. He run sword through heart and killed her. Women screamed, pressed down on belly, push infant out and pulled the babe rest of the way, take her from mother's body. Bjorn and I attacked Borghild from both sides and slay him, sword in each side. Two of his men come running in, I pulled sword from Borghilds body and killed the one, Bjorn held other man from behind and I put a sword through him.

I look at my Kaja with the sword through her heart. No, this no can be, not believe what eyes see, I go to her, shook her shoulder. 'Kaja, Kaja, answer me,' I beg her answer me, the women were crying and tending the babe. Dorte stood frozen, look at my Kaja, did not move, her face expressed sheer horror of all. I pull sword from her body, took it, in anger stabbed it into Borghild's heart with oath sending him to the fires of hell. He be dead on floor with three swords in him. Bjorn also struck him a second time with sword I used to kill his men.

"I knelt on floor next to Kaja where she lay in bed - I cried and screamed, 'God, dear God, save her! Not take her from me, Jesus Son of God have mercy on me a sinner! I need her, I not live without her!' I cried like a babe I cried, took her in my arms, held her close to me, kissed her face, her hair and eyes 'til Bjorn and Karl, still bleeding of injury took me from her. I heard our babe cry, got up from floor. Roared like a lion, lifted the barbarian with swords sticking up from him. We three carried him to stairs, I screamed, 'He killed my Kaja! Kill the barbarians! Kill the devils!' and we threw body down on rest of barbarians who fall under his weight and turn to run away when they gaze upon his body with three swords. They leave him there, why they not take him? I go after them, pull a sword from body and chase them out of castle, out of courtyard, out of realm, throw sword, kill another as he mounted steed. Steed took off as rider fell to ground. Our soldiers still fight them, 'til all be killed or run." Aksel sat back shaking with the memory, took a good breath, exhaled . . . .

"That how she die, murdered by barbarian who wreak vengeance on me. She make fool of him, she make him think I dead, he come to steal my realm, my wife, my life. Come again after many years gone by – to fight this time, to win my realm with swords, kill my wife. If he not have my realm, not have her - he kill her. I be there to protect her, but he kill her, I not protect her well." Aksel rose slowly from his chair. "I not protect her well." he repeated. He killed her, while I be there." Kaja followed him as he walked away, fighting the tears she shed for his pain.

His sons sat and looked at each other, fighting their own tears from the story their sire

told them. "It must be horror. It no wonder our sire not able to forget, cannot put it behind him," Unne said softly. "Feels guilt, he not protect her."

They had heard some of what transpired when their mother was killed. They were there - held off the rest of the barbarians from entering the stairs, but Bjorn and the women did not expound on what happened in the birthing room, their sire asked them not to. Bjorn did not speak now, did not trust his voice to speak now, his sire's vivid description of his marm's death brought it all back tenfold.

He raged with grief in his heart, he too, had not protected his marm well.

They all silently climbed down the steep steps to the chamber below where Aksel occupied Kaja's smaller chamber that housed all their babes when they were small. Bjorn has the kings chamber with his spouse and his daughter. Kaja, was given the birthing room where her mother had been killed, the room where she was born, the room where Aksel and Kaja loved each other and slept for many years.

"I be lost when your marm die – it like I die. Friar Kristoffer try comfort me. I argue with him, 'I be a good husband, good king to my people, fair to all, work hard to make life good. Why God do this to me? Why he take my wedded wife from me. She a good woman, good mother, be a good wife, have me to care for her, love her. All loved her.

Friar said, "It be not God who do this, it be barbarian. Barbarians not think of people who be good, only want to make evil in the world - like the devil do. He want what you had. He could not win what you had, so kill what you had.' Friar said, 'Look to God for love and sympathy. He be there for you. You have little lassie to care for, to love and you have daughter named Kaja now."

They continued to slowly walk and took the path past the church on the rise, over to the garden area and the open fields where men were working. The people were happy to see their old king walking with his family and greeted him pleasantly. It had been many moons since they last saw him walk about with his fancy wooden stick to help him on his bad legs. He had taken to his chamber much of the time these last several months.

Aksel walked to the ridge that overlooked the country-side where he first spoke to his wedded wife after his father died, where they had met on common ground to get to know each other and start their life together. "Daughter Kaja," he paused and looked at her, "the first time I saw my Kaja, she just 12 birthdays, a skinny lass who look just like you. I be willful prince, promised to her sister who died of fever. I come to claim and she died. I anger at her loss, she a beautiful maiden, more beautiful than my Kaja. I take my riding crop, whip my stallion and her wise man try stop me. In rage I whip him - Kaja saw this. She struck me with her fist on my chest, hollered, 'You no whip wise man, you be no less an animal than your steed.'" Aksel mimicked the young Kaja of old and gave a smile which turned to tearful sobs. He paused and continued, "As be custom, her sire promise Kaja to me when she be grown.

"First time I see my baby daughter, Kaja, she be wrapped in a soft cloth after born. She squirm in Dorte's arms with sound of squeaking little mouse. First time I hold my baby daughter be when show her to her dead marm before we lay her to rest in ground. We walk to her grave aside wagon, Dorte hold babe Kaja in her arms. Took you from her, knelt alongside body, show you to her. I tell you, 'this be your marm, her name be Kaja.' Tell your marm, 'this your new-born daughter, I name her Kaja so I have another Kaja about me to love and care. She remind me of you always.'

"Dorte be like mother to you these many years, care for you, love you. Frode taught you when a little lass, as he taught your marm – 'til he, too, go to Jesus. He gone now, like my Kaja gone. Dorte be good mother to my daughter, be a good wife to Frode." He thought to himself. *She's a nice plump lady for me?*

"When return to Heborg from Alphild, when my promised maiden die, Ingvar report to my sire her death and of her sister who be promised in her place when grown. He be embarrassed by my bad manners – I whip the wise man. He anger at my willful manner, send me to sea with Ingvar and Karl to learn how men live and rule through the world. Go to Iceland, Ireland, British Isle. Even saw a land further east where found Evocha, a shipwrecked Norseman, and little boy Kyush. -Not know where we be, none know the name. We be gone away at sea more than three years!

"When returned to Norway, my sire be dying of consumption, want to see his son wed and happy before he died. I be more grown, more a man when return from long trip afar at sea. Remember little lass who struck me, wonder how she look now, wonder she be as fair as her sister. In heart know she make good wife for me. True there no other eligible maidens of proper age about. I stop to claim her on my way back to Heborg. Her sire had taken her to promise to another lad who be too young. 'You be gone too long,' her marm said. I begged her marm, 'I have first promise.' Many days pass, Kaja came to Heborg with her family, we spoke together and were wed next day. I not act a husband to her for many suns 'til my sire died. He call my name when I not where he could behold me. I gone so long, he be afraid I go travel again, if he not see me. I stay with him, comfort him, my wedded wife slept alone in her chamber.

"My sire died, I take wife in the night, take her like barbarian the need so strong. I apologized for bad manners, ashamed to go to her, brooded in my chamber many days after sire died, 'til my marm spoke strong words to me. I walked for long time, thought much - up here on this path - walked in the cold wind. I sent a young lad to Kaja, to tell her come to me. She came, we walked, I talked, she talked. Talked together, came together as one – it be good," he paused and spoke softly. "We found much love together, much understanding."

He paused again, gazed out onto the countryside below, sadness in his eyes which were still filled with tears. His face turned to anger, his teeth clenched in hate, "Have much hate for barbarian who kill my Kaja, so much hate I fear my God send me to hell. I must forget and forgive - fear I not even be able to spend eternity with her." He walked slowly back toward the castle with them, relaxing. He looked up at his sons and daughter, "It give me great comfort to walk with all you here where walked with my wedded wife, your marm. Remember how it be when we first loved. She be my saucy green-eyed vixen, I call her that. She like when I call her that, but not when called her vixen when we among others. She scold and told me, 'I be a saucy green-eyed vixen for you, not for all in court. You not fun me in front of all!'"

Young Kaja laugh at her sire, who told his thoughts of her marm, things they did and said. "Be I like her, sire? You say I have the look of her, but be I like her? Have blue eyes as do you, be I a blue-eyed vixen?"

Aksel hugged her to him, she did not come up to his shoulder, "Ya, I think you be like her, you be learned, saucy, sing like a bird and have the look of an angel. Ya, you be like her."

He looked down on her, caressed the hair on her head and gave her a loving smile as they turned to return slowly to the castle. He caressed his sons as he passed them, a loving hug and a fatherly pat on the shoulder. "She be proud of her young men as I be. I have peace and comfort in my heart now. You all know how your marm died, why she died." He paused and said sorrowfully, "I not protect her well."

They found a strange coach in the courtyard when they arrived back at the castle. Aksel recognized the king, who stepped down, as one from another realm of the Alliance with his lady and two youthful lads. Bjorn had invited them at the last Alliance meeting and Aksel was somewhat anxious of their reason for the visit with two youthful lads in attendance. "Greetings to you King Tornekrans, welcome to our realm," Aksel greeted him.

King Tornekrans greeted him in return and introduced, "This be Alvilde, my spouse. Alvilda this be King Aksel of Heborg. You hear me speak of him often, my love."

Aksel turned to address the lady along side him, "It my pleasure to meet spouse of friend of Alliance. You have a pleasant trip? Welcome to you and these young lads, they be your sons?" he questioned.

"A pleasant trip? With two wild, young rascals in the coach! No! We sent one out to straddle horse with the attendant! That be for punishment, make him behave well," Alvilde laughed.

Aksel smiled, "Be he a willful lad or full of much energy he need use?"

"Energy!" Tornekrans answered.

"Willful!" Alvilde corrected giving her sire a strong look.

Aksel gave a short laugh and looked at the lads. "They look to be polite with good manners, can I guess which be the willful one – or full of energy?"

"Surely? Can you tell which be which?" Alvilde asked with amusement.

"We see, I have a moment or two to consider? We enter the hall now, a beverage to quench your thirst?" Aksel was anxious to observe the lads to try to determine which lad was as he had been, a willful prince. Perhaps that would be the one for Kaja? Or perhaps the other who was probably more judicious. Would the sire send the willful lad away to learn to be a man, as had been assigned him as a lad?

Kaja entered the hall as they sat politely making conversation, sat next to her sire who put his arm about her shoulder and gave her a nod. "These be Thorkild and Ditlev, sons of friend King Tornekrans from the Alliance and spouse Alvilde.

Kaja rose from her seat, curtsied nicely to the king and queen, slowly curtsied to the two young lads. Thorkild stood and bowed politely in return, while Ditlev gave Kaja a stare with a willful look and kept his arms crossed in front of him. He rose and bowed only when his mother called his name, somewhat threatening!

Aksel looked at Tornekrans and pointed to Ditlev, "That be the willful one. I be like him when a lad. My sire angered of my willful manner, send me to sea with cousin and Knight-protector to observe how kings rule their realms for good or harm, to teach me to be judicious, to grow a man."

"How many birthdays have you when sire did this?" Alvilde inquired, somewhat incredulously.

"I be eighteen birthdays when we left and not return for more than three years." Aksel made it known.

"Ya, I be willful prince!" Ditlev asserted and looked at the old king.

"I be prince, someday be king," Thorkild said and looked at the old king.

"I be saucy princess," Kaja said and looked at her sire with a fetching smile.

Aksel set his jaw with a smirk, his arms across his chest, looking back at all of them, slightly nodding his head. "I" he paused, reached out to Dorte who was serving them beverages, gave her a resounding slap on her backside as she passed him, much to her surprise, "be willful old king!" He grinned mischievously at all of them, especially Dorte who returned a saucy little smile and gentle nod to him.

THE END

A VIKING AGE TRILOGY
Part One, Aksel's Odyssey
Part Two, Kaja's Angst
Part Three, Harmony & Tribulation

GLOSSARY

<u>Althing</u>, The National Assembly founded in 930 AD (noted in history as Europe's first parliament.)

<u>Asatru,</u> Asa (referring to Norse gods) and tru (troth or faith), usually referred to as Germanic paganism.

<u>Burbs</u>, Were defended settlements (root word for our modern borough) definition was it had a defensive wall or stockade, a mint, and a marketplace. They were laid out in grids often arranged as a square with rectangular distance between the streets, to accommodate industry that passed through the town. Cattle were herded into one street, penned up in the next street, slaughtered in the next, there hides processed into leather goods in the next street, where craftsmen made them into sale items. A busy chain of businesses throughout the commercial streets of town: hosier, shoemaker, soap-maker to sell wares to visitors and citizens and meeting halls where prosperous citizens held feasts.

<u>Chieftains</u>, Powerful men who have authority at the Althing.

<u>Ell</u>, A measured quantity of homespun woolen cloth, used as a minimum barter in trade.

<u>Godar</u>, (singular, godi) The 36 most powerful chieftains who serve in the Icelandic Althing as well as duties in their four home districts.

<u>Grapa</u>, Latin for grapes.

<u>Horses</u>, Imported in large numbers from western Norway and the British Isles.. The Icelandic breed is small,

thin-legged, with full manes, graceful, and docile. Not bred for hauling carts or carrying loads, but move in the tolt (fifth gait - smooth so rider's head does not bob) and have an acute sense of direction. (They can find their way home when taken to a new pasture.)

Law Speaker, Elected chieftain who speaks the laws at the Althing for all to hear.

Mead: Fermented beverage made of water, honey, malt and yeast.

Mulct, Fine, penalty.

Nine Noble Virtues, The Asatru moral code of conduct represents wisdom and codes gleaned from various ancient sources including the Havamal, Icelandic Sagas and Germanic folklore.

Ormen Lange, Norwegian song means The Long Serpent.

Runes, Stories inscribed in stone, wood or metal; quasi-alphabetic mottos never completely deciphered.

Sagas, Prose narrative carried by word of mouth till recorded in the 11th and 12th century, of Iceland's historic or legendary figures and events of the Norwegian and Icelandic heroic age.

Skald, Poet

Thralls, Slaves or bondsmen who work for their owners.

Trell, Slave – owner's property, purchased or bartered much as livestock. Were not protected by the law.

Troth, Faith, Fealty, Loyalty to one's spouse, family, friends, Gods. The highest of virtues.

Tyne, Sharp prong. Used as fork.

Vinum, Wine (Latin)

Weregild, Money compensation for murder.

Other works by Ann McDeed

*****

No Greater Love

A traumatic, dynamic love story of sacrifice and devotion of a lifetime. Having to watch one's life-long love approach the end of life's journey, a devoted wife provides tender loving care to her spouse as he winds down. Moving and inspiring, a tale of true love.

*****

Mariana

A love story of passion and desire, two hearts mature and come together as one. Romance and togetherness among the trials of work, ordeals and misfortunes of life. A great love story set in the flourishing twentieth century. Marianna should bring a smile to your face, a quick beat to your heart, perhaps a tear to your eye or a lump in your throat from a remembered memory of your own.

Available from
www.a-argusbooks.com